I0680944

When Fighting Monsters

By
Edward F. McKeown

AN IMPRINT OF COPPER DOG PUBLISHING, LLC

The Maauro Chronicles: When Fighting Monsters

Moondream Press
An Imprint of Copper Dog Publishing LLC
537 Leader Circle
Louisville, CO 80027
www.copperdogpublishing.com

Ordering Information:
Special discounts are available on quantity purchases by corporations, associations, and others. For details, contact the publisher at the address above.
Printed in the United States of America

Credits:
Author: Edward F. McKeown
Managing Editor: Michael H. Hanson
Creative Director: Helen H. Harrison
Editor: Laura Jean Stroupe
Proofreader: Julie Harrison Saunders
Proofreader: Catherine Van Sciver
Cover Art: iStockPhoto/Tithi Luadthong Art

ISBN:
978-1-943690-28-2 (Paperback)
978-1-943690-29-9 (Kindle)

Fiction: Science Fiction

DEDICATION

"Beware that, when fighting monsters,
you yourself do not become a monster...
for when you gaze long into the abyss.
The abyss gazes also into you."
—*Friedrich W. Nietzsche*

CONTENTS

INTRO

MAAURO IS MY FAVORITE OF MY CREATIONS, THOUGH like a parent I feel bad making a choice among them. Early on, I made the decision to set her story in the same universe as Robert Fenaday and Shasti Rainhell's adventures. This gave me a consistency in storytelling that I felt yielded a lot of benefits, not the least of which was the crossover character of Shasti Rainhell, who has reached the apex of her own power since her days on the privateer, Sidhe. This links the two major works I have done, with the short stories I have written on Confederate Space, allowing me to do some of what Larry Niven did in his "Known Space" universe. There is a certain relief in not having to invent new universes and a comfort in visiting places that have been seen before. It also allows me to deepen those cultures and their interrelationships over time. I work the same vision on the canvas of my words, over and over, like Monet and his waterlilies. The universe grows in complexity, color and texture.

I often feel that I did not create Maauro or her adventures. I tune in on her reality and she tells me the truth of her existence. There are times that I am typing so fast that I feel that I am first seeing the words on the screen. While I have always felt a close and organic relationship with my characters, it is the more so with Maauro. In part that may be because the first person present tense perspective makes her feel so close to me, almost as if she is hovering over my shoulder, watching to make sure I get it right. Wrik with his worries, his troubled past and his constant questioning about his courage was an easy character to reach out to, He's like the rest of us, conscious of his flaws and his coming short in what he wants out of himself. He is Everyman. I have a great affection for him, if not the fascination I have for Maauro.

There have been times in writing her that I have gotten it wrong. I initially had her in mind for that type of Japanese anime "cute gal" character so ubiquitous in anime. She rejected that, insisting that she was a serious person, with a real story to tell and that it was at novel length. So we started doing that. Little did I know that there would be eight novels of her life with no end in sight.

Those of you who have read the evolving relationship between Maauro and Wrik have seen them move steadily, if slowly, closer to a true commitment. That was not quite my idea as I had envisioned him being with Jaelle, but Maauro insisted that his future lay with her. Any attempt to write it otherwise yielded a poor story. When I again committed to her vision of herself and her future, the story began to sing.

Now while I realize that this all arises from the subconscious creative process, it doesn't feel that way. It feels more like she is somehow and someway real, and periodically I am privileged to be in contact with her. I think of her as a friend: resolute, caring and very, very dangerous. I sometimes hope that she does not speak to me for a long time.

—Edward F. McKeown

CHAPTER ONE

THE PROXIMITY ALARM SHRILLED AS *STARDUST* SPRANG into existence in Olympia system, driving post jump queasiness from my mind. My hands snapped onto the controls. We had to have emerged on top of something for the alarm to be screaming the instant after jump. My screen began to populate with images of multiple ships.

"We are not on a collision course with anything, Wrik," Maauro said quickly, but with her usual calm. Little perturbed the 50,000 years old android. She sat, hands crossed on her slender stomach, her huge eyes not even on the instruments. The ship spoke directly to her; indeed, the ship's AI was merely a subset of her own programs.

"What the hell?" Delt said, from the seat behind her. "Did we jump into a convoy?" His broad, sturdy face, under its shock of blonde hair, showed more concern and his hands danced over the communication controls. Like Maauro, little frightened Delt, former leader of my long dead squadron.

"No," Maauro said.

I, despite her assurance, was checking all vectors. We had emerged at .5C and there wasn't much time between detection and collision at relativistic speeds. Sloppy ship captains died young.

"The vessels surrounding us are warships," Maauro added. "I am detecting Confed and OSDF IFF's from them." Her small hands, capable of shearing steel, didn't stir from her lap.

"Do I remember correctly," came Dusko's dry voice, "that when Captain Fenaday first arrived here decades ago, that this occurred and someone fired a nuke at him?" The Dua-Denlenn, who looked like a woodland elf gone to seed, had entered the bridge quietly.

"Thanks for the history lesson," I shot back, satisfied that Maauro was, as usual, correct and we were not going to hit anything. "There weren't any Confed ships here back then and the OSDF was in rebellion. Hopefully history isn't about to replay itself."

Maauro shook her head. Her long, glossy, black hair shimmered like water as it fell over her shoulders. "I judge not. The disposition of these vessels, out of the likely emergence lanes, suggests a defensive posture, as if this fleet is blockading this jump point."

"Incoming message," Delt said. "Switching to the main screen."

I smiled to myself. Maauro would have detected the message before our mere biological processes could have responded, but she had made an art out of not asserting her innate superiority over the rest of us. She probably figured it was better to keep us busy.

"CSS *Vikrant* to commercial starship *Stardust*. Please respond."

I looked at Maauro. She gave a small nod. I touched the screen. "Stardust to CSS *Vikrant*, acknowledging. Surprised to see so many ships here, *Vikrant*. May I ask what's going on?" While I spoke to the starship, a cruiser of the *Alaska* class, our datadump of starmail, inventory and shipping documents radiated out of us to all receivers in the system. I was relieved to see that the cruiser was not interfering with our transmission.

"*Vikrant* to *Stardust*, your arrival was expected. You will be briefed on landing in the capitol. Director Rainhell sends her greetings and a welcome to you all. *Vikrant* out."

"We're expected?" Delt said.

I looked at Maauro.

"When we sent our messages to Jaelle," she said, with an embarrassed air, "I was also obliged to report to Candace concerning developments on Retief and our next destination. They must have sent the messages out by high speed courier immediately."

I suspected that more was going on, but Maauro had been somewhat fragile since Retief. Some of it I attributed to our new found intimacy. We'd become lovers on my homeworld, something that may never have occurred before between an AI and a biological. I also suspected something more had happened on Retief. Something she had not yet shared with me. Maauro had been involved in assisting Confed forces abort a rebellion on there. I knew that, but I also had a growing certainty that was not the sum of it.

Maauro had concealed things from me before, if she felt it was in my interest that she do so. Though I didn't like it, now wasn't the time to address the issue, especially as I'd initially snuck off to Retief to face my past without her. That had been an epic mistake and, to be fair, she'd made less of it than any other female would have, but she really hadn't needed to. For now, I would let the issue lie undisturbed, but not forgotten.

"Candace?" Delt asked, breaking my train of thought.

"Candace Deveraux, head of Confederation Military Intelligence," Maauro said. "We report directly to her, when we work for her at all."

Delt's eyes grew round. "You work directly for the head of MI?"

"We are too important an asset," Maauro said, "to be delegated to anyone lesser."

"And they call her Candace," Dusko said, leaning back against the bulkhead, with his restorative drink in hand.

"She does not share her grandfather's obsession with personal security and uses her own name," Maauro added, apparently missing the irony.

"*Stardust*, this is OSDF *Persephone* calling."

I turned back to the screen. "*Stardust* acknowledging."

"We are preparing to match course and speed and refuel you, courtesy of the Olympian government. Director Rainhell requests that you expedite your transit to the inner system."

"*Stardust* acknowledging. We will maintain course and speed."

"Stand by for refueling in twenty three minutes and fourteen seconds. *Persephone* out."

"Wow," Delt said. "Free gas. You guys really do rate around here."

Dusko shot Delt a sour look. "Aren't you a bit old to believe in free lunches?"

Delt pointed a thumb at the older Dua. "Is he always this cheerful?"

"If he gets any happier he may break into song," I said.

"Now, don't pick on Dusko," Maauro said.

Things are definitely different, I thought with a mental sigh. It still took quite the effort to get used to her being so proprietary about the Dua.

A wave of queasiness swept over me and I remembered my meds, quickly taking them from the compartment in my chair arm. The others I noted had already resorted to their cups and packets, save for Maauro of course.

To my surprise, a light signaled the arrival of a personal message. I thought it might be from Director Rainhell, then saw it had originated on Star Central.

"There is a message for us," I said, with rising unease.

"Yes, I know. It is from Jaelle," Maauro added, a note of dread in her voice.

Delt and Dusko looked at us and each other. Both rose without a word and left.

I sighed and stared at the panel. The message was a hologram.

"Delay," Maauro said, "will not change what the message holds."

"You don't already know?"

"I did not hack the message," she replied. "I believe we are meant to experience this at the same time."

I nodded and tapped the screen. An image of Jaelle Tekala, my friend, ex-lover and partner in Lost Planet, sprang into existence in the air between us. Her hair was ruffed out to its fullest and the business suit was of the finest cut. I had forgotten quite how beautiful Jaelle could be. Her yellow eyes, set in a face perfectly balanced between feline and human, were bright. A pang hit me at seeing the Nekoan; she'd been my first serious relationship.

"Wrik and Maauro," she began, "word has finally reached me that you are both alive and well, despite the troubles on Retief. It's difficult to put my relief and joy into words.

"I have listened to the two personal messages that you sent me many times. I'm glad that you have found love in each other. Truly, I am happy for you both. Please believe this. There is something between you two that will not be denied. You are, in some way, each other's essential other part. No one could stand in the way of that, nor would it have worked had I tried. I accept this.

"To you, Wrik, I am grateful you finally shared with me the full story of who you are and what happened to you. I wish I could have been the one to help you find your way, but as fate would have it, that role fell to Maauro.

"You have asked me if we are to remain consorts. A silly question, but I now better understand the human culture that makes you offer. We are, and we will remain so. You said that though we are no longer lovers, that you love me still. I return that feeling, my consort.

"To you Maauro, you who so swiftly asked if we are still networked—I give the same answer. We are, and I still care deeply for you.

"I do not wish our friendship to end, though it must take a new shape from here. I think that my own culture makes this easier than either of you suspect.

"We three have Lost Planet to run. I will be its public face and handle its trade. You two, and poor Dusko, I suppose, will be up to Gods know what, Gods knows where. I was warned by Confed Mil-Intel to expect that from Olympia there is another job waiting for you. I asked not to be told of it, at least for now. I will sleep better, I think.

"Send me messages when you can. Mine will come to you through Confed channels.

"Maauro, I know you have perfect recall and remember what I said to you on the roof on that day. If you hear it again, it will mean I am in terrible trouble, or Confed MI is no longer to be trusted. Candace may delete this part of the message, but probably won't dare, fearing you would detect tampering.

"There are other messages and reports to follow in this communication on the doings of Lost Planet. We have three ships now running specialty cargo. But I wanted this message to say all that is needed between us three.

"So be safe and return to Star Central when you can. For the meanwhile, know that I send my love. Farewell."

The image froze, and the pent up breath I hadn't realized I'd been holding whooshed out.

"I am intensely relieved," Maauro said. "I had feared worse."

"Jaelle has never failed to exceed anyone's expectations of her," I said, sinking back into my seat. *Wish I could say the same for me*, I thought, then shrugged it off. That was an echo of the old Wrik. I was no longer that person. I realized that the back of my shirt was damp with sweat and stood, letting the air conditioning dry me.

"It helps that she is from a species that does not demonstrate much in the ways of jealousy," Maauro added. "I would not forsake what I have for you for anything or anyone, but it would grieve me if Jaelle severed ties with us over it."

"This calls for a celebration," I said. "We didn't bring enough Reitefan wine with us, but if ever anything called for a bottle— this does."

Maauro went to get a bottle, just as Delt walked back past the hatchway. He stuck a concerned face in through the door, then caught sight of Jaelle's image.

He raised an eyebrow at me. "Everything ok?"

I nodded. "Maauro just went to get a bottle of Mid-star to celebrate."

He looked back at the holo. "So that is Jaelle Tekala."

"Yes, and mercifully, still my friend and consort."

"Remind me why I was feeling sorry for you when you were off planet? God, she's gorgeous. It appears you were up to your eyeballs in the beauties of the galaxy."

I noticed Maauro coming up behind Delt with the bottle. From the look in her eye and her grip on the bottle, it seemed she might bean him with it.

"Of course," he added, with a grin, "none can compare with the Queen of the Stardust, our own dear Maauro."

"Here, here," I said, getting three cups from the restorative cabinet on the table.

"Very good," Maauro said archly. "You spotted my reflection from a monitor."

"Well that, and the fact that you smell like ginger cookies," he returned.

I smiled. The byplay with them wasn't really jealously, just Maauro playing at human characteristics. It was becoming a thing between them.

"Will you join us?" Maauro said. "We celebrate good news. Jaelle remains our friend and Wrik's consort. Lost Planet lives."

She turns to me. "Wrik, there are four of us. Please put out a cup for Dusko. I have called him up."

My eyebrows twitched. There was a reproof in her voice, more evidence that something happened on Retief that I didn't know of.

"Sure," I said, and reached for another cup.

Dusko reappeared and perched on the communications station chair. "There is good news, I take it?"

"Yes," Maauro said. "Our network to Jaelle is healthy and intact."

"Good," he said, scratching his chin. "She was always a smart one." His eyes, blue from lid-to-lid, betrayed little of what went on under his salt and pepper hair, but he seemed genuinely pleased.

I unscrewed the bottle and poured for us. Then, moved by a sudden impulse, I took out another recyclable cup and poured a tiny shot, placing it in front of Jaelle's image.

I raised my glass, "To love, friendship and forgiveness."

Each of us thought our individual thoughts on that subject and savored our wine.

I head to the galley while Wrik handles the inflight refueling with Persephone, something I could have done while I wandered the ship through my interface with it. I like to leave the details of flying Stardust to him. It is very important to Wrik to be a good pilot, and even I am impressed by his skills. Meanwhile, I will work on one of my own developing skills: cooking. It would no doubt have amused my Creators that I, an M7 Mark 2 Prototype Combat Android, would enjoy the act of making food for biologicals, when my initial purpose was to destroy biological life. Well, Infestors anyway. But the small rituals of classic feminine behavior intrigue me. I have built an identity as a female, and while there are many ways of defining female, I enjoy looking after my crew. In this regard, I have the unlikely assistance of Dusko, who left the bridge for his hydroponic garden. We will have fresh vegetables, fruit and herbs tonight.

I briefly consider my menu: lamb, roast potatoes, rosemary bread, peas, onions and carrots. The wine will be a pinot noir. Ice cream and fruit will finish the meal. I hum to myself in the galley until I spot that, as usual, some item of Delt's clothing is hung over a chair by the metal table.

As delighted as I am to have Delt with Lost Planet, I have quickly learned there are some downsides. He has a tendency toward practical jokes, which are more effective on Wrik than I, and he is something of a slob. I have unconsciously been assuming that all men are like Wrik, who I now see is much more fastidious about his person and quarters than the unruly Delt.

Wrik merely laughed when I mentioned this on the voyage from Retief to the jump point. "Yes, he was always a bit of a mess. We used to bunk together in the Kaydets. If I hadn't made his bunk for him, he'd be marching off demerits daily. You have to remember, I've been a deep spacer. There's no spare room on ships. Everything has to be just so. He's had a whole planet to leave his gym socks around on. I think his mother and older sisters spoiled him too."

I privately think that vaporizing a few of his random bits of clothing is not a bad idea, assuming he notices they are missing. Still, I decide to be tolerant. I am not used to this many males in close proximity. Dusko keeps to himself, or his quarters, most times and would never leave anything where someone else might lay hands on it. He seems even more determined to do so since the relentlessly cheerful Delt signed onboard.

I sigh. While I too enjoy the bright presence, I occasionally long for the quieter Stardust. Still, it does me good to see Wrik in the company of his old friend. The darkness that so often clouded his face is much rarer since he's completed his self-appointed mission to confront his old squadron mates. I also know that he is worried about Delt, who has not lived up to his promise as a young man, being also wounded deeply, but in a different way than Wrik.

So I simply remove the offending item and place it in the laundry, then return to my dinner preparations. Dusko greets me with shoots of onions and cloves of garlic.

The remainder of the transit to Olympia is uneventful. Wrik and I spend the days together and make love several times. I am still trying to adjust to being a sexual, as well as a loving, being. I grow more attuned to his moods, to the way that he looks at me. As for myself, I revel in the sea of love that surrounds me. Though I have no libido, being a machine in origin, I do throw in situations where I initiate, which I notice he appreciates. Still, I wonder what it must be like to be in a human body during sex. To be so utterly swept up in something one was made to do, something that most of their culture and art is based in. Perhaps my answers lie ahead on the bright world growing in our screens.

We are cleared for a landing in the capitol city, Marathon and pass liners and other far larger freighters that must be wondering why this small scoutship-freighter is accorded such honor. I fancy that Wrik looks extra proud as he guides our ship into the approach to the spaceport. The automatic landing system takes over, as it does at most spaceports. Both Wrik and I stay in the circuit and monitor. He, because of his professionalism as a pilot, and I, as usual, alert to treachery. There is nothing to be alarmed of and we planet in a perfect fin down landing.

"Well, we are here," Wrik says, stretching and standing after securing us for planetside routine. "Landing time is 1500 hours; weather is sunny and bright on a summer afternoon." He looks at me. The voyage to Olympia was my plan and I have not yet shared with him my reason, nor am I yet ready to discuss it.

I too stand. "We have our invitation from Shasti. I wish to see her as soon as we can."

He looks at me curiously. "I hadn't realized you two had become so close."

I smile. "Shasti and I are much alike. We did not have much time together, but I think we are, well, you might say kindred souls. We were both created, she biologically and I mechanically, and we see the universe in similar terms. I can hardly wait to see her again."

He nods, aware that something more underlies this, but as usual, and I am thankful for this, he gives me the space to unfold at my own rate.

"So, what do you want the rest of us to do?" Delt asks. Behind him, Dusko, who usually prefers his own cabin for takeoff and landings, makes his way into the bridge.

Again Wrik looks at me. "I've made no plans beyond our arrival here. Doubtless we will be contacted by MI, given what Jaelle said, but until we know what they want, it will be hard to plan."

"Nor I," I reply, "but with our lives, it probably pays to have the ship refueled and reprovisioned as quickly as we can. Dusko, will you see to the sale of our present cargo? We will hold off taking on general cargo until we decide where we voyage to next. Of course, you will want to enjoy some leave in the capitol. My AI on the ship can take care of routine tasks."

He nods. I know he will take the time to peruse the market for his own semi-illicit trade in questionable goods. So long as this causes no trouble for the ship, I do not care.

"I can take care of the reprovisioning," Delt says. "I don't know anyone here and I'm sure there will be time for local exploring." He then grins. "I hear the local girls are goddesses."

"And the local men, gods," Dusko added, with a touch of smug satisfaction.

"Always ready to rain on any parade you see?" Delt shot back.

"Maybe you can find a female with poor eyesight," Dusko returned.

"Behave," I growl at them both. Delt merely grins, but Dusko shuts up. In his culture, I am his alpha, only to be displeased at cost. Since his service to me on Retief though, he has been testing his newly expanded limits with me.

Wrik, I notice, is watching me with careful attention. My boyfriend, I think and savor the word, is unusually sensitive and intelligent, he too sees the change.

An incoming text message hits our system.

"A vehicle is being sent to meet us," I say, saving Wrik the time to read it. "We have barely time to change before we will be whisked away."

"We?" Wrik says with a smile.

I stick my tongue out at him. A moment later my outer body shimmers. Then I am standing before them in a taupe bolero jacket, over a deep-aqua blouse that matches my eyes and skirt to match the jacket, closed toe shoes with a three-inch heel and a bow on the side. A strand of pearls hangs about my neck.

In my hime-style hair is a small yellow silk ribbon, confining a fingerful of my hair. A silk ribbon was Wrik's first gift to me, and I have always worn something yellow in my hair since, save in battle. It used to be a larger bow, but now I judge that too juvenile a look for me, given that my appearance is now closer to an apparent age of in my early twenties. My first ribbon was lost in battle before I took such care. I have always regretted it.

Delt whistles. "Maauro, you are the definition of understated elegance."

Wrik shakes his head, "And in the blink of an eye."

"You better get your homely self in motion," Delt said. "You're holding up the parade my friend."

"On my way," Wrik says and dashes off.

CHAPTER ONE

I leave the bridge to Delt. Dusko nods carefully at me and disappears to attend to my orders about disposing of our cargo. I make my way back to our cabin where I have a small present for Shasti, a set of earrings made from an unusual stone found on a plateau of the highlands of Retief. Each is a perfect fossilized miniature shell, in pink and gold. I hope she will like them. By the time I retrieve my present, cunningly wrapped in handmade paper over an ornate wooden box, Wrik has changed and is waiting for me. He wears his best uniform, an officer's dress blues of the Confederacy, modified with our Lost Planet logo. As our commissions are secret, he doesn't wear the military rank he is entitled to in the Confederate Navy, but on his collar is the single star that denotes a ship's master. He wears the full cap with a Lost Planet insignia on it. I think he looks very handsome.

We leave the ship by the main airlock, both of us donning sunglasses. In Wrik's case, it's for protection from the fierce Olympian sun. For me, it minimizes attention to my overlarge eyes. At the foot of our ship, a flitter is already waiting. It bears the insignia of the Olympian Security Directorate. An unmarked vehicle behind it holds two security officers.

A woman stands besides the marked flitter. She is beautiful, with blood- red hair, and stands 6-feet and 3.65 inches. She greets us with a professional smile and firm handshake. "I'm Ameline Girardot from Director Rainhell's office. I was sent to welcome you to Olympia." She gives me a very curious look, and I wonder how much she was briefed about me.

We exchange the usual pleasantries, then slide into the vehicle. There is a uniformed driver, a precaution, as it is automatically piloted. We lift off, followed by the unmarked flitter. I gaze back at Stardust, as she sits vertical on the fins that hold her impellers. Her green and gold colors sparkle in the brilliant sun. Beyond her the city of Marathon, with its blue and white buildings contrasting with taller glass and metal skyscrapers, embraces a wide bay. I wonder how Shasti stays so pale under such a fierce sun.

My knowledge of Earth history tells me the planet was named with Earth's ancient country of Greece in mind for two reasons. The first was its sun-washed shores, abundance of islands and aquamarine seas in its more habitable regions. The second was more ambiguous, a devotion to the art of human perfection, initially by contract marriages between the more "perfect" people and later by genetic engineering. We are here to visit with the epitome of that science; for all that she turned her back on her creators and brought down that government.

I couldn't quite contain my nerves or excitement at the thought of seeing Shasti Rainhell again. Her voyages, both with Robert Fenaday and later, when she in turn captained the privateer Sidhe, were the stuff of legend. That legend might be less popular here, where Shasti and Robert had destroyed the Eugenicists of Olympia and touched off a brief war with their allies, the Voit-Veru, who, unfortunately for them, had been holding Fenaday's wife as a prisoner for years. In return, he atom-bombed one of their cities.

I snuck a glance at Maauro, who sat calm and still in the right seat of the oversize flitter. She wore sunglasses as well and they looked good on her. She detected my glance and half-turned, smiling sweetly, and rested a hand on my arm.

"It will be good to see Shasti again," she said, in her musical voice.

I could only smile back. "If by that, you mean seeing Director Rainhell, hero of the Confederacy, I agree. Though I doubt I will be able to bring myself to call her by her first name."

"Well, we have discussed many personal issues," she replied archly. "We are closely networked."

I wondered if I was one of those personal issues discussed by the two deadliest females in known space and what it was that was bringing them together. I was still concerned about some emotional fragility to Maauro. It took place only when we were alone, but there were times when she was sad. This frightened me, because I thought it might arise out of the change in our relationship. When finally I'd confronted her about it on the outbound leg of the voyage—she'd been genuinely surprised.

"Nothing could be further from that," she'd said.

Thereafter, she'd been more cheerful, but I'd felt that she was just hiding whatever was bothering her.

It particularly galled me that Dusko might know more of this than I did. He'd been with her while I'd escaped to Retief to confront my past and my family. But the Dua would never part with any secret that she'd shared with him. He'd originally lived in dread of her and had almost died at her hands several times during his first months aboard. While it seemed that the nature of their relationship had changed, at the heart of it was his healthy fear of displeasing the "alpha" of his particular little pack.

Maauro put her head on my shoulder, which stilled my sudden impulse to ask her why we were here.

We flew over the bay, circling upward. Our hostess was making sure we got a good look on Olympia, with its population of millions and the rocky shoreline and beautiful bay.

"Is it strange," Maauro suddenly asked, "to have landed in the same spaceport as Robert Fenaday's Sidhe when he came here?"

"It is," I replied. "He wasn't aboard when she landed, having snuck planetside with the attack force the night before. The star-frigate landed in the bay," I pointed to an area seaward of the Stardust. "Shasti landed *us as close to where she landed as she could. Sidhe was a hell of a lot larger than Stardust."*

"But not prettier," Maauro insisted.

"But not prettier," I agreed.

We flew the rest of the distance to the Presidential Palace in companionable silence. After all, I was with the woman I loved, and it was a beautiful day.

CHAPTER TWO

WHILE WRIK AND I CHAT, I AM SCANNING ALL AVAILABLE NETWORKS *and wavelengths. Even on the homeworld of a friend, it does not pay to be lax. The secret of what I am is barely a secret anymore. While I remain hidden from the general public and casual inspection, too many in powerful places have learned of my existence. One of those groups, the Voit-Veru, formerly had much influence here.*

As we fly, I sense Delt purchasing fuel and sundries for the ship. Stardust's AI is inspecting and repairing the ship, using small nonautonomous robots I have made for it. I do not care for other machines much, and these are non humanoid and mostly confined to the mechanical spaces of the hull, seldom seen by the crew.

Dusko has left the ship to seek buyers for our cargo. He will spend the night seeking diversions of his choice. I do not approve of some of these, but he needs a chance to "blow off some steam" as Wrik would say. He will prefer to purchase female company, rather than cultivate it, as he would consider the latter a waste of time on a world he may not return to.

I find myself wondering how Delt will deal with his needs and wants and hoping that he will be less casual. Then I wonder why the thought occurs at all. For some reason, I feel that sex is important and should be a mutual gift and not sold. Perhaps I am being impractical. As one who has barely put a toe into the waters of sensuality, perhaps I should not judge how others swim.

My thoughts are interrupted by a slight jar as the automatic landing system for the palace takes control of us. The pilot sits back. We circle down to an immense building which partly resembles the Pantheon of ancient earth, set among other more modern structures that complement the ancient style. We are well up on a foothill above the city.

"I hate ALS," Wrik says.

"There, there dear, I know. It must be so hard to trust your well-being to a machine." I say. His double take and strangled laugh are most enjoyable.

The flitter settles on the pad. We are greeted by a detail of soldiers wearing the green and gray colors of the OSDF as we disembark behind Giradot. All are tall and we are treated to their salute, which Wrik returns and I nod at. Wrik at six foot –two inches is not tall here and I, eight inches shorter, must look up at everyone.

We are escorted into the large building, past people hurrying about on errands and well away from a tour of school children. Giradot leads us into one of the modern looking buildings to the right. Soon we are in offices, but everyone immediately yields right of way to Giradot, and my suspicion that she is one of Shasti's closest aides is confirmed.

We pause before a door labeled Planetary Security, which opens as we advance. Giradot steps aside and motions us forward. She does not follow us in. The office revealed is opulent and, at a large desk surrounded by holos and monitors, sits Shasti. She rises gracefully with a smile. The years since we saw her last, on the night we returned her wounded grandson to her, have been kind to her. Now 106 years old, only the silver banners in her long black hair and a certain weariness in her eyes betray the age of the greatest of the Engineered.

She comes around the desk, towering over us both. I barely come up to her chest. Wrik throws his best salute. "Director Rainhell, it's a pleasure to see you again."

Her smile turns indulgent, and Shasti extends her hand. She is a personal hero to Wrik and well aware of it.

"Please, Wrik, no such formality between a grandmother and the man who saved her grandchild."

Wrik blushes and manages, "Yes, Ma'am." as he takes her hand. It is terribly cute.

Shasti turns to me, and placing a hand on my shoulders, bends to kiss me on both cheeks, to Wrik's evident astonishment. "And greetings to you, Maauro, without whom all would have been lost so many times."

"I was glad to render aid in such a good cause," I reply, warmed by her welcome. "If it does not cause distress, how is Maximillian?"

She nods. "He is largely recovered, remaining somewhat delicate emotionally. It is hard for him to shake off all the death that being a prisoner of the Destroyer made him an unwilling accomplice to.

"He paints and studies and is content with this." Her face hardens. "I have forbidden anyone to try and involve him in politics, or other thoughts of a career, and in this I have been obeyed."

"I understand," I say. "I too have been a prisoner of programming others inflicted on me."

Wrik places a hand on my shoulder.

"Thank you," Shasti says. "I knew that you, of all people, would understand."

"Please send him my regards, though I am doubtful he remembers me."

"He says he remembers a gentle voice singing to him. It was a great comfort."

"I am glad," I say, unexpectedly moved by this.

Shasti gestures at a veranda, behind what I detect is weapon resistant plas-steel. It reveals a nice view of a garden. The table is set for three. One nice thing about Olympian furniture is that I need not be concerned about my weight. I am not much heavier than the adult men here.

"I've had a selection of Olympian delicacies brought in for an early dinner." She gives me a mischievous look. *"Maauro's consists mostly of deserts. Perhaps it is the indulgent grandmother in me."*

"Well," I say, *"if I end up sitting in your lap, you'll have no one but yourself to blame."*

A chuckle comes from the tall woman as we seat ourselves around the table.

"My husband will join us later," Shasti said. *"It was too much to hope that both of us would be free at the same time."*

Shasti and Wrik chat amiably about ships and spacing as the food and promised deserts materialize on robo-servers. Wrik gradually relaxes as she tells him of her battles in the desperate days of the Olympian rebellion. His eyes shine as he looks at her in a way that could make me jealous, if I let it.

Dinner and especially the desserts are all that could be desired. Shasti asks questions about the Retiefan rebellion and I give her the carefully edited version that is safe with Wrik present.

"I fear that we will see more such incidents," Shasti says. *"Power is shifting within the Confederacy. The lessons of the Conchirri War are lost on the later generations. The central government continues to weaken and the new species that have been added have diluted the old, human-led, coalition. Nothing has arisen to replace it.*

"Have such elements resurrected themselves here?" I ask.

"Not as such," Shasti said. *"With the fall of the Eugenicist cabal, that movement was utterly discredited here. We closed the labs and forbad further engineering of humans. I have seen to it that the Engineered have been woven back into society. Had we become a persecuted minority, there would have been a rich field for the planting of dissidents. There are a few revanchist societies of course, but you have to remember, the Engineered were themselves to be replaced by people like me, a totally mixed human. For the Engineered, who so prized their bloodlines, losing the meaning of those bloodlines was upsetting. It knocked out the underpinnings of their lives."*

At the end of dinner, the door chimes.

"Ah," Shasti says, *"that will be my husband."* She taps a key on a console and the doors swing in to reveal Mikhail Vaughn, President of Olympia. Wrik and I stand as he strides into the room. Even I must admit he is a daunting presence. He is seven feet two inches tall, massively muscled, but on the body of a triathlete. His skin is swarthy under steel gray hair over eyes that almost blaze blue. Vaughn was designed, I feel, to look the part of a king and does.

"Hello, Darling," he rumbles. *"So these are our guests."*

Wrik looks up at Vaughn, his posture suddenly tense. I suspect that Vaughn has that effect on most beings. But not me, and I have placed myself between Wrik and the giant.

Vaughn grins at me, as if aware of what I have done, and Wrik, perhaps realizing it as well, steps around me and reaches out his hand. Vaughn's grin broadens in appreciation at his refusal to be intimidated.

"Mr. President, an honor to meet you," Wrik says.

"And you, Captain Trigardt. May I call you, Wrik? I owe you thanks for the safe return of my grandson, though I must also share those thanks with you." He turns to me with a gleam in his eye. I recognize the combination: interest, intelligence and avarice. I am on my guard.

"So you are the fabled Maauro?" he says.

"I am," I reply, "and the very embodiment of the concept that good things come in small packages."

He gives a delighted laugh. "From only a few seconds exposure, it is obvious that you are no mechanism. Only a fool would entertain the thought a moment longer."

"My boyfriend thinks the same." I reach and shake Vaughn's hand. Mine simply disappears into his, but his handshake, while firm, is careful, as if I was the delicate female I appear to be.

"More each day," Wrik says.

"Ah," Vaughn said. "A spacer with a glib tongue; perhaps I should guard my interests by taking you on a tour of the palace?"

Shasti laughs. "I don't think he is interested in trading for an older model."

"Well," I say, "technically, I'm the older model."

"I am simply honored to be in the presence of Captain Rainhell," Wrik says gallantly.

"I can see why you like him," Shasti says to me. "He is reflexively kind."

"There is a list of reasons I like him," I reply. "It is not short."

We chat amiably as Vaughn repeats his thanks and we tell him directly of the grim adventure on Seddon and the retrieval of his grandson. The huge hands knot at the discussion of Maximillian's suffering.

"Ah," he says. "It is so hard to hear of the pains of one's grandchildren. Would that I had Bexlaw's throat in my hands." This last comes out as a growl.

"You would have to fight me for the chance of ending him," Shasti said.

"Still, enough of that," Vaughn says, visibly bottling his anger. "This is a glad day when we can greet people to whom we owe so much. My son-in-law and daughter are off world, but they send greetings and thanks. If they can get back before whatever duties take you back to the stars, we will all gather."

He hesitates and casts a look at Shasti. "One hopes you will forgive it if Maximillian does not come. Reminders of his imprisonment—

Both Wrik and I shake our heads.

"Think nothing of it," Wrik says. *"The boy's health is all that is important. We have received thanks enough and are glad for a chance to be of service to Captain Rain... to you both.*

Again the grin. "My dear, I do believe this boy is in love with you."

Wrik blushes furiously, "Always an admirer."

"No teasing, you great Ogre," Shasti adds. "He is a fine handsome boy, but quite spoken for."

"And it would never do to incur the enmity of this one, from what I have heard." Vaughn adds.

"No one has ever profited by it," I agree.

He did a double-take on me, but his face is thoughtful. "Of that, I have no doubt."

Vaughn rose from his chair. "Well Wrik, shall I show you around? There is an excellent range in the basement with quite a selection of vintage and rare weapons. Are you a good shot?"

"Yes, with pistols," he replies.

"Well then, shall we try our luck."

Wrik touches my hand, probably aware that this has been arranged by me so I can be alone with Shasti. He follows the giant Vaughn out.

I sit opposite Shasti on the sofa, which handles my weight easily. Shasti sighs as she settles back and lifts a glass of wine. "When I was young, I was something of a night owl. Now, I find the day long enough and look forward to a nice warm bed before midnight. Today began especially early, for reasons we will discuss later."

The admission of the effect of age causes a pang of sadness for me. Shasti is new to my network, but is the oldest being in it. An Olympian might live 175 or 200 years, but she is through more than half of that. This bears on my own journey and the commission I am about to hand her.

"Shasti, I have come to ask a favor of you."

"For you or Wrik? Anything within my power."

I smile. "It is indeed for both of us, but I must ask you not to discuss this with him yet. He does not know my intentions."

Her smile dims slightly. "What is it that you want?"

"We are lovers now in deed and word."

"Then you took the advice I gave you by our little waterfall."

"Yes, I did. Though it took me a long, somewhat bewildering time to do so – yet now I have that which I could once only barely imagine.

"Yet, I find that I want more. Wrik is wonderful to me, but I think he may love me more then desire me. As for me – well, I feel something inexpressible and wonderful when we make love. But I know it is only the dimmest echo of what he feels with his biological body. What you feel with yours. I want to feel that. I want to be joined with him as the same form of life."

"You want to become a human?" Shasti asked. Expressions flitted across her beautiful face: wonder, fear, doubt, amazement above all.

"Not forever," I say. "I have learned something unprecedented in my journeys, a knowledge I purchased with great pain. I believe I can download my consciousness into a human body and back it up to my android body daily. I will live as a woman for the lifetime of the human body and then I will continue in this body."

"Such a thing can be done?" Shasti murmured in astonishment.

"I believe so. I have seen the process. But there's something I lack, a human body. So I have come to the world of greatest genetic biological engineers. Shasti, can you make a body for me – not as a child either? Wrik cannot wait decades for me to grow to adulthood. I wish to start as an adult woman, and as close to my present appearance as can be managed."

Silence follows as Shasti mulls over what I'd asked. "This is a daunting prospect," she says finally. "The technology to do much of this was destroyed in the fall of the Eugenicists. I myself was made in a somewhat similar fashion. No actual parents – I was assembled from the distilled genes of many thousands, perhaps millions.

"But I was made as an infant and grew as a child. This would be growing a human body to full-size with a functioning brain, yet having no personality, no soul of its own."

"Yes. In that last we are in agreement," I quickly add. "I will not take the life or place of another."

"Of course," Shasti said with a raised hand. "The thought did not even occur."

"Oh," I say, "to the owner of a leather-bound volume of Frankenstein?" I cut my eyes in the direction of the bookshelf where it sits.

She grimaces. "For those of us who are made, not born, the book does resonate."

"I know," I reply. "I've read it, though I confess only as data, not text."

"What manner of experience is that?" Shasti muses. "You must contain many libraries in you, but you still read?"

"The best I could render it for you is that I contain these works – I am aware of them and their content – yet I can only focus on so many things at one moment. Think of it as being a very good librarian who knows and has read many of her shelves – yet must draw down a book to enjoy it."

Shasti nods and I know her questions are but to give her time to think of the practical, moral and ethical issues raised in my request. "Interesting, Little One, I don't know if this is possible. Of certainty, much research would be needed. The expense does not concern me. My husband is a largely benevolent dictator. Oh, I mean 'president.'" She smiles. "I have access to black accounts and will bring it in under some pretext.

"But," she leans forward, "we of Olympia have walked this road before, playing God, but without god-like judgment. If we create this miracle – it will be for you alone-for what I owe you."

"Do not fear," I reply. "This would work for no other being than me." This is half true. The psychotic hacker, Lilith, who I fought on Retief, had downloaded a human consciousness into a sextet of HCR bodies, though she remained chained to the life of her original human body. In that much, we are totally different. My original body has no time limit on it.

"This is true?" Shasti asked. The question was asked and answered, but she seems to wish assurances.

"I do swear it. None other than I can use this technique. A human downloaded into a machine body does not escape Death's dominion. When the biological body dies, the person dies." I remember my final conversation with Lilith when I let her escape. Months after my encounter with Lilith, I still did not know if I wished her peace in the time she had left, or merely an early exit from space-time.

"You are sure the same fate does not await you?" Shasti asks, shaking her mane of black and silver hair out of her face.

"There is no complete certainty in this, as in much of our existence. Reality is only a construct of probabilities. Yet, I have very high confidence in this. I would not risk my future, or Wrik's grief, on something where the odds were not markedly favorable.

"Do you not tell him because you fear that he will not want this, or that he will want it too much?" she asks. "The question is woman-to-woman, I will not object if you choose not to answer."

"I see no reason not to. I withhold the information only until and unless there's a choice. We may never come to this bridge, or if it appears before me, I may choose not to cross it. I cannot say for certain what I will do in the future. I am so changed in just these few years – it's impossible to guarantee my future behaviors, but if it is possible then I believe I will do it."

"As for Wrik, I do not doubt him – but he is young and male. I will no longer consider, or allow, that place in what is between us, to be occupied by another, as I did before. But no matter how I work to extend Wrik's life – it will end, and too soon for me. Already this is a terror I must cope with. You are all so appallingly fragile. I can only be amazed at the courage you show in your exploring, your striving, your loving."

"So in what time I have with Wrik, I want everything I can possibly have – it may have to last me for all of my existence."

Shasti rises from the sofa, crosses to me and bends down to fold me in an embrace. I realize that I am on the edge of my seat. My voice, demeanor and posture have revealed my fears. I relax in her embrace, savoring the warmth and the scent of her, wondering if this is how a child feels in the arms of its mother.

"*I am glad you love Wrik, which has always been clear to me. Still more, I am glad that he loves you, which is equally obvious from when I see him with you. Still,*" *she says with a half smile,* "*it's as well that you recognize that he's young and male. Men are like…*"

"*Onions,*" *I add,* "*many layers and each makes you cry.*"

She gives a delighted laugh and sits on the couch beside me. "*Exactly!*"

"*Has it been so between you and Vaughn?*" *I ask, greatly daring.*

"*Ah,*" *she says.* "*You waited for the right moment and got me back.*"

I raise an eyebrow in her own gesture and say, "*The question is woman-to-woman, and I will not object if you choose not to answer.*"

Again she laughs. "*You're a true female, as if there was ever any doubt.*" *Her expression turns serious, even wistful.* "*We have had our times, Vaughn and I. Our love was very passionate, wild at first, as if we were literally made for each other. He is Engineered, but not to the degree I am. No one else is.*

"*But we are in some ways too alike. We have competed for power, and our vision for Olympia is not always the same. We sometimes clash – most notably over our children and grandchildren. He and his son-in-law have that dangerous streak of a will to power.*"

"*And you?*"

"*Of course I have it too, but it is linked with my protective instincts. I will suffer no danger to what is mine.*"

"*In this way we are much alike,*" *I say.* "*I seek no dominion over biological life. I've always wondered why your fantasists always have my kind either enslaving or destroying yours. Why should I want to rule humans or other biologicals? The handful I'm involved with take up too much of my time. Honestly!*"

"*Oh, Maauro,*" *Shasti said,* "*stay up and drink with me. I cannot say when I've enjoyed company more.*"

"*Well, I will happily drink, but I if some more sweets could be found as well…*"

CHAPTER THREE

I WALKED ALONGSIDE VAUGHN, BARELY COMING UP TO HIS shoulder. He spoke easily of the history of Olympia, the founding of the colony and the construction of the Palace. Soldiers saluted as we passed. Many of the civilian staff nodded at Vaughn, or greeted him with, "Good afternoon, Mr. President."

"You've been president for four terms," I said.

"Yes," he replied. "But not consecutively, it's against the constitution. Fortunately, given how long-lived people are, we have been able to hold off term limits. Still, I can only run twice more. I keep talking to Shasti about running, but my wife isn't very political, and while she has mellowed with age, she is still likely to answer an insult with a straight shot to the throat."

"Wouldn't want to stop one of those," I said.

"No indeed," he replied. "Shasti, as you probably know, was the ultimate expression of the Genetic Engineer's art. Pound for pound, she is strongest person ever created; I just outweigh her. By a little too much these days," he chuckled, patting his mid-section.

False modesty, I thought, *by a consummate politician*. There was no softness in Vaughn's middle, the hand had smacked into thick muscle. But I nodded.

We walked down into a part of the building devoid of paintings, statuary and gifts of state. The offices to each side had a more utilitarian look.

"Our history," Vaughn continued, "is of course, not always a pleasant subject."

"You were raised in the Guild of Assassins," I said.

"Just so," he agreed. "As Shasti herself was before she escaped."

"It's interesting," I said. "I don't think many would have imagined that the leader of the Old Guard would end up married to the woman who destroyed the Old Guard."

"Even more than you may think, given that my initial assignment was to kill her, which she of course perfectly frustrated." He snorted a laugh. "Perfectly frustrated actually describes the first couple years of our courtship. I ended up pursuing her half way across the galaxy before my interest was reciprocated.

"Ah, here we are," he continued, gesturing at a huge door. Well, all doors were huge here. This one was marked, 'weapons range.' Inside, sat two men in dark uniforms with red trim. Both stood to attention, but Vaughn waved it away. "At ease. Do me a favor, Bob, get out a few of those old cartridge weapons, as well as my favorites."

"Yes, sir," said the elder of the pair. The younger man followed him out.

"So, Wrik, if I may call you that?"

"Yes, sir, of course."

"You may call me Mikhail, when it is just the two of us. I see no need to stand on ceremony."

"Mr. President, I haven't even managed to call Captain Rainhell by her first name either. It seems....disrespectful."

Vaughn smiled. "I can see why she likes you. I guess it is nice to have such admirers. The offer stands."

"Thank you.

"However, I have a few impertinent questions to ask you before our armorer's return."

"If among those questions is, why we are here, then I can't help you. I really haven't a clue. After I went to Retief, Maauro joined me there and she was involved suppressing a revolution. Then, all of a sudden, she wanted to see Shasti again."

"Interesting, I have a feeling that your Maauro resembles my Shasti in more than just coloration. Both of them keep secrets from us when they believe it is necessary to do so."

I nodded. "She does. I wish she didn't feel the need, but I have to admit that sometimes she's had reason. I might even have pressed the issue except...well, when I left for Retief...for personal reasons...I didn't tell her I was going."

"Ah," he said, wagging his finger. "Your position was not strong. I agree, now is not the time to press. Politics is not that different from relationships. It's interesting to see that your relationship with the young lady... well, she is fifty thousand years old... but she certainly seems like a young lady..."

I couldn't help but laugh. "I think Maauro has made a study of classic femininity, when she isn't battling giant mecha, or dodging missiles. You, at least, are a match for your wife—"

"Not sure about that," he said, scratching his head

"With me, sometimes I feel like I'm the comic relief," I said.

"From what I read, it was you that figured out how to stop the mecha that imprisoned my grandson and was crushing Maauro underfoot."

I nodded with a thrill of pride. "Sometimes the whole is greater than the sum of its parts."

"We feel the same about our marriage."

I sighed. "It's complicated sometimes."

"I had wondered," he said. "She is a fantastic simulation of a beautiful young girl, big-eyed to be sure, but we have such mutations in the Confederacy, especially on Gloaming, the world she originally used as a cover. Yet, her body is made of fantastic alloys and ceramics? How does that work for the pair of you?"

CHAPTER THREE

I felt a strange desire to confide in Vaughn as he looked at me, somber and thoughtful. He'd lived a long time, seen much, and he had Shasti.

"I do not mean to pry," he added. "But like everyone else in on the secret, which I can only wonder how long will remain secret, I'm fascinated by her."

"There's a lot we are working out…as man and woman. Hell, for all we know this is the first time this has ever occurred." I felt a frustration for not having a vocabulary for what we were living through. In a way, Delt was too close to talk to as he traveled with us. Vaughn, I could leave behind.

"Well, I understand about complicated," he said, an ironic expression on his big features. "At least your love life is largely private. My wife ended up pregnant by a man who wanted to kill me, not long after our own affair started."

I looked at him. "I knew she'd had a child with… "

"Robert Fenaday," he grimaced at saying the name. "The tale isn't well known. One of Shasti's differences is that her body could delay bringing a fertilized egg to term. Not that she even knew it. She'd been pregnant in that sense for years by him. Her body, because of the various dangers, didn't allow it to proceed.

"It didn't become noticeable until she visited the Fenadays, while Lisa Fenaday was pregnant. She'd never spent time around another pregnant female, and her body decided it must be safe to bring on the pregnancy."

"That must have been awkward."

Vaughn laughed. "Oh, I would have paid serious money for a video of when the doctor told Shasti and the Fenadays that he was the father." His face showed serious relish at the thought.

"And that child?" I asked.

"Stellan was raised by the Fenadays. Shasti was still voyaging in the *Sidhe* then and we were not yet a couple. Fenaday and I have never been friends, but Stellan is Shasti's child and he treated him like his own. To my surprise, so did Lisa Fenaday, as did his half-sister, Daire. Once, some boys were annoying his "big" sister. Stellan, being engineered, was large and powerful for his age. He threw their bikes into the Shannon River. There was quite a fuss over it."

"Oh?"

"Yes, the other boys were still on them at the time." He chuckled.

"In any event," Vaughn continued. "Shasti and Lisa became quite close. She still visits them occasionally. I've only gone the once.

"Some years later, we passed through our own rather stormy courtship and we had a daughter of our own, Melisande. A beautiful girl, though she inherited much of her mother's willfulness. So I know about complications."

The armorers returned with a selection of weapons. I could clearly tell which ones were for me, as Vaughn's hands would be too large for them. There were revolvers of an ancient pattern.

"Single-action slug-throwers," Vaughn said, "not unlike our modern ones. They used a wider slug than we do because the propellants were not as good and they used metal cases. Just pull the hammer back for each shot and pull the trigger. Here's how you eject the cartridge. Don't touch it afterward as the cartridges are hot enough to burn."

After a few more minutes instruction, we stood in the booths and began firing at various holo-targets that moved and changed appearance. It took me a few shots to get comfortable with the wicked kick of the weapons. The ones Vaughn fired blew back my hair and made me grateful for the sound deadening system. We spent a pleasant two hours, shooting, changing weapons. There wasn't much conversation, but neither of us felt the lack.

Afterward, we returned the weapons. Vaughn had outshot me of course. He'd been a master assassin, and I suspected that even now he had better than human sight.

"It was a pleasure, young man," Vaughn said after we returned the weapons to the armorers. "I don't often have the excuse to practice. Now, if you will excuse me, I must return to those duties that you gave me a chance to escape for a while. Unfortunately, affairs of state take precedence over my social schedule."

"I enjoyed it," I said.

"There is a shower in the back," Vaughn said, "along with a refresher for your clothes. You might make use of it. The ladies will probably not appreciate the smell of gunpowder. Your girl can shut off her sense of smell I imagine. Mine cannot."

"Sounds like a good idea, Mr. President." We shook hands again.

"An aide will be outside the door to return you to my wife. Good bye."

"Good bye, I hope we will meet again before we voyage out."

Vaughn nodded and left the room.

Feeling that the suggestion I shower was more than a casual one, I did and took my time. When I came out, the same aide who'd brought us in from the flitter was waiting. She nodded pleasantly and led the way back. I was glad she didn't disturb me with idle chatter. I was thinking of what Vaughn had said and why I had felt like discussing the matter with the older man.

I found Shasti and Maauro chatting on the couch with a bottle of wine open between them. Both seemed pleased to see me, but I could not help but notice a conspiratorial air between them.

"Would you care to see the gardens?" Shasti asked. Maauro nodded with enthusiasm, she liked flowers second only to the night stars. I didn't care one way or the other, but I sensed that Shasti didn't want the visit to end. So we ended up wandering through roses and other vegetation

I could not identify. I had to admit the gardens were attractive. There was a public section, which had a variety of miniature trains and Mag-Lev's running through tiny villages and cities, that I enjoyed the more.

Eventually, and long after the sun had set on this summer day, we found ourselves back at the main entrance to Shasti's building, saying our good nights.

"Will you come to our ship tomorrow?" Maauro asked. "It may be foolish, but you have served us a meal in your home, I would like to do so in mine.

"Yes, of course," Shasti said.

To my surprise, a devilish smile spread across Maauro's face. "Oh, but it must be a secret, there is a certain practical joker aboard my ship that I want to steal a march on."

Uh-oh, I thought.

"Ah," Shasti said. "Well, it has been a while since I was an operative. I shall have to hope my old skills have not deserted me."

"And you," Maauro said, placing a finger against my chest, "are now sworn to secrecy."

"Never heard a thing," I said.

CHAPTER FOUR

WRIK FINDS REASONS TO ABSENT HIMSELF FROM THE SHIP THE NEXT *day, on the pretext of dealing with ship paperwork and taxes. Meanwhile, I prepare for a very informal dinner-of-state. Dusko remains off the ship, but Delt, having not yet found feminine company to keep him away, evidently feels he is on vacation. Slovenliness is beginning to expand exponentially.*

Wrik returns at the appointed time and toward evening, an unmarked flitter lands next to the ship. I really need not have sworn her secrecy. Shasti's movements are always secret. I note that she is alone, save for her security detail. I assume the President is again busy. Wrik and I go to greet her.

I am again hugged and Wrik respectfully shakes hands with her, though he does seem more at ease in her company.

We walk into the Stardust and I savor my coming moment at Delt's expense. As we round the spiral stairwell to the level with the galley, I see Delt, sprawled across the most comfortable chair, a reader in one hand, a beer and a sandwich in front of him. His shirt is untucked as usual, and his hair looks like small animals have battled in it.

I step up first, holding Wrik's hand. I give it a little squeeze, and he looks at me and rolls his eyes, but cannot contain a grin.

"Ah," Delt says, "the lovebirds return." At that point he spots Shasti's silver and black hair as she steps up to tower over both of us.

I give our unrepentant shipboard slob an evil grin.

He has one frozen moment looking at Shasti, who has a slightly bemused expression, then Delt flings himself into the air in a fashion I would have thought impossible, lands on his feet at attention and snaps a letter perfect salute. "Captain Rainhell, welcome aboard CSS Stardust.*"*

Shasti gives me a reproving look, but cannot hold it and laughs softly. She returns Delt's salute. "At ease, Spacer."

"Yes, Ma'am," Delt says, assuming parade rest.

Again the soft chuckle. "Really, at ease, Mr. Teljard. Though if you wish to be useful, you can bring out a few more of those beers you have there."

"Yes, Ma'am," Delt says, furiously snapping in and tucking his shirt, and grabbing an errant sock to place in his pocket. He runs behind the galley island to the refrigerator.

Meanwhile, we seat ourselves at the table. In seconds, Delt returns with three bottles of the finest Retiefan brew and a plate of cookies.

"The cookies are a nice touch," I say sweetly, "doubtless it will reduce the flogging for laxness on duty."

"Now, Maauro," Shasti says, "you cannot be quite so severe with your crew. They are, after all, only human."

"Well," I reply, "it's really Wrik's crew anyway. He's master."

"You let the two of them play with starships unsupervised?" she returns in mock horror.

It is too much, and everyone bursts out laughing.

"You got me good, Maauro," Delt says. "From now on, it's all shipshape. I swear it."

I wag my bottle at him. "I will hold you to it. I am not your oh, so-forgiving childhood pal."

"Ah," Shasti says, "for such uncomplicated days. Despite all you may have heard about desperate doings aboard the Sidhe, there were times like this too, at least among us in the command crew. It was a larger ship and company."

Wrik properly introduces Delt, whose easy smile and charm are on full display, as usual, when any female was around. Stories are swapped and a second round of beers brought out before Shasti's mood turns serious.

"There is another reason why I accepted your invitation to come aboard and see the ship."

"I thought there might be," Wrik says, settling back and watching her with a carefully neutral expression.

"The times are troubled, more so than many people realize. Much is kept under wraps and must stay that way, lest certain disclosures bring about the disaster that we are trying to hold off.

"I was most grateful to Candace Deveraux when she reached out to me during my search for Maximillian and revealed you to me, Maauro. I knew that such help always comes with a price tag, but for what was done for me, I am more than willing to meet what I owe the Confederacy."

"Candace calls for aid?" I asked.

Shasti nodded. "Much of it has already been supplied. But she knows you are here and has sent someone to meet you. That person will arrive in the morning."

Wrik looked at me. While he had been about his mission of reconciling with his family and former squadron, I had a mission too. Mischance had landed Lilith, a psychotic computer hacker, and a sextet of Humanform Combat Robots on Retief at the same time. It had been the most difficult balancing act of my existence to keep secret and separate, that deadly mission from the flowering of our love on his homeworld. I knew if he became involved, it might be impossible to protect him. I also knew that once he learned of the danger Lilith posed, there would be no way to keep him out of it.

"Tomorrow's problems can wait for then," I say. "As for now, the table is set for four. Time to enjoy ourselves." I pat Delt on the shoulder

CHAPTER FOUR

and the four of us adjourn to the room I have set aside and prepared for the evening.

CHAPTER FIVE

AS PROMISED BY SHASTI, WITH THE SUN CAME A WHITE airvan with reflective windows. There was no way to see who was within until the doors opened. I drew a surprised breath at the sight of the long, blond hair and lithe body of Olivia Croyzer, as she slid out of the backseat. She wore a sharp business suit that accentuated her athletic body and the ubiquitous sunglasses everyone wore on Olympia. The thick, yellow hair fell over one eye that I knew was artificial and saw in other spectra.

"Well, well," Maauro said dryly, "one of your exes is coming."

Delt's eyebrows shot up and he grinned. I merely gulped.

"Exes," he said, "another drop dead gorgeous female? When the hell did you find time to fly? I am through feeling sorry for you, buddy."

Before my relationship with Maauro had evolved to being sexual, I'd had a brief affair with Olivia toward the end of the mission to find Maximillian. It was probably not a good idea to remind Maauro that some of that had been at her urging, given that she had not yet conceived of the role of lover for herself. Olivia had left it at light and fun. She'd wanted to go places and do things that did not necessarily involve me.

I found Maauro's small hand in mine and wrapped mine around it. I stole a glance at Delt. He'd picked up Maauro's signal and his face was now empty of expression. We waited, side-by-side, as Olivia took the smaller elevator to our level on the gantry. She walked over slowly and I could sense that she was looking at our conjoined hands. She stopped a pace away.

"Hello Wrik, hello Maauro."

"It's good to see you, Olivia," I replied.

Her lips quirked slightly at that.

"This is a surprise," Maauro added, "but a pleasant one."

As we were now in the shade of the ship's hull, Olivia took off her sunglasses and slipped them into her pocket. "I'm glad it's a pleasant one. I'll tell you what's not a surprise." She gestured at our hands. "That mean what I think it does?"

"Yes," Maauro said. "It does."

"Good for you both. I wondered how long it'd take you two to figure it out." A smile shot across her face. It looked genuine, and I felt a knot in my shoulders release.

We looked at each other and then back at her. "Nice as this is, you didn't come all this way to tender us congratulations," I said.

"No, though considering what's happened here, maybe somebody should. But before we chat…"

"Yes, sorry. This is Delt Taljard, who joined our crew on Retief."

"Who doesn't believe that an intelligence operative of Confed MI doesn't know who he is," Delt said easily, sticking out his hand. "Welcome aboard."

She gave him a wolfish smile and took the hand. Her expression switched back to neutral quickly, "Major Olivia Croyzer, Confed Military Intelligence."

"When Candace learned you were bound here, she sent me with a FYEO briefing for you two about our new mission." There was a distinct emphasis on the 'our.'

I shook my head. "Delt's part of the crew now—he gets cut in on any deal."

"So is Dusko," Maauro added.

Ah, I thought, *so this is why he came back late last night.*

"Neither of them is MI," Olivia protested. "Dusko is a career Guild criminal. Sorry Mr. Taljerd, but your last commission was in a rebel air force!"

"Well," Maauro said, "Dusko is now my career criminal, and Wrik's prior commission was in the same rebel air force as Delt."

Olivia's one visible icy-blue eye searched our faces.

We looked at her patiently.

"Oh, very well, call for Dusko," Olivia finally said. "I know better to argue with you when Maauro is backing you up."

Ten minutes later we were in the galley, and Dusko had joined us. He'd nodded at Olivia when he saw her, which was the extent of his greeting. Her's was no more effusive.

Olivia set up a tiny holoprojector on the table and slid in a crystal. The image of Candace Deveraux, head of Confederate Military Intelligence, appeared on the table, though it occasioned less joy than seeing Jaelle's holo on the same spot. To my surprise, Candace was considerably thinner then when we'd last seen her. Some of her physical exuberance was gone. I briefly wondered if she had been ill.

"Well, well, well," she said. "Here we are again—though I am only present in spirit. Now that Wrik's voyage of self-discovery is over, I hope you two don't mind doing some work for a change. Your Jaelle negotiated quite a fabulous rate for you. She even tried to charge me for room and board for Major Croyzer!"

"You won't mind this one so much. Your friend, Director Rainhell, brought this to my attention and she has quite a stake in this, so you'll be helping an ally. You'll have passed much of her fleet guarding the entrances to her home system on your way in. She has reason to and we're coordinating Confed Fleet with her.

"Olympia system has turned into one of the great hyperspace transit points in Confed space, with exits to multiple critical systems, including Voit-Veru space and now to the Piola sector—"

CHAPTER FIVE

"Piola?" Delt asked.

His comment caused Candace's image to freeze and the AI suddenly displayed a starmap I wasn't familiar with.

"Piola," Maauro began, "is the newest sector of uncharted space found with viable jumppoints. It has three exits that have been located so far, Olympia, one near the Voit-Veru home systems and one that is only one additional jump from Star Central. This was discovered while we were in the time distortion of the Artifact."

"The what?" Olivia demanded.

Maauro considered her for long enough to make me nervous. Finally she said, "It was an ancient ship, an ark if you will, made by the Infestors, the enemies of my Creators. We discovered it while party, albeit unwillingly, to a Guild expedition to find it. This was the year before we met you. The ark was hiding, well, I could poetically refer to it as a wrinkle in space-time. We were only there for a few days, but five years passed in the galaxy."

"Huh," Delt said. "Is that why you still look so much like a kid?"

I nodded. "I've lived five years less than you have."

He shook his head in amazement; the few weeks he'd been aboard had not been enough to catch him up on all that had transpired during my self-imposed exile from my homeworld.

"What of the ark?" Olivia asked. "There was nothing about this in the briefings I received on you two. You never mentioned it when we were on the voyage to Sedon."

Maauro shrugged. "I did not feel a compulsion to tell Candace at the time. Our network was a much more fragile connection then. After the events, it seemed irrelevant. Now there seems no reason not to tell you. I will save the full story for another time, but the Artifact, the last evidence of my Creator's great enemy, the Infestors, is gone." Maauro gave a chilly smile.

"You destroyed it?" Olivia challenged— her eyes narrow.

"Say rather," I answered, "that we caused it to be elsewhere and elsewhen."

"But back to the briefing." Maauro said and though she made no gesture the recording resumed.

"There has been a big push into the Piola sector and the jump points beyond," Candace's image asserted. "This space is unusually rich in habitable, but unoccupied worlds, some with evidence of a recently fallen civilization. So it's the usual greedy rush: Free Trader ships, breakaway colonials and cultists, the usual wild-catting getting out ahead of a proper Confed survey.

"That came to a sudden end recently. There are seventeen Free Traders and small Combine ships overdue, and no word from any of the wildcat colonies or space stations in that sector. They have all gone dark.

"Confed sent a scoutship and the cruiser *Taiko* to find out what was happening. The scoutship jumped into a system with a Voight-Veru colony and found it intact, but filled with Veru terrified by the sudden disappearance of all shipping. The scout jumped to rendezvous with the heavy cruiser. *Taiko* was sent to evacuate the Veru colony and the scout ship jumped onto the next system. All it found in one was a missing space station, and in another, a deserted colony. No evidence of what happened to the colonials: they were there then they were gone. The scoutship jumped back into Confed space after that.

"The cruiser *Taiko* is overdue and presumed lost, clearly something happened to it when it went for the Veru colony.

"Something is haunting that area of space," Candace continued, "a sector whose jump points lead into important sectors of the Confederacy, including Olympia. The fleet has gathered blocking forces on the jump points into our space, but we do not know that all of those have been located, and we can't keep that much of the fleet in a defensive posture for long. Fleet command doesn't want to jump into Piola space without knowing what is there.

"So," she said, with her usual broad smile, "that's where you come in, Lost Planet. I believe your motto is, *we go where others dare not—*"

"I have a feeling I'm going to regret coming up with that," I said with a sigh, interrupting the playback.

Maauro placed a hand on my shoulder. "I thought it was very clever of you."

I smiled. "Thanks, Dear."

"Our mission," Olivia said, with the tone of someone who would brook no more interruptions, "is to jump into Piola space and find out what the threat is. The Olympian Self Defense Forces and Confed Navy will be waiting at the jump point into Piola, either for news or, and I have this authority, to summon them to the attack. The rest of Candace's message is mere detail to this."

"And I have already downloaded, incorporated and am analyzing all data," Maauro said. The image of Candace flicked off. "It will be sometime before we leave. The ship is to go into the OSDF dockyards to be remilitarized and outfitted for extended voyaging. We'll be supported by automated sleds that will jump to the various destinations we are being sent to – so we may reprovision and rearm in Piola sector."

"Director Rainhell wanted to put you up in the presidential palace," Olivia added, "but MI prefers that you start adopting a lower profile, so its officer's quarters in the OSDF base. A van will come and collect you all this afternoon."

"Wonderful," Dusko said. "I'm heading back into town to get drunk and otherwise indulge myself first. Our missions are usually suicidal, but this one sets a new and unwelcome high mark and stuffs it—"

Maauro raised an eyebrow and a finger. "Language…"

"Should you speak to anyone, or try to desert—" Olivia began, eyeing him.

"On Olympia?" Dusko scoffed. "What a great place for a Dua to hide out, in the shadows of all the giant, pretty humans. Besides, while I am not afraid of you, or MI," he slowly gestured toward Maauro, "I will not risk getting back on her bad side. The first time was enough."

"Have fun in town," Maauro said. "Don't pick up anything I can't cure."

He gave her a sardonic grin, which seemed out of keeping with his professed fear of her and headed out.

"I need to talk to the Port Authority about our being activated for military service," I said. "I'll have to send info to Jaelle so she's not looking for a cargo out of us."

"Yeah," Delt said. "Good news is if the government is reprovisioning us, I can save us money cancelling some contracts. It's back to work for us."

"I will see you out," Maauro said to Olivia. The two exited as Delt and I headed for our coms.

"So Wrik," Delt asked, as we headed to the bridge, "the gorgeous blonde?"

"Major Olivia Croyzer," I replied, "known to the Thieves Guild as, The Witch of Cimer, where she was chief of police. Maauro and I met her on a mission and I recommended her to MI. They took me up on it. Because she knows where Maauro came from, they teamed us on the Seddon mission and evidently whatever this is."

"Personal history? Maauro made a crack about her being your ex?" There was a lazy smile on his face. I recognized this as Delt on the prowl.

"A little, between her and me," I replied, "during the Seddon Expedition. Ironically, Maauro kind of pushed me toward her, before we were prepared to commit to, hell, before we recognized what we were. It wasn't serious either way with Olivia."

"Probably lucky for you, I wouldn't want to share a small ship with a jealous android."

Me neither, I thought.

"Other history," I added. "She's back in the Marines now, but don't ask why she was out being a cop. She'll tell you if she feels like it. Don't press."

He nodded. "Good to know."

"I know this is going to fall on deaf ears, but watch your step. Olivia can be mad, bad and dangerous to know."

"Sounds like just my type," Delt said, with a grin.

"Don't blame me if you get a busted nose out of this."

"God," Delt said, slapping me on the back, "you sound like an old married man." He gave my shoulder and affectionate squeeze and walked off.

Maybe I do, I thought, surprised and pleased by the thought.

"So," Olivia says, as we make our way to the exterior gantry, "you and Wrik?"

"Yes," I reply carefully, "we are a couple. It's developing well."

"Congratulations, I was hoping it would work out for you, if only because he is so stuck on you he'd never move on."

I am not quite sure what to make of this comment, but decide to take it as well-intentioned toward us as a couple and simply nod.

"I trust my brief history with Wrik won't be an impediment to our mission."

"If by that you are expressing worry that I may be jealous, it is an emotion that I cannot entirely deny, but neither am I a prisoner of its irrationality and negativity."

"Good. I will take that as a no."

"In fact, I may enjoy having a human woman along. It could be educational for me.

"Oh?" she says, eyebrows rising.

"If you're not above the occasional bit of girl-talk?"

Olivia's sudden and unexpected laughter makes me again aware of quite how pretty she is.

"I'm sorry, Maauro. It's just that it would have made my father laugh to have heard that. I was such a tomboy growing up, and hardly ever spent time with other girls. So it would be a new experience for both of us."

"From your ability with clothes, hair and makeup, I would say that you found time to acquire those skills."

She smiles, but there is something again wolfish in it now. "I found it useful for a professional woman, at least off the battle field. Females still get judged on their appearance, even now. Which, you surely know, having chosen a perfect body and face. Overdid the eyes a bit."

"Speaking of which…"she reaches forward and takes my chin in her hand. I allow this out of curiosity for what she will do. "I'd swear your eyes are a little smaller. And you've altered your skin tone. It's more realistic— not quite as utterly perfect as your earlier appearance. I'd take you for your early twenties, save for how impossibly slender your waist is. When I first met you, you looked more like a teen."

"The longer I remain in this configuration, as Maauro, the more I can control it and refine its details. I have come a vast way from my original appearance."

"You didn't always look like this?"

"No, originally I was nine feet tall and weighed twice what I do now. My humanoid appearance was rudimentary at best."

"What happened?" Olivia asks, startled.

"I was blown up during my last battle in the service of my Creators. Most of the vanished material was armor and ablative materials *designed to deflect or absorb blast. It took several hours to reconstitute myself and continue the attack."*

Olivia shook her head slowly. *"We shipped on a voyage together and I still hardly know you."*

"Speaking of secrets," I say. *"There is one that I want to be sure you were briefed to keep. While I was on Retief, disposing of the threat of Lilith, Wrik was unaware of my mission. It was accomplished without his becoming so."*

She stares at me. *"You're kidding."*

"Not even slightly."

"I wasn't briefed on it," Olivia says.

"Glad I asked then," I reply. *"Perhaps you were dispatched before my final report reached Candace. I did emphasize that I want this to remain a secret. You must consider that an order."*

"An order, Maauro?" Olivia says archly, *"are you under the impression that you command me?"*

"Don't be tedious, Olivia," I reply. *"Considerations of rank are extraneous. You are aboard Stardust, essentially within my body. Do not imagine that anyone but I command this ship."*

She studies me— her face remote. My own remains bland and friendly.

She finally snorts. *"Ok, but yuck about the body thing, I'll keep your secrets. I kinda like the overt power play though. It's reassuringly human."*

"I like you, Olivia," I say. *"You are brave and resourceful. You may even become my friend in the full meaning of that word. But you serve Confed Military and in all our time together, you have always been assessing me as a potential threat and as to how the military can use me and my technology."*

Her smile is a grimace now. *"So you trust me only so far; you're smart and you're right. Do you think that there is any other way this would have worked? You're incredibly powerful, not just for that body. I might take you with a modern weapon if I could ever get one to track, or fire, in your presence. But I remember what you did in the Voit Veru colony. They provoked you and you would have destroyed the colony if they hadn't returned Wrik. Even if they destroyed you, the latent virus you infected them with was unstoppable if you triggered it. And that's not the limit of what you can do. The only reason you haven't been taken into protective custody is that the casualties for doing it—"*

"Would be quite fantastic," I finish. *"Nor would I be taken alive."*

"Live free or die, eh Maauro?"

"True. And the only thing that would be worse would be if someone tried to threaten Wrik to control me. The carnage then would be beyond words."

"A warning, Maauro?"

CHAPTER FIVE

"A reminder, Olivia." I reach into my pocket and then extend my hand. *"Cookie?"*

For some reason she bursts into laughter.

CHAPTER SIX

STARDUST WENT INTO THE YARDS AT OLYMPIA TO BE refitted. The shipwrights found no fault with her maintenance and even expressed envy with many of the improvements Maauro had made in her. But they added what even the industrious android had not been able to: her original armament suite of a .5cm laser, a railgun and two chainguns. Her missile tubes were reopened and four anti-shipping torpedoes were added. She was as heavily armed as any one of her class ever had been. This would have comforted me more had a cruiser with twenty times her armament not already gone missing.

Maauro disappeared often, usually in the company of Shasti Rainhell. The unlikely pairing seemed to surprise many, but when I saw them walking side by side with their similar coloring, there seemed such a natural affinity between them that they might be family. When I saw them laughing on a balcony, a feeling swept over me. I had not been able to give Maauro much experience of family, with my train-wreck of one. Now, it seemed she might be forming one of her own.

Olivia meanwhile drilled the merely biological members of the crew mercilessly on every known detail of Piola. At times, I thought my head would explode. Other times I thought she might shoot Delt. Studying wasn't Delt's strong suit, both as a leader and a pilot he'd operated on instinct. Still, no one could fly and maintain spacecraft and not master intricate detail, so I suspected that his apparent indifference to the briefings was more a way of stimulating Olivia's interest in him. I thought the tactic a dubious one as Olivia didn't suffer fools gladly. But Delt seemed pleased enough with his verbal sparring with the Major.

Dusko proved the best student of us all when he was there. Having mastered his lessons quickly gave him some additional time. Apparently assured of his imminent demise, he spent this windfall on debauchery in the offport.

As for me, I was careful to keep my time with Olivia professional and usually in the company of others. Her demeanor matched mine and she never made any reference to either Seddon or Cimer. The resurrection of her career seemed to have gone the way she wanted and her connection with Maauro and I had made her an invaluable asset to MI. This mission was not only her dream assignment, but clearly the fact that we would again accept her as part of "Maauro's network" could only make her more valuable in the future.

Work progressed on *Stardust* around the clock. Now that MI had assembled the team, they were desperate to start. Maauro's desire to start seemed little less. "This is something Shasti wishes me to do. We will be helping our friend."

A message came after we learned the ship would soon be ready. Maximillian's parents would not return in time, but the boy, having learned we were here, insisted on a break in his semi-reclusive life and asked for us to visit him.

Maauro and I flew down in Shasti's company to visit Maximillian in his little house by the sea. I found him to be a young, solemn-eyed man, a younger version of his grandfather. In a way, we were meeting him for the first time, after we recovered him from the grip of the Destroyer; he'd been semi-comatose on the voyage back. Maauro had nursed him, singing him to sleep at night.

"I remember your voice," he said, looking at Maauro as we sat on the house's small seaside veranda. "I am glad I remember so little else." A haunted look came into his eyes and his grandmother covered his big hand with hers. They sat silent as the wind ruffled the large umbrella that kept the setting sun from our faces.

"My lack of memory will not prevent me from thanking you both from getting me out of the hell I was confined to," he said finally, shaking off the mood.

"But thanks having been tendered," Maauro said. "Let us leave the past to the past. I am more interested in your artwork. This piece for example, it is quite beautiful." She turned to point at a small seascape hanging on the wall just beyond the open door to the house. "This reminds me of... my original world."

"It's a beauty," I agreed. I'd noticed her standing before it earlier. "I've always loved sunset paintings."

"Then," he said. "Please accept it as an inadequate token of my appreciation." He rose, went inside and took off the wall. He disappeared inside to return with the painting now properly wrapped for transit. "It will be a great comfort to me to think of it voyaging through the stars with you both."

Maauro looked at her new prize like a child on Christmas morning, and I loved her all the more for it.

"Well," Shasti said. "I have to get these folks back to the capitol and their ship. They have another mission to undertake. Their ship is coming out of the dockyard tomorrow."

"I hope that we will meet again," Maximillian said, to Maauro, I noticed wryly.

"I do plan to return here," she said.

I kept surprise off my face and in truth wasn't overly so. There was clearly something between Maauro and Shasti, and I simply had to wait for them to tell me what it was. I sighed mentally.

After bidding Maximillian good night, we flew back to the capitol in Shasti's private, unmarked flitter, I could not see our escorts, but knew they were there. We circled down at the officer's quarters at the OSDF base next to the dockyard. The three of us got out of the flitter, leaving the driver inside. Overhead, the stars burned in a clear sky, limning the few high cirrus clouds. Olympia was one of the few ringed, Earth-type worlds, and the arch of rock and ice crystals glimmered overhead on the moonless night.

Shasti looked up at the arch of sky. "The nights before a voyage are always special, the preparations, the anticipation. I am envious of you, setting out on an adventure. Well, I suppose I shouldn't be. I have had my time out among the stars."

"Would you come with us if you could?" Maauro asked, looking up at Shasti.

Surprise flitted over Shasti's face and she laughed. "Oh, don't tempt me so, Little One. I am a responsible grownup now."

"Who evaded my question," Maauro said, with an impish air.

Shasti turned to me and put both hands on my shoulders, and I too had to look up at her. "You be good to this young lady," she said, with a mock sternness that none-the-less held an actual note of warning. "You will never be this lucky again."

"Yes, Captain," I replied.

She smiled, then bent forward and kissed me on the lips. I couldn't control a furious blush,

Shasti then turned to Maauro and bent further, wrapping her in her arms. "You be careful out there. The Confederacy will always have its own interests beyond what you do in Piola. Be wary."

"Always," Maauro said.

"Come back and visit me," Shasti said, then kissed Maauro goodbye and headed for her car. In moments, the vehicle rolled forward then, with a blast of turbofan, lifted off.

"She's everything I've always thought she would be," I managed.

"And perhaps a bit more," Maauro agreed. "Come Wrik, you must be tired, and I think tomorrow will start us on this new venture."

I yawned. "Yep, good food and good company and now…good night."

In the morning, we moved back into the Stardust. The vessel was loaded with supplies of every sort. Cargo containers were even stacked, strapped and secured in the hallways.

"There will be supply sleds prepositioned in some of the systems we are going to visit," Olivia said at the briefing she gave after we trouped aboard. "But there is no way to be sure where we are going, or for how long."

When Maauro and I settled into our cabin, I turned to her. "So how much crap did they try to plant on us?"

"One feels that the effort was perfunctory," Maauro said, amusement playing on her face. "There were the usual bugs, sensors and spyware. I have already scrubbed and recycled everything, including that which was secreted in our supplies on the theory that we would not go through the discomfort of unpacking everything. As if I would use such crude methods. Really! I am quite insulted. In any event, we are secure."

"I wonder if Olivia knew," I muttered.

"I doubt it," Maauro replied. "It would compromise her for no purpose. The information they seek would not be for her use. Like us, she probably expected it, but knowing me better than most, she also would not expect it to work."

"Olivia to Wrik and Maauro," sounded over the system.

"Speak of the devil," I said.

Maauro raised an eyebrow. "That comment better not come with an image of her in a clingy red suit with a pitchfork and tail."

"I never think of Olivia with a pitchfork," I replied with a grin. "She's too likely to use it."

She gave me a dubious look. "I suppose we had better answer.

"We hear you," Maauro said, internally opening the channel.

"We've received clearance to lift off 0530 tomorrow."

"What is it with the military mind," I groaned, "that has everything happen in the early morning hours?"

"Best part of the day," Olivia said. "So suck it up, Buttercup, and hit the rack at a reasonable hour."

We took Olivia's advice and turned in early, to rise at 0200 and begin preflight. Even this was something of a formality. Neither Maauro, nor *Stardust's* AI, ever slept and every system had been under continuous review since we accepted the ship back from the dockyard. Maauro, after waving a cup of strong coffee under my nose, slipped outside and climbed all over the ship, having changed her color to match the ship's hull. In the predawn darkness, she would be hard to spot, checking the outer hull. She reentered forty-five minutes later having satisfied herself.

"No one will be able to approach the ship now without my detecting it," she said with a touch of smugness.

Dusko and Delt stumbled in shortly thereafter. Dusko apparently hadn't slept, as he wore what I saw him in last. Delt wore a fresh shirt and pants; we didn't have a uniform, per se, on *Stardust*. Olivia came in last, wearing Marine combat fatigues.

"How are we looking, Captain?" she said to me, but her eyes were on Maauro, who wore her usual red and gray jump suit.

"We will lift on schedule," I said. "We could go now, but the orbital window to the accelerator doesn't open till 0530."

Olivia nodded, pleased. She joined us for a quiet and light breakfast. Only Delt, who had an iron stomach, dared more. We cleaned up and headed for launch stations. The tower began relaying the myriad of tasks that came with launch, until they cleared us for liftoff, and I reached for the throttle.

CHAPTER SIX

Stardust began to rumble and shake as the impellers fought gravity and we rose, meter by meter, until we could see the sun peeking over the horizon. Steadily and with more assurance, the ship accelerated until we reached the high blue and then the black of space.

A few quick orbits built up our speed, and we lined up at the giant orbital accelerator that would boost us up to higher speed for the transit to the jump point. We remained in our acceleration couches for this part. The accelerator would bump us up against the limits of the AG field. While the great accelerator, which looked like an endless rack of ribs, was huge, we approached it at such speed that it required careful attention and skill to maximize the boost.

Behind us, an automated sled loaded with fuel and provisions was fired into the accelerator. The unmanned sled easily accelerated to match speed with us. Like most unmanned vessels, it was painted a dull orange and white. This one was almost as large as *Stardust*.

We were on our way.

CHAPTER SEVEN

DAYS PASS AS WE ADJUST TO SPACEBORNE ROUTINE. OLIVIA SETTLES *back into the ship in her old cabin. Dusko retreats to his hydroponic garden. Delt divides his time between Engineering and teasing Olivia, who greets his attention with a mixture of exasperation and appreciation I find fascinating and amusing.*

The voyage out has given me time to think about the gaps in my knowledge of Wrik and his past. He has always been guarded about that, even with me. Now, I have Delt here and time to talk. So I decide to spring my trap as we head out to the jumppoint. With Wrik asleep, Olivia in the part of the hold we have made a gym and Dusko tending his flowers and plants in the hydro, Delt is all mine.

I find him in the galley, seated in front of a plate of pasta and an iced tea. He has been working out, losing the pounds of early middle age that he allowed to accumulate when he was running an aviation repair shop. Wrik had told me how Delt boxed in college. While I think that boxing is too much of a sport and not much of a combat skill, I have watched him workout before and must admit that he hits the heavy bag with power and speed. Delt was always strong-looking, but now he more resembles the lean fighter pilot of his youth. He wears a gym suit and a thin layer of perspiration. I do wonder if Olivia's addition to the crew is providing him with even more incentive to get in shape.

"Hi, Maauro. How is it going?"

"Hello, Delt. All is well. We are on course and all systems are nominal."

"Good."

I dial up a cup of hot tea and sit on the metal bench opposite him. "We've never really had much chance to talk have we?"

Delt eyes me around the mouthful of pasta he's twirled onto his fork. "Huh? What do you mean? We see each other every day."

"That is not the same as having the time and place for a meaningful conversation."

He chuckles. "God, you really are female, all the way down to your toes."

"Why, yes I am," I reply. "I think when I rolled off the assembly line and opened my eyes, I saw through a feminine lens."

He sips his tea and looked at me over the rim of it. "You remember the date of your... birth?"

"Yes, as I remember every detail of my existence that I myself have not deleted from my memory banks. There were some memories of my... combats that I discarded. They disturbed me. I no longer do that, a promise I made to Wrik."

"What was that like?" he asks. "Becoming active, I mean."

"One moment I was not, then I was. When my eyes opened, the first thing I beheld was the stars shining down through a great window in the facility ceiling where I was made, an armaments factory on one of the oldest of the Creator colonies. I do not know where it lies. That information was removed from me lest I be captured. Even my memory of that night sky is scrambled, so it could not be examined for clues on where I came from.

"But it was a pretty world of pink clouds and colorful sunsets. Ah, but the stars were wonderful, even though I knew from the first instant of my awareness that they were immense balls of flaming gas, I somehow felt they were more. Almost like friends."

He puts the glass down. "Over fifty thousand years ago, Maauro, I just can't grasp it. I sit here with you and you're just a pretty girl to me, albeit with the biggest eyes and tiniest waist I've ever seen. I just can't believe you aren't human. Well, except when you are lifting a motorcycle with me on it over your head."

"It was just to chest level," I say, indicating with my hand.

"Oh, was that all?"

I nod. For some reason this makes him chuckle.

"What was it that you wanted to talk about?"

I lean on my elbows, chin in hand. "Tell me about the Wrik you knew. The one you grew up with? The one I do not know."

Delt has some more pasta and tea, clearly considering his answer, "It's funny. I have to work at it to think of him as Piet, the kid I played with. It's a little like Piet is gone forever, and we have Wrik now."

"I have felt the same, and it worries me. The trip to Retief cleaned out many old wounds, but it seems that he wishes to remain Wrik and leave Piet behind, even though his reconciliation was so successful with his mother and sister."

He wags a finger at me. "Don't overthink it. Remember it's as Wrik that he found you, and trust me in this, nothing is more important to him than finding you."

I enjoy the warm glow this brings to me.

"Anyway," Delt says. "We met when he was out hunting with his father, toting a rifle damn near as big as he was. I was immediately jealous and went to my Dad to say, "Look, the Van Zyle boy is out hunting." Dad reluctantly gave me a rifle. Not a monster gun like Wrik had, though. So we started hunting together. Poor Wrik, I remember how his shoulder would get black and blue from firing that damn thing.

"Wrik was always a serious kid. I used to joke with him that he didn't know how to laugh. Seemed he was always worried about something. Then I met his Dad, and, well, you know about his father—"

"He is never forgotten, or forgiven by me." My voice comes out in a growl that surprises us both. I give an embarrassed wave of the hand.

"Owen Van Zyle is a sore point with me. He does not know how close he stood to death after I learned he'd erected a headstone for his son, saved only, and ironically, by the fact he is Wrik's biological parent."

"So," Delt continues, *"his life wasn't easy. Thank God he had a good mother, though she wasn't able to do much about Owen. I guess I remember the good times between he and his sister better than he does, but I saw that turn bad too, and that was hard to watch. I eventually broke off with his sister. Rena has a mean streak in her that can't be trusted."*

I consider that Wrik has placed his sister and her children in my hierarchy as ranked only below himself. Delt's memories of Rena are not as fresh as ours, and I judge that she is more mature now, but I do not contest his assessment.

"Wrik was a good student, always trying to exceed, so the old bastard would finally be proud of him. He was cautious, never one to dive head first into anything. He didn't like to fight, but never once failed to back me up in one of mine."

"Did he have other friends besides you?"

Delt again considers. *"I guess not so much. He always hung with my friends, but they were my crowd. Girls liked him, and he had a lot of female friends for somebody who was kinda shy. I think they saw that he was born old—"*

"We females refer to it as mature," I say.

"Do you now? I am pleased to say that none of you have ever said it about me." He grins. *"Nor likely to anytime soon. Even now, when I've lived five years or better in the universe, while you both were in that wrinkle of time, doesn't he seem the older? The more serious?"*

"Yes, but that could be just arrested development on your part," I muse.

Delt chokes a little on his tea. *"Oh, been talking to Olivia perhaps?"*

"I decline to answer; I must preserve the sanctity of the female network."

"Anyway, I was his closest male friend. After the slaughter...." His face tightens. I reach a hand across and place it atop his. I feel the blast of heat that comes on him with the anguish of recollection.

"We left this on Retief," I say. *"Reverend Janna told you it was time to put that burden down."*

"You yourself," he manages, *"are now too much like us to think that is entirely possible."*

I pat his hand. *"Logical being that I am, regret has bitten me as well. I suppose it is part of the burden of awareness."*

He sighs. *"I said stuff to him. Things I would give anything to unsay. I was too close to it to understand, too foul with my own guilt to be a friend. I threw him to the wolves."* The sturdy face is closed in grief.

I let a few moments pass, my hand still on his, then ask. *"So what things did you enjoy as children?"*

He visibly struggles to shake off the mood. "Oh, anything in the air: kites, flying models, RC aircraft. We moved on to airplane gliders and anything that would fly: flitters, aircars, finally to true aircraft. If it had wings we flew it. Hell, we even built some jetpacks. That damn near killed both of us. Wrik was actually pretty good with one. Wonder if we could whip up some in the machine shop?"

"No," I reply. "They are inherently unsafe and tactically useless."

"Umm, I wasn't actually… we'll talk about that another time."

"When the answer will still be no."

"You're going to be a great mother."

"Unlikely."

"I wouldn't bet against it."

I pat his hand again. "Finish your dinner."

Now why is he laughing again, I wonder?

I allow Delt to slide back into comfortable banality and returned to my daily maintenance of the ship and study of all that is known of Piola. But the work of existing as a living being among other living beings consumes much of my time and power. Sometimes so much so that I reduce the effort I put into it around Dusko or Olivia, who are not as important to me, or as interested in my having a personality.

So the day closes and Wrik and I turn in for the night in our cabin. We go to bed early and make love. I enjoy the experience, but a part of me wonders what it will be like if Shasti Rainbell can create a body for me.

Wrik and I wake in the morning, which means he awakens and I stop considering the 2,523,956 items I am examining and focus on him.

He sighs. "You look as fresh and beautiful as when you lay down last night. I, of course, need a shower and it's time for the weekly depilatory." He scratches at a shade of beard.

"Could be worse," I say. "Males used to drag bits of sharpened steel over their faces in the old days."

"Or the not so old days," he replies. "It's still common on Retief, along with racism, rebellion and other old-fashioned practices."

He heads for the shower as I admire his form, quite satisfied with my choice of boyfriend. He remains lean, but is filling in around the shoulders and upper arms.

Delt and I handle the transshipment of supplies from the sled, easiest for me who is both strong and doesn't need a suit. I finish in a quarter the time it would take the others and we accelerate outward to the jumppoint, able to use power at levels we wouldn't dare with so much distance to cover and unknown perils to face. The Confederacy is desperate enough to provide us with a fleet of tankers. Speed is of the essence, but it is still days to the jumppoint and the ship slips back into her normal routine.

CHAPTER EIGHT

MAAURO AND DELT WENT OVER TO INSPECT THE SLED for a final time before jump, Maauro never being content with any gifts from Candace Deveraux unless she checked them herself. Delt took the opportunity to mischievously paint the name *"Fetch"* on the forward hull. The name stuck and we all took to calling the sleds *"Fetches."*

The *Fetches* had another purpose. There were cold storage chambers in them, if we recovered any survivors, or suffered a casualty, we could send them back to the Confederacy in one. The first *Fetch* would travel out with us and orbit the initial world we would search. The others would lurk near the jump points of the systems we planned to visit. With them, we would have enough range to jump anywhere in what was known of the Piola quadrant.

We reached the standing blockade on the third day on course for the jump to Piola. There a supply ship topped us off allowing us to save the *Fetch One* for later need. I was determined to keep us as prepared as possible. As we passed through the ranks of warships at .9c, *Fetch* remained in formation with us. I drew long slow breaths as we raced down toward the jumppoint. This was a small one, only 1,000 kilometers in diameter. Only the sled was near us.

"Wish some of these formidable warships were going with us," Dusko grumbled.

The reckless smile I'd seen so often back in the Ncome Commando days flashed on Delt's face. "Where's the fun in that, Dusko, my old salt. More glory for us."

"Glory be damned," Dusko said. "I only hope we are getting paid—"

"Fabulously," Maauro interrupted, "quite fabulously and equal shares this time."

"Ah," Dusko said, looking pleased.

"For you mercenaries," Olivia shot back. "Some of us have to be satisfied with flight and hazardous duty pay."

"Some of us had a choice about going," Maauro returned coolly.

"Well, whatever the reasons for going," I said, cutting off whatever was starting up, "we just passed the point of no return. Secure for jump. Forty-five seconds to jump horizon." Everyone, including Maauro, belted in. I reached out with that sixth sense that pilots use. There is a feel to the correct approach to the jump point and it was not totally instrument dependent. The jumppoint distorted space-time and a pilot learned that distortion. Within a specified parameter, the exact approach was up to me. I felt, considered, and adjusted as the clock ran down. We jumped.

The universe reestablished itself around us. Foreign stars glowed down at us from the portals and canopy. Maauro was up instantly, looking out at the new stars, adding them to her mental collection. The rest of us suffered through mild jump disorientation. I gulped my restoratives and anti-nauseants, as did everyone but Maauro. The jump had not been a bad one, but the usual queasiness was present.

Because the jump point was anomalous, we'd materialized back in normal space farther into a star system than was normal. It was only hours to the gas giant that we used for air-breaking. Then, with our faithful Fetch, we headed for the inner system and the wildcat colony that had popped into existence when the new jump point was discovered.

We refueled again from the sled, for all that we'd used little fuel or other supplies. "Bit of an anticlimax," Delt said, his eyes riveted to the scanners. "No hordes of enemy starships waiting for us."

Dusko sighed

"It's not likely that whatever is upsetting this sector would be waiting right here," Maauro said, missing the satire as she occasionally did.

Delt smiled, but let it ride.

The world ahead had no official name, so we used the unofficial one that Free Traders and other colonials had bestowed on it, Windrush. On the fourth day into the system, we came within sensor range.

"It's not the friendliest of worlds, only the equatorial regions approached habitability for biologicals," Maauro said, looking at the planet ahead, easily visible to the naked eye.

"Yep," Delt said. "Looks mostly like cold, dead rock." He was peering into a scanner amped to greater magnification.

"And mostly is," Maauro said. "In the summer time, there is liquid water in the equatorial regions and edible fish in the seas. Some land animals with tradable furs exist, so the first colony was sited there, but it was always intended as a way station for further exploration. When more habitable worlds were found further out in this sector, the expansion here cooled off."

"Was that a pun?" Dusko grumbled.

"Why would anyone want to plant even a waystation on this rock?" Delt said, before Maauro could reply.

"Don't be so delicate," Olivia scoffed. "It has sunlight, air you can breathe, water you can melt, or desalinate, and gravity similar to home. Your body will work tolerably there unless your power fails. You've spent too long on nice planets near Goldilocks Zones around yellow suns. Compared to a lot of places I've been, this is a garden spot."

"Remind me never to go on vacation with you," Delt said.

"You should be so lucky," Olivia returned, but I thought a slight smile played over her lips."

"Anything on instruments?" Delt asked me.

I deferred to Maauro with a gesture.

"Nothing," she said. "No disaster beacon. No calls for help. There was a small satellite system here. I am not detecting any signals from them, or indeed any indication of even dead satellites in likely orbits."

"We'll be coming up on our first approach over the capitol city, such as it was, of Downstairs, in twenty minutes," I advised.

"Funny name," Delt said.

"Maybe all the good ones were taken," Dusko said dryly.

"Maauro," I said, "bring all weapons and ECM on line. I'll leave those to you."

"Better watch out," Olivia said. "I think she longs to try out our pocket battleship's new loadout."

Maauro nodded. "Yep, blasting aliens is my thing."

"You could be in trouble, Dusko," Delt said.

"Ahem," Maauro replied. "To me, you're all aliens. I only look human. Remember?"

Everyone settled after that, eyes on their own boards, as *Stardust* made her first run over the colony world. I dropped us to 2,000 kilometers over the planet's surface. We came in with the sunrise, the light from the system's primary casting a gray and ghostly searchlight over the unlovely world. Wine-dark seas crashed against rocky coastlines under thin clouds. Then a great bay opened under us.

At the middle of the arch of the bay were a spacefield, docks, and the usual low, broad, prefab buildings along with a smattering of local construction. The town of Downstairs lay still, in shadow, and no lights showed. Our vertical perspective gave us no opportunity to look in windows.

Maauro stood over her instruments, manipulating them directly without something as crude as using fingers. Images zoomed and flickered through differing spectra. "Wrik, I see signs of damage. There are fire-engines deployed, but abandoned. I see decomposed bodies in the street." Images of bones and burned buildings began to build.

"Ground fighting?" Delt asked.

"Doesn't look like it," Olivia said. "There's a pattern to such and I don't see it here. It could have been riot, civil disorder or some natural disaster."

"I concur," Maauro said, "the base does not look like it was subject to weapon fire. There is...."

"What is it?" I asked.

"We now know what has struck here," she said, her voice grim. The image changed; we were looking down at the space field. In large block letters, the word, "Plague" was painted in reflective paint in the tarmac.

"My god," Delt said.

"Yeah," I added, rubbing my hand over my face, plague, the dread of the spaceways, an unknown disease.

"Maybe it's just Vibor fever," Delt said.

"No," Maauro said. "There would have been some medications for Vibor, especially on a colony world on the frontier. This is very likely something new and effective on multiple races. Also, it is not likely that some pathogen was here when the first ships came. This world was found by Survey and the usual thorough tests made. It could be something that came in off another ship, or something that came from space. Or it could be—"

"Chemical or biological ordnance," Olivia said. "Broad spectrum stuff like was used in the Conchirri wars. It could be an attack."

"We have no way of telling," I said, "and there's no prospect that we can land and find out."

"There's no prospect that you can," Maauro corrected.

"No," I said, rising.

"Wrik my love, you worry unnecessarily. I am not susceptible to any disease."

"But when you come back—"

"I can coat myself with plasma fire and stand in utter vacuum while I do so. No virus, germ or other contaminant can survive me."

"And the shuttle you would land in—" Olivia asked.

"I will scan it for contaminants, decompress it and if needs be decontaminate it with radiation and anti-biologicals. Even Vibor cannot survive that. There are small risks, but we cannot escape all peril. Our mission requires information."

"But you down there… alone…"

"My Dear, the issue is more your exposure to the disease. I judge the risk all but nonexistent, or I would not even consider going down."

"Truly?"

"Yes."

I sighed. "The pinnace then."

"The sooner I go, the sooner I will be back."

I looked at her.

"Wrik, honestly, I see no danger."

"I am not happy about this," I said.

"I know, but it has to be done."

"Alright but be careful."

"I promise."

CHAPTER NINE

I LEAVE THE BRIDGE AFTER KISSING WRIK AND GIVING DELT a reassuring squeeze on the shoulder. Before going, I take off my small, yellow, silk scrunchie; it would not be safe to take it with me into a plague zone. I head down the scoutship's narrow central corridor to the compact bay where the pinnace sits. The slender, atmospheric, four-seater, with its folded wings, still wears its Confed colors of dark-blue and gray from when we used it at Cimer. The pinnace is quickly made ready, I load my armspac aboard. The dark-gray, boxy, 150 pound weapon has its own rack in the pinnace. With its loadout of armor piercing bullets and AP and HE missiles it gives me more long –distance firepower than is built into me.

While I do not expect to meet enemies in Downstairs, I will use all caution as I promised. Wrik stays at the controls of the Stardust, knowing that even he cannot preflight the pinnace as thoroughly as I do with my sensors. I launch fifteen minutes after leaving the bridge, on route to the dead city below.

The pinnace's nose glows a cherry red as it drops from orbit. Now, I am high in the atmosphere, cooling rapidly and dropping through thin cirrus clouds toward the slate grey sea. No sensors track me, and nothing threatens my ship. I circle over the small city. There are no ships on the field, only the painted warning.

"Maauro," Wrik's voice sounds in my head. "What do you see?"

"Only what you have from orbit. From this point, you will see through my eyes and hear through my systems."

"Ok. Don't take any chances."

"I promise."

When the ship's landing jacks are fully down, I leap out, armspac in hand. I sample the wind; extend every sensor and power up the tiny labs inside my body, hunting the culprit that has destroyed the colony. But the enemy is elusive at this stage.

"Anything?" Wrik demands, his voice cracking with tension.

"I have my biofilters at maximum, but am detecting nothing."

I move toward the buildings and see my first bodies. They are desiccated, partly gone to bone, but I note that the bodies are not scavenged. I extend my sensor array and realize there are no birds, or other animals in the area. Even insects are absent. The destroyer here has been most lethal, even the decomposition is from microbes.

I kneel beside the remains of a middle-aged, human female. Paint is on her largely intact clothes. "This person painted the message. She must have used her last strength to do so."

"Any ID on the body?" he asks.

"No," I reply. "No way to know who she was in life. We can only honor the act, with no chance to honor the doer."

"A soldier known only to God," Olivia says into the silence.

"Not the usual sort of war," Wrik said, "but a deadly battle none the less."

From there, I move into the buildings and find more bones. I exit the small warehouses by the field and walk toward the main port building, a combination of landing control tower and seat of government, typical in a small colony. Wind-blown grit crunches under my feet as I walk over the permacrete. I keep the large boxy shape of my armspac level in front of me. The light remains poor, but this does not trouble me, though for the sake of the others I sometimes beam visible light from my eyes so they may see better. There are small vehicles scattered about. Some have bodies in them. Fire has destroyed part of the main building I am approaching.

I push open the glass and metal doors under a sign that says, 'Welcome to Downstairs'. Inside is the spacefield control station. All the computer panels are dark as are the holo-emitters. Wind-blown debris covers some of the windows. I run a power lead from my body to energize the systems, scanning through the recent entries. All seemed to be well with the colony until 207 galactic standard days ago. A ship in the system broadcast a distress call cut off in midword. Then a shape overflew the colony, blocking out the sunlight. There is little description— just a massive shape, whether ship, device, or something else, the log offers no clue. It was there, then the light was gone as it eclipsed the base, then it was gone. The light returned, but with it came something else. Life itself seemed under attack. Soon animal life of every type withered and died. Only microbic animals seemed to survive.

The local doctor was unable to cope. There were no scientists of any note to help him. People were falling ill. Many raved of a presence, a power that had to be appeased, worshipped even. The doctor put it down to brain distortions caused by the disease. But he had no time for more than recording the initial stages of the plague before he succumbed. From onslaught to the end of recording was merely thirty-five hours.

I take a fragment of bone from the nearby body of a human male and pull it into my labs where it is tested to destruction. Nothing that could possibly be infectious will go back to the ship.

"They had little time," I broadcast to my friends in geosynchronous orbit above me, "a standard day and half from onslaught to the end. The colony was typical of a wildcat operation, not much in the way of records, and what's left is fragmented. The population of the colony might have been 2,743 beings, a mix of most of the major Confederation races. None seem to have survived. I have downloaded all that is in their systems and we can consider it later."

CHAPTER NINE

"Don't linger."

"I will not, but I hope to find a body with more soft tissue here. One that was less exposed to the elements. There is nothing useful in the bones that I have analyzed."

I stalk through the dead colony, opening doors to buildings that once held workers, families, hopes and dreams. All is gray silence. Most of the buildings have no basements and are quickly searched.

The burned building was the infirmary. Whether the fire was a deliberate defense against the disease, or a random accident cannot be ascertained. The fire was fought, so this happened early in the last terrible day and a half.

This building has a basement, and in there, the cool of the earth has preserved the corpse of a Morok male. The blue-skinned, apish alien is intact, at least to the extent that it has much more soft tissue left.

"Maauro," Wrik yells, "the visual cut out!"

"It is all right. There is a body here, and I must do some work that you would find disturbing to watch."

"Am I really that squeamish?"

"Yes, dear, you are."

Moments later, I am done. The sample of decaying biological mass is now in my labs. Every test I can conceive of is run on the unfortunate Morok's remains. I am not idle meanwhile, but finish my circuit of the colony in the fruitless hope of finding a survivor. By the time I finish, I have discovered our adversary. At first, my systems refuse to recognize it as a form of biological life, a pathogen so different that it seems unrelated to anything else that exists. It is a horrid little piece of virus, between crystalline and silicon, well below the size of all but the best biowarfare filters. I consider its lethality in wonder. Is this bio-ordnance, or merely malign nature?

Twenty minutes of analysis gives me a preliminary assessment of how to kill this deadly microbeast and how to protect from it. Antidotes and other methods will take far longer, if they are possible at all. I report all this above, as my labs do their work.

"Maauro," Wrik finally says, "is there more to be gained by remaining there?"

"No, I am finished here. The pathogen that destroyed the colony may still be resident somewhere, either dormant or in some lower animal life. I do not know if it will ever be safe for any biological we know to land here again. I will bring nothing back with me. Even the samples I have taken will be utterly destroyed."

"Then come up as fast as you can."

I gather up my armspac and make for the pinnace. Before I board it, I set my labs to destroy the pathogen sample down to atomic levels. After securing my weapon, I take off and fly to the outer atmosphere. It is tedious to launch in the pinnace, taking much longer to return, than to land. Once out of the atmosphere, I decompress the pinnace and stand outside of it in the clear starshine, which flows down on me like a blessing, after the death below. I generate plasma fire in both hands and run it over all my surfaces, then I route it through my interior. The thorough decontamination returns me to utter cleanliness and I sigh in relief. I wanted to leave the stench of death far behind me.

The inside of the shuttle has plunged into vacuum, but it is designed for it. I inspect all surfaces for any contamination. Then I button the shuttle and skip it through the outer atmosphere causing it to again glow. My caution is perhaps at absurd levels but the green and gold hull I am approaching holds most of my treasure in this existence.

"Hello Wrik, all decontamination procedures complete. I am ready for docking."

"Thank God," he replies. "You're just in time for dinner. Some of my better work, I think."

"Keep it warm," I say, appreciative of this little gesture, "docking in fifteen minutes."

Wrik is waiting for me in the docking area and comes in as soon as the pinnace is secured and pressure reestablished. I am very thoroughly kissed and enjoy this. I suspect that after dinner there will be more than kissing. It gives me something to look forward to.

"Damn," he says. "I know you are near indestructible—"

"And cute," I interject.

"—and can outthink a planet full of PHDs—"

"And very cute." I smile, and raise an eyebrow.

"And very, very cute," he confirms. "I was still scared as hell with you down there without me."

"Imagine how scared I would have been if you'd been with me. Your body would not have survived the decontamination I put the shuttle and myself through. There are advantages to being able to heat yourself to several thousand degrees without damage."

"I'll remember that when I'm old and need to put my feet somewhere to warm up."

I do not allow my expression to alter, but the reminder of Wrik's mortality sets a chill in me. I have happiness beyond anything I have ever imagined before, but for how long?

We stop at our cabin and I gather up my hair-tie and resume a pony tail. He takes my hand and leads me to the galley. The others are already present and greet me with relief, even Dusko. I join them at the table. Wrik has made fish, polenta with parmesan topping and marinara sauce with a side of peas. It is quite good.

By mutual consent we do not discuss the voyage to the dead colony. I enjoy the meal with them, ingesting small portions and savoring the complexity of the cooking. What I ingest, I convert to energy. So I have plenty of room for the apple pie, that to my complete surprise, Olivia has made. The pie is excellent and people enjoy it with coffee and liqueurs. We are savoring the fine things of existence, as if in defiance of death. It is a very deliberate act.

Dusko finally breaches the subject. "What now? We've discovered the reason for this sector going silent, some new plague. Are we going to do the sensible and run home?"

"Have we ever?" Wrik asks. My return has put him in good humor, even with Dusko.

"We know less than you think," I interject, "we know this colony died from a spaceborne plague. We do not know if the other colonies succumbed to the same cause. The satellites are gone. The plague did not get them. Then there is the issue of the sighting of this enormous object that blocked the sunlight."

"Could that have been a delusion by the ill?" Delt asked, as he sipped the coffee.

I shake my head. "No, that observation was made before the plague struck. The object was over the cloud deck, so there were no images of it. The sensor readings were very confused. Some indicated that nothing was there. Others indicated an immense object, far in excess of any atmospheric capable starship. That it could cast such as shadow,' dark as midnight' was the expression, does show that something physical passed over the colony."

"So you are leaning toward an attack?" Olivia said, as she finished the last of the pie.

"Such facts as there are seem to support that theory," I reply, "but it is far from settled."

"So, to answer Dusko's original question, we leave a marker buoy here to warn any other ships of the potential for plague. We resupply from Fetch and then head out to Fenris to check on the colony there, that's where the next colony was. We will skip the system that the scout-ship checked. Fenris is along the route that the cruiser Taiko took when it went to Mana colony to recovery the survivors there."

He looks at me and I nod. Olivia does also, seeming satisfied. Dusko grunts and put his nose back into the strong-smelling brew he favors. Delt just gives one of his wild grins.

"We'll transship supplies and fuel from Fetch and start out in the morning," Wrik says. "We'll leave Fetch I here in the Skerrand system. If Candace's plans are all going properly Fetch II should be waiting for us at the next jumppoint."

"Well, Dusko," Delt said waiving a deck of cards, "want to cut for who does dishes? High card wins."

Wrik stands and takes my hand. We leave the others to clean up.

I have plans for the rest of the night.

CHAPTER TEN

WE EMERGED FROM HYPERSPACE TO FIND *FETCH* NEAR the jump point. I ordered it to full burn and slowed our ship. By balancing the two vectors, I used the minimum of energy to acquire the supplies aboard *Fetch II*. In space, every action has to balance gain against loss; it's the only way to survive.

The orange and white sled matched course and speed with us. As before, Maauro handled the hooking up of the boarding tube and various tethers and hoses in a fraction of the time required for a normal crew to do so. Some of this she did through small repairbots in the ship's hull, some by herself. With the boarding tube secured, the rest of us could board *Fetch II*, which was not anywhere near as comfortable as *Stardust*. Very little of the hull was habitable, and the life support was crude and minimal. It sent a shiver of recollection through me. When I'd first fled my disgrace on Retief, I'd only had money for being shipped in cold sleep. I'd fled as far away as I could, being shipped and transshipped as frozen cargo to end up in Vanceport. The memory was unwelcome, and I shook it off, wondering if anyone ever entirely outran their past.

We unloaded as much in the way of supplies as could be safely contained in Stardust. Containers and barrels were cargo-strapped to bulkheads and in spare cabins, even into passageways. We were far from home and resupply, and at each opportunity I intended to restock the ship to full capacity.

After we finished, I sent Fetch II back toward to the jump point, there to circle against our further need. It would remain there until we unloaded it fully, or until we were so long overdue that its retrieval program wrote us off and sent the sled back to the Confederacy.

We resumed our inward voyage toward another small colony, mostly of Moroks in this system. With our sensors on full, we swept inward. There were no signals to be detected, nothing to indicate a colony ahead.

On the second day, we were all weary from trimming the ship's cargo and supplies, even with Maauro's help and heading to the galley, when Maauro's head snapped up. "Contact ahead, metal object ship size. We are coming up on it in 198 seconds,"

"Dammit," Olivia said. We all leapt up and ran for the bridge, Maauro, as usual in the lead.

"How did it get so close undetected?" Olivia demanded.

Maauro, Delt and I slid into our seats. Olivia and Dusko simply stared into the screens.

"The metal object is not radiating power or EM," Maauro said. "It is 15.673 degrees off our course. While it is not under power, its speed relative to us is .01C speed, a speed that a freighter might use. I judge it to be a derelict."

"We are moving quite slow relative to it," I muttered. "It's falling in our direction."

"Wrik, I believe that we should alter course to pass well within visual range," Maauro said.

I immediately set up the course change and executed it. "Do you want me to dump speed for a link up?"

She shook her head. "No. We would use a vast amount of fuel to come to a relative stop. Let us see what is there. If we need to track back, it would not cost more fuel after we pass it and we can judge if it is worth the effort."

I noted that all weapons had come on line and the ship's compartments all sealed.

"It is best to be fully prepared," Maauro said, in response to my look.

I nodded. It was safest to leave the weapons and ECM to Maauro, who would deploy them at just under the speed of light.

"All recorders and scanners are online," Maauro said. "We will only be within range of visual scanners for a few moments at this relative speed but we can see all we need on playback."

Seconds passed, then Maauro spoke again. "Scanner is picking up what I interpret as a debris cloud, not a complete hull. Visible now, I will slow the playback.

On the main screen, a ship tumbled in space, though it was less a ship than a collection of torn debris in the same area of space. We passed it in an instant, but the sensors slowed the image, showing different angles.

"Maauro," I asked, "what do you make of that?"

"I see what concerns you," she said. "That ship was not struck by beamfire or missiles, nor was it on the edge of an explosion. There are no burns or scorch marks on the hull fragments, at least none that are inconsistent with internal explosions from when the hull ruptured. The metal is torn, mechanically pulled apart is my observation."

"What the hell could do that?" Delt asked.

Maauro only shook her head.

"Can you tell what vessel that is?" Olivia demanded.

"I am doing a reconstruction now," Maauro said. A few seconds later she added, "It is the remains of the *SS Empire Manor*, a small combine trade scout. She was one of the last vessels to be listed as missing before the cruiser *Taiko* disappeared.

"If we are going to stop at the wreck," I said, "we're going to have to initiate braking soon. "

"I see no point," Maauro said. "The hull has obtained absolute zero. There is no power and no section that is not open to space. No equipment aboard could have survived such handling. She is a dead hulk. I will drop a buoy to mark her position."

"Agreed," I said.

"Seems like somebody should say something," Delt said, face somber. "Like to think they would if it was us out there."

I could find no words to say, and Olivia just stared at the wreck.

"You remember our friend, Reverend Janna Lourens?" Maauro asked.

Delt and I nodded.

"She taught me a simple prayer and said that the words matter less than what you feel. I don't truly understand all of this, but if you wish I will recite it."

"I wish," Delt said.

Maauro stood and faced the wreck.

Our Father who art in heaven,
hallowed be your name.
Your kingdom come,
your will be done,
on earth as it is in heaven.
Give us this day our daily bread,
and forgive us our debts,
as we also have forgiven our debtors.
And lead us not into temptation,
but deliver us from evil.

"Rest in peace," I added.

"Rest in peace," Delt echoed.

Olivia and Dusko merely looked on. After a few minutes, we stood and headed for the galley again. Maauro lagged to secure the armaments and presumably download all the sensor data.

We found ourselves, dispirited, collapsing into the galley chairs. Dusko said nothing and just sat in the corner ignoring everyone. Delt stood over the microplate with a package of soup.

"Yeah, I think I still have some of a sandwich left," Olivia said, sounding weary.

"Ahem," Maauro said. She'd entered unnoticed behind us.

We looked at her.

"Is the ship under attack?" she asked.

Delt stared at her. "Uh, no."

"Some other emergency?"

I suppressed a smile as Delt and Olivia looked at each other. Dusko leaned back on the bulkhead, staring.

"No," Olivia said, drawing the word out.

"Then perhaps civilization fell while I was on the bridge?" Maauro looked at me.

"I didn't get the memo about that one," I responded.

She walked in and relieved Delt of the heatable soup and replaced it in the cabinet. "Dinner will be served in an hour. Wrik, would you be so kind as to get a linen table cloth and the ship's crystal. Dusko," she handed him a yellow vase she pulled out of another cabinet, "please pick some flowers from the hydro.

"Shasti gave us a fine supply of Olympian vintages. I will choose something nice for a creamy pasta dish. Delt, find us some nice soothing music. Olivia, you will have time to change out of those greasy coveralls before we sit."

Everyone shuffled to their feet, looking confused.

She looked at us all. "Shoo-shoo. Come back in an hour."

I did my best not to burst into laughter. "Yes, dear."

A bemused trio left, Dusko staring thoughtfully at the vase. I walked past Maauro who was already rustling through cabinets.

"I think it's important to keep up certain rituals," Maauro said, almost apologetically. "It is good for morale and the management of stress."

"I agree," I said, pulling out a tablecloth, "but then I've been domesticated."

She smiled and kissed me on the cheek. "And that's a good thing,"

CHAPTER ELEVEN

MY MORALE BOOSTING DINNER APPEARS TO HAVE BEEN A GOOD *strategy to restore my shaken crew. Which is good, as the next day we find the Morok colony on the fourth world is simply gone. Only a crater remains where once five hundred or so beings had lived. I again journey down in the pinnace, to find no evidence of plague, just the residue of a tremendous blast of heat that simply vaporized the colony. I search, but cannot find any survivors. As best I can determine, this appears to have happened 97 standard days ago.*

We again boost for deep space, heading for the next colony world in the hope of arriving before whatever disaster lurking in Piola Sector strikes again. Because the Fetch III awaits us in the next system, we burn at full speed and return to the jump point for the next colony. The expended Fetch II sets up its lonely watch on the dead system.

Meanwhile we pass the time as best we can.

Wrik and I square off in the ship's gym. "I will set my reaction speed to human levels." I say. "We will see how much of what Olivia taught you has been retained."

"Hey, I've been practicing," he says with a grin.

"Practice without an opponent," I reply, "has limited value."

We engage. Wrik uses his reach to stay back. I judge his speed. While, I have no need to rest or catch my breath, I monitor his breathing levels and adjust my tempo so he gets maximum aerobic benefit.

Still we must pause occasionally. "Wow," he says, "I thought Olivia was a hard taskmaster."

"Oh? Do you prefer working with her?"

"No," he says, smiling at the trap. "But there is the fact that she, at least, is not armored."

"Hmph," I said. "From what I remember, there was a touch of foreplay about your practice with her, and perhaps an element of bondage."

"I believe she called that Brazilian jujitsu."

"Oh, is that what she called it?"

"Not sure I want to continue sparring with a jealous android."

"Well spar you must, but you are not taking advantage of the opportunity."

"What?"

"Wrik, mere rifle fire doesn't even scratch my exterior. There is no need to pull your punches as you were. You can strike at full power. I will simulate the reaction to being hit—"

"No," he says, all good humor wiped from his face.

"My soft outer casing will protect your hand. The training will be—"

"I said, no. Don't ask again."

Something has happened, and I do not understand what. Wrik's face is closed, and he is upset as I have not seen recently. He sits heavily on a bench, facing partly away from me.

I walk over, slowly and carefully, put my hand on his shoulder, dreading that he might push it away. Over time I have learned that if I remain silent next to him, he will speak about what is bothering him. This time he doesn't take long.

He reaches up to take hold of my hand. "My father hit my mother."

Shock.

"Not often, but once was too much. I couldn't... there was nothing..."
He turns and presses his face against me. His temperature is up three degrees, he is badly upset. He does not wish to cry; the culture he was born into stupidly disrespects such displays as feminine and weak.

I rest both my hands on him. Owen Van Zyle, will I never cease regretting that I failed to give you thrashing? Yet, can more violence be the answer to the rot at the heart of Wrik's family, that has spread so much damage to so many?

A sound attracts a minor amount of my attention. Olivia, dressed in gym clothes has appeared at the hatchway, but freezes when she sees us. I give a tiny shake of my head, and she silently fades away,

"I'm sorry," I say to Wrik, stroking his hair. "I didn't know."

"I'm not mad at you," he says quickly, looking up. "The memory upset me; that's all. But, Maauro, I know in my head you're too strong for any blow to hurt you but... to throw a real punch at the woman I love..."

"Shhhh," I say, "it was a stupid idea, and we will never mention it again."

He looks at me, clearly wanting to say more.

"Go ahead," I say, kneeling next to him so our eyes are on the same level.

"Sometimes," he whispers, not meeting my eyes, "I'm afraid that there is a darkness in me. It wasn't Retief, that was just panic. It was Vanceport, the things I did there to survive...the darkness almost owned me. What if it comes back?"

I take his chin in my hand and make him meet my eyes. "You are not your father. There is nothing in you that is not in every other biological. Many go their whole lives without being exposed to the threat of death and never have to face it. I believe you are stronger than this darkness you fear. I do not doubt it. But Wrik, do not doubt this, together we are stronger than any darkness in either of us."

His breath runs out in a rush and I feel him relax. "Sorry," he says. "I'm being stupid. Let's get back to training."

"We will, but not today."

"Ok then, I definitely need a shower."

"Aha," I say, knowing that a playful comment will allow him distance from the emotional rupture. "More proof of my inherent superiority."

"As if we need it." He kisses me soundly, then heads for the shower.

I stand, considering what has transpired. Olivia has returned. She glances in to see if Wrik is gone. "Everything ok?"

"Yes, now."

"Look, I don't want to butt in, but I know sometimes stuff we biologicals do is confusing to you."

I consider. "This one is not. I trod on a mine left over from Wrik's childhood while we were sparring. I wanted him to stop pulling his punches,"

Her eyebrows go up; then a change comes over her face. "Son-of-a-bitch. His father, right?"

I look at her in surprise. "How could you possibly put that together from what I told you?"

She gives a small shrug. "Patriarchal society, not given to female equality, a domineering father, passive mother... it doesn't take that much imagination."

I sigh. "You do not give sufficient credit to your imagination, the non-linear way you process information still eludes me. Did he discuss this with you when you were intimate?"

A cautious look steals over her face. "No, not as such. He occasionally would let slip some detail about his father, who he does not like. I looked up Retief when I learned he was from there. Not much good said about the place."

"His mother never mentioned this to me," I say.

"Most abused women don't, especially in traditional societies."

"I wonder if this happened in front of his sister; that might explain some things as well."

"Even if it didn't, a violent household is a terrible place to grow up. No wonder he has always seemed so old."

"You have noticed this too."

She nods. "He's not like most guys his age. He thinks way too much, about too many things. It's a maturity, but it makes him old before his time."

"Woman to woman," I say, "advice?"

"The usual," she says, "screw his brains out tonight so he stops thinking about it. Tomorrow it will be further away. Distance from memory is one of our protections."

She looks at me as if suddenly struck by something. "I guess it can't be that way for you. Your recall is perfect; everything must remain immediate for you."

I nod. "Yes, the past is as much with me as the present. The only escape I had was to delete a memory. I have not done that since I reactivated and I have promised Wrik that I will not. I must live with all I do, as if I just did it."

"Wow," Olivia says. "I'm not sure I could do that. Wrik isn't the only one who struggles with his past."

"It seems, Olivia, that we all do."

She looks me over. "Mind another question?"

I raise an eyebrow. "Girl talk?"

"Yeah, this one anyway, particularly given the advice I just gave you. So when you're together, I imagine it's pretty much like it would be with any other woman for him. What is it like for you?"

"Are you asking me about sexual climax?"

She gives a laugh, mixing defiant and embarrassed. "Yeah."

'Well, I grant that it cannot be like one of yours: an out of control contraction of muscles—"

"When I'm lucky…"

"—but I find sex deeply satisfying. The intimacy, the connection, sometimes I feel something beyond myself that runs over my circuitry. That should be impossible, but it happens. It is my equivalent I guess. However, it is one of the things that I am curious about and that I envy. Sex seems so all-consuming for you."

"Ah, did you mean me individually, or the species?"

"Well if the lingerie fits, wear it."

Olivia's jaw drops, and she laughs so hard she has to sit down. I smile at her, enjoying the moment of closeness. We chat on for a while about sex and love, but it is an exchange of words, meanings may still be eluding me. Still all data is useful. Later that night, I take Olivia's advice.

The next day, we resupply from Fetch III, emptying the sled and plunge into the jump point. As the strangeness of jumpspace enfolds us I consider the strange state of being that we are entering. My biological friends are in a form of stasis, not an artificial one, simply a suspension of their existence. They are unaware, do not age, or dream. Their bodies are too alien to this place to function or age. Jumpspace is the province of the machine. But even for me, the experience is disorienting. In a way, the ship's original sensor and computer suite are better suited to this task than I am. It is the case of too sensitive an instrument in my case. I see too much into subspace, far more than the ship does even with my improvements. I try too hard to orient and reconcile in a space where this is impossible.

No time passes as the biologicals measure it—nor in truth as I measure it. Yet I am conscious of linear events though I cannot say over what span. For all of my transits I have learned little of this space. I was not made for it by my Creators. Though I was carried between the stars in battle, I was usually inactive to save power.

Now I am active, and control my own destiny. Why should I hold back from my own exploration? I dial my sensitivity down and study the *roiling mass of nonspace beyond the hull of my ship. This is not the first time I have done so. My prior studies have added no objective data to the knowledge of jumpspace.*

But this time, I sense something new. There is a shape in the nonspace, though how this could be I cannot say. All I know is that the contact is outside the ship, that self-contained part of our space that has been dragged here.

What can this be? There has never been any report of a contact in jumpspace before; it has always been a vast emptiness. Only sheer chance gave some ancient race the secret of how to enter jumpspace. Once discovered, the secret had been passed around space as race after race arose and bartered whatever they needed to for access to the stars.

I focus all available sensor power and study the shape. The sensors reveal nothing more and I feel frustration, even anger that I cannot even tell how long I have been examining it. Time has no meaning.

It occurs to me that, when Wrik is close to a jump point, he feels the jump point through more than just his instruments. He somehow senses the correctness of the approach–this arises out of his biological nature. It is similar to how he makes leaps of imagination based on intuition— without the objective, verifiable evidence I need.

What is there? How is anything there and how do I sense it? How does the ship sense it?

Then I realize something. The ship has not registered any alarm— no proximity, no collision alarm, no weapon lock. It occurs to me that while I am a machine— I partake of the universe in a way that the ship does not, cannot. I am a machine, but I am more, an artificial person, perhaps the first there has ever been.

So now I reach out with what I have learned, what I have taken and given with my beloved. I feel. And feeling is almost the undoing of me. I touch something, something anti-life, anti-cooperative, antithetical. There can be no commonality, no communication with this....thing. I recognize only one impression, hunger, acquisitiveness, the desire to consume.

I wrench my consciousness away from the monster, for I perceive it as a monstrosity, out of some other time, some other space and hostile to all I know. Whether this hostility was intentional or just from utter incompatibility I do not know.

The shape has detected me as well. Though I cannot judge out relative position, I sense it move closer to us. Alarmed, I arm one of our four nuclear-tipped torpedoes, setting it for maximum blast. I have no certainty that the weapon will even leave its tube; much less track this unknown enemy. But the torpedo leaves the tube, immediately protesting that it has no target. I must guide it toward my unseen enemy closing in on us. This is maddening; my shots are usually calculated to the micron. Here, I am simply flinging a shot in the dark. Still it is a 100 kiloton shot.

The nuclear bloom spreads across jumpspace and the monster recoils. I sense shock and surprise in its emanations, perhaps it has never been struck at in jumpspace before. There is pain in the sensation, but not enough to assure me of a kill, or even of great damage.

I am in a quandary. My interior damage control is still coping with the effect of my momentary contact with this thing. Now, I am passively receiving impressions from it, and these are buffered and do me no additional harm. If I switch to active fire control and try to recontact it, I might be able to hit with a second torpedo. No—I decide that between jumpspace disorientation and the effect the monster has had on me, I would not last the time it would take to guide the warhead to target.

I bring all weapons on line, though all protest that there is nothing there, no threat to lock onto but I know better and suppress or override all safeties and warnings. I will only fire if the enemy closes on us, waiting until the last possible moment.

How long does this stand-off last? Hours? Days? Weeks. I have no way of telling, but I watch my enemy with all the alertness I can muster.

Suddenly we are back in normal space. My stars, my beloved and beautiful stars are back on their velvet curtain.

"That wasn't too bad," I said, shaking off the effects of jump and reaching for the restoratives. Then I was pressed back in my seat by a brutal acceleration, startled. My eyes darted over the instruments. All weapons were active and a torpedo was gone, fired. The engines were on full.

"Maauro to all crew. Remain secured. Stand by for combat and high-g maneuvers. There was something in jumpspace with us, something hostile and mobile. I fired on it and drove it away. We are putting distance between us and the jump point in case it emerges."

I looked over at Maauro's face. I can see Delt and Olivia behind her. Dusko was riding it out in his cabin. While my hands ache to reach for the controls, I know that in a combat situation Maauro reacted faster than I could.

"What the hell?" Delt said against the acceleration.

"That's crazy," Olivia added.

Maauro looked me in the eye. "Please believe me, Wrik."

"What was it? Did you hit it with the torp?" I said.

Relief flooded her face, a very deliberate act. She knew I believed her.

"Are you certain?" Delt asks.

"Instrument's clear," I say, more for the others.

The acceleration ended and the stars wheeled as Maauro rotated the ship so our weapons faced the jump point receding behind us. A wave of jump dizziness assailed me and I grabbed for the squeeze bulb with my meds in it. The lemony tartness of the restoratives helped quickly.

"Yes, Delt, I am certain. Unlike the rest of you, I and the ship are both aware in jump and I perhaps in a unique way. I cannot properly describe it to you. We sense things too differently –no instrumentation of mine, or the ship, was operating properly. I can only say this. The thing I sensed was a monster in the truest sense of the word. It was anti-life and hungry."

"It wanted to eat us?" Delt asked.

"I do not believe that it craved flesh as such, I only sensed a hunger a desire to consume. I am unsure if it desired us, or the ship."

This caused Delt and Olivia to exchange dubious looks.

"Wrik, I believe this sensation is like the sense you use to trim the ship for jump. Remember how the space itself around the Preon star made you feel ill?"

"Yes," I said. I looked at Olivia, who had shared that experience. She nodded slowly.

"I can only say that these are impressions I gathered— some from a momentary direct contact that caused me system damage—"

"Are you alright?" I demanded.

"Yes, dear. The damage is already repaired. The rest of what I learned was from passive reception of emanations.

"As you surmised, I fired a torpedo at it. The blast alarmed it for all that the explosion was not close. I could only guide it by feel, which was most unsatisfactory."

"This is Dusko," his voice came over the speaker. "Can I join you on the bridge?"

I looked at Maauro.

"Yes," she said. "Nothing has emerged to threaten us, but use the auxiliary jump seat and belt in as soon as you get here."

"Was it intelligent?" Olivia asked.

"I do not know," Maauro said, shaking her head. "All I can say is that it is inimical to life as we know it."

"A creature of jumpspace," Olivia murmured, "could it possibly be?"

I half-expected Maauro to show a sign of irritation at being doubted, but she apparently took Olivia's comment more as amazement than doubt. "I cannot know more on such a brief exposure to it in an environment I was not designed to cope with. What I can tell you is that the Creator's ships and technology for jumpspace was superior to what Confed has. They never found anything in jumpspace. It may be that this monster is not native to jumpspace but merely transits it, and because of its nature, can deal better with the distortions of it than biological beings."

"You say monster or creature," I said gently. "You didn't sense that it was someone in a ship, or something like a natural event, a kind of storm?" I drop the empty restorative bulb in the regenerator.

"A good question," she nodded. "I cannot be certain, but again I drew the mental impression that it was out in space, directly exposed. In the end, all I can say is that there was something there, it was hostile and would have attacked us had I not drove it off."

"I hate to think of a critter," Delt said, rubbing his face, "that could take a 100 kiloton torp."

"There is no way to tell how much I missed it by," Maauro replied. "It felt an effect but whether I was a hundred kilometers off or a thousand, I could not tell. And we were in jumpspace—no one knows how that might affect such a blast. Jumpspace might function like water, compressing the blast to where close proximity was needed."

"Whatever it was," I said, "it seems reluctant to follow us out into this universe."

"That's good," Delt said.

"But it's also just inside the only exit we know of for this system that leads back to Confed Space," Dusko added.

"That's not," Olivia said.

"Always walking down the sunny side of the street, aren't you Dusko?" Delt grumbled.

"Optimism is not a Dua characteristic," he said.

"So, what now?" I asked. "Do we wait here hoping for it to come out into our guns? We're getting further from the jump point every second. If we want to stay in weapon range, we'll have to brake soon."

"Can't say I like the idea of jumping back out with some horror that can eat us in our sleep, waiting." Delt said.

"Maauro," I said, when she does not speak. "I'm not sure that hanging here for an indefinite period makes sense. We'll have to brake hard, use fuel and we will be out of sensor range of the jumppoint before we can get back. We won't know if it emerged during that time."

She looks at me, uncertain, something I have so rarely seen in Maauro. "I'm glad that you consult me Wrik, I am made for combat situations, but this one is beyond my depth. My tactical calculus contains holes large enough to drive *Stardust* through sideways, but I concur. We have a mission and we cannot accomplish it hanging here. Our best guess is that *Taiko* fled this way. Perhaps it encountered this creature and escaped it."

"If it did," Delt says, "it must have done so in normal space. If they had been attacked in jumpspace, they wouldn't have known it. Any more than we would if we didn't have you."

"But that also means a cruiser with twenty times our throw weight had to flee it. That cruiser is still missing, the creature is here. Or there could be more than one," Dusko said.

"Captain Cheerful is heard from again," Delt snorted.

We all turned to look at Maauro.

"Damn if I know," she replied.

This triggered a brief blast of slightly hysterical laughter, even from Dusko.

"Then onward," I say. "Delt, where is Fetch IV?

"It's in formation with us. The automatics picked up on us when we jumped in and it went to full burn. I'll bet's it's a worried puppy given how we hit the gas."

"We should top off all supplies now that we know there is an enemy present," Maauro stated. "I have taken control of Fetch IV and am having it match speed and course with us. I will handle the transfer of fuels. Please all suit up and transfer any sundries and equipment. I realize that we're very full, but let's pack every available space with supplies.

Everyone nodded.

CHAPTER TWELVE

WE PARK FETCH IV IN A LONG ORBIT AROUND THE JUMPPOINT AND *head in toward Tamba, the colony location we have come to investigate. The sled does not have much in the way of a sensor suite, but what it has, I set to watch for anomalous readings, or anything emerging from the jumppoint. My confidence in my watchman is low, the sled's computer system is basic and I have no idea of whether the... whatever, will register on the instruments. Stardust's vastly superior systems had failed to detect it. Only my presence in the systems, with my special abilities and perceptions, revealed it.*

I spend a great deal of my processing power hooked into the sensor suite. Additional hours are spent perched in my accustomed seat near the slender nose of Stardust, my hair spun out to long filaments, making a sensor net superior to the ship's own. I detect nothing, no monsters, no starships, no electromagnetic traffic of any sort. It's another star system devoid of artificial noise.

Tamba is more hospitable than Windrush or Fargo, but was lightly settled, chiefly by Voit-Veru. The planetary rush had spread out by this point and the initial settlers here had been unfriendly to others. We come up on a world with small oceans and more exposed land mass than Earth. Much of it is mountainous, with peaks well into unbreathable heights. The kangaroo-like Voit-Veru had settled in a river valley, near an ocean, the usual preferred site for a colony. Our first pass over the world does not show the colony, there is only a flattened area near the river, the earth raw and turned. Even the course of the river is altered, as if a mass of debris has been forced into it.

Suddenly a sensor lights with a return of a metallic signal, a refined-metal object, 191 kilometers north of the colony site on a high plateau. I focus our full power on it.

"Contact," I say, "a small ship or aircraft. Zooming optic sensors." The others cluster around me and the image of small vessel appears.

"A Confed shuttle," I advise. "It struck and slid across the plateau."

"Can't see it well," Olivia grumbles, "it's in the shadow of that hill."

"Infra –red," I add, "shows no energy."

"Any sign of life?" Wrik asks.

"None, but the image is poor due to the shadow and angle."

"Maauro, send one of the probes down; check the area for plague with those biofilters you updated."

I nod. The probe launches.

"We'll set up for a landing and abort if the probe detects anything," Wrik advises.

The probe returns and is recovered, showing no indication of CBO, so we continue to descend. We drop through the azure sky, heading for the stable outcrop of stone we'd spotted from orbit, near where the crashed shuttle went down. The area close by the wreck is too sandy to risk a landing.

Wrik draws Stardust into vertical and a slow descent. I open the airlock door and step out onto the hull, grasping a takehold and magnetizing my soles. I cannot spin my hair out into full nimbus due to gravity, but fan it as best I can, scanning for any evidence of the plague we'd seen before, and confirming that the outcrop is suitable for our landing. I am not above double-checking and am relieved that the site is geographically stable. Stardust can safely land.

"Wrik," I send, "you can take her down."

"Got it."

Stardust settles with Wrik's usual care and finesse, all of which are needed coming down on an unprepared field. We are far from home or help and anyway Stardust is home for me. The ship lands with barely a jar as her autojacks level her for a prefect three fin landing. The impellers sigh as they run down.

I scan again for any sign of CBO. "I can detect no indication of the plague we encountered before, or of any other chemical or biological agent."

"Wrik to crew, we're landed and level. All systems are nominal and switching to planetary routine. Maauro says that there is no danger of CBO."

I reenter the ship and head for the cargo bay. Quick as I am, Delt and Olivia have preceded me and have the bay doors open and the main power winch ready. I take active control of the three crab robots and move them to where I can hook them up. Delt then winches them to the surface. Then I release them to their own AI's, so they will take station around the ship.

The robots, each half as big as an aircar, retract their wheels into the legs that give them their names and begin to move off. Their pincer claws are folded against the armored hulls, but each sports a multi-barrel gun that, like a searching antenna, is up and pointed skyward. The gray and green standard camouflage changes as the surfaces adapt to a high-desert camouflage of browns and tans.

Delt grins at me. "I can tell when you're controlling something. They don't move with that much finesse on their own."

"Finesse is my middle name," I reply.

"Don't you need a last one first?" Olivia throws over her shoulder.

She does not see my momentary freeze. Perhaps one day I will have one, I think, then shelve the idea. Time will answer the question, and one must admit that, despite our good start, the odds seem long. But now is not the time to think about this even with a brain that can segment and partition.

Wrik and Dusko appear, and we begin assembling the Mule and unlatching Delt's Bush Rebel two-wheeler. I speed to the armory for weapons. Even for me it takes two trips to secure the heavy machine gun for the Mule and weapons for all. I bring my armspac with a loadout of HE and AP missiles.

Olivia is working frantically, the thought that there might be Confed survivors clearly spurring her efforts. With my help, the job is done in 17.43 minutes. We winch the vehicles to the ground, with me riding the four-wheeled Mule down and the others following in the outside elevator or on the scaling ladder.

I look at the countryside as I ride down atop the vehicle, holding onto the straps and quick release that hold the Mule. A small range of mountains lie behind us. Stardust rests on a flat spur of granite from it that extends into the desert. The mountain range is of reddish-orange stone, uncapped by snow and barely softened by vegetation around their base. The desert is curious, more of a veldt of scattered grass and stone, with bands of azure sand that mirror the color of the sky over the small dunes that punctuate the area.

Our Mule is painted in a black and green camouflage pattern that will stand out on the desert landscape. Unlike the crabs, it cannot change, being simply paint on a utility vehicle. Right now it looks more like a frame on an engine then a vehicle. We have not taken the time to put weather shields or covers on it.

The five of us gather next to the vehicles, belting on body armor, helmets and weapons. I raise my hand as Dusko reaches for his.

"Please remain with the ship," I say. "You will have the three crabs and the ship's weapons for protection. The ship's AI will handle defense."

He nods, looking relieved at being left out of the expedition. Well, some things do not change... much.

"Olivia," I add, "you ride with us in the Mule and handle the HMG." I gesture at the weapon perched menacingly in the ring above our heads. She nods and jumps up onto the Mule to stand behind the driver's seat and begins checking the weapon.

"Delt," I turn to him as he slings a triple-auto across his broad back. "Take point with your Bush Rebel." I now make my voice stern. "At all times stay within fifty meters of me. Do you understand?"

"Yes," Delt says. The playful Delt is gone, replaced by a soldier getting his orders.

I pick up my armspac from where it rests in the back of the Mule. I will ride in the back in case I have to leap out and engage some enemy. I look at Wrik. He nods, as always content to leave ground combat situations in my hands.

We pull out with Delt in the lead. I watch Dusko scramble back into the ship sealing it as soon as he is inside. Wrik drives with Olivia standing next to him, her thigh brushing his shoulder as she scans the area over the sights of her HMG.

I too stand in the back. Otherwise my forward view is of Olivia's backside, which, despite Delt's appreciation of it, does nothing for me. I scan as best I can, over the shifting dunes and sandy, rocky soil beneath the sturdy Mule's wheels. Wrik keeps to the firmer soil, using both a good eye, his panel instruments and the track of Delt's two-wheeler.

Fifteen minutes later, I see a rill of white smoke trailing into the sky; it goes up about a hundred meters before a wind takes it horizontal.

"Smoke ahead," I say, over the sound of the engine.

"Survivors!" Olivia says.

"Perhaps," I caution. "It is from the area of the shuttle and there is no reason for there to be fire at the crash site months later.

Delt pulls up and points. I nod. "Pull up on the reverse crest of the next hill," I order. The small rise of land barely deserves the name of hill, but we stop on the reverse slope. Wrik pulls the Mule up so Olivia has a clear field of fire beyond the hillock.

"What are we waiting for?" Olivia demands as I dismount.

I give her a narrow-eyed look. "Use tactical sense, Major, it was trained into you. There is smoke; it thickens, so there is intelligent action behind it, but that intelligence need not be friendly. When advancing into unknown territory, you secure your perimeter and send out a scout."

She blushes furiously, both at the delay and the fact that I am right. Her head nods in a jerk.

"I will scout," I say, before Delt, on his speedy two-wheeler, can offer. "I am the fastest over this type of terrain and frankly the strongest."

"Be careful anyway," Wrik says.

"I promise," I reply. As I move over the crest, Wrik and Delt drop prone with their triple-autos. Olivia again scans the horizon with her HMG. I blur into forward motion, wondering what lies ahead. My speed throws up dust, but my tactical sense is that speed is more important than stealth. Our descending ship was a beacon to anything within hundreds of kilometers. Surprise is not an element.

It takes 25.43 seconds to cover the distance to the last rise of ground before the shuttle crash site. I poke my head over the crest to survey the area. Instantly, I spot two figures, jogging in my direction. Their ragged uniforms proclaim them Confed Marines. Both are male humans, the leader is a tall sergeant with reddish hair. The man next to him has skin that is nearly black, he is wiry and wearing a helmet. Both carry the latest Marine assault rifle. Behind them lays the shuttle, its bottom torn from the long slide it made coming in to its final resting place. From this angle I can now see the graves of six of its complement dug into the hard earth alongside it.

I wait till they are close enough to see me to stand and wave, holding the massive armspac in one hand as I cannot conceal it and do not wish to hide it and come back for it later. They spot me, cry out and wave frantically, then run toward me.

"There are survivors," *I report from inside my head.* "My voice will sound in the headphones of the others. "At least two. You may come up."

I pass over the crest and jog toward the Marines. As I close on them, they slow and examine me, puzzled. Well, I suppose I am a sight, a small girl, carrying an enormous gun, wearing a tight jumpsuit, is probably not what they expected as a rescuer.

They pause a few meters away, wary, but with their weapons pointed either up, or at the ground.

"Are you from the Confederacy? What ship?" *asks the big man, with a pronounced accent that I associate either with Ireland of Earth or New Eire. His name badge says, Cully.*

"God," *interrupts the dark-skinned man, a grin almost splitting his face.* "Are we glad to see you. We've been stranded here for seven months."

"I'm Maauro off the SS Stardust," *I say.* "You're from the CSS Taiko?"

"We are," *Cully said, as he studies me intently.* "I'm Sgt Sean Cully; this is Lance Corporal Abin Troy. You're a civilian ship?"

I shake my head. "We're covert. My rank is that of Lieutenant Commander in Confed Military Intelligence. My companions are following in vehicles and will be here in a minute. We were sent to find out what was happening in this sector and find your ship. Are there other survivors?"

"There are," *Cully says, his voice suddenly weary.* "Glad to see you, Commander. We lost six in the crash. We've got two wounded in a bad way; there are two able-bodied taking care of the wounded. Then there's the Lieutenant," *he hesitates.* "She's not been right since the crash. Not since the thing."

"Thing?" *I say.*

"We didn't get a good look at it," *Cully says.* "Just a big shape that hit us and then took off like a rocket, headed up to the cruiser. We couldn't follow the action, but whatever the hell it was, it chased off our ship."

"Yeah," *Troy replies bitterly,* "they bugged out and left us on this rock."

"Easy, Troy," *Cully says,* "Captain Raglan wouldn't have left us if he had any choice."

"Anyway," *Troy continues.* "Thank God you're here. We're almost out of supplies and our wounded need attention. Man, I really didn't believe we'd ever get rescued. We hot-footed it in your direction when we saw the ship coming in. Couldn't tell what you were from the distance. You can take us off, right?" *His face suddenly hardens.*

"We can," *I assure,* "and we will."

CHAPTER TWELVE

The sound of engines causes the Marines to look up. The Bush Rebel and Mule crest the hill. They pull up and Olivia leaps off the Mule. There is a flurry of handshakes, congratulations and introductions.

"How about we tell you our entire sad story after we get back to the others?" Cully says. "I want them to know the good news. Our coms are out of power so we can't call.

"Sure," Wrik says. "Hop in."

"I'll ride with Delt," Olivia says. She locks the HMG in place and racks her carbine in the back, then hops on the back of the two-wheeler to Delt's apparent pleasure.

The two Marines walk to the back of the Mule. I place my armspac in there and catch Cully looking over it and me.

"That's quite a weapon you have there, Commander," he says. "How much does that weigh?"

I smile. "The weapon was specially designed for me. It's not as heavy as it looks."

"Miss, or rather Commander, though I can't recall meeting an officer of that rank at your apparent age, I've been around weapons my whole life. That's 150 pounds of metal with missiles and an autogun that would break the arm of anyone foolish enough to fire it while standing. You handle it like it's a derringer. Who are you really?"

"I am just who I said I am," I reply.

Troy gives his companion a worried look, but Cully relaxes as he sits back. "As you wish."

"You boys want some power bars?" Wrik says.

"Ta," Cully answers.

He tosses them a ration packet. Cully snags it.

"Hah," I add. "I make far better."

Cully eyes me again. "There's more to you than meets the eye, Commander, or I'm a Bain Sidhe."

"Iced tea," Wrik adds, pulling two plastic bottles from a cooler at the foot of the passenger seat.

Both men are diverted into drinking and eating a food bar.

"Save some for the others," Cully says.

"No need," I assure them. "There will be more than adequate provisions aboard our ship."

"Happy days are here again," Troy says.

"Troy," Cully says, "you ride up front and direct Mr. Trigardt—"

"Wrik has the rank of Lt. Commander as well," I add. "Olivia is a Major of your own service. Delt is a civilian member of our crew."

"Commander Trigardt," Cully corrects.

"Got it," Troy says. "Wow, we gonna have a lot of officers for six enlisted."

We start now with the Mule in the lead. Troy directs us to a small range of hills not far away. As we get close, I see a thin rill of a stream struggling down it and supporting more than the usual amount of vegetation. Above the stream are a few cave mouths in the rock face. A woman emerges from one of the caves, waving and shouting. Another male human appears as we pull up.

"Rainbird, Lacey," Cully says, "it's a glorious day in the Corp. We are getting off this rock."

I study the new pair. Rainbird has short, black hair and a tattoo of a bird's wing on her face. Lacey is very young, wearing a private's bar. They greet us with handshakes and take the other bag of food bars and bottles of tea with enthusiasm. Lacey is almost overcome and Troy thumps him on the back.

"May I see your casualties?" I ask. "I have extensive medical training."

Again comes the searching look from Cully. Wrik merely smiles and shakes his head. "Just believe her."

"This way," Cully says, "Lacey, were you watching the LT?"

"Yes, Sarge. She's not doing anything. Quiet, just like yesterday."

"Watch her anyway."

The young man nods and heads back to the cave on the right.

I follow Cully into the other cave, trailed by Wrik. Olivia and Delt remain behind, speaking with Rainbird and Troy. Inside, a human female and a Morok lie on bedding improvised from the shuttles crash couches. The Morok's head is swathed in bandages; he wears a navy uniform with a communications bar and ensign's rank. He must have run the shuttle's ECM and com.

"He fell about a week ago," Cully said, "bit of damn bad luck on a cliff side.

He starts to explain the injuries, but I wave him to silence, kneel and extend my hands on the Morok first, scanning and testing. "This person has a subdural hematoma below a skull fracture. I will attend to it when we are at the ship. Once I evacuate the hematoma, he should recover."

"So you're a surgeon too," Cully said. "And unless you're a preacher who believes in the laying on of hands, I'd be interested to know what instruments you used to examine him."

I look him in the eyes. "I am the instrument."

"I thought you might be," he says, "though I grant I can't imagine how. You handled that mini-fieldpiece like a popgun, and the other woman, was her name Major Croyzer?"

"It was.

"She switched to the bike because your weapon, yourself and this young man—

"My boyfriend," I say.

"Ah, boyfriend is it now?" he looks at Wrik.

I look at him, and perhaps there is warning in my gaze.

"Now, no offense," he said.

"My boyfriend," I repeat.

"Well you, your boyfriend and your monster gun weigh a bit, and if you add two more Marines, well even a thick-head like Troy might notice the vehicle struggling with the weight if the major stayed aboard."

"You're very observant," Wrik says.

"You don't grow old in this trade otherwise."

I move to the other casualty another human female named Jeiwan. She's lost her leg below the knee and a persistent infection has taken hold. She is fevered and restless. I press my hand against her breast and inject both a mild sedative and a powerful antibiotic. There are internal injuries, so I inject a small number of nanobots to conduct these deep repairs which will be better dealt with without such invasive surgery as I plan with the Morok.

"We used up most of our medical supplies on them in the first few weeks." Cully says. "Jeiwan was fine for weeks after the amputation, but then an infection set back in. She's been going downhill for three weeks."

I glance at him. "You need not apologize. You have done well given the circumstances. The amputation site is properly done and that must have been difficult—"

"Difficult, aye," Cully said. "God grant that I be in heaven rather than have to do such a thing again."

Jeiwan's breathing has become more regular and she settles. I pull an IV out of my body and arrange to hang it and begin replenishing her fluids."

"Ah, where did that come from?" Cully asks.

"I manufactured it inside my body," I reply.

"Did you now?" he says and sits back to stare at me.

"Wrik, give me your canteen; then get me more water. I need to do the same for the Morok and I need fluids to do it with."

"Sure." He looks at Cully. "God as my witness, your people could not be in better hands."

Cully studies Wrik's face. He is about ten years older than Wrik and his blue eyes search Wrik's brown ones.

"I don't lie much myself," Cully says "So I'm not easy to lie to. There's something about you, about the way you hold a man's eye that tells me you shoot straight. Beside's I like her, begging your pardon, Commander."

I smile. "I take no offense and do not stand on rank."

"Is that because you don't need rank to make everyone obey you?" he asks.

"In part," I admit, taking the canteen from Wrik. I drain its contents in one swallow and begin reprocessing it into fluids the Morok needs.

"Who is in charge in your little party?" Cully asks.

Wrik and I point at each other and Cully laughs.

"Later," I say and pull another IV from inside my body. I casually bend some metal into a hanger as Cully whistles.

"I can do that too." I whistle a tune that Wrik taught me.

CHAPTER TWELVE

Cully chuckles and shakes his head in wonder.

"You mentioned the Lieutenant?" Wrik asks. "What's wrong with her?"

"Lieutenant Menoan is a Denlenn demi-female, prefers a female pronoun in our language. I don't think we'd have made it at first without her. But she started to go strange on us. The thing, whatever it is, seems to have had an effect on her. She began making images of it, drawing obsessively, even making a pile of rocks in its image. When we tried to stop her, she got violent. Started raving about us being worthless cattle only fit for sacrifice. After that, I didn't feel I could leave her alone, especially with the wounded, so I relieved her and took her weapons. She went quiet after that, just sitting in a corner, barely eating or drinking."

We follow Cully into the next cave, more of a hollow. Lacey looks up at us, Cully gestures with his head and the young man steps out with a relieved expression. Seated in the back is young Denlenn demi-female. She is tall and well-featured, but her eyes are slack and the body gaunt. Her uniform is fouled and judging by Wrik's face, she smells worse than the other survivors. She simply sits in the back of the cave, not reacting to anything.

I study the Denlenn. "Deep shock. You say that she felt she was in contact with the thing that struck you down?"

"Aye, it's what she said. There's no physical trauma, but she rarely comes out of it. It's been a battle to get enough food and water into her to keep her alive."

I lean forward and place my hand against the Denlenn's chest. Menoan's eyes flutter and she slumps. Carefully I lay her down.

"The anesthetic may help," I say, "and she will be easier to handle until we get her back to the ship and we can intervene more forcefully."

"Do you still have those drawings?" Wrik asks. "The one's the Lieutenant made?"

Cully shook his head. "We needed the paper for fire starters. It wasn't much, just images of some beastie, with many eyes and limbs like tentacles. I don't know where it was from. It looked nothing like what struck our shuttle. She couldn't say."

CHAPTER THIRTEEN

AFTER MAAURO FINISHED HER INITIAL AID TO MENOAN, we walked out to see Olivia and the other Marines.

I looked at Maauro. "Should we move back to the ship, or wait here tonight and start in the morning?"

"I have already sent for the three crab robots," she said. "We can move the survivors to the ship before nightfall."

The look of relief that washed over the Marines faces was palatable.

"Any issue with life-support capability?" Cully asked, apparently determined to suss out any possible impediment as soon as possible.

I shook my head. "We're a *Comet* class scout, original crew capability of twelve but she was military so she's overbuilt by 200% in that regard. We were specially supplied for extended voyaging on our own. Don't worry Cully, we won't be running off and leaving you."

Lacy gave a sour look. "Well, when you've seen your own cruiser hauling ass out of system with a monster on its heels, it's hard to trust."

"Make preparations to break camp," Cully said. Everyone scattered.

"I want to take a look at the shuttle," Maauro said.

"Me too," Olivia said. The pair of them mounted the Mule and headed back the way we came.

As soon as the vehicle was out of sight, Cully reached out and put a hand on my shoulder. "The beautiful little girl with all the magic tricks, what the hell is she?"

I gave him a hard look. "My girlfriend, as she said."

He raised the hand in a placating gesture. "Ok so you're a lucky bastard; she's quite the looker. But she handles a gun I'd expect to see mounted on an APC like it weighs nothing, and she can tell at a glance who has internal injuries and begins pulling medical equipment out of her body. Then, like its nothing, she announces she'll do two surgeries later tonight. Those are the prettiest eyes I ever saw, but the biggest too."

"For right now you'll just have to accept that she's an officer in Confed MI and on your side."

Cully mulled this over. "Who is in charge here? Croyzer, says she's a major, both of you hold the rank of Lt Commander…"

"Command rests with me and Maauro," I said, though I wondered if the addition of a few Marines would alter that dynamic. They were no threat to Maauro, but they could be to me. Then I dismissed that, on board our ship with its compartmentation and her control of the environment, Maauro could handle both Olivia and the Marines if she came to regard them as a danger.

"Huh. Well as long as you keep on this Maauro's good side you mean."

"Been there a good while so far."

"Son, I've seen HCRs up close and I thought they were amazing. They're tinkertoys to your lady."

I nod. "A good point to remember."

"Well, good enough for now," Cully said. He then left to help the others pack.

Maauro and Olivia returned in an hour. Examining the shuttle had told them little. There was no sign of an unusual weapon. Most of the damage was from the crash, and the ship's small computer system has not survived the landing and subsequent exposure to the elements. Maauro returned to the wounded. Cully stayed near Olivia, seeming more comfortable with her then us, and doubtless was pestering her with questions.

The three crab robots slid into view over the hillside and another cheer rose from the Marines. Maauro appeared at the mouth of a cave, casually carrying Jeiwan, stretcher and all, past her staring comrades to place it on the back of the Mule. Maauro had evidently decided that there was little point to concealing her nature to fellow combatants as we pursued whatever was haunting this sector of space. She noticed my look and gave me a cheery smile before heading back to the cave for the Morok.

The Marines loaded up their remaining supplies, one never wasted anything on a space trip, and readied themselves to break camp. Troy and Rainbird went to visit the graves by the shuttle. We would pick them up on the way.

Delt lead with Olivia on his bike as the convoy headed back for the ship. The demi-female Denlenn remained somnolent, but we'd belted her onto a crab bot with restraints. The stretchers were placed on the Mule which Maauro jogged easily alongside. The poor terrain and my cargo of wounded kept my speed low. A couple of Marines offered to give up their spots on the crabs, but Maauro waved it off.

The trip back to the *Stardust* took three times as long as the trip out. Delt and Olivia sped ahead to make things ready. Dusko had used the time wisely, using one of the crab robots to bore a well before Maauro sent for it, and had hit an aquifer. The water was potable and he'd set up an outside shower. While the ship ran at 99.90% recycling efficiency, one never took water for granted. Now, we'd have hot water to waste.

"Maauro," I said, as we drove. "What are we going to do for clothes for these folks? There's some aboard but..."

"I have some of the damage control bots converting machinery into a resynthesizer. I will simply feed in their old clothes and have them reconstituted."

"Oh," I said.

"I have scans of everyone's bodies, if needs be I can harvest plant material to be converted into additional clothing."

CHAPTER THIRTEEN

"You're beautiful, deadly and you can cook and sew," I replied with a grin.

"Delt has said I am the perfect woman," she shot back, eyes shining.

"Yeah, but he says that to all the girls. I only say it to you."

"You'd better," she said.

We top the rise and see the base of the ship. Another cheer came from the Marines. Dusko was outside, his perpetually sour look focused on the oncoming parade, but I noticed that he stood next to a table of sandwiches, pots of soup and drinks next to the shower. Olivia and Delt came out as we pulled up.

I pulled up and Maauro had the first casualty off in an instant. She effortlessly carried the stretcher to the ship, but rode the elevator up into the vessel.

"Ok," Olivia said. "All clothes off and in a pile there, everyone into the shower. We got skivvies and blankets with the hot chow. Maauro told me there will be clean uniforms for everyone in an hour."

"Delt," Maauro said, returning from depositing the first stretcher in sickbay. "Please take the Lt and lock her in the small cabin on the engineering deck.

"You'll need a guard," Troy said.

"The ship's AI will watch her for me," Maauro returned. She unlatched the second stretcher holding the amputee.

"I don't think—" Troy began. Cully tapped him on the shoulder and shook his head. Troy subsided reluctantly.

Maauro took the human female up to sick bay. I followed her in to check on the two casualties. Both were still unconscious but resting. They stank from sickness and difficult hygiene.

"I will wash them before surgery," she said. "Leave this to me."

I nodded and slipped out. Dusko, Delt and I threw the Marine clothes and boots in the machine Maauro's repairbots had created in Engineering, before crawling back into the spots in the hull where they spent most of their time unseen. We threw the stuff in the top, closed it and minutes later a panel opened in the bottom and fresh uniforms, with badges and insignia in place came out. Boots took longer, but we had clothes for all in the promised hour. Dusko brought in the last impossibly foul load from the wounded, but these too came out fresh.

I checked on Maauro, looking into the sickbay panel. Inside I could see her working on the Morok's open skull. Unlike a human, she didn't need to be capped and gowned. She noticed me, winked, then returned to her gruesome work.

I went outside to see the Marines had enjoyed the shower fully. Water ran off onto the rocks and disappeared into the ground, but there was little mud. They were shaved and cleaned up, sitting on rocks or camp chairs, covered in blankets and fresh underwear, devouring the food.

"Coffee," Cully said. "St. Patrick be praised. Real coffee again."

Troy methodically munched on his sandwiches. Rainbird sat back with hers, as if she was afraid it might vanish

"Easy on the chow," Olivia said. "You've been on short rations too long. Fill up the corners with some soup. I don't want anybody sick."

Dusko and Delt appeared with boxes of uniforms and boots. I noticed there were also slip-on shoes for shipboard, a typical, thoughtful Maauro touch.

"Hey," Cully said, holding up a shirt. "This is my uniform! I mean the one I was wearing. It's like new but there's the patch my son gave me. I had it sewn inside a pocket where it couldn't be seen, for luck. How? This was only fit for burning."

"Learn to accept minor miracles when Maauro is around," Delt said. "It saves time."

Everyone hastily donned uniforms, as if normalcy would return with clean clothes and regular food. From survivors, they quickly regained the look of professional military.

"Olivia," I said, motioning her aside. "It would be best for you to take charge of them. Settle them together on the passenger deck cabins. Maauro's already working on the Morok. She'll call me when she's through. Those two will be in med bay for a while. No way we can lift off with someone who had a brain surgery, not for some days anyway."

She nodded, then turned to the Marines. "Alright. Finish what you're eating. Then I want all weapons checked into the armory and I'll get you quartered aboard. All the rations and equipment you brought will go into stores. Maauro will do a med check after she's through with the casualties."

The others looked at Cully, who gave a sharp nod. They began gathering up everything.

CHAPTER FOURTEEN

HOURS LATER WE GATHERED AT THE GALLEY. WITH THE exception of the lieutenant, secured in a cabin and the two Marines in sickbay, everyone was present.

"OK," she said. "If anyone didn't get the word, I'm Major Croyzer. I've heard bits and pieces. Now, I want the full report from the top."

"Yes, Major," Cully said. "But first we'd like to know where we stand. I saw your ID card and they aren't easy to fake, but it's possible. But I've already seen some impossible stuff..." He looked directly at Maauro.

Olivia nodded. "Ok. Let's start there. Maauro and Captain Trigardt are both officers as well, navy commissions. Technically, they're Confed Military Intelligence, but in reality they are mercs, plain and simple. Their chief loyalty is to each other. That said, they were sent here by the highest levels of Confed and are trusted. None of you would have clearance for any code that can verify that, so there you'll have to believe me."

"That's not what I meant, Major. I saw the young lady there carry a stretcher with a 200 pound Morok in it like he was a kitten," Cully said. He gestured at Maauro, who stood unmoving, returning only a bland stare. A human would have likely leaned on something, but she felt no such need.

"I knew what you meant, but since you want it spelled out, here it is. Maauro holds a Confed citizenship as a human mutation—"

Cully snorted

Olivia fixed him with her one human eye and he subsided.

"As I said, human mutation, that's the story. She's covered under the Official Secrets Act, anything you see, hear or learn about her is not to be repeated to anyone other than authorized Confederate personnel or I guarantee twenty-five years hard time. Meanwhile, information on her is on a need to know basis. Better still, after this mission, best you forget you met her."

"No need to make me sound so ominous." Maauro said. "I am a person and have and will keep my secrets. I serve the Confederacy, but am not originally of it. What and who I am, is something I share with few, but Olivia knows most of it. You will find that I combine the strength of a machine, with the speed of a computer and the soul of a person. Before anyone asks, I'm spoken for."

A burst of laughter shot around the room. The nervous looks turned to smiles. I crossed the space between us and put an arm around her waist.

"All right, Major," Cully said. "So you're MI and you were sent to find out what was happening in the sector. You have a special team," he looked at Maauro, "and we're the lucky beneficiaries of that. Another couple of weeks and we'd have been eating each other. I was going to suggest starting with Troy."

Again a laugh, then Cully's face turned serious. "*Taiko* had made orbit over the planet, looking for the Voit-Veru colony. The Captain wanted to get a survey before dropping to a lower orbit and deploying all the landing ships, but there was a storm over the colony site. The XO said they couldn't raise anybody so they sent down an *Archer*, with our squad for security.

"We made it through reentry, and the storm had abated some, when we got a call from the ship. The Lieutenant was upfront with the pilot, when *Taiko* called down. They sent us a vid of this thing. I didn't get a good look, I was too far from the screen, but it was a huge gray shape. It was wallowing around, and then I realized the small things near it were buildings. The damn thing was big, and it was crushing the colony into dust.

"Then to everyone's shock, it lifted into the air. Couldn't believe it. It was pulverizing buildings like they were made out of paper. Ship-metal is the hardest malleable thing we have, but you can't crash a ship through buildings and expect it to function. This thing wasn't damaged at all. It took off and took off fast. *Taiko* told us to move off and clear the zone for inbound fire, but we were too close to the colony. Ensign Long put us into climb, but said the thing was coming up under us and fast, so he banked and dove.

"About that point, Lt. Menoan started screaming that something was in her head. I thought she was just losing it in her first combat action. Now...not so sure. Something hit us. I can't say what, but I saw scorch marks on the upper hull after we crashed. The Ensign managed to get some control back, but we were clearly going in. After we hit, I got out, started pulling the dead and wounded from the wreckage and... then it flew over us...."

Olivia looked at Cully. "So what was it like?"

He rubbed his face, his reddish eyebrows knit together. "How do you describe the shape of Death?"

"Try," Maauro said. "Any data you can give is critical to our success, possibly to our survival."

Cully drew a deep breath. "Huge it was, shaped like a manta ray, if you know what that is, though it was a mottled gray and had no features I could discern.

"How big?" Olivia prompted.

"We didn't have any working instruments to measure it with, and the shuttle's records were damaged. What was working didn't make any sense. I would say it was as long as Taiko and wider than long. To guess as to tonnage, I would have to know what it was made of. It flew over us heading up. It must have spotted the *Taiko*.

"Yeah. When it flew over…" Rainbird shuddered.

"Gah," Troy added. "I can still smell it."

"Smell?" Maauro asked.

Cully nodded. "Aye, a smell that could knock a man flat, a stinking cold draught straight out of Hell."

"Cold?" Rainbird asked, her dark eyes focused on Cully.

He gave her a curious look. "Aye, cold."

"To me it smelled warm and rotten," she said, "like a gut wagon in summer heat."

"No," Troy said. "It was sickly sweet, nauseatingly so."

"Maauro?" I asked.

She shook her shimmering hair. "I do not know. I suspect that this is a psychological manifestation of the thing. At what height did it pass over you?"

"Huh," Cully said. "Well, it didn't follow us down. We were closest to it when we were hit at about 7,500 feet. It was in a full climb there, at least 45 degrees."

"One doubts that you could smell even so large a creature across such a distance," Maauro said. "I suspect that this thing radiates mental impressions. Not telepathy, but something similar. Or perhaps its utter alienness simply makes it seem foul by comparison."

"I don't understand," I muttered. "On Windrush it struck with plague. We had to check for any sign of it before we dared leave the ship."

"Plague?" Troy said. All the Marines shifted uneasily.

"Yes," Maauro said. "It destroyed the first colony we visited with viral plague. One that seems to work rather slowly for something weaponized. Yet there was no denying its lethality across multiple species.

"Here it used a direct physical attack. As it did against the Free Trader hulk we came across," I said. "It's as if it gained confidence or…"

Maauro turned to me. "—as if it delights in different manners of killing."

"I can believe a monster that can knock down a shuttle, but what of the Taiko?" Olivia demanded.

"There, I cannot tell you much," Cully said. "They started firing at it after it cleared the air over us. It must have gone up quickly, impossibly so. Bolton, the Morok handling the coms, said the ship was having trouble locking onto it, like it was no longer solid and had changed into something else. The fighting was high. I've been under warship's fighting in orbit before, and I would swear this was edge of space stuff."

"All we heard after that," Troy interrupted, "was that the ship was damaged and running. Then the com failed. We'd lost half of us and the other half was in bad shape. That's all we know."

CHAPTER FOURTEEN

The briefing from the Marines petered out in speculation and theory. People return their attention to food, drink and the comforts of being back inside the hull of a starship.

I review what we have learned. There is little to base plans or theories on. I decided to check the only physical evidence we had.

"Wrik, I want to reexamine the shuttle and the site of the Marine's battle with this beast or machine. There may be clues that did not yield themselves at first examination." I start toward the hatchway.

Suddenly Wrik is between me and the exit. "At night! By yourself?"

I look at him curiously. "The night does not impede my sensors."

"Not the point. Wandering around alone, on an unexplored alien world where some horror out of space has been rampaging, is the point."

"Wrik," I say patiently, "I could take one of the crabs for company, but as I am the more formidable combatant, it would be more a case of my protecting it, than it me."

"Don't try using logic and sense on me," he replies. "We can go in the morning, together."

"I am quite capable of defending myself you know."

"Who thought of a way to defeat the Kolzin destroyer?"

This gives me pause. More, it would clearly upset Wrik if I continue with my plan. So while I judge the risk of running into anything unexpectedly dangerous as low, the probability of relationship damage is high.

I walk up to him and put my head against his chest. "Yes, dear."

The Marines all chuckle at the scene and I feel Wrik's body relax against mine. I have judged the situation correctly. I am a good girlfriend.

CHAPTER FIFTEEN

I N THE MORNING, AND WITH BOTH ME AND A CRAB ROBOT in tow, we returned to the scene of the shuttle crash. Without the Marines to view it, Maauro felt able to dig it out and with the crab's help, overturn the shuttle body.

"Aha," she said. "This is what I was hoping for."

"What?" I said.

"The shuttle was struck by something from below. The enemy was rising beneath them. This monster may have been intelligent enough to think that the shuttle's presence might limit the cruiser's fire-control options. This mechanical damage is similar to what we saw with the *Empire Manor*. Something strong enough to strike a seventeen-ton shuttle and continue flying, indicates a metal of greater strength than anything your people make. It may even be stronger than what I am made of."

"Not good."

"Indeed not. For one thing, there aren't even microscopic traces of it on the shuttle hull. This should not be possible. No matter how hard the material was, there should be some transfer. Yet there is no evidence of it. I am unable to tell why."

"One damn mystery after another," I said.

"Yes," she replied. "But we have a remaining witness to interview."

"The Lieutenant," I said.

"Yes. Like me, she suffered direct contact with it. If we can get through to her we may learn more."

I got out of the Mule and reached in the back. We had brought flowers from hydroponics and I laid them out on each of the graves. We spent a moment in silence then walked back to the jeep. Behind the graves, Maauro rolled the shuttle back into position to watch over its dead.

I patted the seat next to me in the Mule. "Let's go."

After we drove back, I filled Olivia in on what we had done. I did not want the Marines upset about the shuttle site.

She nodded. "The flowers were a good touch. They saw you leaving with them. I'll talk to Cully. Since you didn't mess with the graves, it'll be ok."

"We're off to see what can be done with Menoan."

"I wish you better luck then I had. She's up, cleaned and fed but not responsive. See what Maauro can do, there's always some magic up her sleeve."

Maauro stood waiting for me outside the Lieutenant's cabin. I was glad Olivia was with Cully, the older sergeant seemed very protective of her. We knocked, but hearing no response, went in.

CHAPTER FIFTEEN

I sat opposite the Denlenn Lieutenant and studied her. "Her" was not quite accurate; Monean was a demi-female, a third gender in the Denlenn species complicated reproductive cycle. Cully had told me that she preferred to be addressed as female in standard. She was about my age, with golden skin and, unusually for her species, blue, human-like eyes. The mouth was thin, and her hair, roughish and golden, was cut short in a military style gone ragged in the time since the crash. She had an androgynous look, as one might expect, but there was a feminine delicacy to her features. Maauro had seen to her basic medical needs, as both she and her uniform were cleaned and patched. She stared blankly ahead and had neither spoken, or voluntarily moved since coming aboard. The demi merely following those commands given to her, not even protesting when taken to her cabin. The door was not locked, though it was under the observation of Maauro's AI constantly. She'd made no effort to leave. A plate of food sat untouched by her bedside.

"Lt. Monean," Maauro began in a soft even voice, "can you hear me?"

The Denlenn simply stared without blinking.

"Are you in pain?" she added.

This time there was a reaction. She blinked and seemed to focus on Maauro for the first time.

"Pain," Maauro repeated, "from some unusual, no, from some impossible source?"

Monean's mouth worked, but it seemed a struggle for her to make a sound. "The Great One," she finally said, almost as if she had forgotten how to speak.

"Yes," Maauro said. "The Great One. Do you know it?"

A tear tracked down the golden skin, though her face remained mask-like.

"The Great One," I added, "it's demanding, isn't it? It's jealous, isn't it?"

Maauro gave me a curious glance, but deferred to me as usual in a matter of intuition. Now I had the Denlenn's attention. Her face twitched as if trying to break free of its frozen restraint.

"We too chanced across the Great One," I said in a conspiratorial tone, glancing around as if afraid I would be overheard. "We were in jumpspace. All of us were in jump stasis of course, but Maauro here is special. She felt its approach."

Monean's eyes wandered to Maauro and again she struggled for speech. "How?" emerged as a strangled sound.

"In am not like the others," Maauro said. "I'm a living machine and aware, to some degree, during jump transits. While in jumpspace, I became aware of something near us, stalking us, something awful and powerful, antithetical to life as I understand it. It tried to touch our ship and I believe its touch would have been death. I drove it off with the ship's weapons but I did not harm it much."

CHAPTER FIFTEEN

A nod, a short, almost savage movement. "It is…it is death, from the time and age of Death's rule."

"Yes," I said, "it's death. It's all of death, isn't it? Its very shadow had the stench of it according to the others. Maauro touched it in deep space, not directly, but through instruments—it hurt her. But you, you were closer to it, in the shuttle when it struck, when it passed over you."

"It didn't," Monean said slowly, "strike us directly. Not directly, or we would not be here. I'm not sure it even noticed the shuttle. We were just in the way."

"But it did more," I persisted. "Like Maauro, you're special some-how— more sensitive, it was aware of you."

Horror filled her eyes and the thin lips pressed hard together. For a second I feared a seizure.

"It wanted…it wanted," the demi gave a deep shudder that shook her whole body. I quickly grabbed a bulb of water and handed it her. She squeezed it into her mouth gratefully, draining it and then nodding her thanks.

"It was aware of me," she said, giving another smaller shudder, "in a way it did not seem aware of any of the others. Perhaps I am weak, I don't know. Or maybe," now the words tumbled out, "I was aware of it." I noticed she was staring at Maauro, the only one with a similar experi-ence. "It wanted me to… to do things. Don't ask, I won't say. But it did want me to hurt those around me. It seemed to revel in the concept of having another to hurt.

"But I wouldn't! I wouldn't!" the voice had gone shrill.

"No. No, of course not," I soothed. "We know this. It's not your fault. Some can hear it, that's all. Right, Maauro?"

She nodded, seeming uncertain. "I more felt than heard it. I can only analogize it by saying that it is similar to what a pilot like Wrik feels through his instruments when approaching jumpspace. But it was vile," she said, her uncertainty vanishing, "unutterably vile. It disordered data within me."

Menoan nodded.

"I think it did the same to you, but the effect differs because of your biological nature."

"It thrust its filth into my mind," Monean managed. "I've never suf-fered the experience, but it must be what rape is like." She blinked and suddenly looked around as if taking stock of her surroundings for the first time. "Where am I?"

"CSS *Stardust*," I replied. "I'm Wrik Trigardt, Captain. This is Maauro and she told you who she is."

"A living machine," Monean muttered. Perhaps only her experience with the "Great One" prepared her for such concepts.

"We're a privately owned ship under military contract for Confed military intelligence. We both hold command rank in MI. There's also an officer of your own service aboard, Major Olivia Croyzer, also with MI. We've recovered all your survivors, and they are in good health or recovering in our dispensary."

"Did I...did I do anything? Did I harm anyone?" Monean demanded.

"No. They said you were acting erratically and had to be restrained, but nothing else happened. After the initial incident, you were more out of it than a menace."

"Fighting it," she whispered, "always fighting it. All alone. Seemed I would always be alone in the dark with it. How I longed for death. I couldn't spare the time and energy to even try. More than anything, I feared being used against my own people."

"Do you feel you are still in contact?"

"No, just with the memory, with what it tried to do to me. That's still in my mind. No, if there was more I would have to die. I could not endure it."

"We don't know where it is," I said. "It seems to have left the planet, perhaps even the system."

"The *Taiko*?" she asked.

"We don't know," I said. "We found a wrecked Free Trader, the *Empire Manor*, but saw no other wrecks or signs of shipping There's no reason to take any but a direct route in and out of a system but even so, with the relative motions of the planets, we could be only a few degrees off and never see anything. Even with the best instruments, and we are a scoutship, you can't search that volume of space. If they flew an evasive course, only luck would bring us within range of a wreck. All we know is that she hadn't returned to Confed before we set out. For all we know, she came back the next day or by some other jump route and word simply hadn't reached us."

"But you don't believe that," Monean's voice was hollow, exhausted.

"No."

"What follows?" the demi asked. "Do we go home?" There was a plaintive note in that.

Maauro shook her head. "We are in pursuit of intelligence on this enemy, lest it strike Confed space without warning."

"Pursuit," Monean said bitterly. "You're mad. You do not pursue a nightmare, it pursues you."

"You may be right," I said. "But this thing is horribly dangerous and it can travel between stars. We don't want its next appearance to be over a Confed world."

Monean looked away. "Listen, if you are going after this thing, leave me here. I can't be of any use to you, and I may be a danger."

"We can't do that," I say. "Even if your people would stand for it, I'm not going to maroon a survivor on an uninhabited world. I could never fly space again if I did. But there may be another way." It was painful to see the hope that flashed into her face.

CHAPTER FIFTEEN

"It was anticipated," Maauro began, "that we would need resupply and refit and would have to send reports, intelligence, samples and even casualties back to Confed Space. In each system we were likely to visit, Confed sent an automated sled. There's one parked in this system that we resupplied from on the way in. They remain insystem until we pass them by jumping out, or until our life support period is surpassed and we are assumed dead, in which case they will eventually jump out and report where we met our end. There are cold storage tubes aboard each for casualties to the crew, or colonists we might have found. We can send you back in one of those."

"There is always a small risk with cold sleep—"' I began

"I'll take it," Monean interrupted. "Anything but encounter it again."

She held my eye. "It's not cowardice. I'm terrified that on a second exposure it will control me, and I could endanger ship and crew. I'll die before I'm so used."

"I know what cowardice looks like," I replied, keeping my voice level. "I'm not seeing it here."

She looked down at the floor. "I'm tired, so tired."

"Enough for now," I said. "There's no reason for you to be confined—"

"No. Confine me. I don't trust myself anymore after that Devil, that monster, dragged me through its filth. Don't trust me. I don't trust me."

"It's not necessary," Maauro said.

"I told you to keep me locked up," Monean demanded, her fists balled. "I don't want to leave this room. I don't!"

"OK, ok," I said, raising a hand. "We'll do it."

She calmed visibly.

I looked at Maauro, but she only stared back, at a loss. "Don't you want to see the others?"

"No. Not now. No, it's enough that I know they are alright. I don't want them to see me. I don't want them to look at me after I failed them so."

"One condition," I said.

She didn't glance up. "Anything."

"You start eating and begin taking care of yourself. Start getting ready to resume your life."

She nodded still avoiding my eyes. "In a bit."

"Then it's a deal."

"Please. I'm so tired. Please go."

"Alright. If you need anything, simply call aloud. Our AI is fantastically above normal and your needs will be known immediately."

Monean dropped back on her bed, an arm over her eyes. I looked at Maauro.

CHAPTER FIFTEEN

"Asleep." she said. "Or rather she has passed out. Given that she has been deeply exhausted, the anesthetic I gave her yesterday would have such effect even the next day."

I lifted Monean's feet onto the bed, removing the ship shoes she'd been wearing in place of her boots. Then I drew a blanket over the unconscious Denlenn and dimmed the lights. I left the sealed meal tray there. It would reheat the contents as needed, or Maauro would bring something later. We slipped out, and the door lock snicked closed behind us.

CHAPTER SIXTEEN

T TOOK TWO MORE DAYS BEFORE MAAURO JUDGED IT SAFE
to lift with the Morok, who had awoken from his brain surgery aboard.
We set the Marines up in cabins and sickbay using every suitable
surface for liftoff. We took off and climbed back into the sky, no one
sorry to see Tamba disappear beneath them. I looped around the planet
to build speed, adding judiciously from our fuel supply to Olivia's evident
annoyance.

"What about a full burn?" she demanded. "Time is not our friend."

"Time is no one's friend," I return, "and in that regard, space is just
like it. They are both actively and always trying to kill you. I don't cut
into a safety margin unless I have to."

"We have the supply sleds," she countered.

"When we see them, we have the supply sleds. Until then, we have
a hope of supply sleds."

Four days later I found out how right I was.

Most of us were on the bridge, sorting through who would return to
Confed on *Fetch III*. Menoan and the Marine who had lost her leg were
clearly going back. Ensign Bolton and the others were arguing about
staying to look for *Taiko*. Menoan, after days of isolation, had finally
come out of her cabin, leaning on Cully, but she made no effort to resume
command of her group. Today, for the first time, she had come to
the bridge.

"Signal on scanner," Delt relayed. "It's the *Fetch IV* right where we
left it."

Maauro turned. "But not as we left it."

"What?" I said.

On the screen next to me, all weapons armed as Maauro asserted
control on the ship. She had left flight controls to me. "Everyone secure
in a seat, or belt to a wall takehold," I ordered. "Now."

"What's going on?" Olivia demanded.

"The signal from *Fetch IV* is diffuse and there is no return of our
electronic signals," Maauro said. "Wait a moment. I am building a visual
from the sensor returns."

The main screen over me flickered and a visual image and a mass
of data appeared on it, but there was no need to study the details.

"Looks like no one is going home," Dusko said.

The sled tumbled on the screens, flayed and crushed, bits if it sparkling in the starlight.

"It was here," Monean whispered. "There's no escape."

"All is not lost," Maauro said. "The sled was emptied of supplies and fuel on our way in. Still it grieves me that we will not be able to send some of you home with the knowledge we have gained."

"Didn't want to go," Cully said, "got a monster to bag and a cruiser to find before I go home.

"Same here," Boulton said, his red eyes squinting. "I got a bill for a shuttle to nail to its ass."

"We left good friends buried back there," Rainbird growled from over Bolton's shoulder. Most of the Marines were outside the bridge on the stairwell leading to it.

"I am scanning at max power in active fire control," Maauro said. "But I do not think that it remained here. My passive sensors have been recalibrated with the information we have gained. I believe I would have detected it with sufficient distance to react to it with weapons."

I looked over her shoulder at the scan. I saw nothing but the debris of the sled dispersing across space. I sighed. "I doubt it's worth our time to salvage any—"

"Where's the LT?" Cully asked.

Suddenly Maauro blurred into motion, lunging across the bridge and into the spiral staircase to the levels below, shoving people out of her way. I raced behind her as the others cried out in surprise. Delt, Olivia and Dusko, less startled then the others, followed first. From the amount of noise Maauro was making slamming into things, she was at top speed for this confined space and could not afford the time to be careful. It could mean only one thing.

Maauro was already out of sight when I leapt over the railing to drop the distance to the level Monean's quarters were under. I ran flat out, caroming off supplies strapped to the bulkheads. I could hear screams and a furious struggle ahead. I burst into the small stateroom. Maauro was holding Monean around the hips. The Marine had wound her bed sheets into a rope and noose and put them over a pipe. She must have leapt from her bed and been grabbed by Maauro the instant before her neck would have broken.

"Let me go!" she shrieked, twisting wildly. "Gods, please let me go. I can't stand it. I can't." The demi-female beat furiously on Maauro's head.

"Wrik," Maauro said calmly, as she ignored the strikes raining down on her and reached up with one hand, while holding Monean around the hips with the other, and whipped a palm blade through the sheet. "Please hold her arms, she is damaging her hands hitting me, and if I hold her any tighter, I fear I will shatter her bones as she struggles."

Monean was incoherently screaming when I grabbed her arms, but the demi-female was stronger than a human female her size and shook me off. Then Delt was there.

"Grab, her other arm," I shouted.

CHAPTER SIXTEEN

The three of us brought her down on the bed. But she fought with the strength of the mad. Olivia leaned in long enough to observe the struggle before turning to stop the onrushing Marines.

"Maauro ," I yelled. "Trank her."

"I already have and with as much as I dare," Maauro said, still holding Monean's legs. "She is in such a state that the effect will be delayed."

Olivia reappeared and got the noose off Monean's throat, then almost nose to nose with her shouted. "Lt. Monean. Snap out of it. To attention, right now, Marine, right now!"

The Denlenn froze in trained reflex. Sanity flickered back into the eyes as she gulped air. We all maintained our grip on her. The doorway behind us filled with questioning Marines.

"Out, everybody out," Olivia ordered. They all fell back, grumbling and anxious.

"Sorry, sir," Monean said to Olivia. "Sorry. Oh no! Miss Maauro, are you hurt! Gods, I'm so sorry."

"Do not be," Maauro said. "I am uninjured. My concern is only for your poor hands, which you injured while striking me."

"I'm sorry," she wailed.

"It is alright," Maauro repeated. "Listen, you are full of tranquilizer that I injected through my palms. Now that you are returned to reason, it will take effect. While you sleep we will tend your hands. Fear nothing. You will be guarded while you sleep."

Monean made as if to speak, then her eyes fluttered, rolled up, and she was unconscious. We all sat back, conscious of wrenched muscles from the battle with the frenzied demi.

"This is entirely my fault," Maauro said in the flat mechanical voice she fell into when truly upset. "I did not anticipate the speed and resolution with which she would move, nor the depth of despair our enemy has driven into her soul. Even with my AI observing her I nearly failed to avert disaster."

"We," Olivia said, "who are much more like her than you are, would have failed as well—only we'd have lost the life."

"Even you, my love" I said, "cannot be perfect."

Maauro sighed.

The other Marines called questions from outside. Cully roared for silence and then came in alone. Olivia tersely advised them what had happened.

"We can put a watch on her," Cully said, "six hours on and six off."

"That will work for a temporary solution," Maauro said. "She needs help of a sort that we do not have here. I will manufacture a cold sleep tube for her. It will prevent her from hurting herself and being a drain on the ship or her resources."

Cully, who seemed to have appointed himself Menoan's watchdog, rubbed his chin. "Can't say I like it, but a small ship is no place for mental illness."

"Meanwhile," Maauro added, "she has injuries that must be attended to and are best done when she is sedated." Gently, carefully, she lifted the tall demi-female.

"Ok," Olivia said. "Enough gawking, those with work get back to it. Cully organize a schedule to start as soon as Maauro says go."

"I'll go with Maauro," I said. I caught Delt and Dusko's eyes. Delt nodded, the Dua looked between Delt and me and indicated with a hand gesture that he'd follow the human. The look that the Dua cast at Maauro seemed to have a concern in it that jarred me.

Olivia had caught the byplay, the way she caught everything, The Witch of Cimer indeed. "Cully, you're with me."

I followed Maauro up the spiral staircase. Then it was only the two of us and the unconscious Denlenn in the sickbay. Maauro got her into the bed and I helped slip her shoes off and cover her with a blanket. She didn't need to activate the monitors around her, being a better instrument than any of them. But she did pull a fine-bone regenerator off the wall and immediately go to work on the Denlenn's hands.

"I wish you wouldn't be so hard on yourself," I said.

"Thank you, but we have come close to losing a life for want of care—this has happened before when I did not understand those around me. It is important that I do so. How am I to care for and love you, when I make such mistakes?"

"Don't you think that a human woman would make mistakes? Don't you think that I do? Maauro, I'll fail a lot in learning how to love and live with you. I already have. I left you behind on Star Central when I went to Retief. Something I can't even imagine now.

"You have to be able to fail. God knows you don't have to like it, but you do have to expect it. Just do what I do."

She stopped and looked up at me. "And that is?"

"Never stop trying to do better the next time."

A small, shy smile played over her lips. "You are right as you always are in these circumstances. I hope you know that I love you."

"I know. I count on it every day."

"And you will continue to love me, even though I am imperfect?"

"Especially because you are imperfect; what need would you have for me if you were perfect?"

"Thank you," she whispered. Maauro put up the regenerator and looked down at the sleeping Denlenn. The grim determined look I had seen before slid over her face. "I will add this to the bill I will present to the Beast when we find it."

A chill shot through me. Maauro had named her enemy and I knew the name was both apt and correct.

CHAPTER SEVENTEEN

WE PULLED OURSELVES BACK TOGETHER AFTER DIS-
covering of the wreck of *Fetch III*. The Marines set a watch on
their lieutenant and none of us discouraged them this time.
Jeiwan recovered and Maauro fitted the young Marine with an artificial
limb that eased her shock at being maimed. As it would take time to
learn how to live and move with even such an advanced artificial limb,
Jeiwan remained in the sickbay and helped with the Denlenn.

Menoan was unconscious for two days and uncommunicative on
awakening save to apologize constantly. Cully's presence calmed her and
the sergeant took double-watches with her for that reason. Maauro and
Delt worked on a stasis tube for the Denlenn, in Maauro's case literally
without cessation until it was ready.

Meanwhile, I put distance between ourselves and the wreckage of
the *Fetch*. There was no way to know where the Beast, and this was what
we all called it now, had gone. Was it still in the system with us? Had it
jumped before us into the system we were going to? Had it jumped the
other way back to the Confederacy?

There was no counsel of war, just a brief discussion between Olivia,
Maauro and I about the continuation of the mission. Both the alpha
females had grudges now and were intent on coming to grips with the
Beast. I, as usual was the voice of caution. We could neither send back
reports or survivors now, save by going ourselves. But I did not need
much persuasion. There was a cruiser out here, last seen in trouble. There
might still be colonists or others needing our help. The decision to go
on was unanimous. Delt and Dusko simply concurred. The Marines only
awaited orders, but their desire to find their ship was such that we would
have had trouble with them had we made any other decision.

Three days voyage brought us to the other jump point out of the
system. Maauro vetoed any jump until Menoan was in stasis, so we'd
slowed our approach to the jump. One did not 'circle' in space without
a body to orbit.

Settling Menoan was not merely a matter of making the tube and its
supporting equipment. In itself, this would have been impossible aboard
ship for anyone but Maauro but there was the issue of installing it as
well. Some of the interior partitions of the ship were structural and made
of the same obdurate metal as the exterior hull. Others were more malleable and intended to allow interior modifications. Only one part of
sickbay had a malleable bulkhead and it was adjacent to power cou-
plings. This was good and bad. The stasis tube needed uninterruptable
power leads, or the occupant would die, but it was a tricky area for

cutting and welding, unless you were an ancient android, who could jet plasma from her fingertips while bending metal with your other hand.

Finally the tube was made ready and the Dua-Denlenn laid into it. I'd hated cold sleep and never had I seen anyone so glad to enter it. "No dreams for me," was all she said. An hour later she was in full stasis. Cully stood by the tube for another hour. There was some affinity between the two that was not military, but the Marine's grim countenance discouraged any questions, none of which I had any right to put to him in the first place.

We'd allowed more time for the stasis tube's manufacture and Menoan's occupation of it then was necessary, and to Olivia's obvious annoyance I vetoed speeding up. "It's a half-day and not worth the fuel," I'd finally said. "Everybody can take the time off and take it easy. God knows what we'll run into on the other side of jump."

She didn't like it, but my word as ship's master was law. Olivia was too adult to huff off, slam doors or otherwise give into her temper, but she was equally clearly unhappy with my caution.

I spent my down time with Maauro. She had decided on another special dinner, again with crew morale in mind. I got out of her way with a promise to return later to help set the table.

Meanwhile, I had curled up with a book and some light music on the bridge, when I heard Delt in the corridor behind the bridge.

"God damn, stubborn, ill-tempered....would have to be the best-looking –" he stopped when he saw me.

"So," I said, "you have a spat with Olivia?"

He snorted. "Who, me, and the poster girl for the Confederacy? How did you guess?"

"Well you were talking to yourself about best-looking, I assume female, and that leaves: Maauro, spoken for, Rainbird, cute enough if you like tattoos, but that would be fast work even for you. And I don't think Jeiwan is feeling up for romance yet. So, Olivia?"

"Good detective work," he said, with a grimace.

"Don't tell me you were lured into talking politics?"

"Not by choice, that girl is Confed Blue through and through. Didn't this come up between you two?"

I shrugged. "I was actually in Confed service when she met me. I never talked to her about Retief and I am not sure how much she was briefed about me before the mission, but she never brought it up. You won't run into many people better at keeping a secret than Olivia."

"Yeah," he said. "Well I'd had about enough of her mouthing off about Retief, rebellion and about how dangerous you two are."

"She trying to convert you?"

"As if," then he ran his hand through his mop of blonde hair. "I don't think that she is really trying. She's just scared of Maauro." He paused, and gave me a frank look. "Are you ever?"

"No. I know you think that is just reflexive and because I love her. You're partly right, but I didn't answer without thinking. Maauro is a great power in herself. I recognize it."

"Wrik, I like her too, but I'm only beginning to realize the full import of what she is, a planetary level supercomputer in a body that is, if not indestructible, is damn tough. I mean she's as cute as any girl I've ever met, so much so that I am frankly envious of you, but there's really no limit to what she can do: control ships, planetary defenses, explode reactors, turn off an entire world's climate control, like she almost did to the Voit-Veru. She doesn't want to rule a world, but what could stop her if she decided to?"

"I suppose she could," I replied. "Her greatest power is her ability to master any computer systems she encounters. She's only grown since I met her on the asteroid, as she learns more of our technology. It's only ever a matter of time before she can infiltrate any system. That's the main reason we were able to stay free of the Guild and as free as we are with the government."

"And you never worry about it."

I laughed. "Well, for the first few hours after we met, I wasn't sure I was going to draw another breath. Remember, I saw her before she changed into her cute Maauro appearance. After she broke free of her original programming, well I just was never worried about her doing anything bad. Hell, even before that she was only dangerous if attacked.

"Somehow I guess I always knew that she was good and could be trusted." I shrugged. "I can't tell you where that certainty comes from. It's just there."

Delt again ran his hands through his hair again, a gesture I knew from our teenage years.

"You have doubts?"

"Not many, Wrik, but I'm not madly in love either. I want to trust her the way you do, and I have never met anyone I liked more on such short notice. Hell, I'd trust her with my life any day. But trust her with civilization itself? That's harder."

"I can't help you with this one, old friend," I said, desperately wanting him to believe as I did. "You have to come to that certainty yourself in your own way."

Delt gazed at me, then his blue eyes unclouded. "You know I wouldn't let anything happen to her."

"She's honorary Ncome commando after all," I said.

"Every damn bit of it," Delt agreed with a surprised look. I'd never brought up the name of our old squadron casually before. "I feel better since we talked."

"So..." I said, "Olivia?"

"Guess I will just have to put up with her politics. After all, the only other beautiful girl not tied up with Confed is spoken for."

I thumped him on the shoulder.

Dinner proved as successful as Maauro could have hoped, even Cully cheered up. With other Marine's onboard, Olivia had returned to the brisk, no nonsense Major Croyzer. Still, she and Delt seemed back on friendly terms.

"That was as good a meal as I have ever had," Cully finally said. "I usually like to jump on an empty stomach, but for this food I'll take the chance."

"Ok," I said. "Everyone not on KP, start getting ready for jump. This should not be a bad one from the records. Just keep your meds handy. Maauro will check everyone and issue a packet at jump minus thirty."

Dusko, seemingly glad to have Marines to boss around, took care of clean up and I prepared the ship for jump, as Maauro readied the crew.

We jumped into the system, which despite its short duration out of space-time, only fourteen days galactic, proved surprisingly unusually hard on the stomach despite the records from previous jumps.

Fortunately, there was no threat near the edge of the system. Only a new Fetch was waiting for us. We rapidly refueled and reprovisioned from it, knowing the orange and white sled would be defenseless when we left. We did not have spacesuits enough for all the Marines. Cully took mine and there were two others that could be modified to fit Rainbird and Lacy. The Marines all confessed bemusement and wonder at Maauro working alongside them unsuited, but appreciated the help.

"We could send Monean back now," Cully said, after they came back aboard. "There are six cyrotubes aboard."

I had looked at Maauro. "I think it would be best to hold that off until we are going out-system again. There may be other people we want to send, further reports, or samples. Once we dispatch the sled, we are on our own again."

She nodded. "Agreed. With the Lieutenant in stasis we do not have disruption to contend with. I would prefer to send the entire Marine team back if we can. We will move the sled further insystem with us rather than leave it here. I do not want it to accompany us, it would use up fuel, but a slow inward fall should remove it from the zone of danger and make it available to us. For now, let us again take aboard all we can." She smiled and headed back to the airlock.

So now I stared out the portal looking at Maauro perched on our ship's nose. I still hated her being outside the ship. We'd been inbound for two full days after refueling and reequipping. The sled had only basic instruments, so it could tell us nothing, but conditions local to the jump point. It would have recorded the emergence of a ship, but likely its instruments would not have registered the monster we feared.

I began to wish that they'd had the foresight to bring torpedoes along but had to admit it would have been a risk to entrust atomic warheads to a defenseless sled. About this point, I would have settled for a conventional warhead.

"Wrik," Maauro's voice came over the speaker. "I'm coming in."

"Got a chill?" I teased, watching her stand, her hair spinning in and wrapping in its accustomed place.

"No, a contact."

"What?"

"Please do not alert the others. I want to talk to you first."

Moments later she stepped through the interior airlock, still radiating both the chill of deep space and that bacon smell that clung to objects exposed to direct space.

"I am warm enough to hug," she said, after a second. I obliged happily. She sighed with pleasure and snuggled under my chin.

"What did you detect?" I finally asked.

"I have picked up the echo of intraship communications, too degraded to reconstruct. *Taiko* was and may still be here." Her face now held a pensive look.

"That's good news," I replied, troubled by her expression.

"It is. As with all news, it has many sides. To this point, all has been harmony in our mission. But Olivia has been sometimes troubled by our caution, our deliberate pace, always restocking at the *Fetches* and our use of cruising versus battle speed. Were she in charge, our safety margins would be far less."

I nodded. "She is a Marine. Hey diddle-diddle, straight up the middle."

She smiled. "If by that you mean that she is inclined to aggressive action with a high risk tolerance, I agree."

"It's more poetic the way I said it."

"In any event, if *Taiko* is discovered, it will alter the dynamic here."

"How do you mean?"

"I control the ship," Maauro said. "Delt and Dusko are ours. Olivia has followed our lead without dispute. She has had to. If *Taiko* is here, that may change. She will have more assets, perhaps decisively so."

I studied Maauro. "You suspect her of something?"

"No more or less than usual," Maauro replied. "You are my priority and I am yours. Olivia has a different agenda; she serves the Confederacy first and foremost. It is the thing that keeps us from being truly networked. Given a choice between our interest and theirs, she will choose theirs."

I hated the truth of that. I'd fought beside Olivia and liked her. Hell, I'd made love with her. It hurt to believe that I couldn't trust her, at least not beyond a certain point. It was also good sense.

"What do you want to do?" I asked.

"What we came here for. To find *Taiko*, gain intelligence on this threat and, if possible, destroy it. But we are Lost Planet and she is not.

We must always be the ones in control of our destiny. Of how much, and how far, we risk ourselves. After all, humans are your people, and serving the Confederacy serves our interests. For now."

"Yes," I replied. "Neither of us wants to risk our freedom."

She nodded. "Just so. I am not urging any course of action against her, or anyone else, but I never forget that Candace's first reaction to me was that I would be best off in a Confederate lab, possibly as parts. There is technology in me that wars would be fought over. Only the certainty that I would inflict appalling damage on the Confederacy prevents their trying. But here we are alone, in the great dark, with a Confederate warship and an operative I respect too much to ever take lightly."

"Agreed," I said. "I presume you relayed some of this to Dusko."

"He follows my orders. I am the greater power in his mind."

"I'm hesitant about talking to Delt. I'm as sure of him as I can be of another man. But..."

"But Olivia is among the most beautiful of women, and in at least the beginning of a relationship with him."

"Relationship is overstating. The find each other fun, but neither of them is the type to settle into a relationship with one person. Olivia's career is her first love. As for Delt, well I've never know him to stay more than a few months with any woman. Still I wouldn't go to him unless there was a real case to be made."

"He will not hear a word against her?"

"Not unless there's evidence."

She nods. "Hopefully there never will be. Shall I inform the others of the contact?"

"Yes, call everyone to the galley. It's the easiest place to get them all together."

Maauro's voice sounded from the ship's speakers. "All *Stardust* crew and passengers to the galley."

"And you didn't even move your mouth," I said, as we headed out.

"I'm a woman of many talents," she replied.

"Oh?"

"Perhaps you will see some of them later."

"Sounds intriguing."

When the others arrived, Maauro told them of the fragment of code she had detected. "It is a single degraded incomplete character. It could have come from *Taiko* or from some other vessel that passed through here recently. As unregulated as Piola Sector was, it's impossible to say."

"No one else pushed this far out," Olivia said.

"No one," I said, "who reported it. But wildcatters, guild ships and free traders trying to hide any finds they made, may well have."

"How do we find a warship that is actively hiding in an uncharted solar system?" Olivia growled, looking out of the bridge at the hard white stars as she tapped her fingers.

"Not used to looking for ships, Ground pounder?" Delt said.

"I'll pound your head in the airlock door if you call me that again." There was no heat in her voice, and the look she gave him was merely playful.

"No need to be embarrassed," Maauro added from where she stood also examining the stars. "You are the only one without a deep space certificate."

"I can fly," Olivia responded, with what I felt was touch of sullenness.

Maauro gave her a curious look. "So you can, but your and Delt's skills are primarily aerospace."

"And," Delt said, waving a finger. "I had a deep space certificate when I was military. Shouldn't have let it lapse."

"Given that it was a Confed certificate," I said, "it might have been hard to do in the middle of a rebellion."

"Always Mr. Picky-Pants," Delt said.

Dusko looked at Olivia, who was silently fuming. "It's like this all the time around here."

"But to answer your question," I intervened. "We have been scanning with passive sensors as we head inward. We're going to air-brake using the super giant Maauro discovered yesterday. Since we lost the Fetch to the Beast, I judge it best to go back to our old fuel scrimping ways.

"The question is where to search and do we go to active sensors, which would tell anyone and anything in the system that we are here."

"While the distances are vast," Maauro added, "there are only a few logical places for the cruiser to be. We saw no sign that she was near the inbound jumppoint, either orbiting or as wreckage. There appear to be only two planets in what humans rather curiously call the Goldilocks zone. Both are marginal at best though.

"Because we do not know how often *Taiko* jumped, or where it may have been in its voyages, we do not know how much relative time she has spent out of the universe. However, even a long-range cruiser such as *Taiko* must be nearing her operational radius maximum, especially if she has engaged in multiple combats with the Beast. The only way to enhance her operational time would be to resupply with raw materials on a terrestrial world."

"Wouldn't it be faster to go to active sensors and start broadcasting a call to *Taiko*?" Olivia challenged.

"It would," Maauro answered, looking out at the stars.

I held my chin in my hand and leaned against the table, massaging tight jaw muscles.

"You're unhappy," Olivia said. "I recognize that gesture."

Maauro's head snapped around, and she stared at Olivia, who did not appear to notice. Delt looked at them both, puzzled.

"Yes," I said. "Once we go active, anything here will know we've arrived. As for probes—we only have the pair. They'll auto return to the ship, but only if we don't have to do an extreme maneuvering while they're out. No scoutship really counts on recovering probes and we have no way of getting more. Like torps, they aren't on the Fetches."

"So it's a commitment and risk," Olivia pressed. "But we are here to find the cruiser and either gain intel on this threat, or end it. You have a tendency toward the slow and safe, Wrik."

"I do," I replied, trying to keep an edge out of my voice, "because we're one small, lightly-armed ship far from home. We probably don't get more than one mistake, if that."

"Too much caution impedes the mission," she replied.

"So does dying."

Dusko snorted a laugh.

"After we decelerate at the gas giant, may be the best time to deploy active sensors and the probes," Maauro said.

"If there is a threat here," Olivia said, "wouldn't it be better to learn of it before we dump speed for entry into the inner system?"

I looked at Maauro, but she said nothing, and I realized that she was leaving the decision entirely to me.

"OK," I said, "active full scan, deploy the probes and start broadcasting a call to Taiko now. If we are going to raise our EM signature that much, might as well go full out."

"In for a penny, in for a pound," Delt quoted. "Kinda glad we are through with the sneaking around stage."

"Good!" Olivia said. "When do we start?"

Maauro gave her a cool look. "Active scanning commenced when Wrik said so, as has the message to Taiko that we are here. I am uploading best course options for our probes as fast as they can take it. Launch in 2.3 seconds."

"Oh," Olivia said

There was as small shudder. "Probes away," Maauro said. "Nothing on active scan, but I would not expect a contact for many hours. While we have narrowed the search zones, the area is immense, assuming that we have narrowed them properly." She resumed sipping her tea.

Hours passed, as did dinner and the myriad tasks of keeping our small envelope of air, heat and food operating even in a ship with Maauro's AI and her rarely seen bots, working to keep us spaceworthy in the bowels of the ship. Finally, Maauro and I turned in. Though in a ship with an ever watchful AI monitoring every instrument onboard, there was no reason to set watches, I knew Delt was on the bridge, working as usual on his deep space First Mate's certificate. Olivia was probably there too, or in the gym, prowling the deck like a frustrated tigress.

I'd be happy when Delt had his certificate. Having another fully trustworthy backup onboard would be useful. There were still system edits that didn't allow Dusko access to all ship functions, without a confirmation from Maauro or I. Likely, he both knew and expected it, as he would have done so in our place.

As I settled down next to her on the bed, Maauro gently ran a finger down the center of my chest. I turned toward her for a kiss that turned into several and then realized her mood. We made love slowly, with Maauro being attentive and innovative.

Afterward, we lay together, her head on my shoulder—something which involved balance on her part so it was not too heavy against me. I cupped her breast, soft, warm and indistinguishable from any human woman's.

"So how much study did it take to get the shape and texture right?" I teased.

"Oh, it was quite simple. I just popped into the shower and felt up Olivia."

A laugh burst out of me then, "You didn't really—"

"No, but the stirring of a part of your anatomy tells me that the idea appeals to you."

"Ah," I replied. "That was just a twitch."

"So how do I compare with her, given that you have sampled both?" she asked, peering at me through half-closed eyes.

"Ahem," I replied. "Well, it was quite a while ago—"

"Oh," Maauro said. "Were they not memorable?"

"Er," I said,

"I am merely curious as to how our bodies felt to you. Perhaps I can make adjustments."

"I think you're perfect as you are."

"Well, hers are larger, as is her ass, but she is a physically bigger woman and muscular—"

"Maauro, honey, why are we discussing Olivia's ass?"

"I am simply studying the characteristics that give her such a high level of sexual desirability. For example, given my small frame, my measurements are actually—"

"Does her being on the ship bother you?"

"Why? Would you throw her out the airlock if I said yes?"

"I might, given the way this conversation is going."

We looked at each other for a few seconds then Maauro sighed. "This afternoon, when you were rubbing you chin with your hand, Olivia recognized that as a gesture signaling inner conflict. You were nervous, uncertain. She picked up on that before I did. That upset me.

"Somehow, she had a link with you, at that moment that was closer than mine. No, don't deny it just to comfort me. It was true.

"This gave me pause. Was that cue something that she picked up because she is so similar to you? Or was it from the intimacy that you enjoyed as lovers on Seddon?"

"Perhaps mostly the former," I said. "We had spent months together on a small ship."

"Yet I, who had spent years with you, did not make that connection."

"Honey, there isn't a question that you and I reach across a vastly bigger gulf to be together than two humans would, more than a human and a Nekoan, or any other alien. In all of known space there is only one artificial person. Don't think of the tiny little details of what still has to be learned between us. Think about the light years of progress we have already made across a gap no one else has ever tried to cross.

"We just made love, something that as far as we know has never happened before us between our kinds."

"Well, you humans do manufacture sexbots," she sniffed.

"No one of which does anything other than follow a program designed into it. No one of which has ever said, 'this is my person.' I am the gift for them alone, and no other may have me."

Again she sighed, but there was a happier sound to it. "You are right, as usual, in emotional matters and I am being childish. I suppose that was an actual moment of jealously, sneaking up on me unexpectedly."

I kissed her thoroughly. "Olivia is my past and Delt's rocky present. Let's not worry about her. Likely after this voyage we won't see her again."

"There, my boyfriend, you kid only yourself. MI prizes her relationship with us and loyalty to them too much. But in any event, we should shower and dress."

"Ah, well we just went to bed and I was hoping to get some sleep."

"We could, but since I have found Taiko on the scan—"

"What?" I said, sitting bolt upright.

"Yes, unexpectedly she is not in the inner system at all, but is in orbit of the large gas-giant that we are on course for."

"When?"

"About ten minutes ago," she replied.

"Ah, you kind of didn't mention it ten minutes ago."

"We were having an important conversation. *Taiko* isn't under drive and we are hours from simultaneous communication range. Nor did she react immediately to being pinged by the probe."

"Yes, well, maybe the others would like to know."

"Hence we should shower and dress as I suggested."

I hopped up and she followed me into the refresher.

"Any response to our message?" I asked, as steamy mist and suds enveloped us.

"No, I would have said," she answered, hot water sluicing down her body.

I decided not to comment on the way she prioritized information and simply made quick work of the shower. We were air-blasted dry and emerged scrambling for our clothes or rather I did. Maauro went from nude pattern Maauro, to black jumpsuit Maauro in a moment.

"Now?" she asked.

"Now, please," I said, as I struggled with my shoes.

"All hands to the bridge," her voice sounded over the speakers. "We have discovered Taiko's location in orbit of the gas giant ahead."

We slipped out of our cabin, which was only one level from the bridge. Delt started to stand when we came in but I pushed him back down in the seat. There was no maneuvering that needed to be done, and if any came up, Maauro could do it without sitting.

Pounding feet sounded behind us. Dusko and Olivia came up, followed by Cully and the others. There wasn't room for all of them on the bridge, so Olivia had the Marines wait outside. She must have been lifting weights as she wore an exercise outfit that showed off her taut body. Mindful of the last conversation with Maauro, I tried not to notice, and given Delt's appreciative grin at Olivia, I felt I was off that hook.

Dusko, who was right behind Olivia, didn't give her a second glance. Perhaps human women did nothing for him.

Maauro projected a map on the main screen. Taiko glowed as a small spot in close orbit of the gas giant.

"Why down so far?" Olivia murmured, as if to herself.

A close-up of the ship's silhouette appeared, green and empty.

"As the sensors return information, and we and the probes all close on her location, the image will fill in detail. We will know what she looks like before we can see her." Maauro said.

"Any response?" Olivia demanded.

"None," Maauro replied, "which is not good news. That cruiser should have registered the sensor sweep the instant it touched her. It has been seventeen minutes of active contact and still no reaction."

"She may be derelict," Dusko said, ignoring the glares from Olivia and the Marines stacked up behind him.

"Unlikely in so low an orbit," Maauro said, "but possible."

"When will we reach her?" Cully called.

"We are already on this course," Maauro replied, "but while we intended to airbrake, it was not to stop, but to slow. We will have to go into retrograde and burn fuel to stop at this destination."

"If we need dock," Dusko said.

"We need," Olivia stated. "Even if derelict there will be records, logs and other information aboard. Taiko is—"

"—Registering power," Maauro interrupted. "Her EM signature has changed and she is emitting a weak active scan—" she paused. "Incoming message. We are detected. Message coming on speakers."

From overhead a male voice sounded. "This is CSS Taiko to CPSS Stardust. We hear you. Be warned that there is a hostile alien life form capable of high speed and ship combat in this system. In space it manifests as a form of plasma and energy in a rhombus-shape larger than a cruiser. This life form is deadly and implacably hostile. Be prepared to flee at the first sign of this enemy.

"Prepare to receive a full download of *Taiko* logs and findings. These must reach Confederate Military authorities at all cost."

"I am receiving them," Maauro told us. "I will commence an immediate review."

"Recommend," the voice continued, "that on full receipt you break off approach and flee out of system."

"The message cycles after that," Maauro says. "How do you wish to reply?"

Everyone's eyes were on me. Olivia started to speak, but stopped when Delt shook his head.

Maauro simply waited and watched. Again the call would fall to me.

"To Captain Raglan aboard CSS *Taiko* from Captain Trigardt on CPSS *Stardust*, we are aware of the nature and some details of the enemy and some of this information has been returned to Confed Space by automatic sled. We are now 14:31 hours from a braking entry to the gas giant and a rendezvous at estimated 13:12 hours tomorrow. We will contact you as soon as we reach simultaneous transmission range. Please report your status, damage and casualties. Please note that we have recovered Lt Menoan, Ensign Bolton, Sgt Cully, and troopers Troy, Rainbird, Lacy and Jeiwan."

Time crawled by as the messages propagated at light speed between the ships which narrowed the distance every second. Meanwhile Maauro continued her analysis of Taiko's records. Everyone else got into uniform and got some food.

We gathered in the galley, the only space other than a hold that we could all be comfortable in. Maauro briefed us on *Taiko's* sad tale.

"She was attacked in close orbit as we knew. She delayed firing on the Beast as the shuttle was too close, until it was high in the atmosphere. As they locked on to fire, the Beast changed. It seemed to be dissolving, but in fact was converting to its spaceborne form: a vast shape of plasma and energy in the same manta ray shape Cully saw before, but 4.339 kilometers in diameter and length. Solid sabot shot simply went through. They were too close for a nuclear weapon, so the battle was fought with lasers. The Beast replied with some form of positron weapon that it wielded in whip or beam form, depending on range. There were apparently psychic effects on a small number of the crew. Some attacked others, some went apparently mad, others simply stopped reacting. Captain Raglan tried to open the range after his ship's hull was breached—

"Incoming text message," Maauro interrupted herself. "Captain Raglan to Captain Trigardt: appreciate your efforts, but this is now an order. Break off your approach before you are detected, and return with the fleet. Godspeed. Message repeats."

I looked at her. "Reply thus and with the necessary codes. *Stardust* to *Taiko*: Negative on order. We are not subject to your authority, but are empowered by Fleet to command any and all Confed assets in Piola sector. Please make all preparations for docking at your orbit."

"Wrik," Maauro said, gesturing at the scan image on a nearby screen. "*Taiko* is badly damaged. Her logs shows killed in action 73, wounded 24 and that, out of her crew of 512, all but sixty are in cold storage to lessen the load on the life support plant. She took hits in her machine spaces, sensors and life-support."

Growls and curses from the *Taiko* Marines and crew drew a sharp gesture from Olivia.

I nodded. "Add to the message to send us a list of essential spares and supplies. We're stuffed with ten years worth of food. We can't refuel something that big, but our machine shop is intact and we have you. Maybe we can get *Taiko* back on her feet."

"Done," she said

"God dammit," the Morok ensign said. "I should be aboard helping."

"We all should," Cully added.

"You will be," I assured them.

Hours crawled by and messages shot back and forth as we started making inventory of all we could do for the cripple. There was some initial incredulity over our having the rank to command *Taiko*, but the codes supplied put an end to that, at least temporarily. Maauro and Delt spent their time in the machine shops, while the others, under Dusko, scoured the corridors and holds, locating anything that could help.

Meanwhile *Stardust* fired her engines to slow. The AG field made this imperceptible to us, but we would all have to strap in for the brutal air-braking that would finally slow us to where we could match orbit with *Taiko*. Before that though, we finally reached simultaneous transmission range. This time only Maauro, I and Olivia were on the bridge when the screen lit up to display the bridge of *Taiko*, its lighting subdued behind the graven-faced Denlenn male.

"Captain Trigardt," Raglan said.

"Captain Raglan," I replied, "we have come a long way to find you."

"I am very grateful for your assistance, Captain, but surprised to find such a junior officer potentially put in command of me." His eyes searched Maauro, who wore a black jumpsuit devoid of any insignia of rank or affiliation.

"Yet, this is the case," Maauro said. "There is surely no question of the authenticity of the coded orders we sent you."

His gaze flicked to Maauro as he studied her. Raglan was too professional to further express his feelings at being addressed in such a manner by what he probably thought was a girl in her late teens, or early twenties, with no rank showing. Yet, his orders would show that Maauro ranked above everyone here.

"What are your intentions?" he asked.

"To rendezvous with *Taiko*, trade what information we have and continue operations against the enemy. If that proves impossible, then to extract your vessel from this system and return Taiko to the fleet."

"I fear we may be too badly damaged to escape with you. We have tried several times since entering this system, but the Anomaly, which you call the Beast, always intercepts us. We have no idea how it is able to do this in real-time. It seems impossible, but somehow it is aware of when we move, without a light-speed delay.

"In our condition we dare not engage it again. It learned from that first fight, where at close range, we managed to hurt it. Even that is supposition. All we know is that it has avoided close fights with us after that, preferring to exchange long distance fire, where it hits harder than we do.

"In its plasma form it has a turn radius of effectively zero, always giving it the advantage and making a nuclear strike difficult. It hit every long distance missile we fired at it. However, it seems reluctant to risk closing in. It would sit over the jump spot forcing us to advance against it, through its fire. We could do nothing."

"Yet, you have survived," Maauro said.

Again the piercing regard to Maauro. "I successfully broke off the last action in the vicinity of this gas giant. It seems unwilling to pursue us into its gravity and radiation fields. Why, I do not know."

His gaze shifts to me. "We named the gas giant Menoan, in the Lieutenant's honor. I am glad that this is not posthumous. May I speak to her?"

"I'm sorry, Lt Menoan was a psychic casualty of the Beast's first attack. She fought a long and lonely struggle to avoid being used against her crewmates and was prepared to sacrifice her life if needed. Regrettably, we had to put her into cold storage for her own safety."

Raglan seemed to struggle for composure for a second. "There is no honor to compare with commanding such fine young people."

"It is my intention to recommend her for a commendation for valor for resisting the Beast," I added

Raglan nodded. "However, while I note your coded orders and the authority that they convey, I would like to speak to one of my own people."

"Major Croyzer," I said formally, "would you call Sgt Cully to the bridge."

"Major?" Raglan asked, seeming to notice her for the first time.

"Major Olivia Croyzer," she rapped out, "Confed Star Marines, TDY to MI."

"Ah," he said, almost in relief "a regular officer."

"Don't worry, Captain," Olivia said. "These folks are who they say they are and, hard though it may be to believe looking at them, they're unbelievably formidable. I'll get Cully for you."

"I have already called below for him," Maauro whispered to her. Olivia leaned out of the bridge hatch and evidently caught sight of Cully hot-footing it up. She waved him in.

Cully jumped the last few steps and braced to attention with a quick salute. "Reporting sir. Good to see you."

"As it is you, Cully. We are all glad beyond words that you and the others made it. Lt Menoan…."

"—Has been given the best care possible, sir, as have we all. She's in cold sleep now: there was no other choice."

"These people?" Raglan asked.

"Real thing, sir. We'd have lost the Lieutenant without the young lady here," he gestured at Maauro. "She's full of surprises, this one."

"Thank you, Sergeant."

Cully's mouth drew into a slit. "I did all I could to look after her, sir. My best wasn't good enough. I let you down."

"I did all I could too, Cully. It wasn't enough either. Thank you for watching over her."

"Yes, sir," Cully managed.

"Captain Trigardt, Ms Maauro, Major Croyzer," Raglan said. "I look forward to meeting on the deck of Taiko and expressing my thanks in person. To you particularly, Ms. Maauro." The image flicked off.

I met Cully's eyes and held them. The Marine's mouth was still pressed in a grim line. He stared back for a few seconds than said. "Denlenn relations are complicated, given three genders, but the closest I can make it is that the Lieutenant's something like his niece."

"I see."

"And I'm returning her to him as an icicle."

"Nothing more could have been done," Olivia said. "Get everyone ready."

"Yes, sir."

As we moved inward, messages flew back and forth. Maauro and Delt returned to the machine shop to continue furious work on the parts *Taiko* desperately needed. With Maauro's ability to manufacture almost any small part in her body and Delt's skills with the artificers, we made progress quickly. Cully and the Marines under Olivia prepositioned all they had found that would help the crippled cruiser, near the airlocks.

"We're coming up on atmospheric breaking," I said. "Olivia, get everyone secured. This is always a bumpy ride."

The air-braking was as bad as I expected. The ship grew hot and bucked and belled as it contacted the outer edge of the gas giant. Our approach had been even more complicated by the thin cirrus rings that wrapped the planet. They were rock and water ice, and I didn't want to contact them at this speed. Finally *Stardust* settled down from her thunderous approach, and slowed as she looped around the gas giant, easily five times the size of Jupiter.

Taiko appeared as a dot on the screens as we closed to visual distance. The cameras finally brought the damaged cruiser into a focus that caused Olivia to swear and Delt to whistle. The sensor picture had shown us much of this, but it was not the same as seeing it directly.

When *Taiko* had left for Piola sector she had been 650 meters of lethal warship in haze gray and blue with a crew of over five hundred. Now the gray and blue hull was pitted and blackened with one whole section open to space. Even her pointed bow was partly crumpled. Her weapon suite showed damage as well.

"God, she's beaten up," Delt said. "I'm surprised she's holding atmosphere."

"The damage is less severe than it appears," Maauro observed, with a professional air. "Her armor has spared her interior, though her weapons suite has taken severe damage. There have been piercing shots to her interior, notably her machine shops. Still, while not technically crippled, she is heavily damaged."

The cruiser's running lights glowed as we reached 10,000 meters. I drew closer to the big cruiser, doing all the maneuvering. Compared to the cruiser, we were little more than a launch, even at our 112 meter length. *Taiko* would rarely land atmospherically, usually in water and with the brute power of her engines slowing the huge mass. Larger ships than her didn't make planetary landings in atmosphere.

"We will be docking in 193 seconds," I added. I lined up on the cruiser, tapping the attitude jets gently to close the distance. Maauro stood next to me, pleased as always by my piloting skill. With an almost imperceptible jar, we touched the docking ring and the clamps engaged with a thump. I hit the control to extend the boarding tube, not wanting to chance the cruisers beaten up one.

"All hands," I called, "docking completed. Boarding tube is extended and green. Dockside routine is in effect. All systems secured."

Maauro and I made our way to the main airlock. Olivia was waiting, in full uniform, with all of *Taiko's* Marines and the Morok ensign with them. It seemed no one was going to wait for permission to reboard the *Taiko*, regardless of the life support situation.

I opened the tube at our end and we trooped in. The airlock door sealed behind us. Unless the override was hit— both doors on a boarding tube would not open at the same time. The far end opened and armed Marines looked in on us. Since Maauro and I led the parade, our presence and perhaps that of Olivia, kept the situation formal, but I could see people looking past us at the shuttle survivors with grins and nods.

A human female in a navy uniform walked up to us briskly. Her brown hair was short-cropped, but her yellow-eyes and muscular build marked her as a Polphorean, an old colony mutation. She seemed uncertain about saluting us, but did so after a moment. "Lt Commander Abalaf," she said, "*Taiko's* executive officer. We're damn glad to see you, Captain Trigardt." Mutant herself, she'd barely given Maauro a second look.

I nodded. "Wrik Trigardt, my executive, Maauro, no last name, and Major Olivia Croyzer."

"I'll take you to the captain in a moment." She walked past to shake hands with the shuttle survivors, starting with the Morok ensign. Everyone else seemed to take this as the sign to relax, and Cully and his group were surrounded with people shaking hands, pounding backs and trading insults.

Abalaf turned back to me. "Like I said, Captain wants to see you, but he also desperately wants those spares, especially the positron pumps. How the hell you could manufacture those without a Class A factory I have no idea."

"We're full of surprises," I replied. "Cully knows where everything is situated. My First Mate, Delt, can give you the pumps. They are in engineering in a vacuum chamber."

"You're a godsend, Captain." She gestured over her shoulder, and Taiko crew in engineering uniforms came forward eagerly. "Cully."

"On it, XO," Cully said. He waved the others forward and ducked back into the boarding tube.

"Follow me, please," Abalaf said. We followed her into the vast honeycomb of passages and spaces of the cruiser's interior. It was immediately obvious this was a ship in trouble. The corridors were cold, dank even, and the air smelled peculiar. In the delicate biosphere of a spaceship, this was a hallmark of looming disaster.

"Captain's on the bridge," Abalaf threw over her shoulder. "Practically lives there since our last battle with the Anomaly."

"We call it the Beast," I said.

She looked back as we reached a metal stairway. "You've seen it?"

"No," I replied, "but we have seen its works and made contact once."

"How?" she demanded.

"Perhaps it would be best if that conversation was told only once in a secured location," Maauro said, as some crewman clambered down the stairs next to us.

Abalaf gave Maauro a searching look, but nodded. "Sorry about the roundabout route. We took a lot of midships damage and had to decompress some of the adjacent compartments to lessen the strain on the airtight sections. If those positron pumps you made, work, we should be able to get atmosphere recycling working better and some of the 3D printers and artificers. We'll begin to resemble a warship again."

"They will work," Maauro stated.

Again the searching stare, surprised perhaps that it was Maauro and not me speaking. I only smiled.

We finally reached the rear of the bridge by way of a broad metal staircase that led up to a space twenty times the size of *Stardust's* bridge. Unlike ours, it was lit in a subdued red lighting. About two dozen crew manned various consoles, some sitting some standing. All of them looked at us as we came in. In the center of the bridge, on a raised seat surrounded by screens, Captain Raglan sat. He rose as we entered and came over to greet us. Raglan was tall, even for Denlenn, and I had to look up at his face, etched with worry and fatigue. His hair had silvered in the same way a human's did, but would be premature for a Denlenn, and there was a touch of gauntness to his face.

"Greetings Captain Trigardt, Ms. Maauro and Major Croyzer," he said.

Olivia threw a salute. As a Marine major she did not rank a warship captain on his own deck. We were entitled to receive a salute, but there was no need to make this point now. I extended my hand, and Raglan took it human fashion. Maauro did the same and he held hers a little longer than was necessary, giving her a searching gaze.

"Let's adjourn to my space cabin," he said, gesturing to the port side. We and Abalaf followed him to a small cabin that held a table bolted to the deck, chairs and a curtained space behind which I knew would be a bunk and small washroom that the skipper of a warship, unwilling to be more than a few steps from his bridge, would commonly use.

A steward was placing coffee, water and a plate of cookies in the center.

"Thank you, Flores," Raglan said. The steward nodded and slipped silently out, as we seated ourselves.

"Damage control and the engineers are getting everything that they have prepared for us," Abalaf said. "We should hear about that positron pump shortly."

Maauro looked at the yellow-eyed woman. "You need not be concerned. The pump I made for you will function at factory specifications or above."

"Sorry," Raglan said. "We do not mean to look a gift horse in the mouth, but how you're able to manufacture a spare of such size and complexity aboard a scoutship defies us."

Maauro only smiled and reached for a cookie. Abalaf poured coffee and Olivia opted for water.

"We can spare you supplies of food that should feed your remaining crew at full rations for months," I added. "We should be able to cover 65% of your spares and equipment needs. Only fuel and fluids are beyond us."

"The crew will be grateful for the food especially," Raglan said, "rations have been both short and monotonous. We are all right for water, given the nearby ice rings. We've rigged up solar panels to harvest some solar power, but it is a poor source this far out in the system."

"But to more substantive matters," Raglan said. "It was a comfort to me to have Cully vouch for you, even with your codes and orders. Major Croyzer's presence is reassuring as well, but you two? Well, pardon an old line officer's skepticism, but you seem to be a very young man commanding a small scoutship and you are actually second to this even younger lady here. Your crew consists of five people on an older model scoutship we only use in the reserves. How is it that you represent a significant force in a battle with an interstellar nightmare we have only barely survived, mostly by fleeing?"

"Sounds like it's time for your speech, Olivia," I said.

She shot me a look. "What Captain Trigardt means, is that while they are private contractors to the government, I'm regular military as you noted. So it falls on me to deliver an order straight for the Head of Combined Military Intelligence and countersigned by Fleet Command." Olivia rattled off a code and handed Raglan a data crystal. He inserted it in a nearby screen which lit and text scrolled on it. Abalaf read over his shoulder and after a few seconds, whistled. Raglan looked startled and kept glancing at Maauro, who was nibbling a second cookie.

"Revelation of any of what you have read, or learn of Maauro," Olivia said, "is a court martial offense and will result in decades of prison time. As for the rest, well Maauro, save us time and show them."

Maauro nodded and finished her cookie. Her hand then began to glow blue with a plasma fire that warmed the room.

"Do not be alarmed," she said, in her soft voice. "I am an artificial person, not merely an AI. I was made by a species that disappeared from space while humans and Denlenn's both dwelt in caves. My computational and software abilities exceed anything that you have ever encountered."

"So you're actually in command," Raglan said, struggling to comprehend.

"No, I share command with Captain Trigardt, quite seamlessly I think. We are usually of a like mind on most matters."

"And you people are private contractors?" Abalaf said, looking frankly horrified at the idea.

"If by that you are expressing surprise that I'm not in Confederate control, I'm an independent, thinking being, with free will and will not be owned by anyone or anything," Maauro said. "The Confederacy has recognized that I'm better courted with citizenship and a commission, than confined or otherwise harassed. This has been a mutually beneficial and sensible choice."

"By which she also means," Olivia added, with a touch of grimness, "she's already ensured her safety aboard your ship by infiltrating every system on *Taiko*, probably before we boarded you. You'll find that no weapon will track on her ship and she can control any system on Taiko from weapons to reactor containment."

CHAPTER SEVENTEEN

"One finds that difficult to believe—" Raglan began.

The lights in the room went out, save for the glowing green of Maauro's eyes. Then they came back.

"I can arrange suitable demonstrations more impressive than manipulating lighting if you insist," Maauro added dryly. "One would hope our orders and codes would obviate such necessity. In addition, we are all allied forces here, even if in our case it's by virtue of being paid."

"Allies or not," Raglan said. "We will scrub any unauthorized software from our systems."

Maauro gave him a pitying look.

"No, you won't," Olivia stated against the building storm. "In the first place, no one has ever even been able to detect any intruder program she's launched, much less counter it. Nor has any but short term defense ever worked against her.

"More to the point, Captain, reread your orders. She is authorized software. Like it or not, she and Trigardt rank everyone and everything in Piola sector. Period. If she wants, she can legally relieve you of command. Argue that point and it's not even insubordination, Captain, the charge will be mutiny.

"Maauro and I are here to help, Captain Raglan," I interjected, "so perhaps we have spoken enough about our prerogatives and ranks and can turn to how we help you. In that regard, Maauro is the big asset we bring to the table. The greatest supercomputer ever known, in the toughest machine body anyone has ever seen."

"And you control her?" Raglan asked, still trying to orient himself in a new universe.

I chuckled. "Hell, no. But she will listen to me if I have a good idea."

Raglan gave Maauro a challenging look. "Why? If you're the superior intelligence, why?"

Maauro met his gaze. "Because I love him, and he has many good ideas. The one I appreciate most is that he loves me too."

I wasn't sure what a stunned Denlenn looked like, but Raglan was probably the image of it now.

"It would be best to start getting over all of this now," Olivia added. "Command didn't do any of this lightly. Maauro and Wrik have been death and frustration to thousands of enemies of the Confederacy. I once watched her force a rebellious colony world to surrender when they were holding Wrik. She would have destroyed the colony by detonating reactors and climate alterations even if they had succeeded at getting her, which I don't believe they would have."

"But as Wrik says," Maauro continued, pouring a coffee for herself, "we are here to help. It was I who made the positron pump for you, the heart of which I had to create within myself in my internal factories." She delicately sipped the coffee.

Raglan's expression softened as he watched her. "It seems I must learn to accept the impossible in the universe. But let me say that you are a far more pleasant and charming impossibility then the Anomaly, and I do not mean to damn with faint praise. You are enough to amaze any being."

"A living machine," Abalaf said, "indistinguishable from a real person."

"She is a real person," I said.

"Of course," Abalaf said.

"Captain, while Maauro has already digested all of what you have sent us from your logs." I said, "for those of us with merely biological brains, it would be useful to hear your story directly from you."

"Which will certainly give me time for another cookie," Maauro said

"Leave some for others," I said.

"Wrik, we brought plenty," she protested.

"Sorry," I said, "she is inordinately fond of sweet things."

Abalaf laughed, and after a moment Raglan followed suit. It took a while for them both to run down.

"Miss Maauro," Raglan said. "I now believe we may be saved, and I must beg you to forget my suspicions and any lack of welcome I displayed. It has been a long and grim time aboard *Taiko*, and there has been precious little laughter. We owe you thanks for so much, but in this I must particularly thank you. I cannot recall when I last laughed."

"Does this mean I can have the cookie?" she asked.

Raglan smothered another laugh with a hand across his face. Abalaf looked as though the effort to not burst out might kill her.

"Yes," Raglan said, "please enjoy as many as you wish and I will have more brought if you want."

With a demure glance at me, Maauro said. "One more will do."

Even I never knew how much of Maauro's charm was studied tactics for influencing biologicals and how much was innate, but she had clearly passed the tipping point of winning over the Captain.

Suddenly the lights brightened, and the whir of machinery grew louder. The air began to stir.

Abalaf touched the headpiece she wore. "Engineering reported the positron pump went in like it was custom-built, twenty-five percent increase in power to be followed with a forty-percent improvement in life support."

"That is excellent news," Raglan said, some of the strain in his face easing. "Miss Maauro the list of things that I must thank you for seems to be growing."

"I am pleased to be able to help."

"We have found only one other jump point out of the system," Raglan continued. "We have no idea where it goes. I sent our one functioning probe into it, transmitting all the way. But the Anomaly, no, the Beast, I think of your name as the more apt, detected the maneuver and damaged the probe. Perhaps that is the reason the probe did not return. So we do not know where the point goes to, but it is beyond hope to imagine that it goes anywhere useful in Confederate space. We dared not jump further away from home; we're near our limits already."

"I would like to see the data from the probe," Maauro said.

Raglan gave her a curious look. "If what Major Croyzer say is true, then do you not already have access, Miss Maauro?"

Maauro looked slightly embarrassed. "It seemed polite to ask. But yes, I already have the data. Regrettably, the only thing I can analyze is the approach telemetry and the first signs of jump effect. I will continue analysis.'

"After you finish your cookie," he said.

This time it was my turn to laugh.

We spent the next forty-eight hours in furious labor aboard *Taiko*, with the crew of the ship working in the stores we'd brought. Everyone, however, seemed to want to make time to meet and thank Maauro. Clearly the Marines, while perhaps not violating the letter of Confed law, had not been entirely silent about Maauro either. There was also no concealing the minor miracles of damage control that were unfolding on the grievously wounded *Taiko*. Maauro was quickly adopted as the ship's mascot, and almost a touchstone of hope of better days coming.

In some cases it simply wasn't practical to keep her secret, particularly from the ship's surviving engineers, too few in number from a devastating hit that had pierced the armor over the machine shops and engine room. The senior surviving engineer, Saito, would have followed Maauro every waking minute if I hadn't appealed to Raglan to restrain her.

"Wrik," Maauro said late on the second day, "I am beginning to realize that the old human saying that, 'three people can keep a secret if two of them are dead' is most apt."

"I thought you were the one getting tired of all this secrecy about your existence?" I teased. "Beside's I'm the one who should be worried. All these Navy guys seem to dogging your every step, despite Olivia's warnings."

"I think in Saito's case, her desire to see me with my clothes off is nonsexual. While I have found it irksome to conceal what I am, that has always been counter-balanced by the need for security for both of us. We are coming to a time when it may be necessary to start releasing a series of worms that might either destroy records and images of me, or perhaps even spread disinformation."

I looked around, but we were alone in the corridor. "I've had some similar thoughts. Not now, but sometime in the future, we may want to leave Confed service and disappear off everyone's scanners. They will not want to let you go."

She smiled up at me. "An exit strategy?"

"Just so, as you like to say."

The smile broadens. "I like it that you are aware of such details. Is that very feminine of me?"

"Yes," I replied, bending down to kiss her.

The voices of crew suddenly sounded behind me,

I sighed. "Your admirers are back."

"Well, they won't be able to follow me where I am going next. Saito is going to admit me to Reactor Room Two, if I am able to fix the containment issue and get the reactor on line, Taiko's situation will be dramatically improved."

"You're sure this is safe for you? *Taiko's* repairbots couldn't take the radiation, much less the crew in anti-rad suits."

"Oh, please. *Taiko's* repairbots? I am vastly more protected than they are. In fact I will absorb and reprocess the radiation in there."

"I think you are hot enough as you are, baby."

"I love it when you talk like that," she said, winking at me.

Maauro proved as good as her word. Eleven hours later, she'd resealed the containment vessel with a patch of extremely dense hull metal she processed in her body, then bonded in a way that was ninety percent as strong. She then repaired the other systems damage. I didn't understand how she scrubbed the compartment of radiation. She just did it.

Saito just stared in disbelief when Maauro opened the compartment, insisting on using three different instruments to check before she admitted the crew and even then initially only in anti-rad suits until, to Maauro's obvious amusement, my presence and her crew's annoyance made her relent.

"Well," Saito finally admitted, "if you are going to let your boyfriend run about in here, I guess I'll just have to believe it."

"Rest assured," Maauro said. "I would not allow Wrik to be exposed to any danger. You may count on that, if nothing else."

Saito gave me an envious look and headed back into the compartment. Within hours, the Number Two reactor was back on line. With this and the auxiliary reactor Maauro's positron pump had repaired, *Taiko* was back at 75% power. The air began to smell better, the ship was no longer dank and cold. Raglan even took some more of his crew out of cold sleep, given that our supplies had ended his food problems.

We were treated, during a brief break in the frantic pace of repairs, to a dinner with the ship's officer's, most of whom, knowing Maauro was with me, had switched their attentions to Olivia. Delt needn't have worried. The Major was not impressed with the junior officers competing for her attention.

A few of the female officers found Delt a far more receptive audience, and if that bothered Olivia at all, it didn't show. I suspect she didn't care. Dusko excused himself early. While Raglan was cordial, Denlenn and Dua-Denlenn were not fond of each other. The cousin species ethical systems were so utterly opposed, even commerce between them was minimal. As there were no other Duas aboard; Dusko seemed to prefer his usual solitude aboard *Stardust*, now blessedly empty of human Marines and the Morok. His withdrawal caused no dent in the party.

Maauro and I headed home to our cabin, notably Delt did not. Olivia came last of all, Maauro informing me just before we turned in, that she was back aboard.

The next day, with *Taiko* recovering additional systems and defrosting more of her crew, we came up against another problem.

"With all the damage to our sensor suite," Raglan said, "even if we could get to the jumpspace point, we wouldn't be able to make a controlled entry. God knows where we'd end up, if we didn't explode on entrance. I don't know that even the miraculous Maauro can recreate a full sensor suit from raw materials?"

"She needn't," Delt said, snapping his fingers. "We recovered our probes on the way in. If we mount one in a torpedo tube, you can use its instruments to serve as the ship's primary sensors."

"Most excellent, Delt," Maauro said. "While I could recreate one from materials here, even for me it would take weeks and use vast stores of power we can ill afford. We do not dare delay our escape from this system by that much."

"Then you do not see how we can continue operations against the Beast," Raglan said. I was certain I detected a note of relief in his voice.

"No, even with all we have done," Maauro responded, "*Taiko* is far too badly damaged to risk an engagement. The Beast appears to have been toying with you. I judge that it could have destroyed *Taiko* in the last engagement, given the firepower that it has displayed. Something stopped it from finishing you. What that is, I am uncertain at this time."

"So then we must make our escape," I added.

"All our previous attempts failed," Raglan said. "The Anomaly...the Beast, is always there ahead of us. It is as if it is aware of our movements by some method that does not suffer from light speed, impossible though that is in normal space.

"We have thought of telepathy and other esper talents," Abalaf said, "but so little is known of this. It does exist. There are studies of the few verifiable accounts, such as among the Skurlock, who reached across space to contact Shasti Rainhell. Most of their espers died in the final fight with the Evolvers. Generally, what little we know of such talents outside the Skurlock species, indicates that most espers require proximity to their contact, or some form of intimate relationship. None of what we know has provided us with any defense, if that is how it is keeping track of us."

"I resisted," Raglan said, "the thought that the psychic casualties of the crew might be the anchor point. There was some feeling that if those so, 'infected' were disposed of, rather than merely put in cold storage that we might escape. While I command, that will not be done."

"Nor will it be considered by us," Maauro added.

"But then how do we make our escape without plunging headlong against a monster that hits harder than the strongest cruiser ever fielded by the Confederacy," Abalaf grated.

No one had an immediate answer to that problem.

It was just us of the *Stardust* crew, back on our own ship after another day of frenetic work. Dinner had been good, if more simple than Maauro usually served and was quickly cleaned up. We gathered around the table, considering our future, if we had one. It occurred to me that while Maauro ate with the rest of the crew religiously, I rarely saw her power up with one of her extensible cords any more. I wondered about it, but decided to leave well enough alone.

"The creature appears to have learned from its battle with *Taiko*," Maauro said. She was the only one who didn't look weary from working with the crew of *Taiko* to get the cruiser ready to flee, for all she had done a hundred times the work of the rest of us. "It has never again manifested in a physical shape where the balance of *Taiko's* weapons can be effective. For now, we are limited to coherent light and nuclear blast, and those have not reached it, or done little when they did. I cannot think of a way that we could lure it into a planetary atmosphere where it would revert to solid form."

"Could we envelop it in space?" Delt asked, nursing a glass of beer. "Add our torpedoes to *Taiko's*, attack from different vectors in pincer attack? Detonate weapons for proximity damage?"

"A good thought," Maauro said, "but in its plasma form, the Beast has very low mass and is much handier in space than even *Stardust*, much less *Taiko*. The odds of our being able to maneuver the enemy to where it can be saturated are low, given its success at hitting missiles. Still, it is the most promising conventional tactic. It has shown great resistance to conventional weapons in normal space—"

"Almost as if it wasn't there," I murmured.

Maauro turned to me, "What do you mean, Wrik?"

"Almost as if," I continued, "as if, when the laser strikes or the blast wave rolls into it, that it takes refuge somewhere else?"

"What?" Olivia said, sleepiness seeming to vanish.

"There are things this monster is doing that defy what we know of physics," I said, "it seems unusually resistant to weapon and blasts, it moves to block *Taiko* in real time with no light speed delay, all impossible in normal space."

"That's it," Maauro encouraged, "do what you biologicals do. Make those non-linear connections amongst the data."

Delt gave her an amused look. "You know that's not really a thing, right?"

"Of course it is," Maauro said. "Wrik does it all the time."

"Oh, that Wrik," Olivia said, dryly, "he's so wonderful."

Dusko snorted a laugh.

"Handsome too," Delt said, with a grin.

Maauro looked uncertainly at everyone, but seeing my embarrassed smile, made no comment.

"All right," I said, "knock it off. But I do have an idea."

"This should be good," Dusko said.

"What is the most unique aspect of the Beast?" I asked.

"It is the only natural life form ever encountered in jumpspace," Maauro said.

"What if," I added, "if it can enter it from far more places then we can? What if some part of it remains in jumpspace all the time? When it's struck by weapons fire, it withdraws from normal space, like a turtle pulling its head into a shell."

Delt shifted. "That might explain some of the other things it does. Jumpspace is the only place where FTL is possible. If it has a constant connection into it, it may have some sense, whether telempathic or otherwise, that allows it to track *Taiko* at faster than light speed."

"It fits the fact pattern," Olivia agreed.

"If it knows where *Taiko* is," Dusko said, "why doesn't it attack?"

"Again," I said, fighting a mounting excitement, "look at the whole picture. What is required to enter jumpspace?"

Delt shrugged. "Low field density, minimal gravitational effects."

Olivia snapped her fingers. "Of course, *Taiko* dove into a super giant's gravity field when she fled the last battle. The Beast broke off."

"High gravity," I said, "intense radiation."

"Worse than Cimer's 1.8G," Dusko mused, leaning back against a bulkhead. "Maauro, how intense is the giant's gravity?"

"It rounds down to 7.418G," she said. "This one did not miss becoming a small star by much. Radiation is intense, only active EMG shielding is making our presence here survivable. Only a warship, or a purpose-built vessel, would dare such proximity for an extended period. The extreme gravity of this area of space might interfere with its ability to retreat into jumpspace, or even to maintain communication, if you are right, with that part of it that resides in jumpspace."

"Let's look at the other factors," I said, struggling with an idea that was just beyond reach. "The monster is usually found in the zone of habitable words, bright sunshine, and moderate radiation. Here it's dark and cold and all but sleeting rads.

"The monster can move onto habitable worlds, but it takes a solid form when it does so, becoming more vulnerable."

"What else do we know?" Olivia said.

"That it must expend enormous amounts of energy," Maauro said, "to move in normal space and to either enter jump space, or maintain whatever connection it has with jumpspace. Even if its nature makes it easier to enter jumpspace, it still would require great power."

"So," I added, "assume that its nature is such that it is most comfortable in an inner system, where it gets sufficient light and radiation in manageable amounts to recharge. We have been unconsciously assuming that this is a planetary animal, with its solid form being the default. What if it is the other way around, and this is a native of deep space, possibly even jumpspace. It descends on planets, either for more energy or raw material or…"

"To indulge its desire to harm and destroy others," Olivia said. "Maauro, didn't your brief contact—"

"Yes," she said grimly. "It seemed to have no interest in others beyond tormenting them."

"And it can endure a planetary gravity field at least around 1G long enough to hunt for what it needs, or entertains it," Olivia added.

"We have a working theory then," I said, "a spaceborne creature that can endure gravity to 1G and rads comparable with planets in the Goldilocks zone. Solid, while on a world, plasma in space, it can either duck into jumpspace or has a connection to it. So it enters jumpspace easier than we do. It can absorb and channel immense energy so that it hits harder than a cruiser, but it must tire. Hence it broke off its attacks here, unable to absorb radiation at the volume present here. To the Beast, it may be like drinking from a fire hose. Its connection in jumpspace allows it to keep tabs on *Taiko*, even if the disturbed crewmen are in cold sleep. Possibly even over interstellar distances, as it jumped back to the system we were in and destroyed the Fetch."

"Does it know we are here?" Dusko demanded.

Silence fell and we all looked at Maauro.

"We brought Lt. Menoan with us," she said. "If it distinguishes between its victims, it may realize that another vessel had to have done that. But I think what you are really asking is, does it know *I* am here?"

Olivia nodded.

"Insufficient data," she answered. "However, unlike a biological, I am able to shield myself in ways you cannot. While we must plan for the enemy's capabilities, to the extent that we understand them, I do not believe that it is aware that I am here. My brief contact with it leads me to believe that it is only barely aware of us. Like a child burning up a nest of ants, it enjoys the struggle, but is not aware of the identity of any individual ant.

We called Raglan. Maauro and I went to see him, thinking our theory might bear more weight if presented in person. We found him in his space cabin by the bridge. He greeted us warmly, as usual having a cookie handy for Maauro. Our theory was greeted with less skepticism then I feared.

"This makes sense, but I am not sure how to apply it. *Taiko* is severely damaged," Captain Raglas said, "even with the improvements and repairs we've made, its still been necessary to keep many of the crew in cold sleep. Our life support remains marginal, and there is no chance she will survive another round of combat."

"So we cannot beat it in space," I said. "We thought as much."

"No. After our initial success, it proved invulnerable to our attacks in space. Perhaps, if we could catch it in the more solid form it took in a planetary atmosphere, but in nine months of cat and mouse, we have not succeeded in doing so." Weariness lined the Denlenn's face, "and I fear I have used up this ship and crew's luck in trying to.

"Then we must try to escape," I said.

"Yes, but every damn time we approach the jump point, it moves in on us. We must slow to make a proper jump entrance, especially with our ad hoc instrumentation. It would be upon us before we could jump."

"But now we are two ships," Maauro said. "It cannot pursue both of us."

"True," Raglan said, "but it would surely just destroy the larger target."

"Perhaps not," Maauro said. "The Beast may choose to engage me. I think I can intrigue it enough to choose my ship."

"Wonderful," Raglan said dryly. "But how will this help us? Even adding the firepower of your hopped up scout to our—"

Maauro shook her head. "A fox that chases two rabbits risks catching none. We will leave orbit at the same time and remain in close convoy. When the Beast approaches, we will lunge for the system's two jump points. You will return with your wounded ship to the Confederacy. We will draw it after us to the other jump point."

"You will only exchange our purgatory for one of your own," Raglan said. "Even if you reach the jump point, we do not know where it goes to."

"The preliminary work you did," Maauro said, "indicates that the jump point is not a long one, it does not generate the signals of a "deep" jump. We cannot tell if it is a short jump, or just a fast one, but the indicators do not promise us years out of the galaxy."

"You realize," Raglan said, "that such readings are at best guesstimates, and in several cases have been proven wrong. There is no certain way to tell about a jump short of diving into it."

"We have instrumentation of our own," she replied, "and it confirms your own work. We can take a realistic chance on it. Beyond that is the fact that your vessel is exhausting its energy and life support, as well as its fuel. We are too small a vessel to refuel a cruiser. While there is some fuel aboard the sled at the edge of the system, there will be no time to get it this side of jump. Though, if it is not destroyed, it can jump with you for later fueling.

"You have fuel for only one more high-speed run if you are to have any hope of returning to Confed Space."

"We are in the land of poor choices," I add. "But you have a crew still on a ship nearing the end of her operational time. We have to get you out of here while you can still run and fight."

"But what of you?" Raglan demanded.

"We will run before this enemy until we devise a way of destroying it," Maauro replied.

The Denlenn sighed in a human gesture he must have learned. "Were it just for me, I would not ask this of you. For my crew and my ship, I must accept. It grieves me beyond words that I leave you to this fate."

"Sooner is best," Maauro said. "How soon can you get underway?"

"We are ready now," he said.

Maauro looked at me and I nodded.

"Then we leave as soon as we return to *Stardust*," she said. "Let us brief the command staff. I have summoned Olivia as well."

We cleared orbit of the gas giant named for Menoan within the hour with *Stardust* trailing *Taiko*. While both ships possessed the same top speed; we could out accelerate the massive cruiser. Maauro's plan called for the ships to travel so closely that they would appear as a single blip on a normal sensor screen. We could only hope our enemy saw no better than we did at a distance. To prevent the enemy from overhearing any conversations, we took the highly unusual stop of running a thousand meters of wire between the vessels. Our circuit was closed and eaves-dropping hopefully impossible.

"We have three days voyage before we must part and take our separate courses to the jump points," Maauro told everyone during the briefing. "If we do not know where our enemy is, there is some danger of his intercepting both of us. Therefore we hope to encounter it before we separate. If we do not pick it up on passive sensing, then on the third day we will deploy our best sensors and generate enough EM activity to either lure it out, or detect it."

"Wouldn't it be better just to try and sneak out?" Abalaf grumbled on hearing the plan.

"What if it is at the Confed bound jump point?" Maauro answered, "The significance of which it has learned by your several attempts to get past it. Then we can only flee out the other jump point with it on our heels. No, we must know where it is before we commit to our strategy.

CHAPTER SEVENTEEN

Stardust and *Taiko* maintained their best speed heading for the two jumppoints far out in the system but mercifully not far from each other. Maauro spent much of the time on the outside hull of *Stardust*, her hair spun out to its maximum use as a sensor array, integrating data from both ships with her own systems. I didn't like her being out on the hull for so long, even though the radiation attenuated as we drew away from the immense super-giant. The ship's EMG screens rerouted radiation from the interior hull, but she was outside. Maauro denied any suffering, or damage from the radiation, but I wasn't sure I believed it. I spent a lot of time watching her through the porthole.

"You know," Olivia said, "a girl could feel jealous of how much you care for her." She'd come up behind me as I watched Maauro

I smiled wanly without taking my eyes off Maauro. "What? Isn't Delt paying enough attention to you?"

"Oh, your handsome childhood friend is diverting and fun, but that is all he and I are going to be. You two are something that happens only rarely. And I'm not referring to her being an android."

I couldn't help but laugh. "Thanks, I think. I do love her. I just wish there wasn't so much arrayed against us, everything from the Guild, to governments, to the nature of our own bodies."

"I doubt there's much the pair of you can't overcome."

I gave her a sidelong glance. "And here I was, never sure if you liked her or not."

"I like her well enough. We may be too alike in some ways for real closeness and maybe too unalike in others. But there is something more. The Confederacy has always been my highest value, my Holy Grail. Maauro doesn't care about it all. She's a citizen, but that means nothing to her. She only cares about you. If you were to die, God know what she would become."

I was surprised at the intensity of Olivia's response. My comment had been meant as a joke. "Maybe you are right, but how then do you account for her willingness to risk Stardust with me aboard?

"Even that is about you. She knows that you won't hide behind her, and that you need some form of work that you find fulfilling. Unfortunately for her, you're not a schoolteacher. She has the same problem. At her highest expression of herself, she's a combat AI. She needs to exercise those capabilities."

"She's more than that."

"I didn't say she wasn't, but it's the core of her being. The only other personality factor that even rivals that is her relationship with you. So she's interested in you, your friends and family, but not a lot more. When you're not around, Wrik, she's a lot more machinelike. She just doesn't invest the effort and energy the way she does when you are present. It's like she's going through the motions. Ever see her plug in to repower anymore? She does it when we are around, but not when you are. Ninety percent of the cute, adorable Maauro occurs when you're in sight.

"Even when we were girl-talking about you and Delt—"

"You were talking about us?"

"Shut up and listen. This is important. Even that is about you."

"You realize that she could be listening to this whole conversation."

"Be damned to her if she is," Olivia said, eye sparkling. "She's always telling us that she keeps her security parameters below the level of her conscious awareness. Whatever the hell that means. Supposedly, she grants us privacy. But Wrik, we both know that she has something in common with humans in this regard. She lies when it suits her purposes."

"And what do you want me to do?" I snapped.

"Start by being aware of it. You two exist in your own happy little bubble-world. You clearly love her, and if I can tell anything at all about her, she loves you. That makes you partly responsible for the most dangerous individual in known space.

"So right now she loves you, cares about your friends and family and this ship. I don't know that it will always be that way. You could die, you could fall out of love—don't interrupt, it happens. You could end up cheating on her. I know you two are sexual, but is it as good as it was with Jaelle? With me? She's a machine pretending to have an orgasm, I imagine. Will that always satisfy you?

"How much has she changed in the time you've known her? She went from a programmed war machine that almost killed you, and yes she finally did tell me the story, to your girlfriend. What will she be like in ten years? We live a long time nowadays but a hundred years from now, you'll be old and she won't. One hundred fifty years from now, she'll be here and you won't. What will be going on in that armored skull then and will it have anything to do with the good of humanity, or even of the Confederacy? She damn near drowned a Confed world because a rebel element on it threatened you. Collateral damage is not a big issue for her.

"What holds her to the rest of us if you're gone, or you change? Or do you care?" Olivia looked almost exhausted by the torrent of words.

I turned back to the porthole looking at the stars beyond. The conversation unsettled me in a way I had never imagined. Finally, I turned back to her. "I don't rule her life. I just love her as best I can and have to hope that she genuinely cares about the things that I care about. Maybe we will just all have to deserve Maauro's love and allegiance."

"You'd certainly better," Olivia said. "That may mean turning down a lot of temptations that will come the way of a wealthy and powerful male."

"Are you going to test me, Olivia?" I shot back, trying to unnerve her as she had me.

"God's no, because I think I could succeed and I'm not going to do anything that would alienate Maauro. In fact, if you were starting an affair, I'd have the other person killed."

"What really scares me now is that you sound half-serious."

"Listen to me, I am entirely serious. You and she are a class of threat not much below what we're chasing. I would do it in a heartbeat, except for the fact that Maauro will spot you straying long before anyone else will."

"Oh hell, Olivia," I shot back. "On Seddon, it was Maauro that kept pushing me toward you. I don't think she's that territorial."

"That was before she decided that place belonged to her, nothing in common with now."

We stared at each other, breathing hard. I was angry, and I knew some of what she said was true. I loved Maauro, but that hadn't turned off my awareness of other women, not Jaelle, not Olivia, but how was that different than for any other man?

Olivia broke our gaze first. "Listen, I'm sorry if you feel that was out of line, but I've been worried about it since the Voit-Veru colony. I do like Maauro, and I want things to work out for you two, but Wrik, for Christ's sake, don't you think I was in love with my first husband? He was everything to me, until he cut and ran when I was court-martialed. I've never gotten over it. And compared to you two, we came out of the same mold. So many long-term relationships end badly, but yours could take a few billion people with it if things get out of hand."

"I do occasionally lie," Maauro's gentle voice sounded. Olivia and I turned, startled. "I try not to, but I find it unavoidable."

Maauro must have reentered the ship while Olivia and I argued. She walked over to us, passing Olivia, who looked ready to bolt or fight as needed.

"So," Maauro continued, "I do not spy on you in the shower, or listen to your conversation normally. I have literally programmed a sub AI in myself to do that, but not to tell me things that do not pertain to my security." She sighed. "However, this conversation penetrated those levels. Maybe it should not have. You should feel free to doubt me, Olivia, and my intentions. I have my own interests. They do not always align with yours, or the Confederacy's. I certainly feel free to doubt yours."

I moved to stand next to Maauro and took her hand, but said nothing.

"There is much that you said," Maauro continued, "that I suspect you intended for my ears. You are devious and clever, though I also believe you are mostly sincere."

"Mostly sincere," Olivia said, "that will look great on my tombstone."

"If you mean to express by that a concern that I will be the reason for that tombstone, than I have done an even poorer job of being a friend than my limited skills in this area justify."

"I'm not mad at you Maauro—"

"No. But you are quite sensibly afraid of me."

"Who wouldn't be, with your powers?" Olivia blazed.

"Well, Wrik for one," she said. "He wasn't really afraid, even when I was merely a programmed machine. Somehow, he never believed I could harm him."

"Does that immunity extend to others?"

Maauro smiled sadly. "And if I told you it embraced you as well, Olivia, would you believe me? We both know I can lie."

"Maybe," Olivia said, after a few seconds.

"And maybe not," Maauro said. "You can no more know what is truly going on inside of me, than I can tell with you. Less even, as I can dissemble with no physical reaction, such as a human has when lying.

"But think of this, if you fear for the failure of my primary relationship, how much more do you think I fear it? If Wrik loves me with perfect purity and unchanging devotion, all a lot to ask out of the first human male to love an AI, what do I have? A century, maybe? At most, the better part of two centuries? If I'm not destroyed, I must face existing without what I have now. If I can."

"So you may be right in more ways than one. I think of friendships as networks; it is part of my basic being to see it that way. And it is likely that the wider my network is, the stronger it will be for me. So, I will make more of an effort, even when Wrik is not there, to be less the machine and more the person. I will try and be a friend. I will try to care about the wider world as, and if, I can.

"Remember, that most of my existence, a period that took your kind from caves to the stars, I spent alone, a neglected war machine with tens of thousands of deaths to my credit. In the few years since I reawakened, I have had to learn to be an independent person. To my own utter shock, I had to learn to be a lover. It will certainly take a lot longer for me to get any good at any of it."

Olivia stared at Maauro for a second longer, then took three long strides to her, and put her arms around her. I let go of Maauro's hand and stepped back, leaving the two of them in the embrace.

Finally, Olivia let go of Maauro. "Sorry," she whispered and spun on her heel to walk off.

CHAPTER EIGHTEEN

WE APPROACH THE JUMP POINT. NOW, I MUST DARE DIRECT CONTACT *with the Beast. We must know where it is before we commit the damaged Taiko to her final run. I have fortified myself by every means conceivable: compartmentalization, automatic reboots and corrective software. I've updated and expanded my backups as far as is possible. In the event of complete failure, I've made a complete copy of all my memories of my life with Wrik and isolated it internally. It will allow me to essentially recreate myself from static storage. I hope.*

The Beast will likely pursue the cruiser unless I draw it to me. I ready my attack though I have no assurance the Beast will even notice. I have never aimed a cyber attack directly at a biological before, but the Beast is like nothing we have ever encountered. For all I know it might be more like a machine, but even there I have to share the language of the other machine, else it is like shouting at a deaf person. Still, I am a cyber intruder of the first water; once I can establish a commonality, my intrusion becomes exponential.

Yet, I dread the coming conflict. The Beast struck me so hard in our first encounter. The last time I suffered so badly was as a result of my own stupidity when I stumbled into a trap set by a Guild gunner named Lostra. To have survived all I'd had and to nearly be done in by that cheap tramp of a gunner! The very recollection makes me burn with shame. The Beast is an enemy so far beyond Lostra as to be unimaginable. Can I win against it?

I have so much to live for. Yet, I could be destroyed or worse, the disarrayal of my data is akin to madness in a biological. I could lose myself.

Do I need to? This sudden thought freezes me in utter shock. No one but I will know if I even reach out to the Beast. It is pursuing Taiko; we are the smaller target and can easily out-accelerate the bigger warship. We could double-back and make for the jump point to the Confederacy. We could escape back home. I need not risk my sanity, my very identity and my future happiness with Wrik. I know that Wrik doesn't want to take this risk. Only the threat to his species and their worlds has made him consider it.

But do I care? What do other humans, beyond the handful I have befriended, mean to me? Why should I risk myself for a warship of a government I do not trust and owe no allegiance to, beyond that which serves me? They would break me down for my technology in a second merely to advance their power. Only the danger I present to that power stops them from doing so. They suspect that I have infiltrated their planetary and military systems with intruder programs and that these will spring to the attack if I am seized. They are right. I have laid such traps all through the Confederacy and beyond.

Still, I am contemplating such a risk for them? I am afraid of the Beast. I am afraid of what I will lose, the life I love and have fought so hard to earn.

No one will know. We can just run away. No one will ever know.

More shock, more realizations tumble in. This was what Wrik felt in the sky over Retief, with an avalanche of enemy warships coming down on his squadron. His plight was the worse; there was only small chance of surviving the engagement. He dove away, thinking that no one would know.

I could lie. I could say I reached out, but either couldn't contact it, or make it notice me. I could tell Wrik it couldn't be done.

I am locked in a struggle with myself. I have lied to Wrik before when I believed it was necessary. Is it necessary now? Is this cowardice? What am I doing? This is no calculation that I can make in tiny fractions of microsecond. In this I must reason no differently than Wrik. This is an emotion-laden decision about what I value, what I love. A sensation of panic begins to surge through me.

Five hundred and seventeen lives balanced against mine, balanced against Wrik's, against my network with Olivia, Delt and Dusko, frail as it is.

Wrik's suffering hangs like a warning in my mind. It took years and all the help I could give him to recover himself as a person he could live with. It didn't matter that he was among people who knew him, valued him, even loved him as Wrik Trigardt. He could not outrun Piet Van Zyle's load of guilt.

Would it be the same for me? If I decide, whether through selfishness or cowardice, to serve only myself, who would I be then? Would I become someone that Wrik could no longer love? Would I become someone I couldn't love?

I look at the last sensor contact of the Beast's location.

"I hate you," I think. "God, I hate you. How dare you put me where I must make such a choice?"

I look at Wrik from the corner of my eye. I know that if I voice my fear, he will give me the benediction of saying, 'Don't do it. We'll find some other way,' knowing full well that there is no other way. He will elect to preserve me over all others.

Yet, if the positions were reversed, he would choose to call the Beast down on himself. He would not allow that he be preserved over all these other lives. I know how he struggles to hang onto his courage, but he has never failed since the day he rescued me on the asteroid.

Rescued me. Yes, he rescued me, a chance companion of mere hours who had even threatened his life earlier. Still, he had charged in an unarmored suit against an Okaran about to destroy me. That moment, when he found his courage was when he said he had begun to live again.

I stare into the abyss and now know that in the depths of it, the Beast awaits me, laughing at me, tempting me with flight and dishonor. Run away. No one will know.

A strange peace settles over my soul. I am Maauro. I am loved. I must deserve to be loved as I am. I should not lie to Wrik. I should not do dishonorable things that I will regret. I will not enjoy the life that I can purchase with disgrace.

Beast, I will not forgive you for the darkness into which you very nearly thrust me!

"Preparing for contact with the enemy" I announce.

Wrik reaches across to place a hand on my arm, worry in his warm brown eyes. How I long to banish worry from him.

I turn and smile at him. "I love you."

"I love you too," This I will hold firmly to as I move into the abyss to grapple with our enemy.

I launch my cyber attack at our enemy at full power, armed with the hatred it raised since it tempted me in the darkness of my own journey into the desert. My attack is also limited to light speed, radiating out of me—only slightly compromised by Wrik's flat refusal to consider that I be outside the ship spinning out my hair into a superior sensor array.

"I've never said no to you about anything that you thought was important," he had said, "but I am saying it now. We don't know our enemy's capabilities. It could strike unexpectedly and I will not have you outside the hull of a wildly maneuvering starship, while we maneuver into a jump point. Don't even think of arguing with me about this. I will not accept such chances with your safety."

He has rarely ever spoken to me so. I am moved by his devotion, if somewhat annoyed that I, a deadly weapon of war, feel the need to listen to him. Still, of such compromises is love made. So using the ship's systems and from the seat next to Wrik, I broadcast my challenge.

Time drags by.

Shock, contact, the enemy is in touch with me and Wrik's theories are confirmed. The enemy has responded at faster than the speed of light. Its reply, its sheer awfulness, its no, not hatred, its massive indifference to the fate and needs, the very concept of "the other" crashes over me.

But I am forewarned and forearmed this time. All my defenses swing to my aid and I block and parry its probes furiously. The battle is not subtle like the one I fought in cyberspace with Lilith, the master hacker I defeated on Retief. She'd appeared to me as a sexually provocative giantess, towering into the virtual sky. I had stood against her as my prosaic, gray and red suited self.

Again I am merely me, though I wear my black suit with its golden details, as I stare into the vast, shapeless darkness that holds my enemy.

CHAPTER EIGHTEEN

Gradually, in a place where time has no meaning and images are shaped by thought, I discern my enemy, a vast shadowed shape in a loathsome green with a dozen eyes, in a misshapen head, that glows with an unhealthy light. Its body is, somehow obscene, with its odd collection of assemblages. I cannot tell why it appears as it does to me. This is no form we have any report of and I have no atavistic racial memory. But thus it appears, and the eyes, empty of any empathy, indeed empty of life, focus on me.

It sees me and I must hold my data, my very conception of myself against its terrible regard. To it, I am less than a bug for it has no concept of a bug, nor of any right a bug might have to its own existence.

"I deny you, Filth!" I shout. "You are nothing. You build nothing, you love nothing. You add nothing to existence. You are nullity. Valueless!"

My accompanying barrage of deadly computer virus spirals around the vast, ancient Other, unnoticed. It is not a machine, and even if I spoke the same language as it, with its utter sense of self, its horrid egotism, it would not be influenced by them. Can there ever have been something so grotesque in its conceit that it believed it was all that mattered in God's creation?

It does not speak to me; such a concept is beyond it. It only hungers for pain, for the suffering of others, without ever being aware what others are, as if their sufferings were only salt for the meat of its tedious existence.

So it seeks to make me suffer, eager for my pain. It reaches for me and I strike as I can, but mostly I resist and simply do not suffer. Finally after an age, after millennia, after a moment, I perceive something: confusion, beginnings of frustration and the initial colors of anger. Like a spoiled child denied a toy, it is vexed. It focuses the awful attentions of its eyes on me.

Now I must break off. I have attracted the attention of this miserable vastness, the emptiness with its filthy craving to be filled. I cannot endure the dreadful pressure and break the connection, shutting myself down to all exterior stimuli further than the length of my arms.

I focus on my suddenly tinier universe- the well-lit bridge, the interior of my home, my Stardust. At the center of that world is Wrik, with his brown eyes filled with worry. I realize that in an emotional sense, I am cold, chilled by my exposure to so much emptiness and waste, such selfishness need. He unbelts and leaps to my side. I struggle to sit upright.

"The Beast," I say in pain, "contact with it is bad, very bad. I feel so disordered." I reach to Wrik, "Kiss me."

His arms wrap around me and his lips press to mine. Warmth returns to my existence. I am loved and this is my strength, my flame, relighting places in my soul that have gone dark, polluted by the utter foulness of the Beast.

"Maauro, my love, are you all right?"

"Yes," I reply slowly. "I have succeeded. The Beast is aware of and now focused on me. It turns to follow us. No matter what happens, we have given battle, and Taiko will live."

"Then you've accomplished much, sweetheart, a cruiser full of lives to our credit and all the information there is on the monster. Who knows how many you may have saved?"

"We may have saved," I insist.

"Now we have only ourselves to worry about."

I surprise myself with a small laugh. "As usual."

"Yeah," he answers with a grin. "Just us, Lost Planet again."

"And Olivia," I add.

"Honorary member, no dues though."

"Then we will face the Beast together," I say, "take the measure of this enemy and make it pay for the death and degradation it has spread."

"God damn right we will," he says, his voice rough. "It's hurt you twice now and this I cannot forgive. Not from it, or anyone else."

"Tell the others for me, Wrik. I would rather not see anyone just now."

He nods and reaches for the toggle. "Wrik to all hands. Taiko is making her escape. Maauro has drawn the Beast after us. She's...ok.

"We are four hours from jump at the alternate jump point. Where we go, we don't know. Prepare for jump. We'll gather on the bridge after depending on the jump effect. Make sure you have your D set of meds and restoratives handy. There's no way to tell what this jump will be like."

"Delt acknowledging, kiss the little princess again for me."

"Olivia here. Tell her... god damn it—just tell her she's the best."

"Dusko, I expected nothing else. Let's try not to die."

"Thank them," I whisper. The warmth of Wrik and their concern for me fans the fire of recovery within me. The Beast's grip on me recedes.

Wrik glances at me. "She says you aren't bad for a crew of misfits and screwups either. Wrik out."

CHAPTER NINETEEN

A T MAAURO'S COMMAND, I SHEARED AWAY FROM THE damaged cruiser. Taiko heeled over in to a more stately turn in the opposite direction. The cruiser's massive engines glowed with full power as she thrusted for the Confederacy. We, accelerating far faster, headed for our jump point into the unknown, 35 degrees to port and 97 degrees relative down.

Maauro slumped in her seat. With the ship on a straight course and the scanner right next to me, I could safely unbelt and move to her. I grabbed her hands, which to my shock, felt cold, and metallic.

I held her against me, having to struggle with her weight. This told me how much harm had been inflicted. Maauro hated to let me feel her full weight, always countering it as best she could. In a few seconds, I felt her become light again as she managed her balance. Warmth and malleability returned to her hands.

"Kiss me," she said and I do.

"I am feeling better moment by moment," Maauro said.

"You're sure? Dammit, I should never have allowed this."

"No, Darling, we need to be sure, and I am likely the only intelligence that could link to this thing and survive even the short exposures I have dared."

"But I love you," I said, my voice shaking. "I can't risk you like this."

"Let's try and avoid it in the future," she agreed.

I informed the others of our success but Maauro and I remain alone on the bridge her face against my chest for a long period. I stroke her long black hair.

We are not going to live like this, I think. I am going to find us a quiet little valley somewhere and we are going to just be together. Someday.

As we approached the Beta jumppoint, we received confirmation that Maauro's gambit had worked. The long distance sensors Maauro had recalibrated showed the Beast had changed course and speed. It was not going to overtake us, but was slowly closing the distance. Perhaps it was low on energy; perhaps it was wary of Maauro. There was no way to tell.

Meanwhile, Maauro recovered her usual optimism and cheer. She resumed monitoring our instruments and systems as I set up the jump. Ahead, I could see via my scanners, a well-defined jump-point, a veritable hole in the fabric of space-time, spiraling down to jumpspace. I'd studied every reading *Taiko* had made in its close pass of the jump point, and it was all matching nicely.

All I could tell from this, was that it showed the shape and characteristics of a single exit jump—what we pilots called a 'chain point' as opposed to a multi-exit nexus point. The good and bad of that was, that chain points rarely led to long jumps, but there was also no prospect that the monster would end up in some other system than we would.

Maauro and I had debated coming to a stop on the far side and seeking to ambush the Beast as it came through the jump point after us. She'd vetoed the idea finally. "The point will not be less than 10,000 kilometers in diameter. Depending on the enemy's angle of descent into the jump point, it might arrive on our heels, or weeks later. Given its extreme maneuverability, should we fail in the attack with our three torpedoes, we would be out of options."

Reluctantly, I gave in to her logic.

The sound of the others coming up the gangway made me look back.

Delt entered first. He flashed me his usual confident fight-jock grin, but his look was more serious as he rested a hand on Maauro's shoulder. Her own came up to pat his; and she smiled back at him before he headed off to belt himself in.

Olivia only had eyes for Maauro, who nodded and gave her the same smile she had for Delt. She nodded and belted herself in. What face Dusko was wearing right now I didn't know, as usual the solitary Dua preferred riding the jump out in his cabin.

"I'm steepening our approach to the jump," I said. It'll make it rougher, but I want to minimize the danger the Beast could come in steeper and overtake us. There's no way to guess the Beast's capability. It's a creature of jumpspace. What can't it do?"

We drove on at our best speed. The stars begin to go strange, as gravity twisted and failed. I turned to Maauro, looking into her calm green eyes. "See you on the other side, love."

She nodded. "I will protect your sleep, Wrik."

The universe explodes into the discord of jump with a mélange of colors, shapes and scents.

I stare at Wrik as he sits unmoving, eyes open between heartbeats. I could turn my head and see the others, but do not feel the need. Perhaps, as Olivia has chided me, I am too Wrik-centric in my existence, but it is his arms that encircle me, his breath against my neck at night. More than that, he always sees me a woman to be loved, no matter that I was made and not born.

Yes, I must pay more attention to other beings, but I will enjoy my time studying my Wrik, now.

Even I have not found a way to reckon time in this realm. So I sit by Wrik and my friends, yet watch vigilantly at the instruments. The enemy has followed us into jump. I sense it hovering at the edge of my passive sensors. I do not risk a third exposure of direct contact. It similarly seems unwilling to press that attack and is content to follow.

So we journey though jumpspace in nontime. I'm content for it to be so. For when this interregnum ends, the battle begins.

The universe crashed in on us again, along with the wretched sickness of a bad jump. The ship's instruments settled back into normal parameters but my vision was blurred. I grabbed my bulb of restoratives and quickly drained it. Then I pressed a tab of anti-nauseants against my arm. It hissed and injected the meds into my system, leaving me to clench my teeth until they could take effect.

I met Maauro's eyes.

"All is well," she hastened to say. "Nothing troubled us in jumpspace, though it did follow us in."

"Mixed blessings," Olivia said.

"Rough jump," Delt said, draining his meds. "How long were we out of space-time?"

"Only four months and a mere 5.81 light years," Maauro said, "rounded off, as you people do so hate going more than two decimal points."

A bitter chuckle raced around the bridge.

"Dusko," Maauro called over the speakers, "how are you?"

"Pleased I wasn't eaten in my sleep by a monster," his ironic voice sounded.

"It's the little things," Delt said,

The excitement of moving into a new star system began to replace the terror of the Beast, as we continued inward. Maauro felt no sign of the Beast's presence so we had no idea of when the thing would make its appearance. Though it was impossible to see anything with the naked eye, everyone spent time at the portals watching this new space.

"It's a pretty part of the universe," Olivia said, looking at a flaming, blue nebula.

"Provided that we don't eat a bit of rock, or ice, at a high percentage of C," Delt replied.

"Is that the sound of you worrying, flyboy?" Olivia said, with a grin. "I thought you left all that to Wrik?"

"Who, me, worry?" Delt said. "We're only burning a hole in uncharted space."

"I am doing all I can to remedy that," Maauro said. "Between our active sensors and occlusion studies, I should have all that major bodies in the system located in hours. I could do it faster if we detach the probes, but I agree with Wrik that it is premature to do so now. There are burnouts in some of the visual spectrum and short-range scanners. I am prioritizing those, but must direct most of my effort to make sure we are in no danger of collision."

Maauro was, as usual, true to her word, and later over lunch told us that she had located a large gas giant inward of us and two more Neptune like bodies further out.

"Any Earth-types?" I asked, trying to contain my excitement. The bounty for finding habitable worlds was large enough to end any financial concerns Lost Planet might have for the foreseeable future.

"Difficult to say as yet," Maauro answered. "But this is another immense gas giant and being as far into the system as it is, it is possible that there are habitable worlds inside the orbit of it. We can use it for air-breaking if we want to slow, loop around it and try hitting the jump point back out. While the Beast followed us in, we do not know if it has emerged yet, and we may be able to slip past it, if it has."

"Hmm," I said. "We may as well head for the gas giant and the inner system. A habitable world fee…"

"Always thinking of the bottom line, Wrik?" Olivia said, an edge in her voice.

"Yes," I said dryly. "You're part of something big, Olivia: fleets, divisions of troops and an economy to pay for it all. We're part of something small and precious to us. Money is our defense against everything: the Guild, the Confederacy's enemies and the Confederacy itself. It's our liberty. The money means nothing to me else. Do you see me living in luxury on some safe inner world? We just risked ourselves to get one of your cruisers away."

The look she gave me turned sad. "*Taiko* was your ship too."

"Not so much, Olivia, and not just because we came from a rebel colony. If we were just ordinary citizens, maybe, but we're not. Your boss sees us as only marginally less dangerous than what she uses us against. I don't question the Confederacy's essential goodness, but it's a greatest good for a greatest number and the sort of people at the top are like the sort of people at the top of the worst governments. They want power for its own sake. We won't permit ourselves to be at its dubious mercy."

We stood, facing each other, Olivia opposite Delt and I, and Maauro just looking out at the stars, as if none of this concerned her.

Finally Olivia sighed. "There is some truth to what you say. Probably, if I were in your shoes, I would feel the same. Freedom's your only religion, you and Maauro, and Delt was your friend from childhood. But I have seen the results of too many people deciding that their way is the only way, too many pocket dictatorship's set up. Or have you forgotten: Olympia, Cimer and Zeltah?"

"Do you still fear us so?" Maauro said into the stillness.

"Sometimes," Olivia said, "sometimes not. You are both the best and the most dangerous thing in creation, Maauro."

"Well," Delt said finally, "now that's settled back down again, at least as much it's ever going to, shall we see if there are valuable worlds ahead, new people to meet, maybe even some answer to the monster that's out there behind us somewhere?"

"Yes," I said

"Yes," Maauro added. She turned to face Olivia. "What say you?"

"Yes, onward," Olivia said, with a half-hearted wave that smacked of an apology.

Dusko walked in on us, looked on the tableau and stopped. "Did I miss something?"

"No," Maauro said. "All is well."

Hours later, I joined Maauro on the bridge, still in my gym set and with music earbuds in my chest pocket, to find the others already there. Dusko had placed some flowers in a magnetic vase on Maauro's accustomed station. He was always proud of his hydroponic garden. I looked at it and just shook my head in amazement. Times change.

"The burnout in the long range optical scanner has been repaired," Maauro said, as she lay down a tray of drinks at the small foldout table at the back of the bridge. "We had more than the usual share of system errors after the jump."

"Stardust has been running hard," Delt said, frowning as he worked on his communications panel.

"And is going to have to keep at it," Dusko said. "There's still no sign of our monstrous friend." Behind him, Olivia made a face at his back.

"I had to prioritize repairs," Maauro said, "but this is the last major system. I wanted weapons and short range sensors back at 100% in case we were attacked. I had the long-range radar next so we could watch out for asteroids and such.

"The image of the gas giant will be available shortly," she continued. "Sensor returns have been fuzzy, which is not unusual with a gas giant. Coming up on the main screen now."

"It'll be nice to—

"No!" Maauro shouted, dropping the drink table.

We all froze. The idea that Maauro would drop something was so impossible, that we could only stare.

Out of the side of my eye, I caught the reason for her horrified expression. The planet ahead was ringed. Three rings circled it, but not all in one plane. It looked like a child's drawing of an atom.

Memory crashed in on me, Cimer, the gas giant where we had ended the Ribisan conspiracy to manufacture Predictors. Maauro destroyed both the research and the last living Predictor. But before he died willingly at her hands, he'd shown her a number of possible futures. She'd never fully shared what she saw in those futures, but I knew that on a world ahead, circling the atom-like gas giant, death awaited one, or both of us.

I remembered her, shaking and crying for the first time in her existence, when I asked if I needed to know what she has seen.

"No." she'd said. "So many of these were only possible futures and with what little I learned we might as likely dodge into the trouble we seek to avoid. Nor was all I saw perilous. There are wonders and beauty ahead if it is our destiny to travel those timelines.

"Yet…have you heard of a world surrounded by three rings in varying planes all at different angles to each other?"

I had shaken my head.

"We must avoid such a place should it ever be found," she'd demanded then.

"We must turn the ship," Maauro snapped. "Now." She started toward the controls.

"Hey wait," Olivia said, grabbing Maauro's shoulder.

"No," both Dusko and I shouted.

Too late, Maauro simply flung Olivia off her. Delt showing the speed and coordination that made him an ace, leapt up and caught her, they both crashed into his station, cracking a panel. Dusko dove behind his chair. I jumped to my feet. Since I was between her and the instruments, she could not avoid me. I enfolded her in my arms.

"Stop," I said, calmly.

She froze in my embrace, not daring to move for fear of injuring me.

"I know," I continued, as if nothing had happened, "that you can command the ship without using the controls at all, but I am going to ask, ask you as the woman I love, not to."

"Wrik," she replied, "you are going no closer to that horrid world than you are at this moment. I will not have it. I will not let you die there." Behind her, a stunned and bruised Olivia was helped to her feet by Delt, who stared at Maauro as if she had gone mad.

"Wait, Maauro," I said. "We have to think this through."

"No, we don't. You die there. I will not allow it. We turn back now. We will face the Beast if we must."

"You said the Predictor only saw possible futures. They could be changed. Remember?"

"Yet the world we fear is there, before us."

"I know you love me, and you arc only thinking of protecting me—but think, that world ahead may not be the worst danger we face. The monster chasing us is so deadly even a cruiser couldn't handle it."

"I am unmoved. You will not set foot on a planet where the three-ringed planet is in the sky." She looked up at me and there was anguish in her eyes. "I will not allow it, even if I must use force and you do not love me anymore."

"Stop that," I demanded. "I love you. I love you now and forever. Your eyes won't open on a day that I don't love you. But I've told you before, I am through with running. I am much more afraid of the long death that follows that, than anything else."

I pressed her head against me. "You may be right. Maybe the danger ahead is worse than the danger behind. Maybe it's the same danger. But we can't decide in a panic. We likely have only one shot, whichever way we go. You didn't want to tell me what you saw through the Predictor, because you feared we were as likely to dodge into the trouble as away from it. Consider if you could be doing that now."

I looked over at the instruments to see we were still on course. She hadn't seized control. I stepped back and placed my hand under her chin then gently raised her face so we were looking each other directly in the eyes.

"We have a crew to consider," I said, "one of whom you just injured and owe an apology to. Beyond that, we have, I don't know how many lives at stake, if we cannot destroy our enemy. You can't, or rather you shouldn't, just decide on the danger to me. I know you too well to think that you are afraid for yourself."

She slowly shook her head. "Don't be that certain. I have so much more to lose now, than I ever had before. I can be a coward too."

I tried to keep startlement off my face. "Well, I guess then you are getting more like us all the time."

Maauro rubbed a hand across her face in a gesture I recognized as my own. "And not always in good ways, I have never before been subject to panic and blind fear, never almost lost control of myself." She turned shamefaced to Olivia. "Are you hurt, Olivia?"

She stared at Maauro for a few seconds. "No, I get worse in sparring."

"Still, I am sorry, ashamed even. I have struck at a friend."

Olivia looked past her at the three-ringed world. "The Predictor....it showed you…"

Maauro nodded.

"All I am saying is that we have to carefully consider our next move," I said.

Dusko stood from behind his chair. Delt moved out from in front of Olivia, who dusted herself off with a wince that Maauro immediately noticed.

"Forget about it," Olivia said. "I mean that."

"Thank you," Maauro whispered. She turned back to me. "I must be alone for awhile, to do the sort of analysis of the Predictor data that I once did on the data on the Seddonese artifacts. At the end, we will discuss, but whether anyone will forgive me or not, I will make the final decision."

Delt shrugged. "Probably best anyway. You're the smartest here."

"I have not demonstrated that in these last minutes," she said. "I will do better."

She turns back to me. "Please do not be angry with me."

"I'm not," I replied. "As Delt says, you are the smartest, but remember intuition and feelings matter too."

"Do not disturb me for forty-seven minutes," I order.

"You will have the time you need," Wrik says gently, placing his hands on my shoulders. I place one of mine on his, and then head for engineering, the most heavily shielded part of the ship. I seal engineering and settle on the deck, after hooking myself directly to the reactor with the tap I use for repowering. All systems are reduced to standby, and all additional capacity is routed to analytics. I explore the memories of my time with the Agrille, the Ribisan Predictor and all that he showed me of my possible futures. I focus the power of a planetary supercomputer on my future. Each image of a possible future is studied to the greatest degree possible.

Joy. There are differences in the Wrik who dies with me on the moon of the gas giant ahead. My Wrik weighs 182.36 pounds—the Wrik who perishes with me, raising his laser against the unseen enemy weighed 193.7 pounds. My detailed scan of every portion of his anatomy indicates that he is also at least three years, nine months and six days older.

Relief temporarily disorients me. We have a chance—we have arrived on a different timeline, years before we perish in the other timeline. But relief is replaced with rage. I have lived for years with the fear of this day and this place. I will not die here. I will not allow anything to kill Wrik and I. This I vow.

I cool down, both mentally and physically, surprised at myself. Logic and caution must guide all my choices from now. We are here and a deadly adversary may be met. So... we have met and defeated such before. I must believe we will again.

I realize that the time I demanded has elapsed. I unplug and stand, then head for the bridge. The others are gathered there, sipping drinks, staring out into space. They all rise as I enter.

I stand before Wrik, pausing only to put a hand on Olivia's shoulder as I pass.

"What did you learn?" he asks, looking me in the eyes. I see he is braced for bad news.

"Now that we confront the actuality of our encounter with the three-ringed world I have examined every image I retain from my time with Agrille."

I turn to the others. "Olivia, you know some of what transpired on Cimer. Dusko and Delt you know little or nothing. It is time to remedy that, but all that is said here must remain within Lost Planet, or an interstellar war of horrific proportions could result. Do you understand?"

All nod, with looks of dismay and surprise.

CHAPTER NINETEEN

"*The short version is that, for a long time before they joined the Confederacy, the Ribisans had the ability to predict future events and manipulate the time flow to reach time lines most advantageous to them.*"

I pause as this sinks in with Delt and Dusko. Both their faces react as they realize the implications of what has been said.

"*That ability is destroyed now, by me. But before it was ended, I saw a number of possible futures for myself.*" *I take Wrik's hand in mine.* "*In one I foresaw this and to my joy it has happened.*"

Wrik blushes slightly as Delt grins. The look Olivia gives me is more complicated and less subject to interpretation.

"*In another,*" *I hesitate,* "*Wrik and I fight something on a moon beneath the world ahead. Something I did not see, as I was terribly damaged. I beg Wrik to flee, to abandon me, but he will not. My last image is of his raising a laser against our unforeseen foe. Then there is light and terrible heat and we are gone.*"

"*That's it then,*" *Delt says.* "*We go any way but that one.*"

Olivia and to my surprise, Dusko, immediately nod.

I raise a hand. "*I left you all to go to Engineering and concentrate every power I have in analysis. I learned critical information. We are here years earlier than in my visions— at least three years so, possibly more with time dilation—you were older in my vision, Wrik.*"

"*Then there is a chance,*" *Wrik says.*

"*Yes. We are forewarned and forearmed. Whether this will be enough, I do not know. But there is, there must be, a chance.*"

"*One,*" *Dusko says,* "*which may not be worth taking at all, if there is any other course.*"

"*Just as Dusko says,*" *Delt added.*

Olivia shifts. "*Why was the Predictor so forthcoming with you?*"

"*He hoped to live on in me. His own body had deteriorated, and he was nearly as much data as being. I refused, but not without regret.*"

"*Before his death, he said that some people, events and places were nodes that twisted the river of time around them. They change what will and can be.*"

"*You are clearly one of those,*" *Olivia says.*

"*Yes. My instincts tell me that place ahead may be one as well,*" *Wrik adds*

"*We shall see,*" *I reply,* "*though I fear you are correct. Why would the Predictor's ability carry me to such a point if not?*"

"*Did it show any other futures that have not come to pass? That proved false?*" *Wrik asked.*

I hesitate again. "*Yes. It showed me one in which you and Jaelle remain together and I— judging my company unsafe for you—leave. My study of that image indicates it would have occurred one year and fifteen days ago. I could see the night sky. There is no question of the date. That timeline is closed now and never came into being in our reality.*"

"*This ability sounds rather sketchy to me,*" Dusko mutters.

"*It was more accurate in macro events,*" I reply, "*and the Predictor was old and failing when I met him. But when he concentrated on me, he could see me clearly. Still, the river of time is like every other river, it resists containment and alteration.*"

"*Anything else,*" Wrik asks quietly, "*that I should know of what you saw.*"

I look up at him. I will not, I cannot, speak to him of my vision of his death, far in the future, in our home. I will not.

"*No, my dear.*"

He knows I am lying, and he knows why and lets me do it. He merely lifts my hands to his lips for a second.

"*I still say we turn around and fight our way back,*" Delt says. "*It gets us all or has none.*"

"*We don't know that an attack in space is the better choice,*" Dusko answered.

"*The paths ahead and the paths behind may be equally dangerous,*" Olivia said, turning to stare out into space. "*We have our mission for Confed. Going back accomplishes nothing for that. Whatever is out there could find its way into Confed space. Maybe it's not alone either. Imagine that monster on a densely populated, inner world.*"

Dusko waved a dismissive hand. "*Duty, honor planet—it will all come down to what Maauro decides, and she will decide based on what is safest for Wrik. Just as I would do in her place.*"

I smile at him. "*Are we then so much alike?*"

He shrugged. "*In protecting what we value, yes.*"

"*Just so*"

"*But,*" Wrik says, "*as I have said before, I do not exist just to be protected. My life has to have a value beyond that, to be worth my living it. There were over three thousand people on that colony, more on all the ships gone missing and the other worlds. I spent too much time fleeing my fears before. Never again. I say we go forward. There is something waiting for us on the moon beneath the rings. We have to face it.*"

I hang my head. I knew he was going to say this. His grip on my hand tightens. "*I'm sorry. You know I love you more than anything, but I can't do otherwise.*"

"*I know,*" I reply. "*As Olivia said, all paths hold peril now. The one behind may be the worse danger.*"

Now I meet his eyes. "*Whatever happens to us, we will meet it together, stand or fall.*"

"*Yes, all stand or all fall,*" he says.

"*All the way around,*" Delt says, "*stand or fall.*"

"*All for one and one for all,*" Olivia quoted with a lop-sided smile.

CHAPTER NINETEEN

After a moment's silence, Dusko spoke. "Ah, Hells. There is no chance I would make it back on my own anyway. All stand or all fall."

CHAPTER TWENTY

SO WE PROCEED, AGAINST MY WILL, ON COURSE TO THE GAS GIANT *with its horrid rings. I am not yet decided at all on what we will do: slow, use it to boost our speed and look for another jump point, or try to speed back the way we came. As we close in, we see that the three-ringed world has its own system of seven moons, and one indeed is Earth-type, orbiting far enough away not to be scoured by radiation. Winters would be brutal on it, save in its equatorial regions. It will barely make Earth class, but Wrik chortles over the money to be made, as if we were already safely back in Confed space.*

"Well," Olivia said. "Shouldn't we give them names?"

"Yes," Wrik says quickly. "The earth-type world will be called Phoenix."

I look at him, taking the classical reference and smile. We divide up the planets. The three-ringed one is left to Delt by luck of the draw. He calls it Reset and I again appreciate it. Olivia names one moon for her mother, Jana. Wrik names one for his, Eldra. Dusko had to be talked out of naming one Payday, and elects for Breksel which he declines to elaborate on. I name two: Starfall and Daisy after two flowers I like.

I make a special dinner for Olivia that night, with all her favorites, a mute apology for flinging her across the bridge. Though she shrugged it off, I can see stiffness in the way she moves and winces when she thinks no one is looking. Delt has been both solicitous of her, and cool to me since the incident. This is the first time that I have experienced a rift with him, and I find it very painful. The dinner helps, especially as Olivia makes an effort to cheer me up, even slapping me on the shoulder. This seems to reassure Delt, and his stiffness toward me begins to relax.

We rose after a few hours sleep, having moved closer to the massive three-ringed world and our first orbit of Phoenix. Despite the appearance of our own mortal omen, the day started the same, rummaging around for socks and underwear, at least for me. Breakfast was a quiet affair: things were still mending from yesterday's explosion. Afterwards, everyone was on the small bridge, but people were pensive and more than usually polite.

Maauro froze for a second then looked at me. "Wrik, something impossible has just happened."

I turned to her as amazed as any of the others, who, mindful of her earlier outbreak when startled, did not move.

"There is a signal coming from the moon below," she says slowly, as if unable to believe her own words. "It is directed to us both by name."

Now it was my turn to be shocked. "What! How? Who could know we are here?"

Maauro mutely gestured to the main screen. An instant later, a face I had never imagined to see again appeared. The eyes, a chill grey like a winter frost, gazed from a petit face, smooth despite her age, capped with silver hair that almost looked metallic. Madame Ferlan, the Guild-master known as the Collector, gazed down at me.

"Wrik," she said, "where have you been? I've been waiting and waiting." An impish smile crossed the delicate face.

Words failed me and I could only imagine how foolish I looked with my mouth hanging open.

Behind me, I heard Dusko spit something out, doubtless a curse in his native tongue. He too had been a prisoner on her ship the *Hummel*, when we landed on the Infestor artifact, but the strange friendship that had sprung up between Ferlan and I did not include him, and the Dua had suffered more at her hands. Ferlan ignored him.

"You're alive?" I whispered.

"Why yes, I am. I suppose I must thank your Maauro for that. She took up so much of the Infestor Queen's attention that I and a few...too few, of my crew were able to regain the ship, before Maauro did whatever she did, that caused the Artifact to disappear."

Maauro stared at Ferlan with no friendliness in her face. "I tipped it in time and space, so that it plunged out of our dimension of space-time and could no longer threaten us."

"A wise and excellent course of action, my dear," Ferlan said. "I must confess that my overwhelming desire to find out the secrets of the universe rather got the better of me in that adventure. Still, I offer you thanks for my escape."

"You need not," Maauro replied. "I did nothing for your benefit."

"Of course," Ferlan said, with a nod, "yet I am practicing gratitude these days, so I offer the thanks anyway."

Ferlan turned her gaze to me. "And you Wrik, you look fit. My, you have filled out. You are no longer a gangling child. But then something like ten years has passed in the galaxy and what, five or six in your timeline? Star travel plays havoc with time, even without the influence of something as baleful and unexpected as the Artifact."

"How long has it been for you?" I asked, fighting off the sense of unreality gripping me.

"Only a short span of weeks," she returned. "When we reappeared in normal space, we were near this three-ringed world. I decided, especially as we had no idea of any jump points, that we would settle down here and wait; a decision not universally popular with my crew."

"I'm glad you escaped," I blurted out. The others, including Maauro, looked at me in surprise.

Her smile turned indulgent, but there was sadness in her eyes. "You are too kind for the times we live in, Wrik, but thank you. I don't suppose that I ever apologized for kidnapping you and for your treatment aboard, well, before I became fond of you. I tender those apologies now."

"But how?" I asked. "We were a thousand parsecs from here and nearly a decade of galactic time ago. How could you possibly be here?"

"In truth, I do not know. I suspect much however, and it all centers on your lovely Maauro. Oh, congratulations to you both. What a wonderful love story!"

I looked at my lovely Maauro, who looked back at me and gave an expressive shrug. Ferlan had known Maauro and I were close, but back then, Jaelle had been my lover, and even Maauro had no inkling of what was going to happen between us.

Ferlan's musical laugh brought her attention back to her. "Yes, I know something of you two. It may surprise your Maauro, but I do not believe it will surprise you, that I do not want either of you to die here. Perhaps it is the reason I have been spared the fate I all too richly deserve."

"You know!" Maauro cried.

"Yes, dear," Ferlan said, something welling in her eyes for a moment. "I saw your last stand on this moon. I watched as Wrik refused to leave you and raised his weapon. I watched the terrible heat fall on you both. Ah, but it must not happen!"

I don't know what used up my limited supply of surprise, the fact that Ferlan knew everything, or that it caused her such anguish.

"How could you know such things?" Maauro demanded, less charmed by Ferlan's display than I was.

"Well, the universe is a vast mystery, and you, Maauro, may be the most mysterious part of it. I feel somehow that you bend causality itself in your trip through space-time.

"As we lifted, and as space and time convulsed about us, I saw the vision of this place and what happens here. Then the Artifact disappeared, and we spun through something I have no words to describe, then ended up in orbit of this world.

"There is more to tell, but perhaps we can discuss it over tea on my ship."

"I believe," Dusko said sourly, "that the human expression is— 'said the spider to the fly.'"

"I see why they kept you with them," Ferlan said, turning her chilly smile to the Denlenn. "Doubtless Maauro has been reaching across space to cyber-intrude my ship's controls. I will make it easy for her and drop our cyber-protections." She reached off screen. "In moments, she will have access to my ship, certainly enough for you to be secure from any move I would make against you.

"So Wrik, Maauro and Dusko, will you come for tea?"

"Do you have any cake or cookies?" I asked.

Ferlan laughed, delighted. "What Wrik? Have you developed a sweet tooth?"

"Not me, Maauro. A good sweet will go a long way toward improving her opinion of you." From the expression on Maauro's face as she turned to me, it would take a major treat to begin to move that needle.

"Ah, well, so incentivized, I will certainly do my best."

"We will land at 13:41 standard," Maauro said.

"I look forward to meeting you in person," Ferlan replied. Her image faded from the screen.

Silence reigned on the bridge for a few seconds. "Wrik," Maauro said slowly, "I am not sure how many more shocks like this I can stand. I feel like the laws of space time and indeed, of causality, are failing about me. I no longer understand what is real." She walked over and sat in the flight chair next to mine.

I put a hand on her knee. "I'm sure that there is an explanation. We just need more data."

"A lot more data," Delt said.

"Data out the wazoo," Maauro muttered.

A ragged laugh raced round the bridge.

"OK, who the hell is that?" Olivia demanded. "What ship and what is the story!!"

"*Hummel*," I said slowly, "is the home of a High Guild official, Madame Ferlan, also known as the Collector. She'd moved into as much of a retirement as the Guild offered, though she ran enough of her old crime empire through subordinates as she needed to keep the ship in service. Retirement on *Hummel* allowed her to relocate frequently and avoid any who wanted to make her retirement more permanent—while keeping her collection of antiquities and alien artifacts with her. Above all else, Ferlan collects ancient knowledge and secrets. She would have loved to add Maauro to her collection, but believe it or not, she was after even bigger game when she kidnapped Dusko and me. She was after the Infestor Artifact itself."

Maauro picked up the tale from there: the desperate fight in the immense hallways of the ancient hulk, the awakening of the Infestor Queen and the capture of the Collector. As the others digested this, I remembered those bitter, chaotic days in the wrinkle of space that held the vast Infestor Artifact, a ship whose very existence activated Maauro's original programming, returning her to the M-7 warbot she had been made as, and locking her into a suicidal battle with her ancient enemies.

Maauro in return would have cheerfully added Ferlan's head to the wall on *Stardust*. My own feelings toward Ferlan remained conflicted and confused. When she ruthlessly kidnapped us and subjected me to drug interrogation, I'd hated her. Yet somehow, afterward, her solicitude toward me had eased that anger. I'd been given the run of *Hummel*, frequently taking tea with her.

I remembered the night that she revealed that her knowledge of my failure in the skies over Retief. Others had condemned me as a coward. She denied it. I don't know why, but the utter irony of Ferlan being the first to say this to me, had created a strong bond between us. She'd even revealed some of her own past, the death of her son, who had been my age when he died in a Guild operation.

It was a little like having Lucrecia Borgia for a grandmother. Still, I found myself oddly relieved by her survival and almost looking forward to seeing her.

I am losing it, I thought.

I turned to Maauro. "Dare we land?"

"Dare we not?" she countered. "Yet, we must take precautions. Our enemy followed us in. I dare not reach out to see where it is now. I fear it learns too much about me in each contact. It has never reached out to me, or if it does, I am insensible of it. I do not believe that it knows where we are, but it may suspect that we would seek refuge as *Taiko* did, near a gas giant, if and when it detects a world with an Earth-type atmosphere, it may come running."

"We must not be caught on the ground by it," I said.

"Yes, I will launch our two probes into geosynch orbits so that all approaches to the planet are covered. I have recalibrated the sensors to pick up the energy field of the Beast. Having Taiko's readings has made that much easier. It will not sneak up on us, though we may not have more than a few hours warning."

"OK, final approach setup commencing," I said aloud. "Everyone strap in. It'll be the usual."

"Getting blasé," Delt asked, "couple of thousand degrees of reentry and 40,000 kph approach just not exciting enough for you?"

"Excitement has not been an issue this trip," I said, with a rueful grin.

We roared into the chilly blue skies of Phoenix. Somehow, it always seemed that each Earth-type world had its own unique palette of colors. The blues were never quite the same.

"Ferlan has been as good as her word," Maauro said. "I am in all of *Hummel's* systems, including her extensive, internal security apparatus. A crew of fifteen and Ferlan are aboard. I have disabled all weapons and control the intruder control systems. The crew's personal weapons are more difficult, however I have ordered all Guilders, save one, to remain on the mess deck or face immediate termination. My orders are being complied with. The one will meet us on the ramp."

"Tell me, Maauro," Dusko said, "is one of the Guild survivors, a simian-looking creature called, Maurice?"

"Yes," she answered, giving him a curious look.

"Well, that was too much to hope for," I said.

"Seems so," Dusko sighed.

Maauro's expression hardened and she turned to me. "Is this someone I should kill?"

The question, posed so casually, struck a chill in me. I knew she would do it. "No."

"Yes," Dusko said.

We looked at each other.

"Not yet," I amended.

"Very well," Maauro said, "I will watch this one with special attention."

Dusko made a face.

The landing approach was no worse than usual, just feeling longer because of all the mysteries at the bottom of this particular gravity well. But we thundered over small oceans filled with islands, heading for the wild uplands where the Collector had landed. We came over grasslands, then a delta broken by small rivers, the largest of which tracked toward the mountains where *Hummel* had landed. This had the air of a high desert, a chaparral where a few stunted trees and coarse bushes dotted the land.

I made a pass over the *Hummel's* landing site.

"There she is," Maauro called and flipped up a real-time image of the *Hummel* and zoomed it.

"That's a base she's landed near," Olivia said, "about eleven kilometers away."

"Guild?" Dusko demanded, alert as usual for treachery.

"No," Maauro said. "It is old and covered in blast damage and erosion. Cursory inspection indicates that it is a minor military installation from a space-faring race not native to this world, or we would have detected vastly more evidence of civilization from higher orbit. Given natural conditions, I would say this base was attacked some 112 to 117 years ago."

"Rounded off," I said.

Maauro rolled her eyes, but smiled. "Rounded off."

"That means yet another new species out here somewhere," Olivia said, eyes flicking around as if the newcomers might spring on her, "interplanetary, or more likely interstellar, given the lack of radio and signal laser traffic in this system."

"Or," Dusko said, "possibly blown out of existence, or at least of space travel, as Seddon was."

Delt sighed. "You forgot to add, that the Beast could have eaten their civilization, to your catalog of possible disasters."

"A good point," Dusko said. "We don't know how long the Beast has been rampaging in Piola sector. It may have been here before us."

This time it was Delt who rolled his eyes.

"No sign of significant damage to *Hummel's* exterior," Maauro added, ignoring the byplay. "There is some cosmetic damage, but she appears flyable."

"Then why are they here?" Dusko said grimacing.

"You do not credit her story that she was waiting for us?" Maauro asked,

"Bah," he said, "it's madness to believe her."

"Any less mad then seeing *Hummel* here in the first place?" I asked

Dusko could only grunt a response and stare sourly at the freighter grounded below us.

The prosaic, white and gray hull of the large roll on/roll off freighter, sat, leveled by her landing jacks, on a broad shelf of granite, not far from the wide, shallow, river that bubbled over exposed rocks. Maauro had drawn the landing information directly from *Hummel's* databanks, but we used our own sensor suite to guard against treachery or, for that matter, incompetence. It was way more wasteful of fuel to dry land *Hummel*, which often would land in water, but she was in far less danger from unstable ground than the vertical *Stardust*. So I carefully pulled my ship to vertical and settled down about three hundred meters away from the *Hummel*.

Stardust's interior, which in places shifted from the horizontal plane to vertical as she landed, hummed as the planetside changes took place. We settled on our own landing jacks, which adjusted to level us. After a few seconds, I eased off the last of the power, leaving the ship solid to the ground. It took fifteen minutes to secure to planetside routine with even the abbreviated version of that.

Meanwhile, I studied *Hummel*. It seemed the crew lived aboard ship, but there were a pair of pipes leading to the river, doubtless for water and sewage. They had not set up homesteading, but had prepared for an extended stay.

"OK," I said, "Maauro and I going over to deal with Ferlan."

"As am I," Olivia said.

"Delt, I'd like to leave you at the controls."

"Why? I'm not going anywhere until you're back on the ship. Maauro's AI can run the ship anyway."

I looked at Dusko. He grinned. "I'll happily mind the store. Give my regards to the ape-man."

"Yeah," I said, "everyone into arms and armor, just in case."

Fifteen minutes later, the airlock doors rolled open and the smells of an alien world greeted us as the cold air bit at our exposed faces. Maauro simply leapt from the airlock door to the ground below. The rest of us, wishing to use our knees and ankles in the future, rode the small elevator down. Delt, showing off as usual, wrapped his legs around the fireman's pole that ran alongside the elevator and slid down.

We were armed to the teeth as we stepped off onto the gritty soil of this new world. From the open hold above us, three crab robots deployed down the side of the ship, using cargo and hoisting points to reach the ground. They took up positions between us and the Hummel, but their weapons were pointed skyward, as if there was no threat on *Hummel*, that we needed to take notice of. I hoped they were right.

The sun stood high in the sky, far smaller than in Earth's sky. It gave only a weak, wintery light, illumination with little warmth. We were all glad for the heating element in our clothes, and the gloves we wore, though the thin covering over trigger fingers let the chill in. On the opposite side of the sky, thirty degrees of arc were taken up with the crescent of the gas giant, its colors washed away by the blue sky. The three rings showed clearly, even in daylight, and Maauro gave them an angry and worried look.

Our feet crunched on alien soil, tan and gray, with scruffy grass, daisy-like flowers and something that looked like a circular cactus, as we approached the open front ramp of *Hummel*.

Hummel's exterior showed no signs of the treasures hidden within. She was several times the length of Stardust and many times the bulk, a type often made into auxiliary merchant cruisers in war time. I knew that she had missile racks and railguns hidden inside, but Maauro had control of these now as we approached. Maauro led, with me on her right and Delt on her left. Olivia trailed us.

A figure moved out of the shadows of *Hummel's* giant maw.

"Well, well mes amis," Maurice's voice boomed. "I bet you did not plan to see me again?" The apish human, easily six-feet tall, wore a long-sleeved sweater that showed his bulging muscles. He wore his usual incongruous black beret over his shaven skull, and his small eyes glared at us in contempt, over his bristling mustache. His belt was noticeable, empty of weapons, a condition Maauro had no doubt set.

"I'd happily pass on seeing your ugly mug again," I returned evenly. My hand was not far from the butt of my laser. The long-armed Guilder was one of the strongest humans I'd ever met, and even unarmed I was wary of him. Still, I had come too far, through too much, to cringe before the Guilder. We walked up the ramp, and I hated having to look up at him.

His eyes flicked to my hip as if to say my courage rode there.

"Who's the monkey?" Delt asks, pausing a pace away from Maurice. His stance was easy, loose and able to punch in a second.

Maauro interrupted the simmering cauldron of resentment and anger. "He is of no consequence, an underling."

She met his black stare with unconcern. "You will remain silent unless I bid you speak. Disobey me and I will render you incapable of speech, likely permanently. Do not think for a moment that your part in our past troubles is forgotten or forgiven. Take us to Ferlan. Now."

Maurice's jaw muscles clenched, but he was smart enough to keep his response behind his teeth rather than risk losing them. He spun on his heel, and we followed him into the ship. A plastic curtain hung inside the overhead, sufficient to keep the weather out and most of the heat in, while the ramp was down. We pushed between the plastic slats into the ship proper. The cavernous hold behind had been full of combat cars and transports for the expedition into the Artifact. None had returned and our footfalls echoed. We took a short stairwell to the next deck and then walked aft. I remembered the way to Ferlan's hall near the center of the ship. All we heard was the humming of blowers, most of the huge crew had met the same fate as the vehicles. Ferlan had said only fifteen had survived, it was not enough to run so large a vessel for long. I noticed that some sections were unlit and that yellow lights glowed on some indicators. Hummel was not the healthiest of ships.

Finally, we reached the corridor outside Ferlan's hall. The door was open and lights glowed inside. Maurice walked in. To my surprise, he did not greet her as he had usually done before and merely faded to the side of the room. Olivia kept an eye on Maurice, though with Maauro in the room, it was hardly necessary. Still, I did not discourage her.

We went down the other side of the huge, ornate wooden table and the chairs, locked down in their tracks so they wouldn't be flung around during high-G maneuvers. One chair was neither delicate, nor ornate, and made of metal, clearly intended for Maauro. At the far end, in her red-damasked chair, Ferlan sat. The tiny woman, wearing a gray dress with a short cloak over it, rose. The light reflected off the metallic silver of her short haircut and the cool grey eyes. I did not know how old Ferlan was, she was a mutant and age didn't sit hard on her. She was slender, but did not appear frail. Her face was smooth, though the skin did have the papery look of age.

"Greetings and welcome all," she said, "please have a seat." She glanced at Maurice, who stared impassively back. At a gesture from her, he left the room to return, moments later, with a small cart he wheeled back to the table, placing it by her elbow.

"Thank you, Maurice," she said. "You may leave. I will call for you if I need you."

He grunted and, without a backward look at us, left the room.

Maauro stood behind the chair intended for her. Her expression was blank. This in itself was a warning she was in no good temper.

"Oh dear," Ferlan said, "you're still quite cross with me, aren't you? Wrik, perhaps you could intercede on my behalf and request a small dose of forgiveness?"

"Should I?" I replied.

"Please. I promise no more tricks, no more issues. I no longer wish to collect anything for myself or for the Guild. I am just an old woman on a damaged ship, far from home."

"The day has not dawned that you are helpless," I returned.

She smiled, seeming glad for a little of our old wordplay. "Well, I did not say that now, did I?"

"Let's sit," I said to Maauro. "She does make an excellent cup of tea."

Maauro sat, and the rest of us arranged ourselves around the table. Delt looked like he wanted to put his laser on the table. I gave a minute shake of the head. He grimaced and put the weapon back in its holder.

"My staff is considerably reduced," Ferlan said. "So with your permission, I shall play the part of mother."

She moved to the cart and drew out a unique cup for each of us. Each one seemed to have some connection with the person it was set before. Maauro's cup was metal and ancient in appearance, with some gems built into its handle that seemed to wax and wane in brilliance. Delt's cup was a sturdy clay mug, brown and with unknown glyph's molded in it. Olivia's was a radical shape, somewhere between a flute and cup, with a black and white pattern that rose, flower-like about its structure.

Mine was similar to Ferlan's own, a white and royal blue cup and saucer, limned in gold. Her own was the more delicate and feminine.

Ferlan placed several small plates of white cakes on the table, then began to pour the tea from a beautiful red, white and gold pot. We all waited in bemused silence as she did so.

"This is a fine charaku tea, not suitable for milk, I am afraid. You need not fear anything in the tea or cakes. Ms. Maauro has already sampled air molecules from them for safety's sake, I am sure. And if not, I give her leave to do so by any means she chooses." She finished by pouring for herself. It seemed the Collector was using her collection to its fullest.

"Ah," she said, sitting with a sigh. "Now we have tea and refreshments and may discuss things like civilized people."

She and I sipped her tea, while the others just stared at their cups, until Maauro took a sip of tea and reached for a small cake.

"How remarkable you are," Ferlan said, watching Maauro nibble her cake, "a living machine, one capable of emotion, even that most complicated and novel one, love. Why, compared to you, my entire collection is mere dross."

Maauro cocked her head at her. "You realize that I am not an object to be collected."

"Of course," Ferlan replied, raising her hand. "You are a person. Though there are some who collect people in the Guild, I was never one such. Beyond that, I incurred your enmity once and only barely survived. Even then, I was not your target. You battled the Infestors and, while it is a sting to my vanity, I was never more than a distraction to you."

"True," Maauro said, "but for Wrik's presence among your convoy, I would have destroyed you quickly. However, I note, but do not understand that your survival, if not that of your crew, pleases my boyfriend.

I can only conclude that he found some merit to you that has eluded me to this point."

"Well," Ferlan said, raising her delicate cup, "I am glad you are open to the idea that I might have some merit." Ferlan's smile was unforced, even playful.

"You're different," I said. Everyone turned toward me.

"Well, Wrik, you are certainly not a coward—is it not possible that I should cease being a villain?"

I scratched the back of my head. "I have rebuilt my life on the faith that a person can change."

"For me," Ferlan said, her eyes distant and contemplative, "I feel as if I am in a different life entirely, or perhaps a purgatory, where I must atone for what my life was, before I am allowed to move on. Little of what has passed before has any meaning for me. I am like a ghost, working on my last great regret. I did tell you, just before what I thought was the end, how much I regretted forcing a conflict between us, Miss Maauro."

Maauro considered, covering this with a brief sip of her tea. "Just, Maauro. Yes, you did. While I am not one for forgiveness, I will forgo our former enmity."

Ferlan nodded her head. "I am grateful. I will give you no cause for regret."

For a second I thought Maauro might say, 'better not' but, in apparent deference to Ferlan's sophistication, passed.

"So," I began, "please continue the story about how you are here, halfway across a galactic arm from where we saw you last, a prisoner of Infestors."

"Let me begin at the beginning," Ferlan said. "When you escaped the surface of the Infestor Artifact in your *Stardust*, the Infestors had overwhelmed the survivors of my command with their mental control. They wanted my ship and sent myself and most of the command crew, helpless automatons all, in an elevator and boarding tube to the *Hummel*.

"When we entered the bridge, we were quite exhausted from running. The Infestors had no care for our bodies, and my own heart felt like it was about to seize. Anyway, their Queen's control wavered. Clearly, it was preoccupied by you, or maybe had realized what you had done to its stardrive. We had barely time to reach our chairs and fire the engines, with no more direction than up.

"We cleared the artifact's surface, but not the effect of whatever Maauro did to it. You saw this, I imagine."

I nodded and sipped my tea. Maauro said nothing.

"As I have mentioned, I am a mutant of an old Terran stock and an esper in a minor way. It is more a talent for telling for what others are feeling, rather than mind-reading. I often sense dangers before they strike, though I confess this utterly failed me on the Artifact. Perhaps the Infestors were simply too different to sense.

"In any event, in the moments before the Artifact vanished, we were caught in its wake and, well, I was thinking of your Wrik: the small kindnesses you had showed me—an enemy, of how...of how you reminded me of my own lost son. I was thinking of how foolish and selfish I had become with my absurd collecting.

"As I thought of you, a vision came of the awful day of your final stand over a fallen Maauro. Then the vision changed and I was touched by a mind so alien to my own that I could barely comprehend it. This was the Predictor. Its mind was bent on you, Maauro, in the vast disturbance that you had caused in causality, the ripples had reached through something that is not space-time, and caused it to see you."

"You saw the Predictor?" Maauro asked. If an android could look surprised, she did.

"Yes. But it seemed that I was swept along by the power of this Predictor. Perhaps the tremendous power of the Predictor is what saved us. It may have tunneled through space-time and causality to bring us here. Somehow, I have been given a part in your and Wrik's fate. I cannot say anything of the how or the why."

"Nor can I," Maauro said slowly, as if still caught up in disbelief.

"My circumstances are much reduced," Ferlan added. "I have this ship, but it is undermanned and our armaments are only slightly greater than what your scoutship boasts. Yet, we are here. Even I, great cynic that I am, cannot believe that my escape from death, and being cast across a decade and a thousand parsecs, is mere chance."

Maauro met her eyes. "Are you then an agent of God?"

"They say that he moves in mysterious ways," Ferlan returned. "What could be more mysterious than to use an old villain like myself?"

"Do you have any knowledge of our enemy," I asked, "anything that can help us?"

"No, Wrik. I saw nothing more than the two of you did. Nor have we found any relevant information on this world. We have explored the old base, eleven kilometers away. There were some interesting artifacts, but nothing that seemed to pend on our situations. The base was owned by an unknown species, humanoid, from an image that we found among the ruins; they look like hairless humans. We have found no information on what destroyed the base, which is far more extensive then seen from space.

"I am here," she said, spreading her hands, "and you are free to make such use of me, or my assets as you can." She cast an eye at Maauro, who had started a second cake, "even if it is only as a baker."

Tea, cake and conversation consumed hours, but yielded no plan. We briefed Ferlan on the nature of our enemy. She didn't whistle, but her pursed lips made it look like she might. She shook her head in amazement.

"If you are right, that it must become much more material when entering the atmosphere of an earth type planet," Ferlan mused, "then we may be safer here on the ground, than in space. A direct assault into your nuclear torpedoes would clearly be dangerous to it, or so I guess, but perhaps my thinking is too conventional."

"It matches my own thinking," Maauro said. "Our conventional weapons are apt to be most effective in this environment, which is why I accepted our planeting. I have taken control of your weapons and slaved them to my fire control. It will substantially increase our firepower, and we have the crabs outside as well."

"Well," Ferlan said, finally, rising. "You young folk may have more that you wish to do, or talk of, but I find myself a bit weary. You have given me a vast amount of data to study, and in return, all that I know of ancient mysteries is laid bare for you, Maauro. I will think on all you have downloaded, perhaps another day's sunrise will bring us additional wisdom. Meanwhile, unless you wish to guest on *Hummel*, may I suggest you return to your ship. Darkness comes early and the cold is bitter. I wish to secure *Hummel* for the night."

We declined the offer of a night on her ship, which I thought disappointed her slightly. The silent Maurice reappeared and escorted us back to the ramp. None of us spoke to the Guilder. He'd already sealed the ramp, and we exited from a small access lock next to it. Ferlan had been accurate in her forecast. The sun was westering into shadows, silhouetted by mountains. Above and to the east the gas giant and its rings glowed in a beauty even Maauro could not deny.

But we had little leisure for sights. The cold was severe already, despite the auto heat elements in our clothes. We hurried back to *Stardust*, coming back with as many questions or more, than we had set out with.

Later, I lay on our bed, my head buzzing with all that we had learned from Ferlan and our fears of the Beast, somewhere in the system with us. *Stardust* was on a thirty minute standby for liftoff. Maauro's inspection told us that *Hummel* could not be brought up to such standard, but had to stand ready with a four hour liftoff clock.

"Impossibilities abound," Maauro said, from where she stood at the plast-steel port, looking out at the running lights of the *Hummel*. "How am I to plan for eventualities when causality seems ripped like an old sheet?"

"Causality rips," I said, snapping my fingers and sitting upright.

"What?" Maauro asked.

"All the multiple impossibilities that have erupted around us," I continued, as the idea crystallized in my head, "have two elements in common, you and a rip in causality.'

She cocked her head at me. "I do not understand. What are you saying?"

"Three impossible things have happened around you. First, is your own existence, a living machine, not merely an AI. We don't know when the spark that made you more occurred, but it occurred in Vance system, where the Murch used their transdimensional drive, when they arrived millennia ago and crashed. Perhaps they came out of trans-dimensional space near the asteroid where you lay all those years."

"It's possible, Wrik, but there is no shred of evidence for it."

"Follow along with me," I insisted. "The next impossible thing occurred when you tipped the Infestor Artifact into transdimensional space, using what you learned of the Murch technology."

She nodded.

"Perhaps, when causality ripped the second time, the Predictor, what did you say his name was?"

"Agrille."

"Perhaps Agrille detected you then. Maybe he realized that you would be a significant factor in his future and that of his entire species, wrapped up in causality as you are. The Collector, who we now know is an esper, was also present, herself already in a battle with a vastly more powerful esper, the newborn Infestor Hive Queen. And all of us were caught in that wrinkle in space-time in which the Artifact had hid itself. When the Artifact disappeared to wherever it was going, the Collector's ship blasted off on another vector.

"At that moment, with the Predictor focused on you, and causality itself failing, Ferlan may have seen this world and our fate on it. That might have been enough to bring her here, possibly altering the time line so we came to this place, a place the Predictor described as a 'node' one of those that could bend the river of time around you."

"So," Maauro said, with an ironic air. "You think that the rips in causality caused by the two times the Murch drive was used in our dimension, set up a chain of events that led to my becoming what I am and tied the Collector to our fate?"

"And possibly altered the time line to where we arrived here years early. We may actually owe her our lives. It holds together and makes sense."

"With not a shred of evidence? Without a single verifiable fact?" Maauro's tone was incredulous. "I have been surprised by your ability to find patterns in the absence of evidence before, but honestly...."

"Well," I said, blushing, "we do have some evidence, observations of what has happened, if nothing else. Unless you're telling me you want to believe in coincidence?"

"No," she said firmly, while walking over to me. "Even for me a super-computer, calculating the odds is almost insurmountable, essentially a googolplex to one. Very well then, even without verifiable evidence, we will accept your theory as a working theory, but it's not very scientific."

"I'll tell you something else that isn't very scientific. When the Murch first emerged in our universe, I think they brought in an element of non causality, a bit of magic if you will. You are that magic."

She smiled widely. "Ok, Wrik, that was poetic."

I stroked her hair. "I have my moments."

"What are we to do with this newfound font of knowledge that you have discovered?"

"I was thinking of making love to the magical part of it."

Maauro slid onto the bed next to me. "Good thinking."

CHAPTER TWENTY ONE

I N THE MORNING, MENTALLY RECOVERED FROM THE IMPOS-
sibilities of the prior day, we held a counsel of war aboard *Stardust*.
I could not help feeling oppressed by time and the roof of the sky
over us. Somewhere beyond the blue, death was hunting for us.

Ferlan attended. I went and fetched the elderly Guildmaster and
brought her to our ship. Maurice clearly didn't like it, but was in no
position to dispute me. We looked stone-faced at each other as Ferlan,
bundled in expensive, warm clothes and furs, rested a delicate hand on
my arm and followed me down the ramp to our ship.

"Ah," she said. "So cold, and I do so hate the cold, but I should not
complain. By any rights, I should be long dead. Now, I may even have a
last chance to do some good in the world."

I gave her a lop-sided smile. "Curious ambition for a Guild
chieftain."

"Perhaps," she said. "But now at the end of my life I find myself only
interested in things that may give me peace in the long rest, if there is
anything after."

She looked up at me. "Do you believe in an afterlife, Wrik?"

"I do, in a nonspecific way. I've never found an answer in any church,
but I guess I can't understand the purpose of our existence if this one
life is all there is to it. I guess one might as well believe, given the fact
that if there is no afterlife, we'll never know it."

She chuckled. "How very sensible of you, I suppose I should adopt
your point of view."

We traveled the rest of the distance in amiable silence and both
entered the warmth of Stardust riding up on the open, unrailed elevator
holding to the stability pole. The others awaited us in the galley. Dusko
and Ferlan eyed each other and settled on mere nods. Maauro gestured
at a chair at the galley table before which steamed a cup of tea.

"Ah," Ferlan said. "How thoughtful, thank you."

"It is only a common tea," Maauro said.

"No matter, some things are common because they are so good that
many recognize the virtue in them," Ferlan said.

Delt handed me a cup of coffee.

We settled in around the table.

"Whatever we are to do," I said. "Speed is clearly needed. We can't
remain onworld, risking the Beast catching us on the ground. We know
that it can handle a 1G field easily enough, but it is leery of higher gravity. We've tossed a nuke at it in jumpspace, which hurt it, but not much.
We have no idea of how close that weapon was went it went off. It fought

a heavy cruiser, again hurt, this time by direct-fire energy weapons. But each time it has had an ace in the hole, a hole we believe is its connection with jumpspace, something that allows it to hide its essential life force in a pocket of jumpspace proof against our weapons.

"The answer," Maauro said, "seems to be gravity, or a combination of gravity and radiation. The creature abandoned its pursuit of *Taiko* when it assumed low orbit of a super gas giant which had abundant supplies of both. It went so far as to even venture out of the system, looking for easier prey, destroying *Fetch III* in a fit of pique. It may have used its telepathic power to keep track of *Taiko*, or it may have just lost interest for a while.

"Is it keeping track of you?" Ferlan asked.

"I do not believe so," Maauro said. "I am a different form of life, with no subconscious mind to access. All of my thought is conscious volition, and I believe this allows me to control whether we become aware of each other. I shielded myself far better in the second encounter, though the experience is one of the most distasteful of my existence, worse by far than being in contact with the Infestors."

"So it does not know where we are, only that we preceded it to this system."

"Can it pick up on those of us that it has not contacted before?" Olivia wondered.

"Again, I do not believe so," Maauro said. "This is just an interpretation of its actions, I have no way to be sure, but it did not seem aware that there were others on this ship. Once my connection with it was shut off, it seemed to lose track of us. I believe that in normal space its sensor capacities are similar to ours."

"Then why not launch and try and get past it to the jump point," Olivia said. "It's a big system; it can't look for us and guard the jump point. We've found a marginal earthlike moon in orbit of a gas giant. Our preliminary scans shows there were two worlds inward of us in the Goldilocks zone. Won't it search there first?"

I shook my head. "We don't know if either is an earth-type world, spectrometry showed some oxygen on both, but that doesn't make either one livable. We can't discount that the Beast may have come this way heading for the Piola sector. It may know this system far better than we. We can't count on it to move the way we want it to."

"More caution," Olivia sighed. "Consider taking the initiative for once."

I raised an eyebrow. "When we need a bayonet charge, I'll call you."

We stared at each other for a moment. In the background, Delt sighed. Maauro and Dusko just looked at the table top."

"So if we launch an attack in open space," Olivia said, returning to the main subject, "it's not likely to work, unless we can lure it near a super giant."

"As a solid object in 1G field it would also be more vulnerable." Delt said, running his hand through his blonde hair. "Maybe destroying the part of it that is in our space-time suffices for our purposes."

"Still leaves it haunting the jumpspace lanes," Dusko said, "most notably ours on the way out of this system."

I sighed. "One could wish for the Skurlock gravity weapon."

Olivia snorted. "Sure, got a black hole and a technology that disappeared down the same?"

I looked at Maauro. "You must have all the records of the gravity lens the Skurlock used—"

"Yes, but Wrik, that technology was lost. Though I could reverse engineer some of the principles, it required a black hole from the collapse of a thirty-four times Sol-size star to power it. There is no answer there."

"Or is there?" I said. "Vast black holes are rare but every starship generates a small singularity with its drive when it enters jump space, the same thing that gives us artificial gravity."

"I see where you are going," Maauro said, with that pleased look she had when I was being clever. "Yes, a ship generates a small singularity in the attenuated field density of a jumpspace entrance, but how would it help us here?"

"The higher the field density," I said slowly, "the more difficult the calculations for maintaining a singularity. It's considered impossible over 1.73Gs, but we are in a 1G field here. Maauro can you do the calculations and stabilize a singularity on the ground?"

"Theoretically, to do the actual calculation to see if it is possible I must divert most of my power to the question. Forty-three minutes should do for a calculation, but to do it for real, I would have to be in the engine room of a ship, adjusting the controls from microsecond to microsecond. A singularity in this much field density is too unstable to last without such control, it will become unstable and implode."

"Well, I don't see where you are going," Olivia said, with asperity.

"A singularity drive going out of control would generate a huge blast," I said. "We don't use them for bombs because they don't do anything that you can't do easier with a regular nuke or even a dropped asteroid. The one thing it would do that a normal weapon wouldn't is generate an intense local gravity field."

Delt snapped his fingers. "A combination of bear trap and landmine."

"Yes," I said. "Horribly dangerous to use, if it is even possible. But, if we can fix it in place by a sudden application of gravity in the middle of an explosion, we might kill it."

"It is the best chance," Maauro added.

"If it is possible," Ferlan said. "One presumes you will use my ship."

"You'll let us?" I asked.

Ferlan gave me an ironic smile as if to say, *how nice of you to preserve the fiction that you must ask*. "I am sure it will not be a popular decision with my crew, but never-the-less I make the ship yours."

"I see where you are going," Maauro said. "If I can work out the math, balance the drive field long enough for us to lure the Beast in and then explode it."

"The plan is mad," Delt said heatedly. "Maauro luring it down. She'd have to stay at the reactor controls until the last few minutes. Wrik, you're not giving yourself much of a safety margin."

"We cannot afford to," Maauro argued. "We have one strike at the Beast and must maximize our attack. Blasts will not injure it without the paralyzing effect of gravity preventing it from withdrawing into jumpspace. There is no matter, as such, in jumpspace underlying our spacetime. It may be able to retreat directly from the planet's surface. We must gain every fraction of G that we can."

"Which would leave us with a shipful of Guilders if you don't succeed in escaping," Olivia said, "not to be selfish or anything."

"An unpleasant prospect," Dusko agreed.

Everyone looked at him.

"What?" he added. "They're no friends of mine."

"And we are?" Olivia said, eyeing him narrowly, arms crossed.

"As long as Maauro lives," he relied, "I have no other Alpha. The Guild has repeatedly failed against her, and these certainly aren't a match for her. Hell, I don't think they're a match for her shipboard AI."

"Good to know," I said dryly

"I cannot see another way of doing it," Maauro said. "While *Hummel* is as computerized as any other ship, she was designed to be used by living beings and is not fully automated. Nor do we have time to alter her that much. Even if we could, her computer systems are not capable of the reaction speed required. We cannot afford any atmospheric distortions, or electromagnetic effects, interrupting my control from a distance. I must be near the instruments."

"Regrettably, I believe you are correct," Ferlan said. "None of my more expendable people can handle the calculations even with a pre-prepared computer. This is beyond our computer science, at least with what we have here. Nor would they be eager, or willing. Willing could be overcome, but a lack of alacrity, no"

"In any event, it is so far beyond biological capability as to be unworthy of further consideration," Maauro added.

"We'll have to move the remaining Guilders aboard," I said. "I won't maroon even Guilders this far out. So get them settled, Dusko. They will have access to their bottom hold cabins, galley and sickbay. They go anywhere else the ship AI will let them have it."

Dusko nodded and left.

After Dusko left, Ferlan turned to look at Olivia. "You realize that should Maauro die, you must immediately kill Dusko."

"What?" Delt said. "Oh, come on. He's—"

"Yes, I know," Olivia said.

"In fact you should dispose of all of us," Ferlan added.

"Very altruistic of you," Olivia said, looking sidewise at her.

"I have no illusions about the value of my crew to the universe at large. As for me, I am an old woman. Should Maauro and Wrik die, I will have failed in the purpose for which I believe I was spared. There will be no reason for me to linger further in the universe. And I cannot imagine that a practical young woman, like the major has not already considered such a detail like myself."

"Detail?" Olivia said with a wolfish smile. "You're the one real danger on *Hummel*."

Ferlan smiled coolly back. "Don't underestimate Maurice. He only looks like a gorilla."

"Not so keen on your former team?" Delt snapped.

"I'm Guild," Ferlan replied. "We have few saints and many sinners in our ranks."

I stirred, breaking the lethargy that threatened to overcome me. "I don't care what you do with the others, particularly Maurice, but I would take it as a personal favor if we don't make it back, that you give Madame Ferlan a lift back to civilization."

Ferlan gave me a bemused look.

"For old time's sake," I said with a shrug. I turned to Maauro. "And Dusko?"

"He goes home, too," Maauro stated, in a voice that brooked no argument. "If I am gone, you must recognize that his nature as a Dua is that he will be a free agent. Attach him to you, Olivia, you are strong and ruthless enough."

"That's enough," Delt said, standing. To my surprise, he looked as angry as I'd seen him.

Maauro looked up startled.

"You're making plans to fail and to die," he snapped. "That's not what we're going to do here. We are going to whip this thing, and then we're going home." His eyes locked with mine. "Do you have that, Ncome?"

His use of our squadron name took my breath away. For a second, I was eighteen again, looking at Delt and the other members of our doomed squadron, back before Delt had ever lost anything, back before we knew fear. I swallowed. "Yes, Squadron Leader."

"Delt," Maauro began, "we must be realistic—"

He turned his hot gaze on her. "Do you have that, Ncome?"

Maauro hesitated. I knew she treasured that Delt had made her an honorary member of Ncome, then, "Yes, Squadron Leader."

He faced Olivia, who, seeming to like what she saw, simply nodded.

"When we flew in here we all made a decision," Delt continued, "all stand or all fall. I meant it when I said it. I led a group of people into danger once and I didn't bring most of them back. It's not happening a second time. We either upship together, or *Stardust* stands guard over our bones, and no other way.

"As for you," he said to Ferlan, "Wrik says you ride home with us, so you do, and that's an end of it. I don't much care for Guild, but if the others behave, they ride back too. They don't and they get spaced. That goes double for the monkey-man. Don't like him anyway.

"Is everyone now clear on what the rest of this expedition is going to look like?" he demanded.

Everyone, including Ferlan, nodded.

Ferlan's announcement that a monster was coming, and that *Hummel* would be expended in an attempt to destroy it, did not go over well with her remaining crew. Maauro's presence at her side, and my promise that they would ride back in *Stardust*, reduced it to dark looks.

Darkest among those looks was Maurice, whose expression, before he shuttered it, was a mix of surprise, anger and, I felt, betrayal. His only comment was to ask for a power line to be extended to *Hummel*. Their auxiliary power reactor was fluctuating and he wanted to shut it down for repair. We didn't need the APU for the plan, but we had no idea how long it would be before we encountered the Beast. Hummel needed to be kept livable and in case our plans changed, flyable. Maauro and one of the crabs ran a heavy duty power cable from the exterior coupling of our ship to theirs.

Ferlan's collection began moving into *Stardust*, carefully and under Maauro's supervision, though the grunt work of shifting it fell on the Guilders. They seemed jealous of this privilege, probably knowing that her prospects for reestablishing herself in the Confederacy and possibly still needing her retainers, rested with the treasure house. Much of the collection are small artifacts, some of which would be ancient even by Maauro's standards. She and the Collector seemed to enjoy discussing the particulars of the oldest artifacts, especially the ones whose purposes and origins were the least understood.

I did not move the Guilders into *Stardust* yet, not wanting the security risk. This meant that though Maauro and Ferlan chose and decorated a cabin for the elderly Guilder, she remained on the Hummel, offering at least some assurance that the others would be taken off when she herself left. It seemed a low cost alternative to having to watch fifteen Guild operatives, particularly Maurice.

The prospect of a long voyage back to the Confederacy with him aboard did not cheer me, but I kept this to myself. In the presence of the Guilders, Maauro was her stern warbot self, mechanical and abrupt, and I found that oddly disconcerting now. I knew that a request from me would end the apeman's existence, but what concerned me was, if I displayed too much unease in his presence, she might act on her own. Despite all she had learned and grown through, when Maauro felt there was a reason to kill, she simply killed. I didn't want that for her, so I kept my peace around the Guilder and ignored him as much as possible. Wary of Maauro, he did the same. With these preparations made, Maauro retreated to Engineering, going so far as to lock them down. "These calculations are almost as monstrous as the thing chasing us," she'd said. "I cannot afford any diversion of processing power if I am to solve them."

I sit in the Engineering room and once again secure myself to the floor, placing a power tap on my midsection to draw directly from the main reactor. The calculations I must do are on a level that I have rarely tried before, even more complicated than the ones I used when we set out to find Sedon and rescue Shasti's grandchild. I shut down as many exterior connections and awareness as I can; I will be working well into the subatomic, even into theoretical levels. As I do not know if the task is even possible, I cannot estimate the time out of contact with the world.

I do not like leaving my crew on their own for so long, but neither the Guild nor the Beast will know of my incapacity. Should the monster appear on the scanners, Wrik will rouse me. We are maintaining a thirty minute lift capacity, which is keeping the biologicals busy. Hummel's crew will be ready to flee to our ship in those thirty minutes, or be left behind.

I plunge into a universe of abstruse mathematics and physics, some of which I am inventing. Failure after failure follows. Time passes as virtual experiments take place in me. The engineering spaces heat up as my casing does, which is extraordinary, given my cooling capacity. Finally a solution presents itself, but it is a very tentative one, amazingly dependent on the physical qualities of the Hummel's structure.

I extend my consciousness through the power tap that we arranged to carry some of the load, with Hummel's APU off line. I study the engine's interior. Relief, her reactor power core is in excellent shape and durable enough for my plans. Yet, the ship itself is too crude, its computer systems and control systems incapable, as I feared, of the near instant responses that will be required to maintain and then explode a star drive on the surface of a world. Without such control, the drive will merely fizzle. I could control the systems directly by routing them through me, but then there would not be enough time to escape.

This brings up the other flaw in the plan. I must attract and compel the Beast to attack me. I had planned to stay on the ship as long as possible, then flee outside to where Wrik would wait with the flitter. We could escape to the base north of our landing – there is a large underground hanger in which we can hope to ride out the resulting gravity-implosion.

But the enemy might detect me relocating. I am unsure if it can attack electronic links but, given its nature, I believe it can. How then to both maintain control and make it seem as if I remain inside Hummel?

I must do something I have not done before. Stardust's AI is a tiny subset of myself, really just improved programs and machinery. Now, I must create a virtual me to exist inside of Hummel. It will not be a full copy, only another full M-7 could contain such a thing, indeed it would be a mere 1.0347% of what I am. That will require me to overwrite and displace virtually every system on Hummel. She will become literally a shell with a stardrive. I set about the creation of this subprogram. I can send it through the powertap to Hummel but it will take hours to install as the Hummel's systems simply could not take the update quicker. I can only hope we are not attacked sooner.

I ruthlessly cull the program down to its bare essentials, yet, something surprises me. As I create the program in this universe of virtual reality, it takes a visible form before my consciousness. I am looking at a miniature version of myself. It stares up at me with curiosity, clad in the all black jumpsuit with gold details that I sometimes use as an alternate to my usual red and gray. I am surprised by the fact that the program manifests a visual image. I know that it is not alive, as I am. I cannot create life, indeed I do not understand how it is that I came to life. Yet, this program is distinct from myself and becomes more so with each nanosecond. I have imbued this program with as much of my personality as I can, given that it is mostly a reactor control program. Perhaps that is the reason why? Or perhaps as much time as I spend with biologicals, I have adopted their tendency to think in analogies. I am creating a miniature of myself to confuse an enemy, what is more natural then that it appear so?

We regard each other in virtual space, and indeed the virtual space begins to take on a shape around us. We seem to float in a blue ball, surrounded by a blackness filled with multi-colored lines that are data inputs to me. A glowing, silver stream glimmers past us, the power tap to the Hummel. The power linking the ships causes its glow. I look down at the miniature version of me, and a pang of regret strikes me. It is not alive, nor self-aware, but it is very complicated and capable. I am sending it to its destruction. Perhaps only I, who live at the nexus between machine and being, could feel grief for it. Or perhaps, in this, I too am falling victim to the tendency to anthropomorphize. I touch its tiny forehead in this sea of data that we both exist in.

"Go," I bid it. "Destroy our enemy, then sleep well, with my thanks."

It nods with a look of resolution on its small face, then steps into the stream of the power tap. Like a silvery fish flashing upstream, it disappears in the direction of Hummel. It will begin to integrate with its systems, not fully yet, or Hummel would cease to operate as a habitat for biologicals. I send it into the power systems; it can see what ails the APU. Meanwhile, I begin to reorder myself into the physical world.

My miniature reports back in only minutes. The APU has been sabotaged with a minor intruder program. I have been tricked.

We had done all we could to conceal the fact that Maauro would be incommunicado. I hadn't even told Ferlan about it. I liked the elder Guildswoman more than I could ever bring myself to trust her. Ferlan had been on my mind since we arrived, her survival, her impossible presence here, her apparently sincere desire to save the two of us from the fate we had foreseen. I'd had a lunch appointment with her that I did not want to cancel for fear of rousing suspicion.

Dusko was already aboard, looking over the hydroponics and other systems to see if there was anything more we wanted to scavenge for *Stardust*. There was no point in letting anything nonessential, yet valuable, go up in stripped atoms with the Guild Ship. Despite the bounties and pay we pulled in, running a private starship was expensive. Beyond that, Maauro and I were building stashes of money and goods known only to us. Since our talk on the *Taiko*, the prospect of needing an exit strategy had solidified in our minds. While we might not ever need it, it could be that we might need to resign from Confed service, running fast and hard and that would take enormous sums. On our return, the world of finance would find it had a new predator, Maauro. But all that lay in the future.

Ferlan could have objected, *Hummel* was not technically derelict, but since she'd agreed to our proposal to use her ship, she'd evinced no further interest in it. A steady stream of goods now left the ship. The Collector's collection was filling the holds of Stardust with things that would have made the any museum curator drool in envy.

A few of the largest pieces were too big for any space that we could spare. These were wrestled onto the crab robots and moved to the deepest underground portion of the alien base. I didn't like using the crabs for this, but Maauro herself insisted that the artifacts were of immense value and needed to be preserved. Given that I was in love with an ancient alien artifact, I wasn't in the best position to argue with her.

The fact that the elder Guilder seemed to delight in Maauro's company, finally charmed my suspicious android. I'd been treated to the sight of them working on a smaller cabin on the same deck as ours, transforming the space into a luxurious, if somewhat fussy and overstuffed, nest for Ferlan. I could only hope the surfeit of cushions, curtains and hangings did not invade our own cabin.

For now, I was walking across the half-frozen ground toward *Hummel*, passing a few Guilders wrestling more of the seemingly endless loot of the freighter. The Guilders looked at me with cool or blank expressions. These survivors knew something of the danger Maauro posed. Even those who had not seen her in action had learned from the others. I, in turn ignored them, my attention more on the ground crunching between my feet and the vast three-ringed planet that took up so much of the sky. At any other time, it would have been fascinating to simply sit and watched something so utterly unique, a wonder of the galaxy. But today I was just hurrying to get to *Hummel*, and wondering if I would ever feel warm again.

I almost tripped over the heavy power cable laid to *Hummel* to supplement her power after her APU failed. Cursing, I stepped over the cable, which, by unhappy coincidence, was essentially the same color as the ground. Another few seconds found me in the maw of *Hummel*, walking up the gangway to the next level. I didn't look for Dusko; hydroponics was in the lowest level of *Hummel*.

I was passing over the machine shop when an unlovely silhouette stepped out of a side passage, weapon leveled at me. I froze, halfway to my weapon.

"No, no mes ami," he growled. "No fast moves."

"Have you lost your mind?" I returned, my voice level, despite the hammering of my heart. "Maauro will tear you to pieces."

"I think not," he said

"This is a dumb play," I said.

"Unbelt your weapon and drop it to the deck."

I did as he demanded.

"Now kick it away."

We glared at each other.

"Everything went wrong after we met you," Maurice growled. "Everything."

"You didn't meet me," I shot back. "You kidnapped me."

"The Madame's orders," he said, with a shrug.

"Which you're disregarding now."

"Bah," he said, "she has gone soft now, this mad expedition into the unknown, away from all of civilization. What profit did we get from the Artifact? Most of the crew is gone and we find we are returned to the universe ten years later. The Madame's holdings are in other hands now. The Guild moves on. Memories for debts owed to one like her are short, if her power is gone."

"So what?" I said, edging toward the nearest hatchway. "You're alive. You'll be back in the Guild in no time."

Maurice gave an ugly laugh. "The government, they will let us go, eh? I'm sure they will be grateful to you for delivering us into their hands."

I considered. "We could drop you off somewhere in Confed space before reporting back in."

"And I am to trust you? Me and the others with warrants out for us, dead or alive? No, we take the *Hummel* and we make our own way. The jump point will not be so hard to find now, we just backtrack your course. Then we are free."

"You forget Maauro," I gritted.

"I forget nothing," he returned. "We have you. She will be a kitten."

I barked a laugh at him. "Just wait till that kitten gets her claws into you."

"I don't believe it will come to that," Ferlan's voice cut in. We both froze.

Turning slowly, we saw Ferlan on the catwalk above us. She leveled the small slug-thrower at Maurice. "I ordered you to stand down."

He glared back. "Once you could have ordered me, not now. Once you were powerful and clever. Now what are you, a simpering old woman?"

"Actually," she said, "what I am is a terrific shot, as you might recall. Unbuckle the gunbelt and drop it."

Maurice did as she bade him, but as the weapon and heavy belt hit the floor, he moved. Ferlan fired at the same instant Maurice swept up a spanner off a tool box and flung it at her. Her shot creased his shoulder, then banged off the hull, ricocheting around the compartment. She toppled over hitting the deck five feet below. Maurice flinched as the bouncing round whizzed by him. I used the distraction to close the distance. He saw me coming and contemptuously flicked a jab at me. I blocked it up and slammed a foot against the front of his knee. He howled, backpedaled and came at me, arms windmilling. Like many overly strong, he'd never learned much technique. My stepping in and blocking then snapping hard left/right combinations at his face caught him off guard. I backed him up, before one of his own straight rights drove me back, numbing the left arm I'd blocked it with.

He grabbed me, but I circled one arm around his and slammed my other palm on his elbow, knocking his arm free. Again, I planted solid shots to the body, and quickly realizing there was no use to that, switched to the parts of the body that were no tougher on him than anyone else, shooting for temple, trachea, eyes and joints. There was no point in hitting him anywhere else. His own shots I stopped with my rapidly bruising arms, and legs, but I was adding up on the monkey man. He hadn't reckoned on the heft that years of maturing had added to my frame and the training I'd been put to by Olivia, then Maauro.

Still, blood was running down my face, as Maurice tried to shove me into a corner, I let him tie up both of his hands by grabbing my shirt front, slamming both my thumbs into his eyes. With a roar, he flung me the length of the compartment, stooped and came up with the spanner, one eye a gory pit and the other focused on my death. I slid to a stop and felt Ferlan's body next to mine. Her pistol lay by her and I scooped it as Maurice charged.

As he raised the tool, I shot him twice in the center of the body. He coughed and gave a surprised look down at his chest, then back at me, as if he had forgotten something very important. I shot him three more times, slow deliberate shots, hitting right alongside the first pair. He took another step, then sank to his knees, his one eye locked on mine. "Should have... should have killed you sooner." Blood spilled from the apeman's mouth as he fell forward on the deck. I looked at him, thinking of every schoolyard bully, every thug I'd had the misfortune to encounter and felt nothing whatever as his blood covered the deck. Nothing, as if he had been so much less than human as to be unworthy of the slightest empathy.

I dropped the empty weapon and bent over Ferlan. Her breathing was fast and shallow, the thrown tool had struck her arm and face. Blood rilled along a narrow, but deep cut on cheek, into the hairline. Her eyes opened as I bent down over her.

"Don't move," I said. "I'll get the aid kit."

She shook her head. "No, secure the ship. He didn't act alone. Delt and Olivia are in danger. He wanted as many hostages as he could get."

I stared down at her.

"Go," she said.

I jumped up, and ran to where I'd kicked my weapon. I scooped up the belt with its extra charges, drew the laser and raced out.

The armored doors of the Engineering spaces slide open too slowly for my need but, as soon as I can fit through them, I lunge into the corridor. I seize control of all ship systems. My AI has not been idle, but it is not me. It detected the sudden attack on the ship's company that Maurice has staged. And I am certain that it is the apeman who has done this. Ferlan would be too smart and not so desperate to take me on.

The crab robots are dispersed on the hills watching the skies or hauling some of Ferlan's treasures to the old base eleven kilometers away. There are three Guilders seated on the one approaching the base. These three are either holdouts, or not trusted by the mutineers, ready to follow whoever comes out on top. Assuming Ferlan not to be our adversary yields twelve enemies. Seven are aboard Stardust. The remaining five are either on Hummel or outside. Maurice has defeated surveillance by an old-fashioned method. His villains have either destroyed or covered cameras a few seconds ago when the mutiny began.

But he has underestimated the speed with which I think and move. Already I am intervening in the attacks on my crew. Olivia has been attacked on the cargo deck, where Ferlan's treasure has been loaded. She is down, trying to get to her knees, having been viciously clubbed. Blood is leaking from her prosthetic eye. Two Guilders are down, one's neck is broken, and he is dead. The other woman clutches her wounded knee as the human male draws back his club, aiming for Olivia's head.

The fire suppression system cannot fire or the halon deluge will suffocate Olivia. I activate a small damage control robot. It launches from its concealed location in an air duct. Two more follow from other locations that will take precious time to reach the combatants. The clubber gets in another strike that puts Olivia face down on the floor, but before he can draw back, the damage control bot bursts from the air duct and leaps onto the back of his head burying a variety of cutting and burning tools in his skull. He gives a great scream and falls over backwards, hands clawing at the device digging into his brain, but only for a few seconds. The woman tries crawling away screaming— it will avail her nothing. The bot or the others swarming to Olivia's defense will finish her. Her other companion will be fortunate not to regain consciousness before the machines attend to him.

I cannot spare time to tend Olivia. I do not know where Wrik is. Delt is on the bridge, struggling with three guilders. These have small knives and other weapons, brass knuckles, bits of pipe, but Delt has found a narrow hatch and only one can come at him at a time. He blocks a knife thrust, getting a shallow cut, but his fists flash out hard and fast, driving a bearded Guilder back with a broken nose. No bot or system can intervene faster than I can, and I am struck with the stark choice. Leave Delt unprotected until the damage control bots can reach him and search for Wrik, possibly losing a friend, or defend Delt and run the greater risk with Wrik. The decision takes an agonizing actual tenth of a second, before I tear upward up the spiral staircase. There is no time for finesse or delicacy. I crash into the rear of the group of Guilders and, in three blows, smash skulls to pieces, decorating the bulkheads with blood and brains. Delt stumbles back, horror in his eyes. I know with grief that he will never quite look at me the same way again.

"Get down to subhold three," I shout over my shoulder as I turn to throw myself back into the spiral staircase. "Olivia is injured." I blur into movement, and open the nearest airlock door, hurtling out into the cold and dark of this world's evening. I drop twenty meters with a jar and sink into the hard ground. My feet tear the surface as I accelerate toward the Hummel.

A missile speeds toward me. I do not know how Maurice managed to get a handheld weapon free of my surveillance. He must have had the foresight to create a cache of weapons before we arrived, possibly worried by what he perceived as Ferlan's aberrant behavior. I damn my lack of imagination, while simultaneously going into a forward roll, coming out of it and leaping left. The homing device on the missile *cannot handle my sudden change of direction and detonates, its fuse realizing that it as close to me as it will get, a spray of metal bounces off my casing, to no effect. Three Guilders are just behind the front landing jack. They too were thrown off by my change of direction. Shots and beams trail me. I fire back with my finger flechettes, my arm auto-stabilized into an effective aim. A burst of fifty flechettes eliminates the ambush team. As I reach the ramp of Hummel, I realize that behind the heavy plastic of the weather barrier, another Guilder with a launcher is lairing. The plastic has fuzzed my sensors. Before I can leap back, there is a flare of light inside. Laser.*

The Guilder falls. A second later, to my intense relief, Wrik steps into view. He has obviously been in close combat and shows bruising that must go to the bone, as well as blood from a busted lip. But his face lights upon seeing me.

"Are you all right?" we both say.

He nods. "Banged up, but OK. What about the others?"

I check through the AI. "Delt is like you. Olivia has more severe injuries. The ship is secure." The damage control bots have finished their grisly work with the live Guilders and are now moving the bodies to a pile outside the ship.

"I took care of Maurice and this other. How many more?"

"There are only three live Guilders left, beside Ferlan. These are with Crab Two in the ruins. Apparently they did not like their odds, or were not involved."

"Ferlan's hurt," Wrik said. "Help me with her."

"I must get back to Olivia."

Wrik looks at me. "She just saved my life. It will only take a few seconds."

We run side by side into the Hummel.

Maauro and I ran into the ship, her preceding me as always, faster and doubtess detecting, by one sensor or another, where Ferlan lay. We found her lying propped up against a bulkhead wall having crudely bandaged her head wound with a strip she'd cut out of her clothing.

Her cool grey eyes focused on us as Maauro knelt down next to her, me huffing behind her.

"Ah," she managed. "Maauro is returned and you live. The battle is won."

"Don't talk," Maauro said. She removed the bandages, pressed her hand against the wound injecting anesthetic and anti-inflammatories and whatever other medical magic she did.

"Ah," Ferlan sighed in relief, "so much better."

Maauro touched the skin around the cut and whether it was with glue, microstitches or something more subtle, quickly closed it.

"How is she?" I asked,

"The injuries are not severe, but she is not young. The shock to the system—"

"Will not kill so old a villain as myself so easily," Ferlan said with her small ironic smile, but a great weariness underlay the words. "Still, I think maybe I shall sleep for a while."

Her eyes rested on Maurice's corpse on the blood-soaked deck. "Ah, poor Maurice. I did not want to do that. He had been loyal; as such things go among the Guild, for a long time. Will you see that he gets a decent burial? Perhaps, when we meet again in hell, he will have a kind word for me."

I glared at the body. "If you wish."

Ferlan glanced up at me. "Do not turn cold and hard, Wrik. It doesn't become you, and Maauro will not like it."

Startled, I looked between the two women and at the pensive expression on Maauro's face. "You're right. He was a living being after all."

"And not the worst of them," she said.

"There will be additional burials," Maauro said. "The Guild now numbers four only on this world, including you. But they will all have proper burials."

Maauro took Ferlan back to the ship. I went in search of Dusko. I found him in hydroponics, bound, and in what was clearly a Maurice touch, left on the compost heap. He did not share Ferlan's sentiments about the apeman's death, spending some time in colorful Dua invective as I cut him loose. When loose, he still gathered up his treasures from *Hummel's* hydroponics before heading back to the ship.

With Ferlan secured in her cabin and the returned three Guilders locked on their deck, I went to see Olivia. I had to wait outside as Maauro continued some work on her injuries. When she finally waved at me, I slipped in quietly.

"How is it?" I said, looking at Olivia, who lay silent and pale on the diagnostic bed. Tubes ran into her arm, which was secured against her body by a thin, but strong sling.

"The injury is significant," Maauro said. "There are skull fractures and an orbital fracture. I have repaired these with mech. Her prosthetic eye was damaged. I can repair this easily enough, indeed I have placed the nanomachines within it to make the repairs, but they cannot be connected until the swelling goes down. There is a severe concussion, but I am ahead of any brain swelling and cognitive damage. She will recover fully in time."

"Thank God," I said leaning against another bed. "We have been lucky."

"Yes," she said flatly. "More lucky then good. Our enemy's cleverness exceeded our preparations."

I knew she was upset that she had not predicted, or ferreted out the plan against us, but now didn't seem the time to reassure her, that, like the rest of us, she couldn't anticipate everything. Olivia saved me from having to come up with something to stay by stirring.

"Do not move," Maauro said quickly. "All is secure and our enemies are destroyed."

"Music to my ears," Olivia managed. "Our losses?"

"None, you are the worst injured. Delt has cuts and bruises. Wrik less and Dusko was only tied up."

"Bah," she said. "I've had worse in training."

"Unlikely," Maauro retorted, "unless you were training to be a corpse. Your wounds have been repaired, but will take time to heal. I have arranged for minimal scarring which we can cosmetically remove later. There should be no permanent effects. Your prosthetic eye was damaged, but will come on line in the next 37 hours."

"Good," she said slowly. "I hate being one-eyed."

Maauro, having detected something, scooped up a water bulb and held it to Olivia's lips.

"Ah," Olivia said, finishing it, "much better."

"Delt," I said, "will be down to see you soon. He's on the bridge doing launch maintenance. Even Maauro's AI can't do everything."

"Mostly because of the need to keep your biologicals warm and breathing," Maauro said. "I could run a really effective ship if it wasn't for all that nonsense."

"Well, excuse me for inhaling," Olivia grumbled, much happier in her more accustomed role.

"Still," Maauro said, "you need sleep. Your own damage control systems work more effectively when your eyes are closed."

Olivia started to say something,

"And even more so while your mouth is closed," Maauro interrupted.

Maauro grabbed my arm, and we swept out of sickbay before Olivia could organize a reply, though I heard some muttered swear words as we headed up the spiral staircase to the bridge.

On the bridge, Delt had opened a panel and was working on it as we came up. It was one in an awkward place for Maauro's maintenance bots, and she had not gotten around to making one specifically for this area. Sometimes, I felt that she left us these tasks just to keep us busy. He straightened up as we came in.

"You should not be bending like that," Maauro said. "Those cuts were long and deep and the repairs are not that strong yet."

"Don't want a system to go yellow with a thirty-minute lift alert," he countered, closing the panel which glowed with a green light now. "I'll take it easy."

"We just saw Olivia," I added. "She's ok."

"Yeah, I'm surprised a club marked that thick hide of hers at all," he said, but the worried look belied the light tone.

"I do not believe we will have any further Guild trouble," Maauro said.

"How did he know when to strike?" Delt said, wincing as he moved his leg. "We did everything we could to keep the fact you would be out of circulation for hours secret."

"In this," Maauro said, "I must admit culpability. Maurice and his team engineered the power failure in the auxiliary power reactor. This caused me to run a backup power line to *Hummel*. He must have deduced that such calculations would cause me to become immobile and turn all my systems to doing the work. In this, he was more than correct. It took every scrap of processing power I had, to do the basic matrix for it, and I am not as comfortable as I would like to be about those calculations. The variables are unpredictable past a point. When the power spiked, as I went into overdrive, even a basic power reader on the line would have shown it. He decided it was his best chance."

"A slim chance," I said.

"Not so slim," Maauro said. "Look how close he came."

"Even if he had gotten the rest of us, he could not have over-come you."

"Wrik, that is the very definition of a Pyrrhic victory. While he held you, I would have been checkmated."

"Yeah. Guess so." I grimaced.

"The situation is now the worse," she continued. "With both Delt and Olivia wounded, we have less options than before."

"The question is, do we wait here for the Beast to find us, or risk another contact between it and Maauro to call it to us?" Delt said.

"For now," I said, "I relieve you, and you can go in and check on Olivia."

"Only for a few minutes," Maauro cautioned. "She will rest better after she sees you."

He flashed a quick grin, handed me some tools, patted my shoulder and slid past me to disappear down the spiral staircase.

"I will check on Ferlan," Maauro said. "She insisted she would be more comfortable in her cabin then Sickbay. She is very nearly as hard-headed as I am."

I nodded.

"I am having the crabs attend to the bodies and have spoken to the surviving three Guilders by com. They understand their situation. On return, they will remain on *Hummel* until after we inter the dead."

An hour later, the crabs moved to an area well clear of both ships and dug a pit. Burials were had. The three surviving Guilders, a woman named Tireste and two Morok brothers named Asabe and Remsab, han-dled the bodies with Maauro's help. They hadn't participated in the fight, but neither had they warned us. Maauro handled the worst destroyed bodies. She glowed blue with plasma after the last of them were placed in the individual graves the crab robots had dug for them. She was careful, as always, not to smell of death.

The wind, which had abated, began to blow with greater force as it usually did toward sunset. The crabots deployed lights to dispel the lengthening shadows as the sun reached the western peaks. We dialed up the heating element in our clothes as Maauro placed a marker for each Guider with their name. A brief service followed with Maauro giving the prayer she'd learned on Retief from Reverend Lourans. None of the Guilders said anything. Ferlan placed some flowers from her own ship's garden on Maurice's grave and said a few words I did not hear.

I looked skyward, discomforted by the whole scene. Maauro and Delt stood with me. Dusko had declined the invitation.

Finally, I turned to the three survivors. "Here's the deal. We'll be leaving here soon. Before we do, we have a monster to take care of. Since I don't think any of you want to homestead here, get your stuff together. We're abandoning *Hummel* to use her as a trap. You'll get two cabins on the cargo deck. You stay there, the galley and sickbay. I think the lesson of what happens to anyone who crosses us, has been learned."

"What happens when we get back?" Tireste asked, looking at Ferlan who turned to me.

"Nothing happens," I said. "The Madam says you three have minor records. We'll arrange for you to be dropped off on Olympia, the Madam has enough credits and specie for you to reach your homeworld and start over." Privately, I thought they would simply rejoin the Guild, but they'd sat out the mini-rebellion and this was their reward.

"Madame Ferlan, where are you going?" asked one of the Moroks.

"I do not know," she said. "Wrik… Captain Trigardt has kindly made room for much of my wealth, but unlike you, my record is… not so minor. Still, if I am allowed, my plan is to retire completely. Age lies too heavily on me now. I do not know how many years I have left but if they can be spent in peace, well, it will be quite enough."

I was surprised by the disappointed, lost look on Tireste's face. The Moroks also looked dejected, in as much as I could tell anything from their simian, blue-skinned faces.

"OK," I said. "Get moving. We don't know how much time we have before all hell breaks loose around here."

The Guilders wasted no time jogging toward the *Hummel*.

"Is there anything else that you wish to move?" I asked Ferlan.

She gave me a weary smile. "No, Wrik. You have loaded most of my collection, which was kind of you. Beyond that, there is nothing on *Hummel* I value. I do not plan to return to the ship. I think I will retire to the cabin Maauro so comfortably decked out for me."

Maauro nodded at the elderly woman. Since the insurrection, Maauro had finally seemed to accept Ferlan as an ally. She offered the tiny woman, three inches shorter than herself, an arm. She leaned on Maauro, as we walked back toward the towering *Stardust*. The growing cold hurried us along, as if to remind us that death owned this place.

We regained the safety of the ship. Delt and I followed Maauro to check on Olivia.

"Wrik," Maauro suddenly said as we entered sickbay, "there is a sensor reflection from Probe 2. The Beast has detected us. It is on its way."

"How do you know?" Delt demanded.

"The sensor returns I am getting from our orbiting probe correlates with the Beast, but is a fraction of its size. I am uncertain, but I believe the monster has subdivided itself, sending small sections as scouts to the worlds of this system, while guarding the exit point. This scout has found us. This explains much. It must have set a part of it or more than one part hunting in Piola. It is how it kept *Taiko* contained, yet destroyed that *Fetch*."

"Looks like I owe you an apology," Olivia said, her voice slightly slurred and her one good eye on me. "I thought you were being too cautious. But if we'd headed back like I wanted, we'd have run into the monster's main body at the jump point."

I shrugged. "No apology needed. It's just how I look at things."

"Maybe I need to pay more attention to how you see the world."

"In any event," Maauro said, "this scout has somehow divined something is here. I felt its mental emanation, like the cry of a hunter that has sensed it prey. Unfortunately, its telepathic ability is not limited to light speed. I have no way to get a fix on where the main body of the Beast is."

"Still, in normal space, the Beast must obey the laws of physics as it moves. It has mass and can neither, accelerate or slow, instantly. The probes should give us some warning. I would say several hours' worth, but this is uncharted space with distortions, uncharted bodies, and energy fluxes it may use to hide. The small monster scout will doubtless await the main body before attacking."

"Dammit," I said. "Worst possible timing."

"Wrik, we can't take off, not with Olivia having a head injury like that. If she has a brain bleed..." Delt said

"Don't endanger the ship, or the mission for me," Olivia managed, through puffed and bruised lips, her one eye glaring. "Leave me here."

"No," Maauro said, before I could even respond. "Do not ask that again."

Before Olivia could argue, I spoke. "Delt, you can't climb out of atmosphere, but if you lift off and run in atmosphere. It won't be much worse than a commercial plane."

"Yeah," he said. "But won't it just chase me, because I am moving?"

Maauro's face grew grim. "I knew I would have to contact the beast to reveal that I am here. To the extent it can understand our thinking, it may accept that you others fled, leaving me behind. It would think that way, if it considers it all."

CHAPTER TWENTY ONE

She turns to me. "Quickly now, we have no time and must bait our trap."

CHAPTER TWENTY-TWO

MAAURO SENT HER CHALLENGE AT THE ORBITING FRAG-
ment of the Beast by radio, betting it would relay the insult to
the main body. Taunted by Maauro into a rage, the oncoming
main body raced into orbit, but in normal space-time, it was a physical/
energy body and subject to the laws of physics that it escaped in jumpspace. It would need several orbits and an entry window to get at us.
For once, its actions were predictable.

"It's on its way," I said to Delt on the bridge of *Stardust*.

"I don't like flying off and leaving you," he said again, his face
grimly set.

I thumped him on the shoulder. "No choice. Maauro is the only one
who can do this, and she has to be locked down in *Hummel* until the
last few minutes. You have to save the ship, or no one rides home. If we
don't make it, hit it with the torps and just run."

He began to open his mouth.

"Delt, it's not running away. You have Olivia and Ferlan to think of.
I don't give a damn about the Guilders. The information on all we have
learned, and all we've tried, has to make it home. We don't have the luxury to do "death or glory," we have to be grownups, much as that sucks
and little as anyone expects it of us."

He looked down, then stuck out his hand. "You get killed, and I will
never forgive you."

I took his hand. "I'll see you with Maauro, or I will see you at Fid-
dler's Green."

I dashed past him. There was no time for goodbyes with Olivia, or
Ferlan. This time, it was I that used the fireman's pole to the ground. I
fired up the green and gold flitter, painted to match the ship and lifted
off to land next to *Hummel* on its far side, so I would be protected from
the wash of the impellers as *Stardust* lifted. With a grumbling thunder,
Stardust climbed out.

I hated that we were separated, with her in *Hummel's* engineering
spaces. I'd drive the flitter inside the cargo ship's massive roll on/ roll
off deck, buying whatever fraction of a second that got us.

"Wrik," Maauro's voice came. "Are you ready?"

"I'm backing in now, engine idling. The door is up for you to dive in."

"The Beast approaches. It is very angry."

"Can you tell if *Stardust* is ok?"

"No, the monster is displaying a new, but not unexpected ability,
electromagnetic jamming. Our signal is too close and strong for it to
interfere between us."

"That's comforting."

"I will be silent for a bit, I cannot spare even the least processing power. When next you hear my voice, I will be running at maximum speed to you. Firewall it the instant I am in. We have no time to spare."

"Understood."

I sat on the quiet deck, the weak sunlight visible just outside the clear plastic curtain that kept the cold at bay. I could see nothing above. That was somehow worse than scanning the skies for our enemy. My mouth was dry, yet sweat ran down my back and I could hear my heart pounding, the blood in my ears.

"Come already, you fucker," I snarled, forgetting Maauro could hear me. She would know it for what it was, terror trying to turn to anger.

"On my way!" Maauro said in my ears. Her voice was only barely urgent; she could have been late for dinner. I jumped as if stuck with a live wire. Suddenly, I could hear her coming, slamming into things she couldn't take the time to evade. Then she was in the flitter, which jarred under the impact as she threw herself in.

I stood on the accelerator. We shot forward, slewing a little, as we roared into movement. We tore through the plastic curtain and reached the flat ground beyond. I hit flight mode the first moment I could. The flitter's nose lifted, its ground-wheels auto-retracting into the body. There was no time to gain altitude. I shoved the throttles past the normal stops into emergency power.

"Where is it?" I yelled unnecessarily. She was just behind me.

"Thirty seconds away, north of us and descending. It thinks us helpless and wishes to grind us to dust. I'm relaying my challenge through the programs I loaded into *Hummel*. It has not realized that I am not still aboard."

A warning whine came from the engine as yellow lights appeared across my panel but the base was in view. I aimed for the hanger mouth to the underground tunnel, hating that I had to slow so much.

"Wrik, it is nearing. Hurry! The containment program is failing."

The light above us faded. Monster or cloud, I had no time to look, but dove into the hanger entrance at a mad speed, then hit the full reverse thruster, not caring if this too burned out in the abused flitter.

The blast went off just as the vast, manta ray shape threw *Hummel* into shadow and we reached the entrance of the underground hanger. A flash burned on my neck, for an instant, before the canopy polarization kicked in, as the instruments danced madly in the EMP of the collapsing stardrive. I dropped the landing gear and we slid along the century old flooring, glad we'd had the crabs smooth the ground. Still, we hit and slid sideways, as the G-bags deployed, cushioning the rough landing. Despite the crash protection, the jar rattled my teeth.

The flitter slid to a halt.

"Wrik," Maauro cried, "are you all right?" The EMP hadn't affected her. She tore through the deflating Gbag and hit the quick release on my chest. "Out, out!"

Dazed, and partially supported by Maauro, I struggled out the flitter door. The ground heaved and bucked like a pain-wracked animal. I glanced up at the cracked ceiling in horror of being buried alive. Maauro dragged me along, her eyes also focused on the failing ceiling, calculating stresses and where it would fall. She batted chunks out of the air, her arm moving almost too fast to see. Her other arm wrapped around me in a sudden brutal movement, everything blurred as she lunged. A massive chunk of ceiling came down behind us.

We reached the arch of the far exit, the strongest, safest place. Above us tornadic winds whipped up black sand and smoke. The wind tore at me, but Maauro was unmoved. She positioned me behind her, then turned.

"Kneel down and press your face against my chest," she shouted, over the howling and rumbling. "Protect your eyes."

I burrowed my face against the softness of her chest. Her body arched over me and her arms surrounded me, offering as much protection as she could. The howl of wind and rumbling of ground subsided, as the unstable black hole behind us fizzled out of existence. The artificial fields having compressed it were gone with the ship that had generated them.

Another pressure built in my head, an ocean of surprised suffering. The Beast, devourer that it was, was devoured by the miniature black hole in the millisecond it existed, before *Hummel's* AG fields compressing it, blew away. It's very mass was sucked beyond the event horizon. It knew pain as it had never dreamt of before. It built and built, eliminating sight, sound and sense and suddenly was gone.

I held Maauro in the sudden and illusory silence, knowing that my hearing was temporarily overwhelmed. I could see dimly through the dust sifting down as the winds over us slowed. Debris was still coming down, but we were well in from the entranceway. Still, rocks and chunks of soil struck and bounced. Standing over me, Maauro had reversed her head in a way nothing human could, and studied the fall, ready to bat away anything that threatened to bounce our way.

My hearing began to return, as did light above. With the collapse of the event horizon, it no longer sucked winds with tornadic force. I looked up into Maauro's concerned face. "I'm ok," I said, standing.

"Certainly more than our flitter is," she said, gesturing back toward the partially collapsed section.

"Damn it," I said. "I just made the last payment on that thing too."

"There, there, dear," she said. "We will simply add it to the bill for Candace under "sundries.""

"And to think I once felt I had to drill commerce into your armored skull. The student has now surpassed the master." I grinned, despite my sudden awareness of a mass of bruises and wrenched muscles, some from where my adorable android had to grab me, without time or leisure for gentleness.

"Let's get out of the underground," she said. "The majority of the falling debris is to the north. Radiation is minimal; it was sucked into the singularity. Our anti-rad meds will handle it. I am more worried about this archway.

"Don't have to ask me twice. We stepped out from under the arch into the swirling dust and walked up the ancient rampway.

From behind us a horrid undulating cry comes from the ruins.

"What!" Wrik says pulling his laser. "It's dead, I felt it die.

"The scout," I say.

"What?"

"The Beast had detached a part of itself to look for us. That part must not have caught up to main body of the Beast and avoided being drawn into the black hole," I say. "I am not in contact with it, but the... pollution it emits is too similar for it to be anything else."

"Do you have any sense of how big it is, how close?"

"By audio triangulation from bounced sound, I make it two hundred and eleven meters from us. As for the rest, I do not know."

He swallowed staring into the murk. "What should we do?"

"The ship will be returning with the crabs and other weapons," I reply. "Until then, we withdraw. Follow me."

We flee at our best speed. While I could likely have outrun the monster for a short period, I could not do so with Wrik on my back. His delicate human body would not withstand the forces involved. I could leave him, and attack on my own, but the truth is I fear the Beast too much to risk battle before I gather every asset to me, and at the least, remove Wrik from the battlefield. So, we scuttle from cover to cover heading south. We hear no more screams, but I detect a metallic sound similar to a crab robot moving over stone and macadam, as if its pads had been worn through, leaving its metal exposed direct to stone.

We reach the southernmost section of the old ruins. Here, the remains of the old base are lower, more tumbled. We crawl into a pile of rubble by a twisted, rusted and crushed hanger door. I scan the ground ahead, a plain of windswept stone and small scrubby vegetation, not totally devoid of cover, but far too open for my taste. I am uncertain if we are better playing cat and mouse among the ruins, or venturing onto the open field. I still cannot call the ship, an issue more on Stardust's end than mine. I hesitate.

"Maauro," I whispered, shifting on the gritty rock while keeping an eye on the remnants of the base in the dim murk. "Mind if I ask you a question?"

"Of course not," she said. Her voice was low, and she remained fixed on our back trail.

"Why did we go to Olympia?"

"Might this conversation be better had after we escape this enemy?"

"It might. But might that also not be your way of avoiding my question?" I kept my eyes scanning the ruins; for all that I knew she would detect anything before I did. I shivered in the chill, but didn't adjust the thermostat in my clothes. I didn't know how much longer we would be out in the cold, and raising my infra-red signature while being hunted was not a good idea.

She sighed. "Very well, I did not want to mention it until I knew if what I asked her about was feasible but—it may be possible for me to live, at least for a time, as a flesh and blood woman."

I could only stare at her in shock, the words whirling around in my head in the hope they would resolve into something that would make sense. "Maauro, what are you saying?"

"I am saying that I love you and that I have learned of a way in which I might download my consciousness into a human body made for me by Shasti's geneticists."

"Why?" I managed

Now it was her turn to look surprised. "Why? So we could be closer of course. I am your lover. While I think that has been wonderful, I feel that there is more that I could know, more that I could feel, if I had a body that was not an armored chassis."

"But...but you would be mortal," I stammered. "Think of all you'd be giving up."

"I prefer to think of all that I might gain, that I might experience love-making as Jaelle, or Olivia, do."

A distant warning bell went off inside me. Maauro had never shown any significant jealously but that was by human standards. She'd now mentioned Jaelle, the only other serious relationship I had been in, and Olivia, who had briefly been my lover on the Seddon expedition.

"Does it bother you that I have been with other females?"

Maauro seemed to consider my question seriously. "No. It would have been unusual if you had not been. Compared to other males your age you may even be inexperienced."

Ouch, I thought internally. But it was just Maauro being truthful, if not tactful.

"This is something else," she continued, apparently having not noticed my wince. "So much of my existence is affectation. I appear to love certain foods, but that is mostly for show. I like sweets for their complexity and for the reaction I get from you when I like them. I profess to enjoy sunny days and cool breezes, but rain, sleet, searing heat are all the same to me. I feel that I miss a vast universe of sensation and experience that exists at my fingertips, but that I cannot touch.

"I am frustrated Wrik; I want to be much more than I am."

"But...mortality," I said.

"Haven't I already existed for over 50,000 years? The first seven I spent as nothing more than a munition. The interregnum was spent fighting entropy alone on an asteroid. Only the years since you found me have had any meaning.

"I fear death, as you term it, but I fear more that I might have to endure centuries without..." she stopped, but I could hear a tremor in her voice and her eyes glimmered from the shadows. Unshed tears?

I hung my head. I knew of these fears of hers, but this was the first time it had hit me so hard. "So many biologicals would trade their bodies to go the other way: to have the freedom from pain and death that you have, the power and ability. How can I see you give up all that for me?"

"My sojourn into a human body need not be permanent. Indeed, I do not plan that it be." Her voice was steadier, and her green eyes reflected the fading light in a way that no humans could have. "If this works, I would live in a human body and back up my consciousness to my machine body. If the human body fails, I would take up residence again in here." She patted her torso, it made the same sound as mine would, but only because she so textured it.

"And if you weren't close to your body?" I demanded.

"There is the risk of some data loss, but only to the last backup," she said, calmly, as if the data didn't mean a tiny death, if nothing else.

"I don't understand. How could you live in both bodies?"

She considered as she returned to scanning the deserted streets. "Darling, we can't even prove the existence of your soul, much less mine. But I think this is better expressed as my consciousness of myself. But no, I cannot exist in both bodies at once. I must be either the android or the woman. While a human, I cannot use that body, save perhaps by remote control. It will essentially be my backup, retaining all my thoughts and memories, what I think of as my soul."

I wasn't sure whether to be amazed, or horrified. "Maauro, the risks!"

"There are some," she concedes, "but I judge them small, particularly against what is to be gained. Are we not here, gambling our lives for money, for freedom to be who and what we are? Is not all of our existence a gamble?"

I shook my head. "You said you were not sure of whether this was possible?"

"Yes. I asked Shasti if a body could be made, adult, and as similar to my appearance as can be managed. Yet, such a body must be devoid of consciousness of its own, but be able to support the brain that would be mine. By definition such a brain must be highly abnormal and still some-how be viable."

"The more I hear of this, the more scared I get."

"Doesn't the thought of holding a soft, light body of mine against yours encourage you? I would be like Olivia then."

Before I could reply with whatever the hell I was going to say, her head snapped around in pure machine motion. "Our enemy is on the move."

This time I heard it, a fall of rock.

Maauro moved closer to me. "I must move forward and engage it. I do not like our odds of fleeing out on to an open plain."

"The hell you will. We'll go together. Maybe I can draw its attention and you can attack."

"That is precisely what you will not do," she demanded fiercely. "You are too fragile to be exposed, and defending you will pin me."

"I won't let you face this alone."

"Then stay back, when I engage, look for an opportunity to get your laser in play."

"OK, but if I say break off and run—"

"Wrik, I should really be in charge here. I am better at this."

We glared at each other for a few seconds, then I said. "Yes, dear."

She kissed me. "By which you mean you will do what you damn well please regardless of my good sense."

"It usually works out."

"Stay two meters behind me."

Maauro advanced, her palm blades extended, her arms held before her in a way that would be awkward for the human she mimicked. I knew that high velocity armor piercing darts were in her fingers and that she could cover forearms in plasma fire and even jet it over short dis-tances. Neither of us had regarded personal weapons as a factor in the fight against the giant Beast. We hadn't anticipated this situation. I longed for a triple-auto rifle, and knew Maauro must be regretting not having brought her armspac.

We moved forward in short rushes between bits of cover. Despite the biting cold, sweat slicked my sides. My lungs strained in the thin dusty air.

Maauro paused by a short bit of wall, holding her arm straight up in the infantry sign for a halt. Across what must have once been a small street, stood more complete one-story buildings. The line of them indi-cated that some had been several stories tall and had fallen in. Beyond the first row were taller buildings and a few cracked domes. The cloud of dust towering over us had dissipated some, but the light had also dimmed in the planet's quick day. The ringed world hung in the sky over us like an evil omen.

Maauro looked both ways, as if considering crossing the open space, then froze. I followed the line of her eyes. At the end of the street lay a slab of gray metal the size of an aircar; it was oddly shaped, almost in the form of a bubble tent. I wanted to ask her if our enemy was behind, or under it, but didn't dare the sound, or the distraction.

Then it moved, and I knew if for the Beast itself. The metal shape pivoted on each of the four corners that bent down to the ground like the feet of a hunting animal. It pivoted slowly, unsteadily. Was it limping?

Maauro and it moved at the same instant. She blurred across the street, up onto the top of the wrecked building, raising dust and chips of debris as she moved. It spotted her, and humped around faster than I would have thought possible. Two spears of metal jetted from its body, toward her. A long buzzing sound indicated that Maauro's fingers were firing a barrage of flechettes. These dimpled the Beast's metal hide and seemed to sting the creature.

The spears of metal missed Maauro, but suddenly flexed into more supple tentacles. Surprised, she avoided one, but another wrapped around her left arm. She slammed a palm blade into it with a great clang and an immense spark, but the metal did not part.

I aimed for the tentacle, realized that I might miss it entirely, or hit Maauro, and retargeted it for the base of the tentacle. The laser licked out at full power and bit in. As with the flechettes, the laser burn clearly caused pain and damage. It might look like a tank but it wasn't.

Another spear of metal launched. I threw myself backwards as it flashed over me, burying itself in the wall, behind me which exploded into flinders of stone, some cutting my face.

I am held in the air by the Beast's most recent trick. As the tentacle whips about me, I am filled with loathing and fear at its touch. I feel the disassociation and disorder that contact with this vile thing brings. For a moment, I consider blowing my own arm off to end the contact, after a savage blow by my palm blade accomplishes nothing. Wrik's laser licks out and the grip on me relaxes as the monster is stung.

It attacks him and barely misses.

"No!" I scream. Plasma jets into my hands. I tear the tentacle apart and push-block another lance of living metal to one side. I hit the ground and leap toward my enemy. I was made for the frontal assault and now want to come to grips with my enemy.

I dodge or block lances of steel, then leap atop the heaving mass of the monster, slamming both my plasma-covered hands into its body. My reactors go into overdrive. I pour jolt after jolt of power into the frantically bucking monster, which careens into the line of buildings. I open every cooling vent in my body, running to full military power.

As much as I attack physically, I also pour my hatred of this filthy monster, killer of thousands or perhaps millions, into it. We know each other now, in this our fourth battle. There is a language of enmity between us. It strikes at me, seeking to overwhelm my defenses and replace my self with its own cruel personality, to absorb me physically and emotionally into it.

But I have been canny with my redoubts and defenses. I hold on and this time my plague of virus strikes and bites into the Beast, forcing disorder into it. The Beast reacts and an epiphany strikes me.

Moral cowardice, the ultimate act of selfishness, an inability to see anything beyond one self as worth sacrifice. The Beast must be a moral coward, existing in a universe of one. Most of it is already dead. How it must be afraid.

In the world of cyber communications, where all moves at the speed of light, I have time to reach out to my enemy and once again to taunt. "You are dying. You are alone and soon to be nothing."

What comes back are not words, or even feelings, but gouts of emotions: the fear I hoped for, more a sense of horror and rage. It wants; it longs, to be administering pain and terror as has always been right and proper in its universe. It cannot understand what has gone wrong. How has the universe become so perverted? It must be me. I am the architect of all evil. I am the devil.

"I am," I whisper to it. "I am all of evil, all powerful and more, so much more. I am infinite. I am all the life that there is that hates you. We are many, you are one. You are dying."

In a paroxysm of pure fear, it manages to throw me off its body. I flip through the air to land alongside Wrik, who is up, firing shot after shot into it.

Maauro landed next to me. Every panel in her body was open. The heat that beat from her was almost unbearable, but I dared not move away. Only she could parry another metal spear if it came.

But the Beast collapsed into a twisted shape of convulsing metal. A small fragment of the Beast turned toward us, its body shuddering and coalescing into a grotesque parody of a human face. The misshapen eyeless head produced a yawning mouth that seemed stretched in supplication.

In my mind, there was a beating force, a need. Not to the point of words, but almost that of an infant, realizing that there was a world beyond itself, a world in which there might be help. It was the precursor to the recognition that the universe held others besides oneself.

All too late.

Maauro leveled her arm, and the plasma that covered her hand when she attacked, was compressed to a jet of force that strikes the Beast in the face. A moment later my laser licked out to join her attack.

Agony flooded my mind as the Beast writhed under the power of the beams, but I keep my finger tight to the trigger even as the weapon heated from warm, to hot, to almost unbearable. Finally, the safety clicked in and the weapon sputtered out. Maauro's fierce beam lanced on and on. Now, I had to move away from her, the ground beneath her feet was sizzling.

I dropped my weapon and put my hands over my ears, but the screaming was in my head. Mercifully it faded; only an echo of pain, fear and wonderment lingered in the air. Maauro ceased fire, but kept her arm leveled at the misshapen lump of our enemy. Heat beat at me from Maauro and the sand under her feet crackled. I couldn't embrace her as I wanted to, so I sank to the ground nearby, as a cool wind bit through the heat radiating off her.

"It's over," she said, weariness weighing down her voice, which holds no triumph. "It's dead."

I nodded. "Time to go home."

Maauro gave me a small smile. "I still cannot raise the ship, but I imagine the heat bloom from the fight will show up on her sensors. They will be here soon." Her amazing systems were cutting in and the panels of her body closed. She never cared to look like a machine if she could avoid it.

We walked from the patch of soil that she had all but fused and sat together in the corner of a ruined building. Now the heat off her was comforting, holding the chill of the world at bay, just as the stone around us held off the wind. She leaned her head on my shoulder and I breathed in the ginger spice scent of her hair. Overhead, I heard the roar of impellers and recognized the sound of Stardust, questing through the gloom, coming to find us.

"I have never contemplated this before," Maauro said.

I winced as I moved into a more comfortable position, my ribs were still sore. "What's that?"

"I have often felt sad about the comparatively brief lives you, my biological companions have. Now, for the first time, I am conscious that there is a virtue in not having infinite life."

I looked at her.

"The thing, the monster, does not come from our time. During my mental brushes with it, I gained data that, because of its horrid nature, and its antithesis to all that we are, has taken time to safely interpret. This awfulness comes from a time in the distant future, so distant that the galaxies have all receded from each other. The stars in them are so immeasurably far apart, that there is no light and little heat left. The ultimate state of entropy approaches, the heat death of the universe is near. In that terrible time, so close to the end of everything, the thing came into being."

"It came back in time? Could there be others?" I demanded

"Maybe it was the last life form. I do not know. But it knew of no other like itself. Indeed, it could not conceive of any other beings as other than food until it encountered us in our space time."

"The thing came from billions of years into the future. All the known history of the species we have met is only a million years. And in that, are vast patches where all that is known is a few stone artifacts. Perhaps, there are others, but it seems unlikely that they would flee to our particular narrow band of known time."

"Unless there is some affinity to our local time that we don't understand," I said, rubbing my hand across my bloodied face.

"Don't go raining on everyone's parade," she said, "that's Dusko's job".

Stardust settled on the plain ahead of us while Maauro worked on my cuts. I knew she must have drained most of her power, but she still produced a cloth and some antiseptic to clean my face.

We walked side by side toward the ship.

"I have informed the others of what has happened." Maauro said.

I nodded, too tired to speak. The ship's exterior hatch opened and the small personnel elevator and the fireman's pole deployed. We rode the elevator upward to find Ferlan awaited us at the top. She held a small tray of brandy and handed each of us a glass as we walked in. Maauro and I both drained ours, she more for the gesture of appreciation, but I felt like life itself was being poured back into me.

"So," she said, placing the tray down on a nearby console. "It seems that you will both live, and the horrid future we saw is gone. You can look on the world of three rings without fear."

"Yeah," I said, struck by the thought and looking out the hatchway. The world we named Phoenix filled the sky with its multi-colored rings and body now beginning to show through the haze and failing light. It truly was beautiful.

"Come on," I said. "I want to see Delt and the others."

We started for the bridge, where I knew Delt would be at the controls, ready for any emergency.

"Oh dear," Ferlan said, staggering.

I turned and quickly lent a hand. "Here, sit."

"Well," she said, as Maauro came up behind me. "I was afraid it would end this way. Still, no complaints. I've had a far better second chance then I deserved and I made the most of it."

"What's wrong?" I demanded, holding her hand as she sat. I knelt beside her.

"Wrik," Maauro said. "I am getting some odd readings—"

"There is not much time," Ferlan said, with a small smile and an urgency to her grip. "Listen to me. I do not want you to be upset when I am gone. You have been very kind to me."

"What are you saying?" I looked up at Maauro. Her helpless expression told me that she had no idea what was happening.

Ferlan's smile widened, yet held a sad wistfulness. "I feel it. The line of events that brought me here has no strength and should never have been in this universe. Now it is coming to an end and I with it. I feared it might be so. I've felt attenuated, like I have been fading since you destroyed the Great Beast."

"No!" I said. "Don't give up. We'll do something. Maauro!"

"Wrik, I don't understand what is going on," she cried.

"Do not trouble Maauro," Ferlan chided. "Even she, a wonder of wonders, can do nothing about this. It is time for things to be as they should be, and I should have been long gone by now." She lay back against the seat, which I realized I could see through her. He hand felt gossamer in my own.

"Farewell," she said to Maauro.

"All is forgiven," Maauro said.

"I will miss you," I managed, unprepared for this last loss.

"And I you, sweet boy. Live long and well, love Maauro and remember me."

"I will, I promise."

"It will not be so bad, I think. I am not afraid."

"Maybe," I whispered, "we will meet again."

"Perhaps," she said, here eyes on mine. "Even in Hades there must be visiting hours."

My hand was empty and we were alone on the companionway. I sat back on my heels and glanced up at Maauro, who, to my surprise, looked as stricken as I felt.

"Wrik, I am so sorry. I could do nothing."

I took a deep breath and stood. "There was nothing to do. Space and time have resumed a course that was interrupted. You could not fight that and she didn't want you to try."

"I know you were very fond of her."

"Yes." A thought intruded. "The other Guilders…"

"—Are gone as well. There are no survivors from the *Hummel* aboard *Stardust*. Indeed her collection of objects is gone as well. I think we will find nothing of her ship aboard."

"You know," I said. "I would like a plaque made, for the back bulkhead on the bridge. I want it to have the names of those who crewed this ship. I want her name on it too.

"I will do it today."

"Thank you," I said. "We've gained and lost a lot on this trip. It's time to go back."

"Where to?" she asked.

"Olympia first, then maybe Star Central," I hesitated. "Will you tell the others what happened? I'd rather not talk to anyone just yet."

Maauro nodded, and placed a hand on my shoulder. I turned and kissed her. She headed for the bridge, leaving me alone with the memory of a woman who I had not understood, but unexpectedly had cared for.

EPILOGUE

STARDUST **RETURNED TO CONFED SPACE VIA OLYMPIA** to report to Shasti. Her greeting to Maauro was more like a mother to a returning child, than to an agent back from the field.

Taiko had beaten us back by over a year, relative time, and had sparked a mass mobilization of the Confederacy as planets suddenly reconsidered separatism, or secession, in light of the new threat. An expedition of a dozen warships was forming to hunt the Beast when we popped back in; one scoutship with a major kill to her credit. We proudly passed the lines of warships, which saluted us and then dispersed to other assignments too long delayed.

Maauro and Shasti became almost inseparable, spending much of the layover together working on what they now called Project: Real Kiss. Only the three of us and her agents has any idea of what had been set in motion by the two women.

Olivia spent her time with Delt, in the usual mix of arguments and fun. But the third day saw her called back to Confed MI. She took her leave of us with her normal breezy unconcern.

"We're too good a team," she said to us. "They'll be rounding us up to save the day again." She kissed Delt, hugged me and bade Maauro and Dusko more reserved goodbyes.

To my surprise, Dusko took Delt out to drown his sorrows. This worked out for me. I had plans of my own now that I knew what Maauro was planning with Shasti. I alternated between anticipation of Maauro's project working and a fear that it might fail, or worse of all, that it might somehow alter the love between us. Love is a strange thing, stronger than steel and as fragile as glass at the same time and never to be caus-ally experimented with. With that realization came the certainty of what I needed to do.

I made my preparations and called Maauro.

"Hello Wrik," she answered. Likely she was talking to Shasti, who had no idea she was simultaneously holding a conversation with me.

"Hi Honey, are you having a good time?"

"Yes, I am. I hope that I am not failing to pay attention to you though."

I laughed. "Well, I will give you a chance to make it up to me. How about we meet at eight at the Starscraper for dinner? Just the two of us."

"Sounds lovely, I will meet you there."

"Only you could be ready for dinner at the fanciest restaurant with no preparation."

"I know, isn't it wonderful. Don't let it get out as I don't want to be attacked by mobs of angry women."

"See you then. Love you."

"Love you too."

I dressed and got to the restaurant early. It had a wonderful view of the vast bay Marathon faced. The sun was down. Early twilight stars were glimmering. It struck me that my love with Maauro was a twilight love, almost a thing of Faery, between and immortal and a human.

Those usually made great tragic love stories, I thought, but I will do all I can to make this a happy one.

Wrik greets me at the restaurant. We sit at an outside table, in an alcove, near the wrought-iron fence around the balustrade. He compliments my rust-red dress. We both love to eat under the stars, so I had generated a little jacket to wear since we will be outside. I do not need it of course, but I try not to draw attention by doing things a biological female wouldn't. There are heaters on the veranda, as the evening is cool. Usually I would have used cloth to do such, but tonight I did not have a chance to return to the ship. The jacket simulation takes much power to make part of my outer chassis thin enough to look at all like fabric, but we are in no danger of a power shortage.

Our table has a lovely view of the bay, which is riffled by the wind, causing the reflected stars in it to shimmer. A few small boats also move through it; their colored lights making a pretty counterpoint.

We order dinner and catch up on the day. By tacit agreement, we do not discuss my project. I know Wrik has reservations. He is showing some signs of tension, yet also seems unusually happy. I am puzzled by this. Dinner is finished and desert ordered when he leans close to me.

"Maauro, why are you considering this – this risky adventure?"

I am surprised that he raises this. "I want to be your lover in the most complete way possible. I want to experience this as you do, so I can understand and be closer to you. Why? Don't you want this too?"

"Honey, I want you to listen to me very carefully. I love you as you are and because of who you are. I want you to understand this above all other things. You don't have to change for me. You are the person I fell in love with, as you are, and with the body you have now."

I look at him steadily, but perturbed. "There could be much to be gained in such a change, much about our lives that we might not experience."

He shakes his head. "I don't feel the lack of anything. Nothing needs to be better than it is right now. I don't want to risk any harm to you."

Now I am troubled and happy at the same time. "I am torn between my great joy at your concern and my desire for this."

He reaches across the table and takes my hand in his. We remain silent for what seems like a long time, the wind stirs the trees beyond the veranda, as the stars burn overhead. Finally he says, "I know that once you have set your mind on something, you are pretty much dedicated to it. But always bear this in mind. If you do this, do it for you. I love you as you are. .

I smile. "Now I love you even more, something I did not believe was possible."

He slides from his seat onto one knee next to me.

I have been slow for a supercomputer. I finally realize what is happening, when he opens the small box wrapped in a yellow ribbon, to reveal a brilliantly cut diamond on its cool band of white gold. I freeze, overwhelmed.

"Maauro," he says. "Will you marry me?"

Do all females feel this way? I wonder, when something predictable and anticipated, is still magically somehow a surprise? Thank whatever Creator designed my programming speed, that my freeze is so brief.

"You mean this?" I whisper.

"I do. I mean it now and will mean it for every day of my life."

"You're sure," she said. "I am so different—"

"I want to marry you now. While you are as I met and have loved you. If you still wish to do this, to try living in a human body, I will support you. Maybe it's just something you have to do. Maybe you are destined to do it. All I want is for you to understand that there is nothing I want to change in you."

I look at my love, my now husband-to-be, "Yes, Wrik. I will marry you and love you always." The feeling that wells up in me is almost unendurable. He slips the ring on my finger, holds me close and kisses me.

Around us other couples seeing the tableau, begin to react to it with smiles and applause. We kiss again and stand. The applause grows louder.

I look up at Wrik and know that what we said to each other on his homeworld of Retief is true. Love has found a way.

THE END

ABOUT THE AUTHOR

EDWARD MCKEOWN is a writer and editor specializing in
science fiction and fantasy with occasional forays into literary and
nonfiction. Ed escaped from NY, but his old hometown supplies
much of the background to his humorous "Lair of the Lesbian
Love Goddess" shorts, as his new hometown in Charlotte, North
Carolina does for his "Knight Templar" fantasy series. He enjoys
a wide variety of interests from ballroom dance to the martial
arts. He has also edited six Sha'Daa anthologies of wry tales of
the apocalypse and a wide variety of short stories. Find him on
Facebook and at edwardmckeown.weebly.com.

Ed is best known for his Robert Fenaday/Shasti Rainhell
series of SF novels, set on the Privateer Sidhe, issued by
Hellfire Publications.

MORE BOOKS BY EDWARD MCKEOWN

FROM

AN IMPRINT OF COPPER DOG PUBLISHING, LLC

MORE BOOKS BY EDWARD MCKEOWN

FROM AD ASTRA BOOKS

CHAPTER 1

I ATTACK THE ENEMY BASE IN THE COMPANY OF TWO OLDER M4 COMBAT *androids. We are launched from a Daggerwing assault-ship and shed our mobility capsules as we land on the asteroid. The Infestation claim the base is a lifeboat station but Intel says it is equipped with heavy weapons and sensors.*

The weapons are there. A disrupter battery fires on us; another lashes out at the Daggerwing and the ships beyond. As we race across the surface of the iron asteroid, a disrupter hits the lead M4. It staggers and slows. Other weapons switch fire to the slowing android. It is destroyed.

I am an M7, the newest combat android, a prototype, faster and better armored. I duck into a crater and return fire from my armspac. Explosions bloom and the disrupter battery is wiped out. The remaining M4 and I crash through the base airlock. Infestor drone soldiers are inside, clad in vacuum suits. They open fire. There is no room to dodge, so we trade fire from our onboard weapons and armspacs. The Infestors' small-arms have little effect on the M4 and none on me. We destroy them and race through the rest of the facility, killing Infestors as we encounter them. I head for the command center. M4 will attack the long-range disruptors firing on our ships.

Explosion. The corridor I occupy shatters, killing those Infestors I have not already dispatched. A mine, or perhaps my weapon, has set off a secondary explosion. I pause for self-repair. I am made of hyper-alloyed metals, ceramics and polymers. My outer casing has ablative layers and sections made to absorb blast damage. I exchange damaged exterior parts for interior and extrude new material to replace vaporized sections. Fortunately, I have taken no core damage. I waste no time on the aesthetics that make me look like a member of my creator's race. I carry enough spare material inside to regenerate two legs and an arm so I can get my armspac and reengage the enemy. I am much smaller now, having used up my spare material.

M4 reaches the disrupter battery, sited atop an arsenal. The bulk of the Infestor forces are arrayed around it. We confer for a millisecond. The battery is firing at our ships in the asteroid belt. I am already damaged, as is M4, and additional resistance is possible at the command post. By ourselves we may fail to take the station and suppress its weapons.

We agree on a plan of action and M4 self-destructs, detonating its plasma generator. The blast destroys the disrupter battery and its supporting forces.

I continue my attack alone and resistance crumbles. M4 may have killed the unit queen with its explosion. I neutralize the command post and mop up the base. In the process, I take seven prisoners. These I drag to a lower level and interrogate. Little useful intel is gained from these low-level creatures. After the last Infestor expires, I cleanse myself of their fragments. Then I delete the memories of the actual interrogation while saving the intel. This procedure is technically against my programming, but the longer I operate, the more latitude I discover in my behavioral routines. I do not know why I feel the need to do this, save that of late I have found the process of interrogation disturbing. I was created to destroy the Infestation and have done so for the seven years of my existence, yet I find more reasons to delete such information as time passes. I function more efficiently without these memories.

I reach the surface of the asteroid and step out under the stars, triggering my recall signal. No answer. I repeat it several times, then extend my sensor net to maximum and pick up a cloud of ionized gas. M4 did not destroy the disruptors fast enough. The Daggerwing, along with the support and repair staff who care for me, are gone.

I detect flashes of nuclear fire beyond my ship's remains. Ambush. The base may have been bait in a trap. Our forces are destroyed or driven off.

Since I do not face imminent capture, I delay self-destruct and continue repairs. I am dismayed by my level of damage even though my exterior chassis is mostly restored. Much of the damage can only be repaired at home base, which now I doubt I shall ever see again.

I consider my course of action. If the system has fallen to the Infestation, they will likely return to this asteroid. I should lie in wait to ambush any rescue party.

I turn my scanners to the sky for a last long look at the stars, which now are my only companions, before turning to walk into the silent base. I switch to minimum power settings. My wait may be long.

CHAPTER 2

I HUNG AROUND IN BARS A LOT. NOT THAT I'M A DRUNK. I
went through a short spell of drinking after I was cashiered from the
service for cowardice. But the bottle is slow suicide and I'm too young
and interested in living for that.

No, I hung out in bars because that's where a human can find work
on Kandalor's Vanceport. The Spacewitch is one of the places expeditions
launch from. Not the big government expeditions from the Confederacy
or the Combines, which wouldn't use somebody like me, but the shoe-
string expeditions from universities or organizations short on cash. I can
fly interstellar. Not everyone can handle the hyperspace visualization. I
can also fly atmo, which a lot of starjockeys can't.

So I staked out a small table in the back, away from the long bar
with its brass and dark wood where the bad and dangerous hang out.
My table sat under a hanging of red-fringed velvet, keeping me in comforting shadow. Square-D, the owner, knew me and would send over
people looking for my type of skills. Square-D didn't care about me one
way or another, but pilots brought trade to the Spacewitch and, he got
a cut.

Luck was with me. Square-D was talking to a tall, dark-skinned
woman in green fatigues. He nodded in my direction and she turned
toward me. She was tall, with a pretty, symmetrical face and an overripe
figure that strained the fatigues. I guessed her to be older than me, perhaps in her late twenties or early thirties. Her vest hung open and I saw
a holster under it. She strode to my table.

"Wrik Trigardt?" The voice matched the body, round and pleasant.

I'd left my real name in the past, with my honor. "Just Wrik." I neither
stood nor extended my hand; manners belonged to another time
and place.

She slid into the booth and rested her breasts on the table as she
leaned forward on her elbows. I got my eyes back up to her dark brown
ones in time to catch the flash of white teeth against her dark skin. OK,
she'd caught me looking, one for her.

"I hear you're a good pilot both on Kandalor and nearspace."

"Farspace too," I said. "I have an interstellar rating."

"Nearspace will meet my needs," she said. "You look kinda young
to me."

I shrugged. "I've been flying since my early teens, military training
as well. As they say: 'It's not the years, it's the light years.'"

I studied her. She had a slight accent I couldn't place. Something about her said Old Colonies or even Home World. "What needs are those, Miss…?

"Name's Candace Deveraux, out from Earth. Call me Candy and I'll shoot you in the knee. I'm looking for a private ship and pilot to take my colleagues to a certain riftoid."

"Treasure hunters."

She raised an eyebrow at me. "Prospectors and salvagers. You have a problem with that?"

I raised a hand. "No offense. I make a living hauling people around Kandalor and the near-rift looking for Old Empire relics and tech. Sometimes they even find stuff."

"But for every one who finds something, a thousand go broke," she quoted, leaning back. "True enough. Before we go much further, I'd like to know a little more about you. I gave you my name and world…"

"My name, you know. I'm out of a Confed colony world, former military pilot."

Her look said she knew this already. "Some people say you're out of Retief, a separatist colony. So why are you—?"

"Talking to a darkskin?" I finished for her.

She nodded. "Boers and Trekkers colonized Retief to get away from any contact with blacks. You regard us as inferior."

"I don't regard you as anything," I said, "assuming I was in fact born there. I take people as they are."

"Yet you fought in the Uprising?"

"As I said, you're assuming I was there. From what I heard, the Confederacy came in and told them to admit darkskins to Retief. Then they backed it up with force. Retief didn't last long after the Confederacy got serious.

"If that's enough 'get acquainted' for you," I said, and then, after sipping my drink, added, "I charge two hundred credits a day with fifty more if I go into vacuum. You pay for port fees and fuel. I get a hundred-credit advance now to reserve my time. You doubtless pulled my flight sheet at the port."

"Doubtless," she said, smiling. "I set the schedules and you learn where and when we fly when I decide."

"Deal." I tried to conceal my relief and surprise. She'd accepted my opening rates.

"Give me a number where I can reach you. You'll get twelve hours warning. Tell anybody where we are going and I'll shoot you in the other knee."

I passed my card to her and she inserted it into a portacomp. A few keypunches gave her my number and me one hundred credits.

She slid my card back to me. "You gonna buy me a drink with any of those credits, spaceman?"

"Uh, sure."

She laughed. "Just kidding. Next time come up with the idea on your own." She managed a nice sashay for a big woman as she walked away. I was tempted to whistle but afraid she might take target practice on my knees.

I finished my drink and slipped out the back of the Spacewitch after leaving a healthy tip with Square-D. Distracted a little by my good luck, I failed to do my customary check of the alley before I started down. I caught the heavy, earthy smell just before a thick, furred arm fastened over my throat and arm.

"So, Wrik, what are we up to?" I turned slowly in Truf's iron grip—there was no point in struggling with the bear-like Okaran—to face Dusko, the tall, Dua-Denlenn who ran a third of Vanceport's underworld. The Dua-Denlenn looked like a woodland elf gone to seed, with pale skin and blue pupilless eyes.

"Dusko," I nodded slowly. "I was just coming to see you."

"Of course, human," Dusko said, looking me over as if I were edible. "You owe me fifty credits."

Sweat trickled down my back. "I have it here."

"How fortunate for you, though perhaps disappointing to Truf here."

The Okaran whiffed a breath in my ear. "There will be other opportunities."

"My cardcomp's in my inside pocket," I said.

"Let him go, Truf. This youngling's too prudent to be dangerous."

I pulled out the cardcomp and handed it to Dusko, who ran his own card-comp over it and made the transfer.

"Who was the offworlder you were talking to?" Dusko asked. "Anything I would be interested in?"

"A rift-haul for a prospector. She's cautious. No up front info from her."

"So no way to set her up," Dusko shrugged. "Doesn't sound worth my effort. You will let me know if there's a chance for mutual profit off her."

"I did last time," I said.

"True," Dusko said. "Their personal effects brought a nice sum. If it eases your conscience, they turned out to be druggers."

I tried not to remember the traders I'd led into Dusko's ambush. But it was either them or my ship and the ship was all I had.

"Good doing business with you," Dusko said. "As Truf said, there will be other opportunities. See you around, human." The languid Dua-Denlenn stepped back into the darkness, followed by his hulking guard. I leaned back against the wall, feeling the night air sift through my shirt and fighting the chill. Dusko was right. I was prudent. I had a knife in my boot and a slug-thrower in my back belt, but I wouldn't try an Okaran with the small caliber weapon at such close range. Throwing down on any of the established Guild was insane, anyway.

I decided to sleep in my ship, an old *Dauntless* class scout I'd named *Sinner*, a leftover from the Conchirri Wars long ago. Before heading out, I arranged for the port recorder to forward any message from Candace Deveraux to *Sinner*.

I hopped a native transport, which was the cheapest transport available. The open cart, towed by two oxen-like animals, was an odd contrast to ground cars or flitters but it was emblematic of Kandalor, which combined poverty and wealth as well as high and low tech. It had been a forgotten world until a Confed expedition stumbled across it and the races of the Old Concordiat. A few native Kandalorians, muffled in their robes, glanced at me with their bulbous black eyes but otherwise ignored me. I returned the favor and tried to breathe shallowly, the smell of the natives competed with that of the draft animals.

Sinner sat at the spaceport's edge under a metal overhang I'd rented to keep off the worst of the weather. She was about thirty meters long, a bulky ovoid with short stubby wings and lots of interior volume. I'd painted her anti-corrosive chrome yellow. Unlike military craft, we civvies want to be seen. I keyed in the secure code and locked myself in, letting my breath go in a rush. On Kandalor you live like a rabbit or a wolf. Maybe I'd have an extra big helping of carrots tonight.

One week later, I was doing some scut-work on a small Indie-freighter when my comp buzzed. I took off my gauntlets and sealed the engine port before answering. "Hello."

"It's Candace. Time to go prospecting. How soon can you launch?'

"I'm in good shape for a Rift run this side of the 38th in four hours. If we are going out farther, I'll need to add wing tanks."

"We aren't going farther. I've got the flight plan on file with the Port Authority. They'll download to you just ahead of launch."

"Cautious, aren't you?"

"Wouldn't want any problems with local interests."

I swallowed. "There won't be."

"Good, I'd hate to shoot such a pretty boy, at least until I was through with him." She laughed and clicked off.

Candace showed up at the *Sinner* early, as I expected. She liked to set the pace. Two men accompanied her. One was tall, with dark, suspicious eyes and a hooked nose over a beard, unusual in someone who expected to use a space helmet. The other was a dark-skinned like Candace, but whipcord thin and balding, with the look of a spacer.

"My associates," Candace said, gesturing to hook-nose. "Harung." She pointed at the other. "Maku Treska." Both nodded.

"We've got a cargo sled coming. My boys will do the loading," she said.

"Long as I check it after," I said.

Treska looked at me. "The kid doesn't trust us to load. I was flying when you were waiting to be delivered."

Candace looked at him with annoyance. "Quiet, Treska. I don't want to fly with anyone dumb enough not to check his own ship's load."

Treska grumbled but headed for *Sinner's* capacious cargo bay. Harung gave me an unfriendly stare and followed.

I looked at her. "No weapons on my ship. Hope you left your knee-shooter in the port lockup. Explosive decompression can ruin your whole day."

Candace grinned at me. "Gonna pat me down, Wrik? I've got a lot of area to cover, many dangerous curves to hide things."

Her smile and manner had probably bent men to her wishes all her life. "Sounds like fun, but I don't think I want to pat down your buddies, though, so we'll use a scanner."

She gave a look of mock disappointment. I could feel my blood stirring. Human women were rare on Kandalor, and I had little to offer one. Truth was I didn't have much experience there, either. Candace's mocking smile told me that she suspected it.

Stick to business, I thought, *you're out of your depth with her.*

I checked the load and scanned my passenger for weapons. We boarded *Sinner* and settled in. Candace rode in the second seat on the flight deck. Her companions strapped in the far less comfortable cargo compartment, grumbling loudly enough to be heard. Candace smiled and shrugged.

Sinner kicked free of Kandalor's surface and started a slow ascent. Kandalor stretched out forever below us, seducing the eye and the imagination. Empires had come and gone on this world while humans lived in caves and waved stone axes.

"Beautiful," Candace said, looking out at the mountain and huge forests beyond the spaceport area. In the distance lay the ruins of one of the many lost civilizations. Haze made the wildly tilting towers appear blue.

"Yep," I said. "You've got spaceports and primitive tribes all on the same world, an archeologist's treasure trove."

"Here and in space," Candace said absently. "Those empires extended out for hundreds of light years. Lots of good stuff out there."

"Going to tell me what we're looking for?" I asked.

"Just drive the taxi, Honey."

"Yes, Ma'am."

Candace talked as we boosted toward the Rift, using my ion engine for a slow, steady thrust. I found myself liking her. I didn't want to; friends are an expensive luxury for a Rifter. I set the autopilot and we turned in early. I had trouble falling asleep, thinking of Candace's lush body in the bunk above me, wondering what it would be like.

We came up on the Rift in the next watch, not that there was anything to see. Even in as thick an asteroid belt as the Rift, it would be unusual for any two objects to be in visual range.

We set course for a large riftoid well in from the edge. One of a million such rocks unvisited by anyone since the planet blew to hell. Gradually the riftoid grew from a tiny point of light to a gray, pitted, roughly spherical rock about 2000 kilometers in diameter. Scanners showed it to be almost pure nickel-iron. A huge impact crater marred part of it.

"That's the one," Harung said. Everyone was crammed into my cockpit, staring hungrily at the pitted gray surface. "Just as I remember it."

"Probably part of the old world's core," Treska grunted. "That would account for all the metal. It'll give it a bit more gravity than you usually get in a rock this size."

We drifted down to the surface. Treska was right; gravity was strong enough that I didn't need to fix anchors. I did it anyway, space rewards the cautious.

"Suit up, everyone," Candace ordered.

I looked at her. "I'm just driving the taxi."

"Don't be like that, Honey. Now that we're here, don't you want to see what we came for?"

"Depends."

"What do we need him for?" Harung demanded.

I sighed. "She doesn't want to leave me behind in the ship so I can hold you up when you come back with whatever treasure you came for." I looked at Candace. "Ever get tired of working with people who aren't as smart as you?"

"No," she replied. "I only like smart men in bed."

Harung glared at me.

We suited up and walked out onto the surface of the riftoid. Treska unlimbered a large mining scanner. Evidently he got a fix on something, as he began moving in quick little hops, kicking up dust. Candace and Harung followed, lugging their equipment. I thought about waiting where I was, then decided it might be safer to stick with the herd. Five minutes later, we found ourselves in a small crater, looking at an oddly-shaped hatchway of yellow metal nearly three meters across.

"What the hell is it?" I asked, excitement getting the better of me. Dust indicated that the hatch hadn't been opened in a long, long time. The design didn't look like anything I'd ever seen.

"Maybe an Old Empire asteroid station," Treska said absently.

I looked around. "Over 50,000 years old."

"Or more," Treska said. "I spotted it when I was here with a freighter that came out of hyper too close to the Rift and had to dump delta-V to avoid a collision. I kept the readings on my scanner to myself. Those Combine bastards wouldn't have given me a percentage of any find."

"Why don't you tell him your life story?" Harung growled as he placed heavy jacks around the hatch.

Candace used a laser drill to place a monofilament probe through what looked like an inspection port. "As you suspected, Treska," she said, "hard vacuum on the other side. Start the jacks."

The power jacks took five minutes to crack the airlock. We used pry bars until we could squeeze through in space suits. A few more minutes on the inner door and we were shining our torches inside.

The interior of the station was familiar looking; form follows function. We saw a rack of odd-shaped spacesuits hung on the bulkheads. Whatever wore them had been much bigger than a human, multi-legged, with a large skull or a need for a lot of headroom. Boxes and tanks lay all over the floor. The metal of the floor worked with our magnetic boots.

"This is a military station," I said.

Candace looked at me. "Why's that?"

"A lot of compartmentation, thick hatches to deal with explosive decompression. Though I'm surprised a military station wouldn't have been dug deeper, for blast protection."

"Maybe it was converted from something?" Harung said.

"Who knows?" Treska shrugged.

Candace nodded. We played our flashlights around the gray and white metal halls, looking at unfamiliar inscriptions and dead light panels.

"It kind of reminds me of the old lifeboat stations they have in Sol's system from before the advent of hyperdrive." Candace said.

"We might find an Old Empire ship," Harung exclaimed.

We started down the sloping corridor and came to a partially opened doorway.

"Christ, look at that." Treska pointed.

At our feet lay a large pile of shredded fabric covered with white dust. Nearby lay boots, though not for any human foot, and a thing that could have either been a power rifle or some sort of heavy tool.

Candace bent down. "Crew. Must have died here in the doorway. Wonder what tore up the uniform?" Cautiously, she pushed open the doorway and looked in, a prybar in one hand and flashlight in the other.

Harung brayed a laugh. "Looking for something? That corpse has been there for fifty millennia in vacuum. The fibers degraded and fell apart. We'll bag what's left for the scientists. They'll pay plenty for material from the corpse of an unknown species."

"Look, a ship!" Candace exclaimed. Her light illuminated a small vessel beyond. It looked like it was made of some translucent, half-melted, dark-green glass. Yet it was recognizably a spacecraft.

"If you're right about this being a lifestation," I said, "there's your lifeboat."

Harung pushed past Candace and me with Treska on his heels. The smaller man accidentally kicked an alien boot. It spun silently away into the darkness beyond our lights. I shuddered.

Candace knelt by the fragments of fabric and the metal implement. "A weapon?"

"Maybe," I said. "It has that look, but I don't see any sights."

"Well, any charge it had must have gone before the pyramids were built."

The space beyond was wide and flat, big enough for several small craft. A hatchway that must have once opened outward formed the roof of the hangar; for all that we had seen no sign of the hatch on the surface. Harung and Treska clambered all over the small ship, peering into it with lights.

"Wrik," Candace called from the far side. I went over. She was standing over a pile of white dusty fabric and more boots, buckles and webbing. The fabric was shredded like the first one.

"What the hell?" I said.

"There's a passage up ahead. If this is like a Terran lifestation, it will lead to the medical and crew quarters."

"After you," I said.

She frowned at me. "You're a bring-up-the-rear kind of guy, aren't you, Wrik?"

"You weren't hiring at Hero's Hall."

We left the others to explore the ship. Our magnetic boots raised a thin film of dust, to hang and fall slowly in the low gravity. Colors here were more vibrant than in the more utilitarian areas. The combinations hurt my eyes.

We reached the crew quarters. Debris covered the area. All manner of odd-looking furniture lay scattered and broken.

"Decompression?" Candace asked.

I shrugged.

IF YOU ENJOYED THIS EXCERPT, LOOK FOR THE MAAURO CHRONICLES, BOOK 1, MY OUTCAST STATE AVAILABLE ON AMAZON.COM AND COPPERDOGPUBLISHING.COM.

Copper Dog Publishing LLC

OUR IMPRINTS:

Pumpkin Hill Press

To find out more about our imprints
and our upcoming releases, visit our website:
www.CopperDogPublishing.com
or our Facebook page:
www.facebook.com/copperdogpublishing